BLOOD RENEGADES

ROSEMARY A JOHNS

They twirled each other round, as they danced out into the courtyard garden, like I'd once danced with Ruby in the carnage and the flames – a kid let loose in the world. No conscience or battle for redemption. Nothing forcing me to grow up and face an adult world beyond my own will, wants and delights.

Together? A fanatical Magnificoe and his wicked witch?

The First Lifers didn't stand a chance.

I0629221

FANTASY REBEL

FANTASY REBEL

ISBN-13: 978-0995557932
ISBN-10: 0995557934

Fantasy Rebel Limited
rosemaryajohns.com

For A.

'There's nothing but snowflake patterns.'

The Light Inquiry

NIGHT 1

Betrayal. Death. Hope. Isn't that how all truly great stories start?

I don't know if anyone will hear it. Governments silence their critics. Censor. Detain. Execute.

Bollocks to them.

The Blood Life Council's atrocities and war crimes--

Mr Blickle, please note: we are not at war.

Yet. We're not at war – yet. And my name is Light.

Very well, Light. We're not holding this inquiry, however, to debate the nature of the Council's actions. Rather those of your terrorist group.

We prefer 'freedom fighters', sweetheart.

And I prefer to be called Liberty.

Having a laugh, aren't you?

You don't think *Light* has a touch of irony to it?

All right, Liberty, but I delivered my band of merry misfits out of slavery – one you wankers sold us into. So labels..? They don't figure.

They never do.

Your band of misfits does have a name?

Yeah, it's called a family.

Captain told me you were cute. *Renegades.* **As you know, we're well aware what you call yourselves. You paint it bloody for us to find.**

Look, you want me to bear witness? I'll bleeding bear witness. I'm a prisoner here anyway with a stake pointy-like at my heart and I'm all about survival. Just don't figure on liking what you hear.

No one does when it's the flayed truth.

You want to be ready don't you? You know what's coming in less than two weeks?

Your trial.

Kangaroo court more like.

Closed court. Nothing's been decided. Yet. It rests on your testimony.

Then where's my solicitor?

You're a terrorist - you've forsaken your rights, as you have your own species.

And the jury?

The material's too sensitive--

Embarrassing. The word you're grasping for, sweetheart, is embarrassing. For you and the rest of the Blood Life Council. So here's a question--

I ask the questions, Mr Blickle.

Bit of respect here: dead man talking. So who's the judge?

It won't help you to know...

It's Captain, right? I'll take your awkward silence as a *yes.*

Bugger.

So let's say Captain doesn't like what I have to say – and he won't – what then? What happens in two weeks? Slap on the wrist? Trip to the naughty step? Bare bottom spanking across his lap until I bawl? Or..?

Execution. By fire. Most likely.

Figured. Thirteen more nights until I go up Mr Bonfire for you nice people then.

You don't know--

Don't play games. Not about this.

That's outside my remit; I'm only here in the council offices with you to take your statement.

It must be nice to fit everything into neat little boxes. Then go home happy each dawn with no dirt on your pretty hands because all you've touched is paperwork.

Hitler's lawyers were good at that too.

If I'm going out in flames, high in their glory, then Christ in heaven will you get my witness: one you'll never forget.

Even though I may only have two weeks to live, it's a truth I'll remember until my second death.

Sod it; bring on the fire and ash.

But before all that dramatic buggery...I'd kill for an e-cig.

When I was hauled in here, like catching your most wanted had sun maddened you into a spot of desperate slap and tickle with your new toy, some bureaucratic bird snatched my e-cig; she also managed to get in a good grab and grope. How many of you pervs does it take to do a strip search?

Perhaps you're just popular.

I've been called many things over the last 150 years but never that.

I tried going nicotine cold turkey once; I don't recommend it. So unless you want one pissed off Blood Lifer, do me a favour and--

Why should I do you a favour?

Seriously? You're pointing at a 'No Smoking' sign?

We're Blood Lifers – glory of the electrifying, sublime, *beat* of the night and burn of the endless hunt – yet you're following *No Smoking* rules?

Wait, sorry... I'm in the greedy clutches of the Blood Life Council. Pale ghosts of Westminster. I forgot who I was talking to for a moment. What do you kids, only decades old to this dark evolution, know of real Blood Life?

I know you're not permitted to smoke.

Sodding hell...please?

You almost sound desperate. Intriguing: for a brutal terrorist leader.

We could negotiate.

Haggling with the Devil never ends well.

It does for the Devil.

And which of us is that then?

You want your nicotine hit; I want to impress my superiors.

An inquiry into the leader of the ruthless Renegades: a terrorist organization fanatically dedicated to eradicating human slavers, thereby endangering our secret world.

That's the remit.

Yet I know I could provide answers to questions the rest of the Council don't even understand they need to know.

This is more important – bigger – than anything they can conceive. But I do.

So I want one truly personal memory every day of the trial. *Your* secrets. Ones

you've never told anybody. Then I may allow your treats.

Memory? You want to violate my mind as well?

That's the deal. Or we could just get on with it. You don't need to smoke.

I abs-bloody-loutely do.

Right, I'll bite. One secret a day. Something I've never told anyone. But I want something else thrown in: vintage '60s motorcycle jacket with gold ace of spades on the back. It's mine, and you wankers took it.

Cold are you?

That coat? It's been through the bloody wars with me, and I've been through the bloody wars to get it back.

What's it worth? One memory – one secret - for one coat.

A sensory deprivation hood is a cracking piece of kit.

Sight, sound, smell. Taste and touch. Wiped out.

Blackness. Silence. Nothingness.

As if you don't exist, or the universe doesn't.

All that remains is the howling in your mind.

I was adrift in the darkness. Giving these shallow, panted gasps. No gag this time, so small blessings.

I could only smell the suffocating stink of leather. Only feel the freeze of the cellar floorboards underneath my shivering skin. Everything was narrowed down – focused – onto the few senses I had left: the strain in my shoulders, as my hands were shackled behind me and the furious *beat*, *beat*, *beat* of my heart.

My blood called to me, whispering *predator* in every pulse, harsh behind my eyelids.

I was lost, however, in the black.

Soon I didn't even feel the pain...cold...floor. My shoulders weren't mine because I wasn't sodding me.

As I said: a sensory deprivation hood is a cracking piece of kit...if you want to break a Blood Lifer, and the First Lifers of the Blood Club wanted us as their pretty playthings all in a row.

The specters of the dead rose before me in comfort: my two human sisters, Nora and Polly beneath our willow tree, my Blood Lifer family and first mate Alessandro, smiling up from a chess match waged against himself. And Kathy: my gorgeous Moon Girl.

Each of them was erased, however, as fast as they were conjured, as if my brain was shutting down.

Loss. Loss. Loss.

Each one abandoned me. Alone in the dark at the end. Because we always bloody are.

Alone in the dirt.

And it was my own wankering fault.

I was still playing the rebel, you see. Because there's no play about it.

You're a born a rebel; you die a rebel.

It's just that moment was looming closer than I'd hoped.

'Prostrate.' *Tap, tap, tap.* I'd risked a quick glance from underneath my eyelashes at *Sir*; he'd been tapping the red-and-black hide riding crop impatiently against his grey-suited trouser leg. A little furrow had been between his plucked brows. 'Prostrate, shadow.'

I'd known that one: drop to the floor on my stomach in front of his bloody Nibbs, and then turn my nut to place my cheek against his black Oxford shoe. If *Sir* was in the mood? It gave him a stiffy if I also kissed it; it didn't matter that *I* was never in the mood.

I'd stayed in *kneel*, however, even straightening my shoulders.

It's hard to look dignified when you're starkers and on your knees before a bloke in a suit, but I like to reckon I pulled it off.

Yeah, deluded prat here.

That shred of Light not yet swallowed into shadow hadn't let me prostrate myself. Not to Mr Poncey Corporate. Not again. I wasn't a trained monkey: even if I performed like one.

Pride: it'll catch you by the balls every time.

Sir had pushed his black framed glasses further up his nose. He'd studied me in disturbing silence. Then the tongue of his riding crop had licked out, welting my right cheek.

I'd yelped.

'Look you, my pretty leech, don't start and make trouble,' a sick caricature of a smile had tugged up just one side of *Sir's* mouth, 'or maybe you're the sort of bitch as likes to make trouble, isn't it? Shall we play a game? See if you're a true hero or just a worthless little leech?'

I'd knelt in silence.

I'm not that much of a nitwit: *Sir's* games were never going to end well for yours truly.

Sir's smile had snarled into a frown. He'd reached behind him excruciatingly slowly.

I'd tensed, my cheek still stinging from the crop's kiss.

That's when *Sir* had pulled out something, which had been tucked into the waistband of his suit trousers. It'd been folded in half, so I hadn't been leery of it until...the smell.

That stink of leather.

And before I'd known it? I'd been bawling out my nancy heart. 'Please, *Sir*, I'm sorry *Sir*...'

'Don't. Move.'

Intense citrus underlined with cedarwood – *Sir's* aftershave – had choked me, as he'd leant closer.

Closer.

And...

I'd shuddered but I hadn't legged it like every instinct shrieked. Fight had already been stolen from me in the fight or flight equation.

Then everything had gone dark.

I don't know how long I was lost in the dark. Time has no meaning in that torture. Our blinding senses are our strength but used against us they become our weakness.

An hour? Day?

In that panicked, gasping void, I lay curled on the freezing floorboards and I shook.

All right, so I was a pillock to nark off the human, who had the power to steal the light.

Yet such extreme punishment, over such minor rebellion..?

We'd been playing cat and mouse for weeks; it's not like I had bugger else to do: starkers and chained in a bricked up cell. A thrashing here, a day or two of starvation there. Adrenaline drenched interludes, in between days of lying on my back counting the blossoming demonic hordes of spores; angelic warriors clashed against them, when I counted the splinters in my fingertips.

Numbers are the only mates who've never deserted or betrayed me.

The game? Somehow it'd changed, and I'd been caught bloody in the cat's jaws.

Problem was: I hadn't reckoned I was the mouse.

White needles pricked my retinas. I screamed, as the hood was wrenched off. I screwed up my peepers against the sudden light; tears tracked from their corners.

I let out a sob of relief; I wasn't lost anymore.

Sir had found me.

Rich mould, thick dust and ancient floorboards; I could smell again in a volcanic rushing overload. It was citrus, however, which was invading every bleeding inch of me. Through my bleary peepers I could see a dark shadow.

Sir was crouching down.

I curled closer around myself but I couldn't save myself: I knew it. Even in the midst of our dance, I'd never forgotten that.

I could feel again: my aching shoulders and numb legs. My body was my own once more.

That was the illusion, however, because I was property.

Possessed by *Sir*.

Then *Sir* was on me; he crouched over me, one arm cradling my thin spine, whilst the heavy weight of his legs held me down. He stroked my cheek with his manicured fingers, lightly tracing where the red welt had paled to pink. If I'd fed? It would have become as invisible as I now was to the world outside, locked here in Abona House.

Sir gently lifted my chin. I forced myself to meet his hard gaze. I was shocked to see it suddenly tender. 'You don't know nothing, you don't. How things work in here. On the Estate. Why I have to...'

Sir tightened his grip; I gasped. 'Now, little leech, you tell me which bitch has been feeding you, like the greedy baby bird you be.'

Sir knew?

The Blood Lifers risking – everything - to feed me blood gnawed from their own wrists, even though blood sharing was like communion, a bond as close as family?

Two Blood Lifers saved me: Hartford, the powerful Long-lived (or angel-haired cupid to the johns), and my cousin Donovan (with slave name *ailill*, meaning *elf* in Irish Gaelic, just to right royally strip away his dignity).

I'd once done in Donovan's sadistic twin, Aralt; I'd saved the world too from his screwed up vision of using our venom in the name of superior evolution. Yet even Donovan, with his dark mop and lilac eyeshadow, blood shared.

We were united in adversity.

True hero?

They were the bloody heroes.

Sir knew?

I shook my nut quickly.

Sir's lips brushed my cheek, whispering wet patterns across the pretty pink of the skin. 'Come on, don't look so frightened. I'll keep you safe, my shadow. Your *Sir's* here. Just tell me which bad bitch is forcing you to feed. It's cupid, hmm?'

Shocked, I startled, but *Sir* held me fast. His long body hard on mine.

I had the sudden flashshot memory of Hartford's tiger-striped arse, bruised from the same riding crop, with which *Sir* had marked me, and then Hartford's brilliant smile, as he watched me suckle at his bloody wrist.

'No, *Sir*,' I blurted.

'Don't lie,' *Sir* jerked my nut back; *buggering hell that hurt*, 'you leeches think I'm stupid, isn't it?' When he laughed, every part of me wanted to crawl into itself and hide. 'Say it. The truth now.'

'No, *Sir*.'

'Cupid thinks he can be a father to you leeches. That he still be worth something. But look you, he be nothing but a whore, and after this offence? I'll send him back to *Master*. There was never no slave he couldn't break. Even cupid. The things *Master* will do when he trains him a second time--'

'No, *Sir*.'

Sir's lips crawled across mine. 'You must love the dark, isn't it?'

I heard a rustle. A movement, like the slither of black tar. Then *Sir* was dragging the hood over my nut again.

I screamed, thrashing side to side like a snared Komodo dragon, but I was pinned tight under *Sir*.

Then everything went black.

I was trembling. Sight, sound and smell: all gone. The scratch of leather was against my lips.

'Ailill,' I whispered.

I'd played the game and come out a fake: no *true hero*.

I'd lost.

Yet I'd made the darkness hesitate. Pause over my lips. And in that moment?

That was a sodding victory.

Then the black was being delicately rolled back: senses returned one by one. To a world I no longer wanted to face.

The Judas betrayal (of my own cousin), sickened me.

I heard *Sir's*, 'good boy,' as he ruffled my hair like I was a mutt.

Yet drowned in my own guilt, it was as if I was underwater. When *Sir* pushed himself off me, giving my cheek a final paternalistic pat, I doubled up with it.

What the bleeding hell had I just done?

The chest looked suspiciously heavy when *Sir* dragged it in. He'd taken off his jacket and sweat patches had formed like growths under his salmon pink shirt. He never sweated. Now he stank but he was smiling.

The smug bastard.

The chest was steel. Strapped shut and padlocked with leather round its middle like a chrysalis. There were also these strange pinprick holes along its side, as if...

The bloody, bollocking, buggering bastard...

Sir dropped the end of the chest hard, and I heard the groan.

I had a gander at *Sir* from kneel, not even attempting to hide the glare.

'Don't fret you,' *Sir* turned his smile on me indulgently, 'he can't hear us.'

Clang, clang.

When *Sir* banged on top of the chest, there was a terrified whimper; it clawed at my insides, shredding them.

'Sensory deprivation, like the hood, see? Hotter though. It's an experiment. Let's see if ailill enjoys the dark as much as you.'

Sir left me alone then. Alone with the chest.

I'd botched up, and Donovan was paying the price. It hurt too much to imagine Donovan as he danced the Charleston yesterday with Hartford around this cell, reliving Hartford's glory days on the hunt in the Cotton Club to the throb of Duke Ellington. Then as they'd snatched my hands, pulling me up too with them. As they'd pulled me out of despair, reigniting the fire and rebellion, which today had led to...

'Please, I'm sorry. Whatever I did...whatever it was? I'm sorry. *Sir*?'

Sir hadn't told Donovan.

Wanker that I am, I was shot with relief. Then I was sick from it. I knew what it was to suffer and not to know why.

I crawled across the cell to the chest as if – irony of bloody ironies – it could hurt me.

'I'm about to freak out here... This is not cool... *Sir*? Let me out... Let me out...'

Clang...Clang...Clang...

This time the banging was from inside the box. It was muted. Padded then; considerate of *Sir*. I reckon he didn't want the merchandise to bruise itself: that was his job.

I raised my trembling hand to the steel side; the heat was radiating in waves like the sun. But I didn't quite touch. The banging stopped. I heard a stifled sob.

'Are you there?' No more than a whisper.

'Yeah, Donovan, I'm here.'

'Is anybody there?'

Christ, I wished he could hear me. 'I'm here, you git.'

'I'm sorry.'

'No, I'm bloody sorry, right?'

'Just, don't hurt Hartford. I...whatever it was...I did it. Me.'

True hero, see?

I threw myself to the corner, as far as I could from that mummified box. And rocked when the screams started. Yet it was worse when they stopped.

Because Donovan's silence was like an accusation.

When *Sir* came back – all I knew by the burn for blood was that it must be days not hours – he found me huddled, with my knees drawn up and my arms over my nut, at the back of the cell. I'd briefly considered gouging out my own peepers, so I wouldn't have to keep looking at that chest – or I couldn't see it staring at me. See how guilt turns you potty?

Lady Macbeth has nothing on me.

Instead, I'd hidden and counted the cost of betrayal.

Then *Sir* was there, crouched like a long-legged spider, stroking my hair away from my mush, as he cooed, 'Is he disturbing you, my pretty little leech?'

I could've exploded in anarchic rage, until the world cowered in its rightful place at my feet. Instead, I twisted my silver S.L.A.V.E ring, as I stared at my dirty toes. 'No, *Sir*. But--'

'Yes?' There was danger in the tightness of that one word.

Family. It makes you weak. That's how they hurt you; shank you through the heart.

Love? It's for berks with neon signs over their goolies flashing *Boot Me Here*.

The world's one tangled web; you can strain against the sticky matrix all you like but you were born inside the nest. You'll die inside it.

I'd reckoned – daft bugger that I am – that my glorious rebirth into Blood Life had burnt through the web, and I was safe on the other side. But that was the lie. The con. As long as we love? We control, and we're controlled.

You don't have to be a slave to lose your freedom. Just look around you – every First and Blood Lifer is a zombie cradle to the grave.

And *Sir*? He was a necromancer.

If I denied family...love...then *Sir* couldn't make my dead limbs dance.

At least, that's what I thought.

'It was my fault I drank from ailill, *Sir*.'

'What a good boy you are. Confessing at last. So you need punishing then, don't you?'

I froze: not the outcome I was going for. *Not the dark, not the dark, not the dark...* 'If I'm punished, you'll let ailill out?'

'Do you want me to?'

Sir was playing with my hair, tufting it up into a mocking pompadour; I hungered to rip off his bloody fingers. 'I'm sorry I was bad and...I want to be good for you.'

I realised I'd walked the right humiliating line, when *Sir's* mush lit up. He stroked my cheek, now pale and perfect, as if to check I was real; I'd been wondering that too, ever since I'd been hunted, defanged and enslaved.

'Of course you do. I'll take that bitch away, and then we'll have some quality time, see? Just us. You'll still need to be punished.'

When I tensed, *Sir* chuckled, as if my conditioned terror was a blinding joke. 'A fortnight without blood. That'll teach you to only drink from one source. I feed you, isn't it? Me. Now,' his too soft lips whispered into my lobe, and I cringed, 'ailill didn't know why he was punished. That can be our secret - just between us.'

I'd been wrong: *Sir* could make me dance any time he liked. It hadn't mattered what I'd said or done. Because family? Love? They hadn't made me weak to *Sir's* magic.

My own bloody betrayal had.

Secrets: we all have them worming at our Souls.

Sir never told Donovan why he'd been punished, but *I* knew, and that's the bleeding point.

Hartford or Donovan.

That'd been the choice at the heart of it. Biological or chosen family.

I'd betrayed my blood, and everything comes down to blood. If Ruby – my Author – had been alive to see it? It wouldn't have been pretty: my goolies and trampling comes to mind.

I tell myself I betrayed Donovan out of fear for Hartford: to save Hartford from *Master*. He survived *Master's* loving attentions once; I barely came back from it. No one – not even a Long-lived – could come back twice.

Deep down, however, there's still that whimpering slave git *what if*..?

What if I grassed on Donovan because of my own unnatural fear of the dark? The black of that hood? *Sir's* control?

You reckon I've ever confessed this sin? Not bloody likely. You're the first person I've ever told.

Donovan is still - as he was then - in the dark.

Secrets stain, fester and ultimately corrupt.

We can all hurt and betray those around us. Even those we love. It just takes the right pressure.

Who do you trust?

You tell me this sob story, and I apologise on behalf of the wrongs sanctioned by the Blood Life Council: is that how this works?

I dare to dream.

There will be no apology, official or otherwise. The Blood life Council

established the human Blood Club to enslave our own kind – that's the *atrocity* you expect to expose? You've already set *Master's* Estate on fire.

What you fail to understand is the justification and necessity.

This'll be good.

Only certain Blood Lifers were selected for slavery: the most powerful lines, Magnificoes and their descendants.

Play another tune, I've heard this one.

You're throwbacks to wilder, darker times. Politically destabilizing to our new world. Fundamentals and fanatics. Our council was attempting to bring in worldwide modernizing regulations with the Highbury Edict. Hartford was the first to refuse.

What?

That's why he was our first acquisition. Hartford was trying to stop... He was in the way of the Council's authority.

Now listen here, sweetheart, there are only two words to justify the cruelty of one species enslaving its own: power and money. All the rest is spin.

Extermination. That's a third word. Captain used it, if slavery didn't work. If the old families couldn't be controlled.

Which is preferable? Slavery or extermination?

That's like asking a bloke how he'd prefer to be castrated: starting at the right or left bollock.

Still, at least it's a choice. Never gave us that, did you?

I don't speak for the Council.

Bleeding sounds like you do.

I'd start worrying more about how you'll sound when this witness is used in court.

Don't think I've forgotten that; not for one second. And it backfired, didn't it? The Blood Life Council's attempt to neuter your political enemies? Screw over the strongest bloodlines? You call us *tamed* Blood Lifers, but who's your Most Wanted now? On your Red List? In chains--

There are no chains, Mr Blickle.

Metaphorically speaking. See, I can use big words too. We Victorian bank clerks are the most viciously pedantic berks you'll ever find.

Shame you sound – and look – like a '60s Rocker then.

Shame you're too young to know we cleave to the times we pass through, nicking what we love best. Babes to this world, your Council don't even know how to be Blood Lifers. When were you elected? A decade ago? I've walked these streets generations before both your birth and rebirth. And the '60s brought me to life. Saved and freed me. I learnt we're not predators alone to nosh on humans as prey--

Play another tune, I've heard this one.

Ha–bloody–ha. How about this then? Us tamed Blood Lifers are the terrorists in your new world. Yet we only enslave, imprison and scapegoat blame those we fear.

You must be terrified of me.

Would you enjoy that? After your period of impotency?

My what now?

I believe you said you knew big words.

Your fangs were removed, as part of Abona's regimen. You haven't had them back for long; I can only imagine how disempowering that must've been.

Does it feel good to cause fear again? Instead of *tremble* with it?

You don't fear me. Why is that? Despite the obvious?

Who are you?

I'm Liberty. I'm born of Captain's fangs. And he's told me all about you - traitor.

I'm the traitor?

See here's the thing: you can betray love, family, country, your own species, the world...or yourself. I've done all of that, at one time or another. Our identities, however, shift like chameleons.

Still, if you're Captain's elected (my commiserations, by the way), then he knows by my fist what it's like to be defanged.

Does that make Captain impotent too?

You can ask him tonight when he returns.

Blinding. I've missed being brutally tortured. Hang on a tick, no, I haven't.

No need to be anxious; you're under my protection. I have the lead on this inquiry. No one'll hurt you for the next thirteen nights.

If you say so.

You asked who I trusted. It made me wonder, Mr Blickle: who do you trust?

You've got your one secret. Isn't that enough? What more do you want from me? Blood? Wait...don't answer that. Just an e-cig and my coat, that'll do me.

This isn't voluntary.

So I ask again, who do you trust?

Betrayed by your own people to your enemy. All it needs is the right pressure..? When it was applied to the Renegades they

buckled, choosing to hand over their leader for burning on Easter Sunday to save themselves.

Don't blame us that you don't like the outcome of their vote. We didn't rig it.

Everything's rigged. If you can't see it, only means you haven't worked out how yet.

For the purposes of the Light Inquiry, I wonder if you knew your family was a nest of Judases.

If they're Judas, does that make me Jesus?

Only if you have a messiah complex. Do you?

Bird once accused me of having a hero complex. Betrayal's a funny thing: it hurts the one who does it, more than the one who suffers it.

Will you still be saying that in two weeks? When you're facing the flames?

I didn't think my death was a dead cert? My witness--

Is the witness of a traitor, terrorist and betrayer. Tell it. See if it saves you.

Don't fret, I get this is my Last Will and Testament.

I won't hide from you, Captain, the Council or the danger of words because I've spent most of my life hiding in the shadows and hoping invisibility meant invulnerability.

But it doesn't.

Remaining the Lost condemned us to slavery.

I reckoned I could keep my misfit family safe by skulking on the edges in the dark.

Yet when you hide in the wardrobe – alone – that's when the monsters come. First Life or Blood.

They always find you.

The Cannibal Tarantula – that's what they called him. The Blood Lifer I met one night in Southwark.

Met? Maybe too strong a word.

The Tarantula was quite a Blood Lifer tourist attraction back in the 1960s. He nested in the crypt beneath Southwark Cathedral choir. I'd crossed London Bridge, prowling through derelict warehouses, which had been bombed out in the Second World War and left to rot, home to squatters and junkies.

Ruby would've delighted in exploring such horrors back when she'd first authored me. But by then? She'd become distracted by her brother Aralt: money and power. Plus blood sharing with him, let's not forget that. I'd been left that summer in '68 to wander London alone.

There was always going to be danger in that.

I jumped the last two stone steps, landing in a fog of bone and stone dust. I spluttered, as it caught in my nostrils, stinking of decay and the merry dance of death.

Just my kind of joint.

I bowed my head under the low arch, peering through the deep black. Corroded lead coffins lined the crypt, which was sealed to humans. We Blood Lifers had our own way in. Sweat trickled down my neck; bleeding hell it was like being baked in a stone oven.

'Mr Tarantula, I don't fancy playing the fly but I've come for tea, yeah?'

No reply, only the faintest rustling at the far reaches of the crypt.

Sighing, I swaggered towards the sounds, which became dry *snaps*, *cracks* and *scraping*, which had my fangs aching.

I needed my bleeding nut examined.

An albino web of bones tangled out of the gloom.

'Bloody hell...'

A Blood Lifer crouched inside the white cage, hiding in the shadows, but it didn't look up... *Snap*... Its long hair covered its mush, but its industrious fingers never paused... *Crack*... A femur was shaped, pushed into the intricate framework of the web... *Scrape*... Just for a moment, glowing peepers darted to mine and then away.

Yet although it was as grubby as any street urchin, it was dressed – *he* was dressed - like a toff, in striped boater jacket and dove grey waistcoat; his socks stuck out comical grimy, as he worked hunched over.

It was as if someone had dressed him up doll-like to keep up appearances.

'Shame of it is, he won't feed from First Lifers.'

'Christ in heaven...'

If I hadn't been so distracted by the sight of a bloke building his own human bone cage, whilst dressed like he was watching a 1920s Boat Race, I'd have sensed the Blood Lifer sidling up behind me in an emerald beaded flapper dress.

She was the type of bint I would've both idolized and been too much of a mouse to raise my gaze to in First Life; her majesty grabbed you by the bollocks. If I hadn't already been leashed by Ruby, she'd have collared me.

The Flapper caressed my shoulder, tracing over the gold ace of spades on the back of my leathers, as if this was a new sign language. When she stroked lower between my legs, I jumped.

'It's a damn bother but he needs Blood Lifer. Blood, I mean. Yet he won't feed from me.' The anguish in the Author's frown made a lie of the studied boredom in her words, as well as her wandering hands, which were crawling over my arse, like she was laying claim to it. How many times had she repeated this routine, like she was the sideman in a freak show? When the Flapper pressed her palm to the web and a bone clattered to the stone floor, I flinched. 'Will you feed him?'

'You must be off your trolley.'

The Flapper's mask slipped; such fire burned she could blaze continents to ash. I took a step back. Then her mush was blank again. She swung her pearl necklace in tense arcs, as if winding a hidden weapon. 'Don't be so horribly wet; put your arm through.'

At the sounds of the clattering bone, the Tarantula had become still. His nut twisted towards us. Then he...sniffed...as if scenting the air.

The bird had circled me predator-like. The crafty bugger was now between me and the way out of the crypt.

How voluntary exactly was this *donation*?

My black t-shirt was sticking to me, like a damp layer of skin, but I wasn't taking off my jacket. Not in this place, no bloody way.

I inched my arm towards the cage.

When, however, was I ever frightened of being bitten?

I thrust my arm into the web, with my hand tightly fisted because I didn't want my fingers to look like delicious nibbles.

A scuffling *scuttle* and...

The Tarantula was there.

His warm breath was over my tender wrist - right over the pulse point.

Blood sharing was intimate, and I was about to break one of those rules with...

He was beautiful. His black hair hanging in matted waves over a mush as pale as his bone prison.

His violet peepers were...blind.

The Tarantula was so thin his ribs showed through like knives. His delicate fingers were searching, smoothing over my wrist in quick motions.

'The darkness,' he muttered. 'The black feeds. Three...three...three...'

Each *three* lit up spectacular explosions in my brain: my magical number. Hearing it gunshot chanted, with the sensation of the Tarantula's soft strokes over my pulse point, was orgasmic.

Shuddering, I breathed, 'Have yourself a good nosh, mate. Looks like you need it.'

Tarantula startled, like he hadn't expected to be spoken to; I wondered how long it'd been since he had been. I don't know why I'd felt the nancy need to reassure this stranger. Why did I give a rat's arse if he shriveled to nothing in his web?

Yet the idea of being trapped tugged at me, awakening a confusion of new feelings.

That's why when Tarantula sank in his fangs deep I hissed, yet – just as fast – I was lost. I closed my peepers in ecstasy.

I could feel the steady suck, the touch of his lips and the swirl of his venom: it was firework in heaven glorious. I was caught in the bond, every molecule alive with it.

Sod it, no hunt or feed can equal blood sharing.

I wondered faintly why Ruby had denied such joy to me – rationing her own bite, as well as other blood sharing – she might as well have forbidden me to wank.

The Tarantula? He was touched. Some of us don't survive the rebirth whole or put a match to our Souls after. Else the snowflake patterns of difference were there to start with and Blood Life merely amplified.

What I couldn't figure – as I swam in the bubbling flow of our bonding – was whether Tarantula had caged himself or *been* caged. Whether he truly was touched? Or if this treatment of him (and didn't I bloody remember it well from Bedlam?), had *turned* him touched?

The dark...

I smiled, sinking deeper into the bond, imagining Ruby's expression if I brought Tarantula back to Advance with me. If I saved him...

When suddenly – agonizingly – the bond was broken.

I shot up.

The Author was standing next to me. A human rib, gory crimson, still grasped in her mitt. She dropped it – *clatter* – so loud in the silence.

Woozy, it took me a moment to...

Tarantula lay on his back in the bone cage staring up at the stone ceiling of the crypt, with his unseeing violet peepers. Red crept out of his waistcoat.

Over his heart.

Where the bitch had shanked him.

I'd been a distraction. A toy to dangle, whilst she did in her own elected.

I don't know whether it was the blood sharing, but I was shaking.

'He came back wrong,' the Flapper whispered, staring down at the boy she'd authored and then murdered. 'The Order of Electors warned me, but I thought it no account. I stole him away, before they could... I hoped I would be enough.'

I didn't hesitate, and she didn't stop me.

When I rammed the same rib through the Flapper's heart, she fell next to the cage like an emerald butterfly. Broken – the same as the kid she'd authored. Her pearls spilled like shining tears into the crimson.

She stretched out to try and touch the Tarantula's fingers with her own but couldn't through the layers of human bone.

How's that for bleeding irony?

It turns out you can't hide in the shadows. You're not safe in your cage. And the dangers in life? They're from those you love, as well as from across the divide of the species.

You know what I learnt that day? There's no way to tell who's the predator.

And who's the prey.

NIGHT 2

I keep my promises; I hope that's duly noted.

No need to get your knickers in a twist, sweetheart, it's only...all right, not *only* anything, but it's an e-cig and a leather jacket. Not the promise to save me from the lick of the flames or to let *him* go.

I thought family made you weak.

I was wrong.

I'm glad we have that recorded: I don't imagine you say it often.

Shows how little you know me. So, listening yesterday were you?

That's why I'm here.

What you do in here is anything but listen. Analyze, twist, manipulate...I haven't figured it out yet.

But not listen.

This bloody room is smothering me: red floors, ceiling, poncey rugs and cherry desk, as if this is an interrogation suite for billionaires. I could sink in my fangs and drain the whole sodding room. It does match your lipstick though...

We're Blood Lifers. Unlike the human slavers, we don't need training on – *interrogation* **– was it?**

Because that, Mr Blickle, is the point of the Red Room.

Red Room? If you wanted to spank me, you only had to ask.

If I intended to spank you, I wouldn't ask first.

I wonder what Sun would say?

Is that like *What Would Jesus Do*? But for Blood Lifers?

Sun's a law unto herself. If I knew what she'd say..?

Maybe you wouldn't be here.

Maybe she'd love me, as much as I love her. Like she's the true sun, and I'm melting every time she looks at me. Like she's the light, and without her I'm in the dark.

Except that's just the hearts and cupid.

The real stuff, deep in your guts, todger, wormed in your brain...like maybe then she'd see what having a life born from my fangs feels like; a screaming, bloody part of me ripped from my Soul. Forever aching. Sensing her move inside me, even after the wonder of her rebirth.

Touching the beauty of her death and sharing my life.

Saving her to be mine.

For the purposes of the Light Inquiry, I'll summarize that you love Sun?

You have no Soul.

It's not been proven either way. We have our scientists and philosophers working on it. Now I kept my agreement (you're

smoking that e-cig, aren't you?), so I require a secret.

How about I'll show you mine, if you show me yours?

I'm not Clarice, and you're not Hannibal. Keep your promise, please.

I always keep a promise.

Your memory's photographic: prove to the Council you have some use. Tell me about this new family of yours.

Hartford: a dangerous Long-lived, dissenter and now terrorist.

A Renegade.

Hartford's long pale fingers wove across the keys of a battered black baby grand. His left hand leapt in rhythmic, Art Tatum style bursts of sheer jubilation.

In open-necked crisp white shirt and indigo blazer, with his golden hair slicked back, Hartford looked like an angelic jazz singer, under the club's weak spotlight.

I was lost in the rattling rawness of Hartford's improvised "Rhapsody in Blue". My spine tingled. Skin prickled. I could taste the notes, each sharp or sour.

When I caught Hartford's eye, I grinned.

Tentatively, he smiled back.

It'd taken months to get Hartford up there: in this club, outside and out of his sleeping bag.

It was a bloody victory.

I'd take what I could sodding well get.

Then a starkers dancer spun between us, and I got an eyeful of dick.

Wait, that doesn't sound...

'Hartford's not some wee lamb to the slaughter. Adorable he is to be sure, but stop mothering him. Get your arse back to work.' The strip club's tiny manager – Aedan – swatted me on the arse with a bar towel, as he pushed me towards the counter.

'What'll it be, mate?'

I heard Aedan *tut* behind me, smothered my grin and gazed up at the posh fellah in sleek grey business suit and even greyer hair. He was drumming his fingers on the counter with repressed frustration, like he yearned to take me over his knee but was having to put up with smiling paternalistically instead.

Guess he liked to play the Daddy.

Daddy looked as if he'd come from the City and a stressed day fleecing folks of their lolly to lounge on Peter Pan's faux crocodile skin and fur sofas and drool over starkers boys, as well as Blood Lifers centuries older than himself.

Still, to the outside world we were young men. So what did that make us?

Fair game.

Not if I could bleeding help it. Not one of these Lost Boys.

My fangs itched. My blood pounded. The urge to hunt – violate the bastard's sagging throat and feast on human blood, breaking my abstention – stole my breath.

I clutched the counter's sticky surface; I knew I was panting.

'Cotton candy martini,' the bloke reached out, stroking the back of my hand; his fingers were moisturized, and for a horrifying moment reminded me of *Sir*, 'shaken, not stirred.' He bayed with laughter, as if I hadn't heard that one before.

'Not sure 007 ever asked for cotton candy. Even at a carnival,' I satisfied myself with pointing out.

See it's like this: black wool dinner jacket, me, bloody had to wear it.

I looked a dead poncey git.

On the first night, we'd huddled in the box room behind the bar, which had nothing in it but a hanging rail of clothes and a cracked sink; it stank of sweat and sex.

Hartford had smoothed down my satin lapels. 'Look at you, mac, all dolled up. Why aren't you the bee's knees?'

'Leave it out,' I'd shaken him off, before glancing at Donovan. 'How's your costume?'

Donovan had twirled. 'Groovy, man, this is gonna be a blast.'

I'd raised my eyebrow.

Donovan was starkers. In just a silk bowtie...and black tube socks.

Because the punters had to stuff the tips somewhere.

'This is your choice. You don't have to--'

'Don't freak out. I wasn't... Blood Clubbers didn't hurt me, like they did Hartford and you. Hartford will play, I'll dance, and we'll get the cash we need. Together.'

I shook the cranberry, grenadine and vodka like it was a missile, rather than a cocktail, pouring it into a glass. Then I sprinkled cotton candy on top, waiting for the magic. It dissolved into the blood red sea, as if it'd never been there.

Mesmerized, it gave me the shivers. Daddy looked unimpressed.

I pushed the martini over to the Daddy wannabe, whilst humming "Rhapsody in Blue". The smarmy bastard slipped a folded note across my palm and then up into the tip jar: a pair of starkers legs with an opening where the todger should've been.

The classy only went so far.

I dropped in a slice of lime, my fingers grubby from collecting the dancers' tips. 'Enjoy.' I smiled around my canines.

Suddenly Daddy's frustration wasn't so repressed anymore. 'Stupid slut.'

And that was it.

The fangs shot from my gob. The predator inside blazed. Howled. He wasn't leashed; I wasn't tamed.

I was free.

The only one holding me back? Stopping this fur-lined operatic club, where the boys never grew up, from becoming a crimson bed of carnage and chaos?

Me.

There was only me now - and that's what was giving me the bleeding willies.

I sprang over the counter in a haze of fury, my tailcoat catching on the edge, like I'd devolved into a monkey. Except that'd be a human; I should say Komodo dragon. When I thrashed to the side, something ripped.

That'd cost me.

When I slammed Daddy back, he splashed his martini down his designer shirt, like I'd already savaged his throat.

He was tall: twice my size. Yet he couldn't push me back.

It was cracking not to be the weak one anymore.

The smug tosser looked as if a beggar had told him to *shove his pound.*

'See, I reckoned I just made you a drink. Barman here. Seems to me you're confused.'

Daddy laughed. It was shaky, but he still laughed.

'I'm supposed to be frightened, am I? Of a little bitch like you?'

'You bleeding well should be.'

I could hear his blood. The rapid *beat*, *beat*, *beat*.

I ran my tongue over my lips.

One quick bite.

Heart attack: his death certificate would read. *Natural causes*. Who would care?

I took a shuddering breath. I was the moral example (and wasn't that a bleeding joke?), for my family. If I slipped, there was nothing holding any of them back from returning to the hunt.

Who was left to stop *me* falling into the dark? To help me become the man I've been striving to be for decades...but...the *blood*...and Daddy was struggling now... Fear smells and tastes sweeter with a hint of terror... *Yeah, that's right, a bit of a struggle, always liked that, gets the blood pumping...*

The piano faltered. Notes fractured and broke.

Hartford.

I swung round, forcing in my fangs.

Buggering hell.

Hartford was having a shufti. He'd seen.

I dropped my nut, unable to meet his gaze.

In my distraction, my quarry had wrenched away; I could hear him bleating to Aedan. It sounded more like a kid telling on his classmate to earn him a caning than an alpha Daddy.

Plus his shirt was buggered. So there was that.

I tensed when Aedan stormed towards me, flicking his auburn braids like whips. 'Your fanboy over there – the squealer – wants you fired.'

I shrugged.

'He said he was playing some head games, and you made a holy show of yourself.'

'Thing is, I'm not his to play with. Not anyone's.'

'That's why I'm throwing out his crybaby arse,' Aedan replied loudly.

'What?' Daddy stomped over, towering behind Aedan.

'Do we have to get the bouncer?' I smiled. 'I wouldn't make us if I were you; she really doesn't like folks touching me.'

Catching the glint in my eye, Daddy hurriedly shook his nut, before stalking away.

'Cheers, I--'

'You know who you remind me of?' Aedan poked me hard in the chest.

'James Dean? Joe Strummer? A young Michael Caine, you know, in *Alfie*--'

'Me.'

'No offence,' I examined the elfin mush of my boss, with his moss green peepers and mouth, which looked like it was about to curl into a grin, 'but we're not exactly twins.'

'When I'd just got away from my ex. He was a bad boy and not in the good way. We'd had quite the carry on. That's when I opened this place.' There was something about the way Aedan had said *got away from*, which made my hackles rise in an instinctive protective response. This was a First Lifer: not family. Yet somehow that wasn't what my blood was calling to me, when it screamed for revenge on the tosser, who'd forced this...whatever this new closeness...not family but *friend* my Soul whispered...to escape.

'So how am I like you again?

Aedan glanced at Hartford, who was settling in for the big finale.

Donovan writhed snake-like down the center arm of the stage to the rhythm of Hartford's music; his slim muscles rippled.

I watched too – teeth gritted – as the First Lifers pressed folded tips into his socks, caressing up and down his oiled thighs. Donovan was grinning and flexing like it was all some cosmic joke, which I hadn't been let in on.

He was high; he was always sodding high.

Donovan was turning, sliding down the stage as if in a mating ritual, never taking his gaze from Hartford, who played like his tune was a returning mating call.

And eye-fucking? I finally got what that meant.

I could sense Hartford's aching fevered obsession. Bloody hell, hadn't I felt obsession like it often enough myself?

Those pounding, pulsing humans were blind to the death playing and dancing as vitally as they'd ever be just...different.

Hartford hunched over the piano, his back as tense as his jazz, like wings were hidden under his shoulder blades, ready to break out and carry him away from the world.

I'd better check on him.

Aedan sensed my slight movement towards Hartford; he rested his hand on my elbow. 'That's how. On edge and about to bolt. As well as looking like Batman and Robin's personal bodyguard.'

'It's the dinner jacket. Anyway, Batman and Robin? Which is which?'

Aedan patted my arm. 'You can't tell?'

'I promised to keep them safe.' Aedan stared at me, startled. I hadn't been able to hide the anguish; Aedan had broken through to it, and now it choked me. 'To give them a home. I promised.'

Listening to the soulful blues of Hartford's set, those chilling snaking improvisations haunted me, as if the specter of our slavery was still on all our shoulders.

In the close swirling heat of the club, as the First Lifers danced to the rhythms of the Charleston, in front of the stage, which was divided by a walkway into the shape of a cross, Hartford was messianic.

Under mirror balls hung in alien-like clusters, blokes sprawled in red looped seats, as if they'd parked their arses in frightened mouths (or twisty todgers, depending how you looked at it). The walls and ceilings were in leather, damask and brocade.

A fantasy. A theatre production. None of it real.

'We all have our histories and pasts. No home but here. Look around you,' Aedan gestured at the other dancers: our real Lost Boys. Brandon with a shock of neon green hair, Kyle with gold nipple rings and tiny Jamie with the stammer. Aedan had taken them in. Like he had us - the daft berk. Didn't he know it was dangerous to invite in strangers? 'How about we close up a wee bit early?'

I gawped at Aedan. 'It the Apocalypse?'

Aedan flicked me with the bar towel. I squawked. 'I'll go tell She-Who-Must-Be-Obeyed.'

Aedan sidestepped the drunks and gropers with the skill of a boxer, before disappearing into the crowd.

Hartford had finished his set. "The Killing Moon" spilled spectral across the sound system. Hartford was dancing with Donovan now in the dark of the club to the mysterious mandarin style bass and cello.

They were lost in each other. Lost to this world. Lost to the First Lifers of this stinking club, as they reveled to be alive in our glorious second evolution.

Their cheeks touched; Donovan's dark mop was falling over his mush. His snake-green eyeshadow sparkled. They were whispering secrets to each other, with these wicked smiles.

Hartford was centuries old: power radiated from him. He glowed. Yet he was dancing with his stripper partner – my cousin – in a human club because I was too afraid to be discovered by our own kind.

But this was my London. The dark and dirty behind the pretty.

Crash.

'Bleeding hell...'

I ducked – just in time – as two black disembodied hands flew by my nut and – *crash* – there went a prime bottle of gin.

And my night's pay.

Gloves.

Black gloves: my brain was just able to untangle, before I was surrounded in black (I forget how tall she is), the soft sway of ash blonde hair and a mouth.

Sun.

I was sodding consumed by her. The life born of my fangs.

She wasn't Grayse.

Grayse had died that night out on the moors, I knew that now, but Sun had blazed to birth on her passing and she was here burning up every inch of me. A life created from me but never less than me. I wasn't her Ruby. I'd authored her but I'd never be more than her equal.

Christ how I'd spent my long life aching to discover that.

Then I whimpered.

Icy fingers had worked their way up the back of my white shirt and were playing my spine like it was a piano. I tried to pull away, but bugger it was Sun powerful.

She smelled of cheap Tahitian Gardenia and freedom - *me*.

Sun nibbled my lips with her teeth. 'It's wick raw out. See what an ice queen I've frozen into on account of standing at the door all night?'

'Suits you.' When those torturing fingers teased their way towards the front of my trousers, I looked up into Sun's flint peepers and was relieved to see the laughter there. 'We could always swap back? You're the one wanted to be the Big Bad.'

'Na-ah, Mr Penguin suits *you*,' Sun flicked my bowtie, 'plus you make more tips in the dick jar.'

'There is that. Aedan takes too many risks for us anyhow; it's not like you've got a license or whatnot..?'

'I'm not a frickin' dog.'

I couldn't quite hide my grin. 'I remember telling you the same thing.'

Disgruntled, Sun snorted.

I grabbed both her cold hands, which felt blinding (and not just because it kept me safe from their torment), as I tugged her towards the dancefloor. 'Come on, or we'll miss it.'

Traditions. Habits. Rituals. Call it what you like, they bond and familiarize. Even the broken, fragmented and lost. Maybe us more than most. There's a risk, however, a danger in every one we add crutch-like.

That we don't control them: they control us.

Blokes in pinstripes, leather or starkers. Brandon's punk hair and a punter's neat side parting. Donovan and Hartford at the throbbing heart: a flash of white and sweating pink. United First and Blood in the musky heat going wild to the club's signature closing song: the creepy, joyful alienation of Echo and the Bunnymen's "People Are Strange".

Caught in the song's rapture, we were laughing, as I drew Sun close. I warmed her hands between mine: she fitted.

For the first time in 150 years I had the one I loved, family and a home.

I had hope.

I was bleeding soaring.

The organ rose to its ecstatic crescendo: lights burst in my mind. The world expanded. Who needed blood when I had this?

Sun's fingers – hot and aggressive now – stroked down my neck. Questing. Her lips seared, as they pressed to mine.

Then we were kissing, as we were crushed amongst those First Lifers jumping to a song, which was warning them to look out for the very creatures in the shadows who were snogging in their midst.

Humans are berks like that.

We broke apart, when the strippers rushed onto the stage for the finale, Donovan amongst them. They writhed and twirled along that cross, as the punters whooped and catcalled, tossing money like confetti - and the grooms were for sale.

Sun's body was entwined with mine; I could hear her harsh breathing. I was losing myself in her.

In those hedonistic moments of psychedelia, we were forgetting everything.

And for me? The human camera?

That's like…heaven.

Christ I hope so.

The world. Our pasts. The pain.

Because right then? We were happy.

We were free.

You'll only truly understand what that means, when you've been a slave.

Forgetting? Losing myself in the music? Dance? The feel of Sun's lips – body – against mine was as good as the sweet opiate of blood.

Almost.

Yet I know in the choice between fight and flight I'd chosen flight. Safety. When you have family it's a Siren call.

A sudden swing of red braids.

Aedan threw himself chimp-like at Hartford, who stumbled back and then laughing, twirled Aedan round: a First Lifer clambering up a Blood Lifer like he was trying to climb the evolutionary tree.

They were giggling. Whispering. Pawing. Two kids escaped to a playground.

Sun hissed, but when I licked up her neck, it turned into a sigh.

I watched over Sun's shoulder in shock, as Donovan dived off the stage and ripped Aedan away from Hartford.

Buggering hell.

Aedan's arms were windmilling, as Donovan's mouth was pressing closer and closer to Aedan's throat.

'Sodding git…' I elbowed my way through the crush of sweating, sexed up bodies – their blood pumping *beat – beat – beat*. I could smell it in every blood bag, beneath their skin.

Bleeding hell, I could drain every one of them dry; Ruby and I would've made a crimson soaked tempest night of it.

I closed my peepers; wet pricked their edges.

'For crying out loud, mac, what's your beef?' Hartford wrenched Donovan by the hair, ripping him away from Aedan's neck.

Was Aedan bitten?

I was panting. The shock or...horror?

Aedan looked dazed. He was rubbing his throat. I caught him around his waist before he could fall.

He didn't seem paralyzed.

Please, please...just...sodding please...

Why did I care if one First Lifer died? Only Kathy - my Moon Girl for over fifty years – had ever truly crossed the divide of species. Why was my heart beating so hard my bloody chest ached?

Hartford was still dangling Donovan starkers by his dark tumble of hair; Donovan was howling like a trapped animal. We were putting on quite a show.

The other dancers were having a gander now: they looked pissed. The punters were amused at the extra entertainment.

'Outside,' I snapped, before reconsidering. 'Clothes on. Then outside.'

Hartford nodded. 'We'll beat it.' Then he pushed a path off the dancefloor, caveman dragging Donovan squirming and squealing after him.

When Aedan stroked my mush, I looked down. 'Now tell me you don't know who's Batman and who's Robin?' Aedan wriggled in my arms. 'I'm not a damsel in need of rescuing; you can let go now.'

'Right, sorry.'

I backed up. Had Aedan been bitten? I ran my fingers down his neck.

Aedan jerked away. 'Cop on and stop being a cock-tease.'

'I wasn't--'

Aedan waved it away. 'Like Donovan wasn't?'

'About that. I mean, are we alright?'

'You mean: are you fired?' Aedan's gaze had hardened.

I sensed Sun at my shoulder. When I glanced back, she smiled; all at once I knew what it was not to be alone.

Aedan shifted, before shaking his nut. 'This is your home, you tool. Now go and sort out those two idiots of yours.'

When I found them in the dank alley behind Peter Pan's, where the pyramid of rubbish bags spilled stale beer bottles and used condoms, Hartford had Donovan slammed against the brick wall, with an arm against his throat...and he was right royally narked.

'We do not eat friends,' Hartford ground his arm into Donovan's throat harder with each word.

I leant against the wall, crossing my arms. Donovan glanced at me, as if for help. I simply raised my eyebrow.

'You're blowing my mind. Since when were First Lifers friends? *Your* friends?'

Hartford lowered his arm; Donovan fingered the blossoming bruises. 'Pipe down, will you? Aedan's on the up and up. Can't you see I'm balled up right now, baby? So Light says *no humans*, and that means we're on the wagon-avous.'

Donovan's features gentled. 'Yeah, man, I understand-avous. But...*friend*? After First Lifers...tortured...raped...' He swallowed carefully. 'We're still slaves inside. You still freak out over nothing: your nightmares and Light's.'

Hartford couldn't meet his eye. Or mine. He was shaking. 'I need this. I just...'

I wished Donovan would shut up or Sun would hurry up.

What we needed?

A good hunt.

All right then: pretend hunt. Get the blood rushing and the predator roaring. Bury the ghosts because they'll never vanish, only fade. You have to learn to live with the unwelcome lodgers.

That's when I sensed him: the other Blood Lifer.

He was lurking – and yeah, anyone who lurks is suspicious in my book – at the end of the alley behind the industrial-sized green recycling bins.

He was watching us.

I was already coiled for the hunt. I didn't even hesitate; I shot off into the black.

The bloke, however, was ninja fast. I only clocked a hoodie patterned with skulls before he was gone. Me? Now I could leg it with the best of them.

I buzzed with the predator freed, leaping over walls and bike racks. I was clouted when I shoved by a pug-faced john with a skanky hooker on her knees. I spun but didn't even pause, as my peeper swelled: the gap was closing.

The wanker was leading me through rabbit warren alleys; the tang of the Thames was sharp on the breeze. Polish music bled from cars into the still of the night. Inside my brain, however, Echo and the Bunnymen was playing on loop, jabbering how sodding strange I was.

I'd have beaten my nut bloody on a lamp post, painting it scarlet – *of course I know I'm strange, have some of that* – if I hadn't been so close.

I caught a glimpse of Blood Lifer – a slice of black.

I hammered my fist against my forehead and sped up.

For one brief moment, his slim figure was silhouetted against Southwark Cathedral. He was having a gander back over his shoulder.

At me.

As if he *wanted* me to follow...

I stumbled, before catching myself.

The bloody cheeky bastard.

So he was playing cat and mouse..?

I prowled back the way I'd come through the frozen streets under the death-white moon, working my way round. Bladdered geezers in blue shirts weaved in rowdy bands. The night stank of beer and desperation.

Typical Saturday night in London then.

I ducked down, jumping over the last wall.

The Blood Lifer was leaning against a humungous gleaming finger up to the sky, which they call the Shard.

He would be – the tosser.

I shoved my hands into my pockets, as I swaggered up behind him.

When I tapped him on the shoulder, he jumped a bleeding mile. He could barely have been authored: no instincts at all.

When he spun round, I saw he was a kid. A bloody Emo: skull patterned hoodie, black and white striped socks and matching scarf. Even a t-shirt with cartoon vampire: cute fangs and bat wings.

Perfect – he had a sense of irony too.

Emo flicked his long black fringe, which was sprayed green like a mouldy skunk; his peepers were rimmed with enough eyeliner for one too.

Donovan would want to swap tips.

Then Emo crossed his arms and tapped his foot, as if I'd been the one who'd been caught out being a bad boy.

And yeah, I was bloody bad but I'd proved I was no boy.

I frowned. 'Who the bleeding hell are you?'

Emo just smirked.

That did it. No more Mr Nice Light.

'Look, you pain in my arse, why were you watching us? Can you talk to me or do you have to go get your daddy first?'

The Emo's smirk widened. Then he head-butted me.

Crack – there went my nose.

Hand strikes – *one, two, three* – so rapid I didn't have time to think more than: Emo kids knocking the stuffing out of you with Kenpo Karate? Now that's not something you see every day.

I choked on the pain blazing in hot shocks where his small hand sliced.

No more Mr Nice Light? *All right then.*

I grabbed the end of Emo's stripy scarf and twisted. His turn to choke.

Gasping, Emo hesitated - *my in*.

Because here's the thing: *I know karate too.* And the moment Emo realised it?

Blinding.

I slammed an elbow strike, followed by swift knife-hands, driving Emo crashing back against the glass Shard. It trembled. He kicked my legs; I gritted my teeth but didn't lose ground. Close now, I went for a flurry of strikes, until all I could hear was his soft grunts and the hit of flesh on flesh.

I'd missed this: fists and fangs. You can't tame a predator – and I've never pretended to be a hero.

Battering that cartoon vampire with its ironic batwings?

Don't knock it until you've tried it.

Reluctantly, I eased back, but kept my hand pressed to the brat's chest.

Emo was panting, yet he still had that *not bothered* expression.

I tilted my nut. 'So now that's out of your system, let's try this again. Why are you spying on us? Who do you reckon you are? Bond?'

It was Emo's turn to tilt his nut, as he assessed me.

Confused, I glanced down: dinner jacket and bowtie.

Sodding hell.

I sighed, easing back from him. 'Names Light. Just...Light. Now whatever this is? Can we get on with it? It's been a long night. I need a kip and a quick bonk. That's not an offer, by the way. I have a girl...'

That's when Emo pulled out the shooter.

For a long moment, I simply stared at it – sleek and dark – between us.

Emo's mush had suddenly stilled. It was strangely blank.

I blinked. 'You're having a laugh.' Emo cocked the shooter. His finger on the trigger. Not *having a laugh* then. 'Stop waving around that todger extension. Unless you're figuring on shooting me through the heart, it can't do me in.'

'You're right,' Emo sounded so sodding young, stood there with a gun and fangs but no clue as to the true power of either weapon, 'but it'll hurt. Won't it?'

Bang.

I screamed.

The barmy bleeding buggering bastard....

Scarlet searing exploding agony. I hunched over, struggling not to hurl.

Emo had shot me in the foot. He'd totally destroyed my boot.

Grayse – before she was Sun – had given me those boots. I was going to pay Emo back for taking that from me.

I stared up at Emo, astonished. 'We don't use guns; they're the humans' toys. Don't you know anything about being a Blood Lifer?'

Casually, Emo shrugged, as he slipped the shooter back into the waistband of his tight jeans. 'I was told you were a rebel,' *sneer* – there was definite sneer in his tone, 'you don't sound like one to me.'

He was examining the gory gaping wound in my foot; his peepers were lit with enthusiasm. 'How does that feel?'

'Bloody awful, you little bastard.'

Emo nodded, as if this was a valid answer, which he was storing for future reference.

I shuddered, before trying to leap at him with my fangs out but only ended up – *clang* - against the front of the Shard, gasping with the pain of my shattered foot, when Emo casually sidestepped, mooching away towards London Bridge.

'Oi, come back here...' I punched the glass. Then regretted it.

Throbbing hand, foot and a long way to limp home? Not exactly how I saw the night ending.

Footsteps. Running. Blood Lifers.

Here was to facing the gallows - or a boot to the goolies.

'Bollocks,' I grunted, as I hit the floor hard, rolling side to side; I curled foetal around my...yeah, bollocks.

I peered misty-eyed up at Sun and then wished I hadn't.

'That's for booking it outta there without me.'

'Point taken,' I gasped, still massaging my privates, as if somehow I could wank the pain out.

Sun was breathless like she'd legged it halfway across...

Bugger it.

I took a shufti at Donovan and Hartford, who were sauntering towards me, their arms casually wrapped around each other's waists.

I reached up my hand, as if Hartford would drag me to my feet in a show of male solidarity, but he batted it away. 'Swell. Now we don't have to kick the poor little bunny too.'

'That's lovely.'

'You're screwy. Still thinking you're the superhero, mac?'

I rolled my eyes, as I slumped onto my back. I didn't know what hurt more: my blown to smithereens foot, pulverized goolies or Hartford's words.

No, the sight of the hole in my motorcycle boot - that did it. I could've bleeding bawled.

'Bit of sympathy; man down here.'

'Not a chance,' Donovan now, his shadow dark over me. Couldn't leave him out: each one lined up to twist the knife. I was discovering it was the role of leader to take it. Must be why prime ministers go grey so fast: have you noticed that? I squinted up through the agony; Donovan was still narked. 'It's not cool. All these stunts. You're not alone; none of us are, not anymore. We're tight, which means no more wigging out. We need you and--'

'Alright, no need to make a song and dance out of it.' I accepted Donovan's hand, and he tugged me bouncing onto my one good leg.

'Bummer,' Donovan examined the wound.

'Chowderhead destroyed your boot,' Sun pouted, before curling her arm around my shoulder, as carefully as if I'd suddenly transformed to china: born of my fangs, she understood.

Even when she'd been mistress, she'd crossed the gulf of both role and species. She'd seen *me*.

Those boots were more than merely the first tentative gift of love – they'd been the return of my freedom. Identity. Soul.

As I limped slowly towards home surrounded by my strange family, I knew I was no superhero.

The people I loved were safe, however, and that was enough to hope.

If that was the only time I'd seen the Emo kid with his skull hoodie and bat wing vampire t-shirt, I'd have been a happy bloke.

But it wasn't.

So you want a secret? Something no one knows?

The next week I went hunting. Hunting my own kind. And emo was my prey.

Did I tell Hartford, Donovan or Sun?

Did I cocoa.

They'll have my balls if they ever find out.

They figured I needed time in the glory of the night to work through the trauma and nightmare of our slavery.

Thing is? You don't *work through* something like that: you survive or adapt.

I'd already done both.

I tracked the psychopathic pillock across Southwark: along the Thames, through Borough Market, which was kaleidoscopic with the fresh scents of fish, chicken and bread, and around the circular Globe that was like a bloody UFO landing. I shadowed him through alleys, which were dives back when blokes got their jollies from bull and bear baiting, and now got them from suck and hand jobs.

Other nights Emo would wander in the upmarket districts with their poncey bars, galleries and gated communities, which thumbed their noses at the rest of the poor sods clinging to the backsides of the housing estates.

Emo never, however, crossed London Bridge. Maybe he reckoned the rhyme was a curse: *London Bridge is falling down...falling down...my fair lady.*

I'd taken to humming it, as I stalked my melancholy ghost.

Here's the thing: I couldn't work out if I was hunting him. Or if he was hunting me.

All I knew? He wasn't going anywhere.

One night Emo led me along a row of cafés. It was freezing. I huddled in my leathers in front of a closed graphic novels bookshop: yeah, I can wave the geek flag. The window was bright with posters: whip-wielding heroines and scowling anti-heroes.

Fantasies.

I'd picked up a black coffee from a street vendor – *two sugars please, luv* – and its warmth was seeping into my ice-cold hands. When I breathed in that mellow wondrous scent, it burst memories through every cell: clasping papa's large hand on a street like this outside a Victorian coffee house, surrounded by fellow scientists, as battle waged over the merits of a latest lens. Excitement and safety both in that world and with my papa.

I shook myself. The scent of my personal specter was still fresh.

My recovery from the sensory deprivation had sharpened my senses. They were raw, as if they'd been flayed.

Adaptation – it's a hell of a thing.

I whistled "London Bridge", before touching my mouth to the lip of the cup for my first sip of heaven.

I didn't notice the tiny First Lifer under the faded tumble of...all right, bloody *comics*...until I stumbled over him.

There was a whimper of pain. Then I let out one of my own.

A mangled ball of black-and-white fur had attached its jaws to my leg and was biting.

Hard.

At least it was above the new boots Sun had half inched from a charity shop.

Gasping, I shook my leg.

'That be wack, man; don't go hurting her.'

A cascade of dusty blonde curls, thin mush and too large blue peepers, like an anime hero had popped out of those discarded comics. Then he sneezed, snuffling the sleeve of his threadbare jumper across his nose.

The poor bleeder didn't even have a coat.

He was fidgeting with a frayed neon and dark green friendship bracelet, twisting the baggy threads around, as if it was a talisman.

It didn't look like it was working.

Passersby were ebbing and flowing around the boy like he was invisible; just another piece of London's detritus. They were adapting around his existence, as they did the empty fast-food cartons and piles of ciggie butts: something not to be stepped in but around.

They didn't see him at all.

I felt the heat of the coffee between my hands, with that *drink me* aroma.

I sighed. 'Here,' I held out the cup.

The kid took the coffee in his small hand. Then he gave me a nod.

The ball of tangled fluff was still making a chew toy out of my leg. I hopped up and down significantly.

'Mutt,' when the kid tapped his thigh, Mutt gave my flesh one final munch with a growl, before padding back to curl next to his master.

I remembered the spaniel pups I'd once craved to buy on Regent's Street, the day I'd run from my papa.

I peered down: the bastard had bitten right through my jeans.

Mutt stared back at me with languid peepers.

I glanced between them. 'Cheers, little man.'

He frowned. 'Will.'

'Light.'

Will took a gulp of coffee.

The poor sod can't have long been a street kid. You could tell.

Then he smiled.

I'd been about to turn back to my hunt and the Emo kid, who was the exact negative image of this one. He could've been the same age when he was elected: two sides of a photograph exposure.

But then that smile was like light...radiance...innocence.

Bollocks.

There's no such thing as innocence. Or sin. We're born animals and what we know best is how to survive because it all comes down to evolution. Who's the quickest, smartest or strongest.

The most beautiful.

We all know it; we just pretend not to. Mask the inequalities. Our world (First or Blood) isn't fair.

And no one is innocent.

Will's smile, however, called to me.

Christ in heaven, no...

I stumbled away from him.

Will's smile faltered. It was uncertain. And that hurt look?

I'd bleeding put it there.

Will ducked his nut, cupping his hands tighter around the coffee.

I wanted to say...something. But what could I?

That he wasn't invisible? That I *saw* him? That I'd tasted his Soul and knew deeper than my heart – in my very DNA – that he belonged to me because he was meant to be born of my fangs?

That he was a new Plantagenet?

Way to freak out a bloke.

It was nothing like the way it'd been with Grayse, which had been a slow awakening; a love growing, until her death had forced my hand. Then Sun had been reborn. It hadn't been a choice. It'd been panic. A fear of loss.

A decision – I'll own it. Yet it wasn't one I'd wanted. Not then and not like that.

This, however, was like being hit – *bang* – with the flowing beauty of another's Soul, feeling the weave of it cleave to you.

Will would be a mix of all four types of Blood Lifer: thinker, beauty, warrior and leader. An individual – as dangerous as me.

Bugger it, I couldn't catch my breath.

It wasn't love: not like Ruby, Kathy or Sun. Yet it *was* love - of family.

I could smell Will's blood. Sod it, I wanted to taste...

My hands shook. I twisted away, grateful not to see Will's pain anymore, as I bent over a bench.

I must've looked a right berk.

'Stinking homeless bastard,' the posh voice jeered. Then I heard the *oomph* of an unmistakable boot to the guts.

Shocked, I leapt round to see Will sprawled in his paper bed, which was sodden now with a sea of spilled coffee, Mutt growling and a poncey git in monkey suit with a bird on his arm, no doubt on their way back from a night of Shakespeare at the Globe, getting in a quick beggar beating.

Everything. Turned. To. Red.

I roared, as I dived at the bastard. He paled to a ghost.

I slammed him back against the comic book shop's window; his mug smashed right up against the tits of some heroine in leather. His gargled pleadings were muffled through the crimson fury hissing *kill* through every protective inch of me.

I twisted the tosser's flabby arm up behind him, ripping that expensive suit.

He screamed.

My mouth was on his neck; my teeth grazed his dry skin. My fangs shot out.

One bite. Just one.

The bitch was shrieking and bashing me on the back with her tote – *thud, thud, thud*. Bruises burst, but even that pain was muted. Her nails were scratching, slicing, scrabbling...

Yet *I* was the predator: these humans were the prey.

I pressed my fangs harder into his skin.

Then there was this small voice tight with fear, 'The po-po, Light.'

It was like being dragged back into my own body. I hastily pulled in my fangs. I could hear the *thud* of the boots.

I flung the bloke round. He was a jabbering mess. There was a wet patch down the front of his trousers; it was dribbling onto the pavement.

I tilted my nut. 'Who smells of homeless now?'

I ducked under the bint's witch claws. Then I grabbed Will and legged it down the street.

First Lifers scattered away from us. They saw us – yeah, they bloody saw us.

Barking at our heels. Mutt was chasing us, just like the pigs. It was all a game to her, as we snaked back through Southwark: hunted now, instead of hunting. When Will collapsed, I scooped him up and over my shoulder.

It was glorious: the cold and dark, and we were free. High on the adrenaline, edge and thrill. The star eyes were watching. Round and round.

I'd run like this from the pigs down Carnaby Street in the '60s: it'd been on the night I'd first realised First and Blood were not as divided as I'd been taught.

When freedom seemed...possible.

Naïve prat, right?

Then Will was giggling, Mutt was yapping, and I was laughing.

I tumbled Will to a heap on the floor of the alley. We were hidden. Alone.

So I bloody laughed to the black night like I hadn't since before Abona.

Afterwards I leant back against the wall, lighting my e-cig. I took a drag. Then I eyed the kid.

He stared up at me like I was a god.

Bollocks.

'That was sick. Are you...' He cuddled tighter around Mutt; his peepers were crystal blue and so bloody large, '....an angel or something like that?'

Like an *angel* then, was it?

I gave him a full twirl – arms out: vintage gold ace of spades leather motorcycle jacket, black jeans (with bite marks), and pompadour. 'Do I look like a bloody angel?'

Will glanced at me sideways. 'Dunno. What do *bloody angels* look like?'

'Oi, watch your language. Angels wouldn't like it.'

Will pulled up his slight frame, as he gave me a sly smile. 'So, like, you *are*..?'

'Not even close.' Embarrassed, I shuffled my feet. 'You know, you shouldn't be out here by yourself at this time.'

'You're not my rents.'

The sudden thought shot through me – like hot poison. 'Where are you parents?'

For the first time, a guarded expression closed off Will's mush; his mouth tightened into a thin line. 'I don't got none.'

I didn't believe him. He knew I didn't believe him. See the games we play?

But here's the thing: the poison cooled to soothing balm at his lie.

No parents meant less guilt when I stole Will.

When, see? Not if.

That must've been what it was like for Ruby with me. An obsession. Every emotion amplified to agony.

I needed Will, the same as I needed the rest of my family: the bonds we form, tie and control us. They entangle us in a web of need, drives and compulsions.

Being alone makes us strong. Yet when you're alone? You're also the weakest creature alive.

It's taken me over 150 years to begin to understand that.

'The streets are dangerous. You should be home.'

Will snorted, giving me this funny look. 'I ain't got no home, bruv. Why you think I out here on my ones?'

Of course he had no home, at least no home he'd admit to: *another game*. Why else would he be out here in this cutting breeze with no coat and half-starved?

'You should be with other...people.'

'I ain't going no shelter: piss, stinky feet and crazy-assed--'

'Not out on the street then. There are predators. All sorts. Find somewhere--'

'Says who?' Will squared his shoulders, tossing his curls defiantly. He had some balls this one.

'Says me.'

Will scrunched up his nose, before giving me that blinding smile. 'Alright, safe.' He trotted backwards, his hands burrowed in his threadbare jean's pockets, as if following an order from God. Mutt jumped after him. 'See you around, Angel of Light.'

Then he was gone.

The little git.

My little git.

And that was the problem - or my new hope.

I'd never felt so alive as I did in the crisp air of that cramped alley in the arse end of Southwark. I buzzed with it.

All because of one young First Lifer.

I made a promise then to protect Will, to save him and (Christ help me), to elect him.

Because I knew – *I bleeding knew* – he was mine.

That's how we control and are controlled – biology, evolution, family or love – call it what you like.

Secrets: they silence us. The more they snare us, the harder it is for us to spill our Souls.

So I didn't tell them - the others. About Will.

Because I wanted to hold the secret precious and safe for just a while longer.

Hope, promises and love.

That night? I burst with them.

And the Emo kid? I forgot all about him. The hunt. Being hunted.

I forgot to fear.

That was my biggest mistake.

NIGHT 3

No blood but black coffee. Again?

You can't diddle me, sweetheart, I know what your game is.

Enlighten me.

Sleep deprivation. Caffeine? It lights up the nerves like fire.

Torture was Ruby's cup of tea - not mine. She'd swum in those dark waters since the Inquisition; I remember her playing with this one poor sod, feeding him mug after mug of coffee. Agony amplified until he was aflame.

Isn't that how you take it? Black with two sugars?

I'm only surprised you don't have the Jade Spider pulling the wings off me. I've heard the rumours about that bloke.

Shame you'll have to put up with me.

All the cruelties of the slavers..? Your Author taught them everything they knew.

Captain loves to see his own species burn. Family? What the buggering hell does that mean to him?

Yet he didn't betray his family. Unlike yours.

Do harp on about that, don't you? Where is Captain? Wanker hasn't spent his quality torture session with me yet.

What..?

Don't tell me you'll have to waste ink redacting..?

Lies don't suit you. You shouldn't say things like--

Redact?

This is a serious inquiry, Mr Blickle.

I'm being serious. Tell Captain to get well soon and I miss him.

No one's fed you?

Don't need to make it sound like I'm a bleeding pet.

Tell me what I want to hear, then I'll ensure--

I'm not killing. Not human.

You still think you're in control? You truly are cute. We're Blood Lifers. It's a shame to see it's true you've been _tamed_.

I have a solution to your little problem. We anticipated your squeamishness; you will drink fresh human but not kill.

First I want your secret.

You're an emotional vampire, you know that?

I'm a barrister.

Guess I'm right.

It's society that teaches us the rules: who to help or ignore. Strangers? Foreigners? Who's fagged if an earthquake or famine does in thousands of those blighters? Yet if your sister gets a cold, then you'd better post it all over the sodding Internet.

We're as connected to every other individual on this planet as we choose to be...or don't.

That's the secret truth, which it's easier to ignore, because once you open your peepers to it – First or Blood – you'll never see your life the same way again.

SEPTEMBER 1866   LONDON BRIDGE, LONDON

'We are gaining supporters to the League every day, sir. My brother says the vote seems like to go in our favour.'

I studied the bloke's earnest bespectacled mush, as he weaved his small hands animatedly. A single brunette curl fell over his right peeper; he brushed at it with a quick smile. Not quite up at Oxford yet, Edmond was only just younger than me.

Yet it felt like centuries separated us.

We strolled in the early autumn evening along London Bridge, which arched elegantly across the Thames; the moon was masked by mist. The air was sharp; my nostrils stung.

I dragged my overcoat closer around me. It was new and shimmered like a seal's skin: I'd half inched it last month from some poncey bloke, who got his jollies from sightseeing on the poor: *roll up, roll up and see the freak show!* When we'd shown him some true freaks? He'd been less keen.

It was a blinding coat.

Even in the dark the roadway was alive with bustle and roar: broughams, growlers, whinnying nags and drivers hollering.

My London: thriving and thrusting.

Birds hurried with bundles of umbrella frames and cages of hats, mingling with dirty coster girls and oily sackmakers with humungous piles of sacking balanced on their nuts. Waifs. Strays. Roughs. Working men and women ebbing and flowing across the great river, whilst the rich rode in their carriages.

Then there was us: one First Lifer and one Blood, in the black freeze of the evening.

I paused against the lip of the bridge, resting my arms on the granite.

Surprised, Edmond stopped. In his top hat and velvet collared evening cape, he looked like a startled but posh bat.

I avoided his eye, gazing out instead over the Thames.

A chaotic shock of houses overhung the water. Through the grey fog was the pencil outline of railway station and cathedrals: chimney pots and cupolas, steeples, gables and towers.

London.

A grey shrouded ghost.

I couldn't help smiling.

All right then, so here's the truth of it: this was the end of a game Ruby had set in motion a fortnight before.

Ruby and I had been in The Anchor, which clung to the banks of the Thames, sprawling in a beer stinking nook, with etched glass and emerald tiles, when we'd overheard the blathering of a pompous ass.

George Darrington.

The puffed-up leader of the Reform League had been spouting claptrap to a rapt audience.

I'd seen Ruby's peepers spark. Her body had coiled, snake stiffening.

Darrington had transformed to prey.

Suffrage for the common man? Democracy? That was the trendy cause back then. Of course, democracy has turned out to be the saviour of us all...

Bugger. That.

It terrifies me the blind faith folks have in the *system*.

This tosser was a hypocrite. He didn't believe in the working man or his vote. Even in the democracy, for which he was battling.

Ruby? She wanted to show the world: unmask him.

Seduce, change his vote, and then kill.

That was the game.

Anyone can be manipulated to change their beliefs. Love? That's the weapon. Ruby was the queen of that sport – and my mentor.

Ruby had sashayed round to Darrington's table. Darrington had been stiff in starched formal suit, with a ginger beard and moustache, like an overgrown ferret. When he'd seen Ruby, he'd licked his lips and grown a stiffy; he'd been hooked.

But George? He had a brother: Edmond.

It was my job to discover Edmond's weakness, turn his beliefs, and then...

What's a belief anyway? Why do we hold close these few mantras, prejudices, or faiths? Anyone can be convinced of anything.

Your mind is your own. Or anyone else's. We're all wide open, if only we knew it.

Tentatively Edmond plucked at my sleeve. 'Even Gladstone--'

'Oh let's not waste a fine evening speaking of Gladstone; your brother has entertained us quite enough.'

Edmond chuckled but then hung his nut. 'My sincere apologies.'

'Who taught you to apologize all the time?' Edmond blinked, his hands fluttering in confusion. 'Afeared of your brother? Of another caning?'

Edmond's butterfly hands flew automatically to the back of his trousers. Then he reddened. 'Sir, I--'

'Your brother's a brutal man. I've seen him blow up at you and I am more than acquainted with the type; I've suffered them.' I couldn't help the shiver: the memory of everything I'd endured at the orphan school because my uncle hadn't sent for me, threatened to overwhelm me. I swallowed. 'Now, however, you're a man. The same as your brother. What are you campaigning for if not freedom? Choices and opportunities? Where are yours?'

It was Edmond's turn to shrug. 'He's family.'

'Bugger family.' I don't know where it came from, this...tidal roar rage against... Except that's the bollocks because deep down? I did. When I met Edmond's gaze, it was understanding. He suddenly looked older than me. Then it was *my* turn to redden. 'Believe me when I say it's not safe,' I urged softly, 'the affairs he's leading you into. He doesn't believe in the League. It's just for the thrill. The chase,' I gave a bark of laughter, 'and I am one who lives by such games. Truly.'

'It's nothing but a diversion. Men's lives are pawns to be played with, between the brandy and cigars,' when Edmond leaned in closer, I felt his breath warm against my cheek. 'I comprehend this, sir. They rant and discourse but then they guffaw, decrying the working men as *brutes*.'

Edmond whispered the last word, as if he'd be caught out and whipped. His hazel peepers were wide at his own daring; his pale mush delicate and beautiful. His ever moving fingers worried at the buttons on his evening cape.

I'd done it.

It'd been so easy. Beliefs are as intangible as mist. They shift and vanish in the light just as swiftly too. It'd taken so little to transfer Edmond's loyalty.

To break him.

Now to the next step.

I had a shufti around the bridge.

A copper was directing traffic in the center. The bridge was blocked. Steaming horses stamped, their hot breaths spirit white, as drivers flicked their reins. An oik, with bruises staining his starkers chest, weighed us up as he limped by; I glared, and he turned away.

Too many witnesses.

I'd lure Edmond into Southwark: there were plenty of narrow alleys, which would do the job.

I should be elated. This was it: time to feast. Yet I couldn't shake this squirming sense of unease.

I could tell Edmond was waiting for me to say something; I forced myself to still his hands, before they pulled off one of those expensive buttons. 'I know you have pluck, but men like your brother? They incite rebellion. Then when it gets bloody? They walk away.'

'We're so close--'

'Other men will campaign. Reform. They always do. But your brother? He'll take you to hell with him.'

My fangs were aching to spring out. I'd gripped Edmond's arm and was hustling him with me south along the bridge, shoving the working girls and business men in their bowler hats out of the way.

Edmond gasped, gripping his tile hard to his nut.

Why was I so het up? This whole lay was intended to strip away the poor sod's beliefs at the moment of death, yet they were the cub's only comfort.

And I couldn't quite do it.

What the hell was wrong with me? I was new to this dark Blood Life, learning to swim in its crimson tide; I wished I had Ruby there to guide me.

This was a test, however, to prove I was a true Blood Lifer.

Guess I was failing then.

Edmond's soft hand curled around my arm. 'You can help me. Please, sir? I know I have no right to ask.'

Edmond wrenched back from my grasp with unexpected strength.

Ruby would be sinking her fangs in right about now, deep into George's whiskery throat. Pumping in the toxin. She'd leave him paralyzed amongst the sheaves of papers he'd forsaken to sign and then feed at leisure.

I imagine politicians taste nasty.

Befriend. Then end. That was the game.

Simple.

So why couldn't I finish it?

I shook Edmond off – he was trembling.

I'd told him to make his own choice and break from his old beliefs.

Looked like he'd taken my advice.

I screwed shut my peepers; Ruby would rip off my baubles if she ever found out...

When I opened them again, Edmond was studying me with deep concern. How long had it been since anyone had looked at me like that? 'I hope I did not distress you..?'

'If I...help you...then you'll have to leave and not merely London. England - forever. No coming back. More than that, you'll have to change who you are.'

To my surprise, Edmond nodded. 'I would happily be someone else. If I can escape this life.'

'Don't go saying that too loudly. Trust me.'

Edmond blushed. 'But I'm hard up; I don't have the needful. You see, my brother doesn't allow me--'

'I'll stump up.'

I don't know why I said it. Why I reached into my pocket and handed over the folded wad of notes from my latest lay. Ruby would give me such a slating, when I told her I'd *lost* the cash during the kill.

Edmond took the readies with unsteady hands. 'I shall pay you back.'

'You shall certainly not,' I snatched Edmond by the shoulder, twirling him towards Southwark with a shove. 'Take a cab, book passage...somewhere and start living. Give me your word?'

Edmond smiled at me over his shoulder, as he pushed his wire-rimmed glasses up his nose. 'Only if you promise me the same.'

Blood Lifer to First? There was no safe answer to that.

I forced myself to nod.

Then he was gone, lost amongst the throng, and I was alone in the dark cold bustle of London Bridge.

No one ever discovered I'd let that boy live.

I reckon he did a better job at changing *my* beliefs, than I did his.

Still, I promised to live and I always keep a promise.

And that? To you? Is a warning.

To me?

It's hope.

Let me check I've understood this correctly. You save a Victorian boy (having manipulated him quite masterfully). Then over a century later you stumble upon a homeless boy and save him too?

That's not--

At least, you want to save Will. By killing and electing him.

You don't have to make it sound--

Is it guilt? So unusual in a Blood Lifer. You're quite the curiosity. Unique: Captain says.

Me? I never buy into hype.

If I did everything out of guilt, I'd spend my whole bloody life rescuing fragile humans.

Don't you?

Guilty as charged, m'lud!

Wait, what's this then?

You were right. I investigated; it turns out you were indeed being starved. That's unacceptable.

So you may feed now from this boy.

You're off your trolley, if you reckon--

The cuts are shallow; he won't die. Suck like a baby, Mr Blickle, no need to let in the venom. He can be your pet snack. Captain is fond of this one; he uses him in the same way. In fact, he uses him in many ways.

Does he now?

He's pretty: such lovely curls. For a First Lifer.

Humans have other uses than--

My, aren't you prudish? I'd imagined after your enslavement as a sex slave--

Don't pretend you know me. How about this? I'm not sodding drinking.

You truly want this dance?

I don't dance.

Then I suggest you drink, or that torture you mentioned..?

Been there. Done that.

Not *you*. The boy.

That's it... Doesn't it feel better to feed directly from a First Lifer? To be *wild* again? Unleashed?

Tell me, Mr Blickle, why do you see yourself as a protector for these humans, when you can never be human again?

Humming "London Bridge Is Falling Down", I sauntered over London Bridge in the dead of night. My skin stung, assaulted by the ice freeze. The concrete and steel bridge bled out into the Thames; light puddled in crimson blood pools. The Shard was bright on the horizon. Taxis honked, as blokes in hoodies with their hands deep in their pockets scurried by.

I swaggered south out of the City, back towards Southwark and our apartment. I'd been scouting the posh shops for clothes to half inch for Sun. She hadn't lost her taste for the designer after her election, but our salaries at Peter Pan's didn't exactly stretch to her old wardrobe.

I had a scarlet Alex Highbury-Lord dress stashed under my jacket, with which to surprise Sun.

I couldn't give Sun the world. Not how I wanted - not yet. But I'd give her every last bleeding thing I could.

Kathy, my human lover for fifty years, had knocked the light-fingered stuff on the head. After Abona, however, and what the human slavers had stolen from us..?

I reckoned we were entitled.

I only took from those First Lifers who had. Like a modern-day Robin Hood. Except *he* never existed, and *I* don't give to the poor. Unless *we* count..?

Family was coming first now. Any rules? I was making them.

I passed where once the severed nuts of traitors had been displayed impaled on iron pikes (boiled and dipped in tar first, of course), when I clocked dusty blonde curls and intense blue peepers.

Will.

Hunched over in the cold, Mutt padding at his heels, Will was hurrying over the bridge too.

'London Bridge is falling down,' I sang softly, as the hunt began.

So here's the truth of it: every night since that first one outside the comic shop, I'd been following Will. I lied to myself that it was pretend hunting, just to keep my hand in.

Yet that was the bollocks.

It was to keep the little git safe, and I knew it.

Then there was the ache - like being edged, when you're not allowed to come. It was this desire to Author, yet also knowing it had to be his choice because wasn't that what I'd always preached? Didn't I despise Blood Lifers who elected kids too young to understand the glories of evolution?

As Aralt had done to Alessandro?

I watched as Will drifted down the side of the bridge to the embankment, above the river's marshy estuary, as he had every other night.

'...Falling down...' I hopped after Will down the embankment, crunching on the gravel. Will disappeared under the bridge; he was swallowed into the darkness. '...My fair... *Sodding hell...*'

A shank.

Right between my shoulder blades.

It'd bleeding ruined my leather jacket.

I scrabbled frantically behind me but I couldn't reach the blade.

When I heard a *snort* of laughter, I twisted round.

A First Lifer bird with a huge Afro, khaki military jacket and low-slung trousers was assessing me with crossed arms and a smirk. 'Problem, wasteman?'

'Little help here?'

She raised her eyebrow.

Writhing like a snake, I managed to curl my fingers around the shank's handle, before wrenching it out with a holler. When I chucked it into the glass surface of the Thames, it disappeared silently. 'You're no lady knifing a bloke in the back,' I felt the ragged rips in my jacket, remembering everything it'd been through with me since the '60s. 'This is bloody vintage. Bleeding kid like you wouldn't know decent clobber if it bit you on the neck. Bugger me, that hurt.'

'Yeah? I shank to kill, you get me?'

She'd edged closer to the embankment but her fight was still up.

'Should learn your left from your right then. The heart's not... Sorry, no, you shouldn't. You ever considered not going around assaulting innocent...men?'

'You ain't no man.'

Interesting.

'That right?'

Suddenly, she was up in my face. A tiny fury of hair and gangster. 'You be slipping. Lucky I ain't got my gat, you hearing me?'

'Not bloody guns again.'

'Why you following my Will?'

There was something about the way she said *my*. The possession and protectiveness, which I recognized.

Hated.

I wanted to tear out the bitch's throat. And that? Terrified me.

I shrank back. Not from her but myself.

The bint's peepers, however, lit up. Like she'd been the cause and was reveling in scaring the monster.

Power: anyone who says they don't get off on it is a damn liar.

She shoved me in the chest, hard enough to send me stumbling backwards into the freeze of the Thames.

Splash.

Sopping wet, I dragged myself up.

A woman in a scarlet dress was drifting south on the currents.

Shocked, I was about to dive after the bird (all right, so maybe I do have a hero complex), when I remembered Sun's gift: the Alex Highbury-Lord dress. My reason for being out here and away from family. Why I was now bleeding out from my back and shivering like a bastard.

Whilst Sun's present wraith-floated away.

I stalked out of the river. This time? I couldn't stop the fangs shooting out.

I hadn't expected the giggles.

'Drowned rat, innit?'

Not exactly the *big reveal* moment. Deflated, I retracted my fangs, sweeping my dripping hair back from my forehead. Grumpily, I shrugged.

'My mandem – Will and others from the streets – we close. Move to me, blud, and you click get shank. Again. 'Cos we know what 'tings in the shadows.'

'Do you now?'

Her gaze was hard. 'You eat us.'

I shuffled my feet. I hadn't figured on coming face-to-face with a *hunter*. We were the Lost: camouflaged predators.

It looked like we were doing a piss poor job of it.

Hunters weren't meant to exist. No hunters, torches or pitchforks. If they did? This wasn't how I'd imagined the meeting going down: an awkward chinwag, whilst I dripped with stinking Thames water.

I circled the hunter, whilst she prowled round me. 'Kids like you – homeless – hearts must give out all the time. Tragic. So--'

'I'm poor; I ain't stupid. Hidden in doorways: we see. We be invisible even to you. We watch and we die; the same as the suits and the rich bitches with the bling.' The hunter raised herself on tiptoe. Her lips were dry against my wet. 'You suck us too. How we taste?'

'Lighter,' my mouth brushed against hers at each word, but like a confession I couldn't move back, 'diet flavor. Not as rich.' The hunter slammed towards me. Her headbutt stunned me. 'Truth,' I gritted out, 'never bloody easy, is it?'

She was breathing hard. 'You ain't like the others.'

I rubbed my bruised bonce. 'They're not like me. No one's like me. And I don't eat you First Lifers. Not anymore.'

Confusion fluttered in her peepers. Then she grinned. 'Who be you? A tamed bitch?'

I burned to smash the knowing look off the hunter's calculating mug. 'I'm Light and all I want is to get the little man safely back. So he's staying here? You're keeping him...looking out for him? I am too.'

But it was a lie because it wasn't all I wanted. I bloody knew it.

Somehow the hunter seemed to know it too. She gave me an intent stare, before nodding. 'I be Trinity, and this be my yard. Will? He be blessed with us.'

I glanced towards the dark mouth underneath the bridge.

Will's new home: with Trinity, her shanks, gats and crew. I tried to suppress my scowl. 'So if I skulk sometimes, you cool with that?'

'Yeah, but you owe me another shank. Does Will know?'

'What?'

'That he has a guardian angel.'

I sighed, as I shook the water from first one boot and then the other, preparing for the long walk still left back to *my* home. I mustn't forget the dawn: I didn't reckon my welcome to Trinity's crew extended as far as sleepovers. 'Don't go calling me that: it'll give God a coronary. And no, he doesn't.'

'Yeah, he does.'

Bloody hell...

Will poked his curly sunshine nut out of the shadows. He was shaking from the cold; I'd have to nick him a wool coat next time. Then Will bounded towards me with a grin. 'Safe, man, my own angel.'

'For the last time, I am not an--'

'So what are you?' Will was beaming at me but then bemused, patted my arm. The leather stuck to my skin clammy. 'Why are you wet?'

'I felt like a swim. And let's just say I'm something you kiddies shouldn't know about.'

'Who you calling kiddie? Shanked you, bruv.' Trinity licked her lips.

Will launched his slight form at Trinity. It would've been comical, if he hadn't been in deadly earnest.

Trinity held Will back with one hand and a bored expression, before finally snapping, 'Enough, boi.'

I scooped Will around the waist, spinning him to face me. His peepers were gleaming, like he was fighting to hold back tears. 'None of that. There's no harm done, except there's a bloody big...'

I shucked off my jacket...and found Will stroking over the hole with quick light fingers.

'I can fix it and that if..?'

'That'd be blinding, cheers.'

I wondered if Will felt it too. This belonging. A need for family after a lifetime of rejection, loss and abandonment. I needed that more than anything; I reckoned maybe – just maybe – Will was the same.

Fantasies.

We live in dreams our whole lives.

It's why we can convince ourselves of anything.

Trinity was considering me thoughtfully. 'If you ain't feeding, then you be in the market for blood. So come to my yard to see your boi, then we talk. Maybe we can come to an arrangement?'

Redemption?

Sometimes the choices we make for our family mean we sacrifice personal morals, even our chance of being saved.

'Don't bogart the blood, man.' Donovan jittered on his seat like an excited toddler.

I took a single lick, like a cat, at the red liquid, blinking rapidly, before passing the brimming disposable coffee cup over to Donovan.

Donovan was quivering with need. Excitement. Vibrating with an addict's first hit after years of forced abstention. He was already flying from the smell alone.

We were huddled on the dusty oak floorboards of our tiny apartment. We'd stuck strips of cardboard to the windows: now we lived in a perpetual twilight. The stars were lost; we couldn't see the bright open tapestry of the skies.

You've no idea how much that booted me in the goolies. Because locked in the dark I'd dream of freedom, and it looked just like the crystal sharp night sky.

The apartment's walls were painted sky blue (as if to compensate). They were punched with random holes. Faint screams and creative strings of swear words floated up from the couple below us. Somewhere a baby wailed.

The electricity was off again: three cheers for the slum landlords of London. We'd balanced candles in used teacups; the flames cast wild shadows. Sun had been narked we couldn't afford scented candles, so I'd nicked a load the next time I'd been in the City. Except they'd been incense, so the apartment stank like a medieval cathedral.

Sun hadn't spoken to me for a week.

We'd shoved the one sunken scarlet sofa back and were sitting in a Wiccan circle: the only time we felt safe.

Hartford's navy sleeping bag stuck out from behind the sofa because after a decade of imprisonment he could still only sleep in confined spaces. Donovan? He drank, smoked whacky backy, stripped and shagged more than the psychotic bastard ever had because that's one escape.

Me?

I had the nightmares.

You can free a slave, but if you don't free his mind?

He'll always be in chains.

Donovan was taking these quick, panting breaths, as his tongue lizard-licked his lips. '*Human*, right on. I never reckoned you'd...' He glanced down at the thick crimson.

'Ethically sourced. So no snacking. This is all there is for now.'

With difficulty, Donovan nodded. Then he passed the coffee cup to Hartford, without even taking a sip. I couldn't help noticing how hard his hand trembled.

'Aw, that java for me, baby?' Hartford took a deep swig.

Then I had to dive for the cup.

Donovan caught Hartford around the shaking shoulders. Hartford's peepers rolled back, as he juddered like he was demon possessed.

Alarmed, Donovan stared at me. 'He's wigging out--'

'It happened to me,' I couldn't meet Sun's eye, 'when I was with *Master*. Human blood after so long. He'll be hunk-dory by tomorrow.'

'Tomorrow?' Donovan hissed, clutching Hartford to his chest. Hartford was convulsing with cramps.

I shrugged. 'Maybe. Get him to drink it all down; he needs this.'

I stared across at Donovan's stormy mush and Sun's stony one. The incense was a choking entity between us. Frustrated, I shoved myself up, breaking the circle. 'Why can't you trust me? Hartford's a Long-lived. He shouldn't be tame. I promised to free you - all of you. And I will.'

I swung the Triton towards London Bridge and the embankment, cutting across the tangle of traffic in a hail of furious *honks*. Parking up, I hopped off, unloading my precious bundle under my arm. I couldn't help the grin.

The others reckoned I was working another shift at Peter Pan's. Instead, I was sneaking off to see my...*mine*. Let's leave it at that.

My snake betrayal coiled inside. Secrets – I was tangled in them.

I knew that Emo kid was still in the shadows. Hunting. My new obsession, however, was wound too tightly around my heart to let go.

I was weak as any junkie.

Obsession has always been my heroin, and I was hooked.

Sand skittered away in fine storms, as I scooted down the embankment. Before I could even holler, Trinity was in my face – all swagger and despot style – waving a brown paper bag of fresh blood like it was groceries.

The *stash*.

Trinity – our new dealer – snatched the crumpled bag back. Her smile was razor sharp. 'What's the drilly, cuz?'

'Let's just do this.'

'Alright, blud.' Trinity ran her hand down my chest, circling my nipples with her long finger. 'Tell me, Mr Angel Man, how our Will taste?'

'What?'

Then I chucked up in my mouth... *The needle pricking into Will's too thin arm... The crimson drawn out... Life from him to us... My single lick...Then Hartford drinking...*

My predator roared retribution. Possession. Revenge.

Except I did remember that one sublime taste: the bubbling universes meeting all at once and then exploding – end of days and dawn of new ages.

I didn't know if it made Will prey or bonded him closer than anyone before.

Yet Hartford had tasted too, and once we've got your scent, we never forget the hunt.

'You promised,' I gritted out, 'our deal was for my protection; I'd keep all of you safe. In return, no blood from Will.'

'I lied.'

I flung myself at Trinity, crushing her against the embankment. The paper bag crumpled between us. When I looked down, I saw the steel shiv pushing hard against my heart.

I knew it was a mistake to teach her that.

'This is mine, I believe,' pulling together my tattered self-respect, I snatched the brown bag with an air of dignity, before backing away.

'Don't be vexed. The rest's got no Will flavouring, you get me?' Trinity crossed her arms. 'That was bare jokes – you were shook.'

'Dead funny: this is me splitting my sides.'

I threw the two finger salute, before spinning on my heel and marching towards the bridge.

The bint made me feel like we were siblings: ones who bloody hated each other.

I peered into Trinity's dark world underneath London Bridge. Smoke stung my peepers from fires, which were burning in overturned steel barrels, built-up from scrap wood. I coughed; thick smoke wound into my nostrils and lungs. Through a watery haze, I made out blurred ghosts, who were living on the banks of the salt-brine Thames.

The wind blasted from one end to the other; battling against both smoke and wind, I staggered between sprawled meth heads, who were huddled over sweet smelling foil chasing the dragon (and who could blame them for seeking an escape from *this* reality?), a bloke who was ranting at an invisible adversary and a gang of kids.

A heap of curls and tiny body: my Will.

He smelled...like mine.

Will was scrunched against the wall under a nest of cardboard, like a mouse. He was as far from the others as possible. Mutt was by his side, a wag of black and white fluff. Will was fidgeting ritualistically at that neon friendship bracelet again.

I sighed, before lobbing my gift at him.

Will jumped out of his bloody skin. Mutt didn't even wake up.

I laughed. 'Easy to hunt, you are.'

Will tried to pout but then broke into a broad smile. 'Only 'cos you ain't hunting me, innit?'

'Touché.'

Will nudged my gift with his foot, before glancing up at me hopefully. 'That for..?'

'It's a tent. Pop-up. There's a sleeping bag too; I reckoned with it being cold at night...'

I hadn't expected the armful of First Lifer. I stiffened. Then I heard sniffling.

Buggering hell.

I patted Will's back. 'Alright?'

'Yeah,' Will disentangled himself, before hunkering down to investigate the tent.

Good luck with that: I didn't have a scooby.

'Here,' I chucked a luxury bar of chocolate at Will.

I'd been carrying it around since last night, when Hartford had given it to me as a peace offering or a *cheers for the unleashing*. Maybe it was a breaking abstention pressie.

Donovan still looked ready to rip off my goolies.

Hartford, however, was buzzed. All singing and dancing. A Long-lived in the world once more.

Regrets..? Helping Hartford back from the dark wasn't one of them.

Will caught the chocolate with one hand – *good reflexes* – *whooping* like it was bleeding Christmas. When he ripped open the golden wrapper, however, the blanket shifted.

'What's this then?' I plonked down the blood, snatching up the long handle of a gangster-sized shank. I waved it like it was confiscated contraband in front of a naughty schoolkid. 'Little man..?'

'Protection.'

I tucked the blade into the back of my jeans (and that's one place you don't want it to slip). I thumped my chest. 'Here's all the protection you need.'

Will was picking at his chocolate, his nut twisted away from me. 'You ain't always here.'

'What does that..?'

'Just put it back, yeah?' It was hardly more than a whisper.

Reluctantly, I drew out the shiv. Kid like Will shouldn't even have touched a shank: no kid should. Real rebel, right? All these *shoulds*.

There's no such thing as *should*, yet we still pretend.

Kids like these don't exist. Hidden under bridges, down alleys or in squats. They're invisible as we stroll by and every day we choose our own reality, escaping into coke, meth or acid. Puff on joints or shoot up. Medicate on alcohol or prescription pills. Hide away from the real world in TV boxsets or the Internet.

Because who asks for help in there? Who needs you to be strong?

Will took the shank from me with trembling hands, before burying it under his blankets. Then he drew something back out with a flourish.

My jacket: mended.

I twisted it round first one way and then the other. You could barely make out the rent.

Will was blushing, staring down at the syringe littered floor.

I tipped his nut back with one finger. 'I won't forget this. I promise.'

'Filthy whore.'

A hyena burst of laughter.

I hadn't missed it. Even over the birds yapping into their iPhones, the rumble of traffic and hip-hop blasting in bass thrumming beat out of the bar on the corner.

It'd come from the bench outside the comic shop.

Where my Will sat.

I raced towards the over-excited cluster of bladdered suits. A pinstripe platter of red mushes *hawing* to themselves, as they booted and grappled with the whimpering figure at their feet. Swollen with power and coke, they stamped their place in the world by stamping on someone else.

And the crowds thronging either side, whilst these business men got their jollies with a homeless boy?

Didn't do a sodding thing.

'Oi, you!' The blokes glanced up at my holler, which was when Mutt launched her attack.

Growling like a bitch possessed, Mutt didn't know which bastard to bite first. So she circled the whole pack, snapping at their ankles. Until one tosser kicked backwards, and I heard a *crunch*.

Then Will's only defender was lying still.

'Mutt!' A muffled wail from the pile of blood and bruises trapped beneath the suits.

Not Will's *only* defender because then *I* was there.

The boss turned to me with a smile, like he recognized another predator. His thinning hair was sweaty, and his grey tie askew: beating on kids is a good workout. He knelt next to Will, flipping him onto his stomach with what could only be practiced ease and ripped down his jeans. The other wankers cheered like they were at a gallery opening.

Will began to sob.

Then the boss leered up at me. 'Want to join in the fun?'

He had no idea.

I smiled too. The blokes cheered again: another damned soul for their club. Before – dead slowly – I let my fangs descend. 'How did you guess?'

There was this long moment: not one of them moved. Then they screamed - I'd say like little girls, except that's an insult to women - they screamed like coked-up drunken rapists, who'd just had their illusory power crumbled to ash. They legged it, stumbling, falling and grabbing onto each other: predator to prey on the turn of a coin.

The boss, however, I had by the neck. He scrabbled at me, scratching and gouging at my mush. He stripped piercing shards of pain down my cheeks. I didn't loosen my hold. I could hear the *beat* of his galloping heart and feel his sticky sweat.

One bite.

My lips were on his madly fluttering artery...

'Don't.'

That was all it took.

Will. His humanity - my humanity - I no longer understood the divide or why it mattered. Only that Will did.

Will had pulled himself up onto his knees; he'd dragged his jeans back on and was hugging his stomach (broken ribs, I reckoned). He was watching me through swollen peepers.

I shoved the bastard away from me; he probably would've given me heartburn anyway.

The boss crawled away but before he could scarper, I said, 'Apologise.' The bloke's nut snapped round. I could tell by the lemon sour of his mush that he was struggling to get out the words to a homeless kid. 'Or I could just eat you.'

'Sorry, OK?'

'Alright, toddle off then.'

Managing somehow to look affronted, the suit dusted off his muddy knees, straightened his tie and shakily wove away towards London Bridge and the City.

I turned my attention to Will. He was a mess. 'Bloody work of art you are.'

He tried to shrug but stopped with a gasp. *Yeah, broken ribs.*

'I ain't had no shank. If--'

'Not gonna happen.'

I suddenly realised my fangs were still out.

I don't know why I was ashamed of them. After what happened at Abona? With *Master*? I shouldn't have any shame left.

Except I did.

When I ducked my nut, Will's fingers shot out, touching a fang.

I wrenched back.

Will cringed. 'I ain't mean nothing...'

'They're toxic.'

Yet it was more than that - a violation.

Humans had taken my fangs once, and no one was touching what was mine again. I guess Will had felt the same with the suits. The only thing was?

I was no longer powerless.

'You said you ain't an angel?'

'Want to know what I am?'

Will studied me gravely but then his smile was back. 'Nah, man. You're still *my* Angel of Light. You're safe, all that matters, innit?' I blinked rapidly to hide my shock. 'He got you good and that.' Will pointed at the crimson beaded tears streaked down my mush. Guess I wasn't exactly in tiptop condition either. 'You alright?'

Something caught at me. A whispered memory of a bird called Susan. She'd asked me if I'd been *alright,* helping me believe someone could care if I hurt. So maybe I should too. All it took was that hint of tenderness. To be treated like it mattered if I hurt, broke and bled.

Will was looking at me like I was...human. No: like it didn't matter that I *wasn't*.

No way was I letting him see me bawl like a nancy. 'Where's your teenage rebellion? Your Marlon Brando--'

'Who?'

'The world hates you,' I couldn't help it. The words were spewing out; I couldn't hold them back. 'Look at it: what it does to you. What it's done. Where's your rebel fire?'

'Reckon you've enough for all of us, innit?' Will turned away, his dirty fingers – little one dislocated

– stiffly playing with his frayed jumper. 'The world has a beef with me? That's wack, 'cos I ain't got no beef with the world. Just so you know.'

I was a wanker and feeling half an inch tall.

Just then I caught a glimpse of a black-and-white body.

I scooped up Mutt, laying her next to Will. At least she was still breathing.

Thank Christ for that.

I half-convinced myself I only gave a rat's arse for Will's sake.

Will stared up at me like I could perform miracles. Resurrect the dead.

Oh yeah, I could.

I swept my hand over Mutt's furry body. She was surprisingly soft and warm. I rubbed my hand backwards and forwards. Her heart was thudding, slow but still beating. I laid my head close to hers.

Something wet slobbered across my mug from top to bottom.

Mutt was awake, and I'd just experienced a Mutt tonguing.

I glowered at her. 'Bad dog.'

Will, however, was grinning. 'Good dog.' He tried to wrap his arms around Mutt but groaned. No way was his walking anywhere.

'Let's get you to hospital because that's the craze for you humans.' Will scooted away from me on his arse, however, squeaking with pain. 'Bloody stop it now.' Will stopped but still eyed me warily. 'No hospital?'

Will shook his nut.

'I'm not taking you to that...under London Bridge.'

'I ain't asking you for nothing.'

'You don't have to.' And he didn't. It didn't mean I wouldn't tear the world asunder for him, lie to my family and betray promises. Give him my very blood if he'd have it. Sodding hell, I wished he'd be ready for election soon, and that he'd want it - unlike Kathy. The waiting was agony. 'Come back to my home.'

There – I'd said it. Exploded myself out of the water; it was too late to go back.

I was buggered.

'Not cool man,' Donovan whispered, glancing at the closed bedroom door.

Scarlet candles dotted the floor in upturned beer bottles, their flames votary offerings in the black.

It'd been Hartford who'd offered to take the bloody pile of rags and curls from my arms and sweep Will into the kitchen to patch him up like my latest stray, before the hollering could begin; Hartford had an uncanny nose for that.

See here's the thing: that coffee cup of thick crimson – human – blood? Will's blood? Hartford acting all demon possessed on the floorboards?

Don't reckon I hadn't figured on one unleashed Long-lived scenting Will's grazes and thinking *grub's up.*

Yet there was something about the way Hartford took Will from me – Will's skinny arms transferring from my neck to Hartford's, as if he'd always known him or he was family.

Like he trusted him.

And trust? It's harder to find than love.

You can lose it too, twice as fast.

Donovan's intent stare could've set the chipped bedroom door aflame. 'You told us you were at Peter Pan's? You lying to us now, man?'

Heat flooded my cheeks. 'Sorry.'

Sun was sprawled on the lumpy mattress, her hands clenched in the faded sheets. Her ash blonde hair hung in a veil masking her mush; I could just see the laser slits of her peepers. She was dressed in a tight pair of jeans and a flint-speckled top, which she'd returned with from a charity shop. Wearing them, I always reckoned, was a protest.

'Sorry?' Donovan shook his nut, 'What's happened to you and my baby? These First Lifers..?' He spat out the words like they were venomous. 'Bringing one into our *home*..? Unless he's a snack...' I had my hand around Donovan's throat, as I slammed him backwards and onto the bed, so fast I didn't even know I was doing it, until we were both breathing hard and staring into each other's startled peepers. 'Hey, no need to wave the fangs around.'

Surprised, I licked my teeth with my tongue and then yelped. I drew my fangs back slowly.

Donovan could've kicked my arse, if he'd chosen to take offence at my alpha display. He was one step up the Plantagenet bloodline and Plantagenets are...stronger...faster...*bastards*.

I include myself in that.

I hoped I'd never meet that wanker Plantagenet. He probably wore other bloke's fangs as trophies: or poncey cravats.

I eased away from Donovan, who edged away from me.

Donovan was eyeing me warily, like a bloke who discovers a rattlesnake in his boot.

'No one eats him,' I ordered, 'the boy's hurt and our guest.'

Sun shot up. 'Ya huh! We can't afford him.'

I should've known. The bottom line. The profit margin.

'If I take on extra shifts--'

'Where the frig were you tonight?'

I shifted awkwardly. 'I've kept you safe so far. We've this place and jobs--'

Sun's laugh was so sharp it could've cut glass. 'You're soft if you reckon I'm grateful. This place should be, like, condemned on account of it's a slum.'

Right on cue came the *scrit scrat* of Mr Rat.

Cheers, mate.

It wasn't meant to be like this: Author and elected.

I wanted to plan such fantasies with Sun. To thrill our dark pleasures. To know if I couldn't be mentor, then we'd swagger side by side into our Blood Life together.

I forced myself to saunter closer to Sun. 'If you figure you can do better, luv...'

'I do.' Cool and considered.

Devastating.

'What?'

'Reckon I can do better.' I kept my expression blank: I didn't want Sun to know how brutally that one had hit home. 'And you want a pet? Human? That's a whole notha deal.'

'Funny you should say that,' I wiped my hands surreptitiously down the back of my jeans to wipe off the scent of wet dog. Sun still wrinkled her nose. *Oh yeah, my mush snogging by Mutt.* 'What's that..?'

'Will's not a pet. He's--'

'You know what'd be mint? If I start trading again. Then we'd be wealthy enough to afford your young First Lifer.'

Bloody hell, it was like the burbs arguing over popping out another baby. And somehow? I'd become the sodding housewife.

Donovan had thrown himself back against the pile of black satin cushions, which I'd nicked to poncey up the place. His arms were linked casually behind his nut, like a teenager getting off on his parents' shouting match.

'First,' *reasonable voice* (I was not the nagging wife), 'we don't have the readies; you're not getting your mitts on our wages either. Second: you're dead. Your daddy killed you; I know because I had to watch, before I sank my fangs into the bastard's throat. So no identity. No Grayse.'

'You don't reckon I know that?' Sun's voice was dangerously low.

'I was only saying--'

'I'm *dead* 'cos I chose you. And I'm alive? 'Cos *you* made me.'

I swallowed. Even Donovan had tensed. I tried to reach out to Sun, but she backed away.

'I'm sorry--'

'That you elected me?'

'Never that.' I tried to smile but it came out wrong, as twisted as my insides. 'Don't be such a daft bint. I love you.'

Sun slammed her palm – *slap* – against her own thigh. I flinched. 'Then why are you frickin' chaining me?'

Terror moth fluttered in my belly. Tremors shook every nancy boy inch of me. Because what Sun had said, gave wings to the torment I'd suffered under Ruby. For a hundred years I'd been happy, lost in the fug of a false freedom. When in fact all along I'd been – *chained* – by her love. I'd sworn I'd never control another First or Blood Lifer as she had.

Never *chain* them.

'It's to keep you safe,' I spluttered, when all I wanted was to hold Sun – snog her – force her to take it back. Make her swear she was free and I wasn't the same as my Author. Because I wasn't, was I? 'If you traded now, the only bleeders you could deal with would be other Blood Lifers.'

'I know. Donovan told me.'

When I shot Donovan a look – *no whacky backy for you tonight, mate* – he shrugged. He didn't seem to be enjoying our set to much now either.

'These Blood Lifers? Bankers, traders, financers? They're the most powerful tossers there are. Money and power: this is Light 101. They control everything.'

Sun's gaze was mocking. It burnt me. 'Fear, huh?' I startled, when she sidled so close her dry mouth brushed my lobe, as she whispered, 'You're infected by it.'

I tried to jerk away, but her arm was tight around my shoulders, holding me in a false embrace.

Then Sun was shoving her wrist, in its thin sweater, in front of my nose like an accusation.

'Gonna need to breathe any moment.'

'You smell it?'

I sniffed.

Stale smoke, baked beans from dinner woven into the fabric and the fake tang of Tahitian Gardenia: the exotic sharpness of the perfume I'd managed to buy with my first pay.

Bought - not nicked.

It carried me back to Grayse's apartment in Primrose Hill, when we'd been mistress and slave, and the scent of her posh candles had freed me, even if only in my mind.

Now we were truly free.

Sun might not smell of gorse and sunlight anymore: but that had been Grayse. The aroma of Fernando's perfume.

Now she was Sun? She wore mine: and she smelled of freedom.

I grinned. My lips were soft against the scented threads.

Yet when Sun pulled back her wrist? Her mush was cold. 'That? Is the stink of poverty.'

My smile faded. All the sodding light from the room faded, along with the feeling from my body.

When were Blood Lifers caged by labels? Rich? Poor? When had I become trapped in a nightmarish rerun of my First Life, when I was sticky Post-it noted by my *poverty*?

In this twilight world – caught tame between First and Blood – in which we'd found ourselves, it turns out even freedom costs.

'Hey man, you wiggin' out?'

A tunnel of grey.... Me at my orphan school... Memories unkindled for decades roared monstrous. Abuses long suppressed awoke to shank cruel.

I stumbled backwards, my heel catching an empty Guinness bottle. It skittered over, rolling with flying hot wax. The scarlet candle flared extra bright, as if it'd escaped.

I dived on it, stamping it out with my boot – *stamp*, *stamp*, *stamp*. The wax stuck like dried blood to my sole. The flame died under my boot.

When I looked up, Hartford was leaning in the open doorway, watching my fire dance. His mush was very still.

Then I realized.

No Will.

Lucky I can't have a coronary.

'Where's my Will?'

'Ankled it out of this joint once all the hollering started.'

'And you didn't...I dunno...stop him?'

Hartford's expression was troubled. 'Say, mac, was he our prisoner?'

Why did Hartford always have to be so bloody right?

I found Will on London Bridge. Or I hunted him there – I no longer knew the difference.

What I did know was that his feet were dangling over the edge of the freezing curl of the Thames. He was just as battered as before, but I'd underestimated him. He'd taken some bootings in his life to be counted amongst the walking wounded.

It's never a good sign when you know how to take a beating.

Him and me both.

Will's arse was parked on the ledge.

A fine drizzle wetted us in tears. Pedestrians pressed by but not one of them stopped. That's London. There was the *rumble* of buses and the *rattle* of black cabs. All a watercolour wash: nothing but background.

Because my kid (what was the point in pretending?), was hanging over the Thames.

I was going to kick his arse.

'Alright?'

Will shuffled closer to the edge. 'Why are you trying to stop me?'

I took a drag on my e-cig, holding it between trembling fingers, as I tried to lean nonchalantly against the granite. 'Maybe because you're a stupid little git.'

Will's nut twisted round, his swollen peepers shocked. 'You ain't gotta bother, man. Go back to your fam.'

Family.

Will hated that word, as much as I had at his age.

'They're not perfect; this isn't simple though, and Hartford's--'

'Safe,' Will reluctantly shrugged one shoulder, 'but you got a home, and it be shabby.'

I imagined the holes in the wall, faulty taps and Mr Rat: Sun's dismissive *slum*. Then I saw it through Will's eyes; compared to living in that world under London Bridge, it was *shabby* (and I was pretty sure in Will speak that was a *good* thing). He'd smiled – just for a moment – anyway.

Now Will was hugging his wrist close to his chest, stroking that green snake bracelet like it was all he had to say goodbye to.

'That's why I took you there, until you had a case of the runaways.'

'I ain't gonna lose you fam, wifey and home. Or cause you bother; it's all I do.'

'Save the sodding self-pity. I'm a big boy; I can make my own decisions. Now you're going to turn your arse around and come over to me, or you'll discover what a truly pissed off angel looks like.'

The smile was back - sly now. Will looked at me through his curls. 'Thought you ain't no angel?'

'I can be anything I bleeding want. Now get a wiggle on.' Will swung his legs back but too fast. For one breath catching moment he was slipping on the damp over the dark mouth below. Then my hand was bunched in his thin sweater. I yanked him – none too gently – to me. Then I was cradling him. Sod the fact I was babying him. Will didn't pull back. 'Do that again and I'll...tear out your bloody heart.'

'No you won't.'

Will was vibrating, like a mouse when it's played with by a cat.

Problem was? I was beginning to reckon *I* was the cat.

Reluctantly, I set down Will. Of course, he immediately legged it - or tried to. His knees buckled, however, and he hit the pavement.

I took a drag of my e-cig. 'Now that's out of the way, let's have a chat.'

Surly, Will glared up at me from his heap on the bridge. Then he gave a cautious nod.

'What's up with this business then?' I pointed at Will's bracelet: two entwined greens knotted together. An eternal snake. I don't know what made me ask, except there was something about it, like there was with my leathers. The one thing Will had held onto at the end.

Will jolted, as if I'd cattle prodded him. His left hand shot out to cover the baggy bracelet. Then he shuffled closer. I hunkered down, until our mushes were close. I hadn't seen him look so solemn - or less like a kid.

'My sis made it me when we were...' Will's voice dropped to a whisper, 'I done run from the rents; that be why I ain't going no hospital. No po-po, no going back and no kiddies' home neither.'

Poison roiled through my chest, melting my heart to a swirling pool. 'Hold your horses, little man. You told me--'

'Foster, yeah?'

I could've sung hallelujahs.

'Why?'

Will was caressing those green threads again, as if they were strands of hair. 'My sis. She's safe. All that matters.'

I'd caught it, however, the darkness in Will's peepers.

I knew it was in mine as well.

I was going to sodding dismember those bastards. Slowly.

Then I was frightened by the inferno of my own rage.

Will must've read it in my mush too because suddenly he was slipping off that bracelet and forcing it over my left wrist. It dug into my skin. As if Will – his humanity – was touching me, even when he'd pulled back. I blinked my confusion. 'Now you be safe; I ain't need it no more. I have you.'

NIGHT 4

'You have sisters and whatnot? First Lifer?'

Finish your coffee, Mr Blickle, I'm on a schedule.

Puppies to torture before midnight? Sisters, have them?

One sister. Had.

Ate her?

Of course not. Why would you..?

Knock that holier than thou look off your mug; I didn't nosh *my* sisters. Orphan school kid, wasn't I? I didn't go to private--

Boarding school, actually.

It's just what some Blood Lifers do: blood's richer. The DNA intimate-like, almost blood sharing. It's as close to eating yourself as you can get; Freud would've had a field day. Plus what with working here...

And that means...what precisely?

Blood Life Council: the babes to Blood Life who give the rest of us the willies. You should make that your slogan.

You're the Big Bad Wolves.

Captain made a weekend feast of his family. I wouldn't look it up: the photos aren't pretty.

So why *had*?

She's no longer my sister.

Depends how you look at it. Ever been to just look at her..?

Your meal's getting cold. Captain was most insistent--

You can't run from the past. Believe me, I've tried. It'll find you out and carve you up bloody.

Here's a question: if you now know I'm not the Renegades' leader--

Supposition.

Then why am I still here?

Spartacus.

Bless you.

I mean, you're an example. A slave crucified for the sins of your tribe. If your own family wish to burn you, then who are we to object?

Truth doesn't get a look in?

We both know truth doesn't exist.

In ten nights I'll be sacrificial slaughtered. Why are we still playing our parts in this sick charade? You scribbling away on those papers; it doesn't do my ego any good when you doodle fangs in the margins.

Inquiries must be written: it's tradition. The testimony becomes more potent - magic.

You had me up until *magic*. When you write something down, you're granting it an authority, which it hasn't earned.

Lies transformed alchemic into truth.

That's why bastard politicians get stiffies over inquiries, yet erase the parts, which don't fit with their narrative.

I'm not figuring on mine fitting.

Breakfast now, please.

Black coffee and blood to be licked from some boy's arm? You do know how to treat a bloke.

Stop shaking.

I didn't know I was.

Not you: Pet. If you dare spill Mr Blickle's breakfast--

I wouldn't finish that sentence if I were you, sweetheart. Hey, Pet, look at me: what's your favourite band? You like The Animals?

I swear, Pet, Captain will play hunt the human with you again if--

Unless you want to find out whether your blood shows up in the Red Room? Stop talking.

Do you wish to know *my* favourite band, Mr Blickle?

I don't have one. Songs are simply sound; other people's voices used to fill up their emptiness.

Why are you empty, *Thomas*?

How do you know..?

You are hiding behind the music, aren't you?

Whoa there, I was just chinwagging about bands, and this has suddenly turned--

You weren't, though, were you? You never *just* chinwag.

So tell me about why you need so much noise in your head. What are you trying to drown out?

Everything, you stupid bint. Is that what you want..?

Everything.

What do you reckon it's like to remember every...single...moment? The glories and the wonders but also the monsters and the... Every scream...crunch...their deaths sticky under your nails and you can't ever wash...

Everything.

Thomas?

My family, all right? Sisters. Mama. Dead papa. Their voices.

Our last day.

Look, breakfast's over. Send Pet out. You want secrets? That's just between us and this inquiry.

JUNE 1855   WATFORD

We'd escaped - Nora, Polly and I - to the willow tree behind the tall arches of our gabled villa. Mama was out visiting friends, stiffly perched in some overstuffed drawing room, sipping tea and gossiping about society's latest disgrace. Whilst *I'd* freed my little sisters from their stuffy tutor, who looked like he'd been starched head to toe (even his tortuous whine).

I'd unchained them from their tutor's lists of accomplishments: piano, watercolours and posture. My sisters were more than that, even if he couldn't see it.

I'd sneaked them out of the bay window, shunting at the sash. Polly's cotton pinafore had snagged; I'd flinched at the *rip*. Then we'd torn down the manicured lawn – every blade of regimented grass saluting – to the willow at the bottom. Our refuge. Before we'd tumbled in a giggling heap of arms and legs.

I stroked through Nora's long locks. Papa had once pinned a primrose there on our walk up Primrose Hill, once we were out of the fog smoke of the city and gazing over the vast world of London: Barrow Hill Reservoir, cottages, zoological gardens and St Paul's Dome.

Nora had pressed that primrose between her heavy Bible: *I don't wish it to die*, she'd whispered.

Yet when the primrose's creamy petals and sun heart had shrivelled to mummified brown, I hadn't been able to stop myself: I'd stroked its moth wing strangeness. It'd been dry, desiccated - dead.

Under my touch, it'd crumbled.

Shocked, I'd tried to hold it together, but some things can't be saved.

When I'd forced myself to look up into Nora's teary mush, I'd been as devastated as her at the loss.

It was Polly, however, in defence of her sister, who duffed me up.

Their tutor would've been horrified.

Here's the thing: I never was one for mates. In First Life, I didn't have one. Instead I was my papa's apprentice in his experiments into the science of photography; our adventures were of the mind. Around kids of my own age? I stumbled and stuttered; all I knew were beatings and contempt. My sisters were dolls, with which I could play.

And today I intended to initiate my sisters into the secret club of the den.

I flicked open my Swiss army knife. The sun glinted off the steel. As my sisters encircled my waist with their small arms (their familiar weight pressing against me like choir bursts of gold), I cut branches, stripping them with quick efficiency. Sweating, I shifted, the light ghosting the garden pale.

When there was a pile of birch branches, we swept them up in our arms, carrying them under the veil of the weeping willow. Our world. Nora and Polly chattered in their own language, which I'd never decoded, whilst we built a birch igloo, weaving the branches together with nimble fingers. Nora clapped with joy at our creation, as Polly crawled inside.

I grinned.

They were filthy; their pinafores and cheeks smudged with dirt. Their hands as black as a chimney sweep's. When mama saw? I was going to cop it.

We were together, however, and happy. Gold flowed like a wave over me; I wished I could always be bathed in its warmth.

Until I heard the tutor's outraged bellow. 'What in heaven's name is going on here?' He strode towards us like a man on a mission from God himself. 'Girls, inside. The state of you! This is…despicable…a disgrace…wicked. Such unwomanly behaviour is unbecoming. And you, boy?' When he grabbed me by the ear, wrenching hard, I yelped.

Nora and Polly jumped up, but I waved my hand to stop them terrier-like savaging their tutor. Reluctantly, they trailed inside, glancing back at me. They were gripping each other's hands, tears dancing down their cheeks.

I felt as guilty as hell.

The tutor's long mug and blazing peepers was mottled crimson. When he booted the den, it collapsed.

I struggled, but he twisted my ear harder; he was going to bloody pull it off. Then he was stooping down and snatching up a wicked branch, waving it through the air – *swish* – like a switch.

I swallowed.

'Hands against the tree.' At last, the tutor let go of my ear.

I edged towards the trunk, placing my palms against it. It was dark so far beneath the willow. I shivered.

The tutor's hands were around my waist (so different to my sisters'), undoing the button flies on my trousers. Then he slid the jacket from my shoulders, tossing it over my destroyed den, before sliding off my braces and trousers and pushing down my flannel drawers.

I reddened, all the way from my cheeks to my chest.

Even though I was only a kid, inside I raged at the humiliation, the punishment I knew I had coming and at my powerlessness.

I stood there motionless.

And I waited.

'You're spoilt,' the tutor's voice was hard, close to my ear. His hand was caressing my bare arse: *backwards*, *forwards*, *backwards*, *forwards*. I trembled. 'Your papa indulges your eccentricities, but I will not. If I had the misfortune of having you as my son? I'd have you shut up. The whip and the dark. Bedlam. That's what you need, boy.'

I shook, terrified. What if papa listened to this man's poison?

Because what if he was right?

I was different: I always had been.

What if I was destined for the dark?

'Boys need the rod to teach them,' with one hand the tutor was reaching between my legs – *touching* – with the other he was swishing the *switch*. Its cut was cruel through the air. I jumped at each *swish*, expecting the red-hot brand to light up my arse. I was tormented by the anticipation. 'I intend to give you the thrashing of your life. Beat the devil out of you. Count each stroke.'

Then he wasn't at my ear. I felt him move back, allowing himself space to truly swing that sodding switch.

I clenched: every muscle tense. My fingers curled against the smooth trunk of the willow. My peepers screwed shut, as I prepared to have the life whipped out of me.

But the stroke never came.

Confused, I shifted, glancing back over my shoulder.

Papa was standing, like a vengeful Zeus, gripping around the upraised switch with white knuckles. The tutor was stilled, his gob open in gormless surprise.

Neither was backing down.

At last, the tutor lowered his arm.

Papa inspected me, before trying to smile, but I could see the strain. I forced myself to smile back. 'Please make yourself decent, Thomas.'

Hurriedly I yanked up my trousers, fumbling over the buttons. I slipped on my braces, tucking in my shirt with shaky hands. I retrieved my jacket from the collapsed den, before dusting it down and pulling it on.

The tutor waved his arms in horror. 'You do not understand, sir. This contemptible boy--'

'I understand quite well. His sisters came to me in the study. It appears my son was teaching them engineering.'

The tutor blinked rapidly. 'But...they're *girls*. Surely you must--'

'I am only disappointed their endeavours have been broken. They may rebuild again tomorrow.'

I laughed. Then quickly looked down. 'Thank you, papa.'

The tutor stared between us, like he actually had stumbled into Bedlam. 'You're not saying you encourage..?'

'What I am saying,' Papa towered over the tutor, who quailed back, mouse-like now he wasn't intimidating kids. Powerless? I was learning there were strata to these power games in the grownup world - and I bloody wanted to be the man wielding it. 'Is you will not strike my son. He's,' papa paused, considering, 'my little Light.' Papa smiled down at me, as he took my hand, leading me out of the willow's veil and into the sunlight.

Except we never did build that den again because that was our last day together.

The following morning everything changed. One gin-soaked hansom cab driver and papa was lost.

After that, all I knew was orphan school.

So Will? If he didn't want foster or a kiddies' home, I'd give him a glorious new world instead.

Because when you remember the good, it hurts twice as much as remembering the bad.

In First Life I'd lost everything. In Blood Life..? I've lost it several times over.

Abandonment issues? Don't even bloody start.

Yet the secret childhood fear always worming at the edges..? That the dark would come for me and catch me at last, swallowing me whole.

I wouldn't let that happen to Will.

Cold sliced across my skin, as I ran beside the Thames. Even here CCTV recorded every hunter's step; London was a watched over city. Predator energy, however, roiled through my bunched muscles, as I pelted down the pavements, leaping over damp benches, whilst The Animals in all their gritty glory beat through my iPod.

I was lost in the past. In wild joy. In a time when I'd been...

Free.

I was bloody free.

At last I slowed under the orange-sun of a streetlight, gasping for breath.

Footsteps.

Then small fingers wormed out one earbud, like a claim of ownership.

Will: he was burrowing the earbud into his own ear, sharing the bluesy beat and guts of the music. I shook with the sudden intimacy. The shared experience was like blood tongued between us - sacrosanct. The music twining between us was a bond.

The track transported me to 1965, when things were as simple as my Triton on a clear black motorway, with Ruby at my back and hot First Lifer blood thrumming through me.

I licked my lips. The zing was intense...thrilling...*overwhelming*...

Abruptly, I shut off the iPod, tearing away the earbuds from both our nuts.

Will was staring at me – his peepers colourful in black and purple – with this look of wonder. 'The song...that's you, ain't it?'

'What did I tell you about bloody angels?' I grinned, flicking a quick bit of fang.

Will shivered.

I still had it.

Then I felt like a tosser.

Wankering conscience.

I shoved my hands into my pockets. 'That a new look for you?'

Will had magicked up from somewhere black jeans and a t-shirt. He was still wearing ratty trainers but points for trying.

I'd never been anyone's role model before.

Daft kid.

'Come on, I need to see a man about a dog.'

We strolled away from the Thames, through the dripping arches and towards the parade of shops with broken awnings and faulty neon signs. The rich doughy aroma of the bakers warmed the streets in sticky waves, as the *beat – beat – beat* of dance music thudded from the solitary cocktail bar on the corner.

When I heard a strange metallic rasp, I turned to see Will unscrewing a battered flask. He sneaked a glance at me, before taking a swig. Then he choked. I could smell the stink of cheap vodka on his breath.

Quick high kick...the flask was history.

I crossed my arms. 'Not bloody milk that.'

'I ain't no baby, and you drink.'

'Playing copycats, is it?' I studied Will's determined mush speculatively. 'You don't drink to escape.'

'Whatever.' Will flushed. 'What would you know anyway?'

'More than you'd think.'

I sauntered further down the parade, with Will scampering awkwardly after me. He was still hugging his arms around his middle.

Broken ribs.

Of course, he didn't follow me, until he'd made me wait a minute or two's sulky protest.

Teenagers, yeah?

Then there was a *snick* of a lighter, flare of flame, curl of smoke and...

The little git was smoking.

One spear hand later – *stamp* – and the ciggie was dead.

But my nicotine craving had flared to life from the grave.

Will was staring at me with wounded doe eyes; I could've strangled the blighter.

'Those?' I pointed at the smouldering fag, 'Don't hurt me but they kill you. Try and smoke again? I'll ground you. We have an understanding?'

'You like a ninja or something?' Will had edged closer. He'd gripped my wrist and was stroking over the green strands of his sister's bracelet; I don't reckon he even knew he was doing it.

'MMA. How about I teach you?'

The fragility of First Lifers - I'd forgotten that - the decay, mutation and dangers.

Death has stalked me, and I've stalked this world as death.

Even now I could see the bruise reminders of Will's beating; my blood couldn't regenerate his cells. I couldn't heal him faster but if I could teach him to fight..?

Then I thought of Sun. How she was my elected, yet it was Will who needed me.

'Safe, man.'

A flash of cartoon fangs, and a green stripe on long black fringe.

The Emo kid was stalking us. If I hadn't been so distracted by the boy who sang to my Soul, I'd have realised: we were now the prey.

'In here,' I shoved Will through the first shop door we came to: a fast-food restaurant. The stink of chicken and greasy fries both disgusted me and made my mouth water. I watched through the smeared glass: Emo prowled first one way and then the other.

No mistake then.

Donovan *had* sent me out for some grub.

'What do you fancy? My treat.'

Will reddened, as he shook his nut.

'Give over, you're sodding starving. I'll order everything in large.'

It was when my order, in a humungous brown paper bag, was being slid over to me that I clocked we were being hunted...twice.

An officious geezer in snazzy tie and trousers (his name tag thingy read *Kev*), was hovering just to one side of Will; he was herding Will away from the other customers, as if he was going to nick something.

Because those ketchup sachets were worth a bomb on the black market.

Will's shoulders were hunched but he didn't say a word. The boy wasn't stupid; he knew what *Kev* was getting at.

You know your place in society, when you're not welcome in a fast-food restaurant.

I snatched the grub, passing it to Will; he clutched it to his chest. The manager's mouth tightened.

'Kev, is it?' Surprised, Kev stepped back, as if he'd never expected his prey to talk back. I stalked closer, before catching him by the tie – not hard enough to choke but enough to stop him retreating again. The *beep* and *clatter* of the tills continued like infernal machines. The other customers didn't look up from the wet *munch* of their chicken burgers. But Kev saw me - and only me. 'When you're warm inside, paying your rent by serving this muck? Do you think about the kids, who are cold and hungry outside your window?'

When Kev didn't answer, I let go of his tie with a shove; he stumbled backwards, compulsively stroking over the silk like he could wipe it clean.

He'd been touched, however, it was too late: the dark of my world had infected him. If I couldn't kill the bastard? I'd settle for that.

At last Kev opened his gob to reply, but I grabbed Will's hand, dragging him after me out of the shop.

Kev was no predator. The real one was out here - waiting for us.

Will stopped dead.

Emo stood nose-to-nose with him, his skunk scrutiny assessing.

Will grinned. 'Heavy crepes, man. Check out mine,' Will waved his tattered trainers in disgust. Emo's mush was blank, as he remained motionless. 'My crepes be clapping, innit?'

'Shot some kid. Drank. Took his trainers.' Emo nibbled at his chipped black nail varnished fingers thoughtfully. 'I like your jeans.' When Emo smiled, his fangs were already out.

I dived to seize Emo by his stripy scarf but then I heard Will's furious growl.

Will launched himself at Emo in a bizarre imitation of my high kick and spear hands; the fast-food splattered over the pavement. I only just stopped the splutter of laughter in time.

Surprised, Emo still stepped back.

Will was panting like he'd gone three rounds in a MMA final; I patted him on the shoulder. 'Well done, champ, but best leave the fighting to those of us with fangs now.'

Emo tilted his nut. 'A mini-you. He your son?'

'He's none of your business, you rat, that's what he is.'

Emo pursed his lips, as if considering, before pulling out the snake sleekness of his shooter.

'Now don't you be wishing we had my shank?'
Will hissed – *oomph* – elbowing me in the ribs.

'Let's not go through this again: you've got a bigger gun than me. And by gun? You mean todger. Got it. Now stop playing with it in public because my boy here's a First Lifer; he won't just hop away and heal like me.'

'He shot you?' Will's peepers were wide with terror. He'd grasped my wrist –around the bracelet – as if I'd disintegrate to ashes. When I realised that terror was for me? It booted me in the gut.

I shrugged. 'Yeah. A little. In the foot.'

Emo tittered

I glared at the brat. Then gasped as the bones in my wrist were pressed together; Will was holding on so tightly, I could see the bone white of my skin between his fingers, but it wasn't terror – it was rage.

If looks could kill? Emo would be a flayed bloody mess in black-and-white socks splayed on the streets of Southwark.

I prised Will off my wrist. 'Look, I got better. Fast.'

Emo examined me, as if wishing he'd had me strapped down on a lab table to watch my poor foot heal - only so he could do it all over again. He cocked the shooter.

Bloody hell, sometimes I wish I was wrong about the psychos.

'Where shall I shoot you next? Knee? Hip?' Emo smirked. 'Groin?'

'You ain't gonna do nothing,' Will's breathing was harsh, but I'd never heard anyone so definite; I wish I'd ever been certain of anything, 'I'll bring arms house to your ends...'

It's like when a kitten pounces at a tomcat; the tomcat doesn't even bother to bat them back.

Emo studied me calculatingly. 'What will hurt most?'

'Behave or I'll send you to the naughty step. Just tell me why the buggering hell you're following me. I'm tired of the games.'

Sulky as Will earlier, Emo booted a discarded coffee cup skittering.

Yeah, teenagers.

I watched the shooter weave casually through the night air, as if Emo was conducting a silent orchestra.

No one had noticed: the passersby, the streams of cat-eyed cars, black cabs and red night buses or the customers through the glass front of the chicken emporium. Here we were held up at gunpoint on the night-time streets of London.

And nobody had a scooby.

'Can't. Won't. Don't want to.' Then the smirk was firmly back in place. 'And you will like my games. Soon.' Emo levelled the pistol at Will.

Straight at the heart.

None of us moved.

'Don't,' I breathed, 'just...please, don't.'

Emo's finger was pressing down on the trigger. The shooter was going off.

Bang.

I threw myself in front of Will - in front of the gun – and the bullet.

I encircled Will with my arms, as we crashed to the pavement.

Will howled, when I crushed his ribs but he was alive; I was flooded with simple joy, whilst I waited to die.

Will was sobbing and calling my name.

Angel of Light, Angel of Light, Angel of Light...

Then he slapped my mush. Hard.

I opened my peepers.

What the sodding hell?

When I clutched at my chest, my hand came back clean: no gory crimson.

I twisted round to look up at that strangely blank expression on the Emo kid's mug.

He'd tucked away the gun. I had the feeling of being a bug under his scientist's gaze. 'Blanks. No bullets. Interesting reaction. How did it feel to face second death?'

Don't forget me...Sun entwined around me like a steel snake; her bite into my jugular was explosive rainbow end of days. I panted, squirming and gasping. Trapped in her embrace, I juddered. Then Sun was snogging me and I could taste my copper blood... *Don't forsake me*...

I could feel the vibrations of Hartford's anguished plea in his soulful song through every fevered atom. We curled around each other on the black cushions, which were piled on the lounge floor. Donovan was sprawled on the sofa, smoking wacky backy, serenaded by Hartford's new routine for the club. But it was meant for him because one thing I knew..?

Love.

...*Live for me*...

Hartford was singing to Donovan: the dead bloke he craved to resurrect.

I twisted Sun, splaying her over the cushions. She laughed in surprise. I'd forgotten how young she still was. 'My turn.'

I bit but gently. The moment when my fangs slid through her ivory skin was divine. Her blood was like coming home. Her body was quivering... *Don't forget me*... and we were snogging, both our bloods bonded as one... *Don't forsake me*... our hearts beating united... *Live for me*...

Crash.

Splintered door. Black balaclavas. First and Blood Lifers. *Shooters.*

'Bloody down.' I threw myself over Sun, shielding her. I couldn't hear anything over the *rat-rat-rat* of gunshots. The sofa's foam sprayed like snow.

Screams.

Christ in heaven, *Hartford.*

I peered up.

Dark shapes, like black ghosts, were thronging through our flat. A dozen at least.

Hartford was huddled by the wall: he was riddled with bullets. His breathing was laboured; crimson was seeping down his white shirt.

Donovan had dived from the sofa and was stroking Hartford's cheek, snarling at the bastard, who had his semiautomatic pressed to Hartford's forehead.

Enough was bleeding enough.

I stood up, straightening my shoulders. As if with a collective mind, the black balaclava bastards turned their shooters to point at me. Apart from the one who had his trained on Hartford. 'Reckon there's been a bit of a mix up, gents. So why don't you pack up and get your arses out of here. By the way, what type of Blood Lifer brings either a gun or a First Lifer to a barney?'

'That'd be me.'

Bollocks.

Captain neatly stepped through our smashed front door, as if appalled to discover it in such a state. He brushed at his peak of strawberry blond hair: he still had the dimples.

Sodding baby-faced wanker.

'Found an even more morally outrageous way of fuelling your ambition at the Blood Life Council, than enslaving your own species?' Hartford was taking agonised gasps – how many times had they bleeding shot him? When I caught movement out of the corner of my eye, I hurriedly gestured for Sun to stay still. We'd seen what Captain could do; I didn't want a repeat. 'Like taking over the banks? Or going into coalition with the First Lifer Government?'

Captain sauntered in front of me; in sky blue jacket and shirt he was the only colour in a sea of black. 'I have a busy day, absolutely back-to-back with meetings. So, precious as you always are, let's get down to it. Do you remember knocking out my tooth?'

For the first time, I smiled. 'One of my happiest memories.'

'I'm so pleased because I'm certain this shall be one of mine.'

A steel knuckleduster was slipped with practised precision over Captain's right fist. 'Fangs out.'

This time I couldn't stop either Sun or Donovan shooting to their feet. 'Bloody well stay back,' I hissed at them.

'How cute,' Captain was weighing us up one at a time; I felt like I was at a slave auction and remembered the file Captain had written on my weaknesses to help the slavers capture me, 'a Plantagenet has made himself a family.' He eyed Donovan. 'Excuse me, *two* Plantagenets.'

'You want your tooth for a tooth? Sodding well get on with it and stop boring us to death.' I couldn't let the others see what it was doing to me to force out my fangs, knowing they were going to be stolen from me again.

I glanced at Hartford. When our gazes met, I saw he was silently weeping and I knew it wasn't from the pain: it was because he knew what this meant to me.

When Captain stroked my cheek, I flinched. 'You see, I decide what happens. I'm in charge. If you can get with that programme, well then, we'll get on swimmingly. But for now? You need to take your punishment.'

Captain raised the knuckleduster. My fangs ached. I fisted my hands, as I screwed shut my peepers.

Bloody do it...

Then softly I felt Captain's finger tracing over each fang. It was...a violation.

My peepers snapped open.

Captain was watching the way his finger outlined each fang with fascination. The knuckleduster, however, had disappeared. 'I don't need to take your fangs, Light, I already own them. Now since your firebug impression with the Blood Club (an administrative headache by the way), we've been at war. Terrorists have been inspired by your brutish example to free the remaining Blood Lifer slaves and to work against us at the Council.'

'Terrorists? I don't..?'

Captain caught my chin between his fingers hard enough to hurt. 'You're delicious when you're playing innocent. But this is how I own your fangs.' He clicked his fingers.

Suddenly two Blood Lifers snatched Donovan on either side, bundling him out of the apartment.

'Don't... Stop...'

One moment Donovan was there. The next? Gone.

All that was left? Hartford shaking and shouting from the corner, 'Donovan! Donovan! Donovan...' Until he made a lunge for the door, shredded guts and all.

'Want to see what a brain-dead Blood Lifer looks like?' Captain gestured at the goon, who pressed the gun to the back of Hartford's nut.

'Alright, you own me. What do you want?'

Captain smiled: bleeding Cheshire cat. 'The Renegades. Their leader served up on a platter, so I can put them on trial for their crimes. You were asking about power? A celebrity inquiry..? Now that's power.'

'We've been keeping a low profile. No playing Spartacus. I haven't even heard of these wankers.'

Captain glared between us then. From me, to Sun and finally at Hartford: there aren't many blokes who can hold a Long-lived's gaze, especially one blazing with the type of grief and fury, which was threatening to sear Hartford open in more places than he was already shot.

It's a dangerous thing to underestimate a bloke; Captain might be a babe to the black waters of Blood Life but he was a shark.

Captain shrugged. 'If you don't hand over the leader of the Renegades? We'll have to – sacrifice - Donovan in their place. Your call.'

'This is what you're reduced to?' My voice was low and raspy with tears. 'Joining forces with corrupt First Lifers? Bastard guns because you won't dirty your fangs or fists? Kidnap?'

Captain tilted his nut, considering. Then he slugged me in the gut. I coughed, doubled over. 'I dirty my fangs and fists but only for pleasure.' He wiped his palms down his dun trousers, before slapping his thighs. 'Best be off, busy, busy, you know how it is.'

When Captain pulled out his iPhone, we all jumped. Then he jabbered into it, as if we were forgotten, even though he'd torn apart my family, destroying my home. His silent army trooped out after him.

Numb, I stared around at the shattered remains of our apartment: the door swinging on its hinges, busted cushions, exploded sofa...and Hartford in a tangled heap of blood, tears and impotent fury.

I fell to my knees next to him, Sun on his other side, as we wrapped our arms around him like we could absorb his pain.

Except it wasn't enough.

Because one of us was missing.

I rubbed my mush against Hartford's hair, as we rocked him. 'We'll get him back, I promise; I'll get Donovan back.'

Family, you see, they do make you weak. What's there in life, though, if not love?

Captain? What's he ever loved except power?

Does he even love you?

NIGHT 5

Love was always your greatest weakness, wasn't it?

Not family, loyalty or obsession.

Love: the fear of losing it.

Come on, Thomas, wake up. There are only nine more nights before your trial. You must give me something more than dead papas, homeless boys and--

Kidnapped cousins? Sorry to bore you, sweetheart. How do you know my weaknesses flayed bloody? Seems you've been reading Captain's file on me.

Sod it, I'm right?

There were photos in there; *Master* got off on telling me. Starkers ones of me: chained, collared and leashed. Enjoyed them, did you? Had a good laugh?

Or did you touch yourself instead?

Mr Blickle, I assure you--

Right cozy feeling to know my torture and enslavement does it for you.

What would *do it* for me, would be some tangible evidence. You dance around like a boxer. This is your second life: I'm trying to save it.

I investigated, and you were right: you were being starved and sleep deprived. Plus of course, you're no leader for the Renegades.

I'll be off then, shall I?

We still need our Spartacus. Yet I don't like being tricked, as much as I do like a puzzle.

That's what this is to you?

Isn't it to you? A vast world of infinite puzzles? A continual search for a challenge worthy of that astounding brain, which you attempt to hide behind the banter? Come, we're not so different.

I've been around for 150 years. I've learnt a few things, like when you struggle – sacrifice – and finally open that puzzle box, and it's empty..?

It wasn't worth one single bleeding thing you lost.

Silence. Crimson. Cold.

I couldn't stop shivering. Water trickled down my back, through my soaked t-shirt. When we'd dashed out of our flat into the freezing rain, I hadn't even paused to grab my leathers.

Hartford's pale body gaped with wounds, like an abused voodoo doll, scarlet against the pale. He lay motionless on the top of Aedan's stripped bed, in the flat above Peter Pan's. He looked so small on the grand four-poster, underneath the kitsch mosaic of Adam reaching (and failing) to touch God's outstretched finger; Hartford's damp hair was as golden as the thick wallpapered walls.

Hartford stared at the ceiling, but he didn't even blink. For a horrifying moment, it was like we were back at Abona House, and he was laid out after some sadistic john had got his jollies from shooting holes in him.

Aedan hovered at my shoulder. All things considered, the chinwag when we'd turned up as if out of a warzone, hadn't been as awkward as it could've been.

'So what gobshite did..?' Aedan's green peepers gleamed, as he waved into the bedroom. He was whispering, like Hartford was sleeping - I wished he had been. 'So I can ball him, before I castrate him with my teeth.'

'You'll have a bloody long queue,' I patted Aedan on the back. 'Cheers for this and sorry for...'

'Not being human?'

I shifted. 'Never for that. Lying. Missing work. Getting blood all over the bed.'

'No bother, I'll dock your wages,' Aedan grinned, slapping my arse.

I could hear Aedan nattering to Sun, as he tramped downstairs. There was the stink of pigs' blood – alien, thin, *wrong* – after breaking abstention. Hartford wasn't up to sinking his fangs into me, however, for his fix, so the 24 hour butchers it was.

Hartford would heal but only if he drank.

I perched next to Hartford, sweeping my hand through his hair. 'Hey, helmethead.'

Not a flicker.

'Tasty blood - alright, pigs' blood - but it'll take away the pain.'

Still nothing.

I leant closer. My clothes stuck to me, as cold tremors shook me. I couldn't – didn't want to – think of Donovan with Captain. What Captain was doing to him.

My predator roared. My fangs were owned - again. I was an idiot to think I could be free; we were none of us free. Donovan was abducted, whilst Hartford was silent and unmoving.

Frustrated, I threw myself up from the bed. 'Not bloody good enough. Snap out of it.'

Nothing.

Furious, bubbling, impotent rage, which had been repressed from the moment Captain had slipped on that knuckleduster, whilst holding a gun to Hartford's nut, erupted. I swung my palm.

Slap.

Shocked, I stared at the crimson handprint on Hartford's white cheek. His motionless doll cheek.

'You're a Long-lived. *Sir* didn't break you. *Master* couldn't. After everything they did to both of us – our species – you protected us all. Then you tore those bastards apart, remember? *You*. I know this hurts; I'm bleeding out here too. You need to transform that pain to rage because what we did to the Blood Club will look like child's play by the time we're done with the Blood Life Council. I promise. Right now? It's fangs and fists; it's not time to hide. Please, Hartford?'

And then?

Hartford blinked.

He saw me; he heard me. He was a Long-lived once more.

'What's the plan, mac?' Hartford's voice was croaky but determined.

There was a sound in the doorway; Aedan was behind me. He'd heard. At least...enough. He simply slipped to Hartford, however, his red braids swinging over his cheeks, as he pressed a mug of blood to his lips, like it was the most natural thing in the world.

Confused, I no longer knew who was predator or prey: Blood or First.

Yet I did know my family were both species. And that?

Sodding terrified me.

'Grayse Cain, upon my Soul. Where the frak have you been?' Fernando (perfect prat that he was), glared out of the smeared screen at the Internet café.

In checked shirt, which was buttoned up to the top and backlit by a tech lab of computers, which were glowing as if they'd bloody invented sunlight, it was like Fernando had been trapped in amber: unchanged from when he'd helped us take down the slavers. Maybe the whole world was in amber, and it was only Sun and I – under the false light of the café's computers – who'd moved on.

Evolved.

Grayse Cain had. Now she was Sun.

Only Fernando didn't know that...yet.

Sun shifted next to me on her plastic seat – *squeak, squeak* – as awkward as me. 'Hey, 'sup Prof? I know this is fried, but we had to book it outta there that night and--'

'You forgot my number?' Fernando's mouth was twisted like he wanted to twist something else. By the way he was casting these furious glances at me? I reckoned it was my neck. 'Like I've just been sitting on my thumbs waiting..?'

'Shut your mush.' To my shock? Fernando actually did. 'There are bigger things here than your petty pride. We had to keep safe.'

'Whoa, calm down there, little man,' Fernando fluttered his long dark eyelashes, as if *he* was the reasonable one. *All right, point made.* 'Why were you hiding?'

I bristled. 'Don't call me *little man*.'

'Can't you tell?' Sun leant in closer to the computer. The bustle and chatter of the café was suddenly too loud; the neon blue of the streetlamp reflected through the glass was too bright. The sweaty stink of the teenagers, who were pressed up next to us intent on their fantasy multi-player game, was too powerful. Sun licked her lips. How was she getting off on this? 'Your family were mine on account of I was alone in Harvard. Your cuz? He was like my brother. But would they have me over for a keg party or lobster roll *now*?'

Fernando pushed himself closer to the screen as well, as if he was able to climb through it. 'You're one of *them*,' he hissed.

'Not *Invasion of the Body Snatchers*.'

Fernando's dark gaze flickered to mine. 'Yah, it is. You murdered Grayse. So I don't know how but I'll have vengeance.'

'Think that line's taken.'

'What do you want? Humans working here.' Cold and dismissive. Fernando's mask melted in the golden warmth of that humming lab.

Now it was Sun, rather than Grayse?

The tosser didn't give a monkey's.

Somehow Sun had known.

'Ya huh! You don't pull that one on account of Blood Lifers are dying here. You study this: evolution. So you wanna study that or extinction?'

'Always were a drama queen, whoever the frak you are now,' Fernando sighed. 'What miracle do you want my magic fingers to pull off this time?'

'I have the brains; you have the...ethical hacking. When I was at Mann with that right bastard *Master*, I broke into his study. Paid for it mind. I found a list though: all the specialist slaves sent around the globe, their masters and locations. I memorised it. You hack--'

Fernando frantically waved his hands around like he was swatting an invisible wasp. 'Wanna say that word any louder? Another time? Unencrypted? Where even are you? You're not on a private computer...'

'How do you know? Been *hacking* us?' Exploding Alpha Geek. I couldn't help hopping in my seat in expectation. Until Sun grasped my hand, and I noticed her stormy expression. All right then, best not to poke the bloke with a stick, whilst you're asking for help, even when he *is* your lover's ex. 'It's safer this way. You don't need to know where we are.'

'Southwark, man,' the pink haired teenager, who was plugged into an online dragon game on the computer next to ours, helpfully offered with a grin, 'our ends, innit?'

Fernando smiled – white and wide. 'London? Why don't you come down Boston? To the university?'

'Nice shiny lab with matching dissection tables all ready for us?'

Fernando tried – hard – to look hurt.

I could see the thoughts, however, whirring; I sodding wished I hadn't given him ideas. 'All we need is for you to h – a - c – k Abona's records. Then match the slave names to the original Blood Lifers. Also see what's been happening at the locations because it turns out some bleeding heroes – the Renegades – have been rescuing these high end slaves. The poor gits who got the same treatment as me, before being sold to princes and billionaires. Trust me, it won't be a hard trail of breadcrumbs to follow because they'll be dripping crimson.'

Fernando examined me in silence. It made me feel like my insides were on display bloody. Then he gave a sharp nod. 'I'm warning you, this time it's not a freebie. If I do this? Here's the deal: I wanna research *him*.'

The glint in Fernando's peepers, as he pointed at me, gave me the willies. I could already imagine the scalpel in his hand. 'Hey now, I've had enough of being poked and prodded by so-called doctors.'

'Then goodbye.'

'Wait, buggering hell, alright then.' I was panting; my heart was thundering.

When had that started?

Sun had slipped her arm around my waist; her fingers dug into me like a claim, as if she'd never let me go. Never let this wanker own me, like the slavers had, the Doctor, Captain...

'*I'll* call you this time tomorrow,' when Sun licked up my neck I jumped; Fernando did too. 'Light? He's mine. You want him? Na-ah, not happening. You find us what we need to know. Then we'll talk.'

The screen went blank.

'Off the hook: that was some serious live action role-playing or something?' The pink haired kid gazed at us in awe.

'Yeah, something.' When I stroked Sun's hand, she eased her death grip. 'Still reckon Fernando's a decent bloke?'

Sun shrugged, but her mush was shuttered. I wished I could've snogged the sun back into her.

'We'll get Donovan back. Sod the Blood Life Council and wankering Captain. Bugger Fernando. We're--'

'Don't you dare say *safe*.'

Sun's murmur was like a slap in the mush. Her python gaze was hypnotizing. 'You don't get to leave me. You're soft if you reckon you can just sacrifice yourself. You're my Author.'

'Am I now? I didn't reckon I meant that much to you.'

Sun's peepers widened. Then she was snogging me.

Her hand grasped behind my neck; her body wound round mine. Her fingers were playing with strands of my hair; my scalp bursting in delicious tingles. I could hardly breathe: nothing but *Sun, Sun, Sun*... The whoops and catcalls from the teenagers sounded far away.

I was soaring. Lost in Sun: her touch, taste, love...

Until Sun suddenly drew back; snake ready to strike. 'Remember that Emo kid, who was spying on us?'

I risked a nod.

'Don't you think it would be wicked strange, if he wasn't connected?'

Reckoning I was hunting Emo but realising he was hunting me... The fight outside the gleaming Shard where he shot me... A shooter the same as the Blood Life Council were using... The games of hide-and-seek ever since, even when I was with Will, except I'd let it go *because* of Will...

Sun was right.

This was my fault.

I must've allowed my thoughts to show because Sun's gaze sharpened. 'No more lies. You knew that something was up?'

'I didn't, luv. But that kid...'

'You saw him again?'

I risked another nod.

'Since when didn't you tell me on account of I'm family? Na-ah, I don't wanna hear it. Ever since that human pet? It's like you're not even with us anymore.' When Sun stood up, I could see she was shaking. I didn't know how to reach her. Not now. 'I wanna get Donovan back. But you? That's a whole notha matter. How am I gonna get *you* back?'

Then she was gone – *bang* – there went the Internet Café's door.

'You just got owned,' the teenager sniggered.

I slumped back in my plastic chair – *squeak*. 'You're not wrong, mate.'

Water tears snaked down the café's front, as I rested my forehead against the freezing pane and shivered. I splayed my fingers, their imprint ghosted against the glass. Rain wormed down the back of my neck. My pompadour dampened to curls.

I sneezed, snuffling mournfully.

I didn't go in the light and warmth, however, to the teenage crews, blokes rewriting their CVs or practising for their citizenships. Not again. That was Fernando's territory. Yet I couldn't bring myself to return to Peter Pan's and Sun either.

Not yet.

So here I was. Dreary no-man's-land. Sodding cold, it was.

Fernando had looked like he was wet dreaming, when the monitor had sprung on, and he'd caught a gander of me slouched on the plastic seat for our meet up...and no Sun.

I'd rather not have known what his come face looked like.

Fernando had drooled over my every word. I hadn't blamed him. No Sun? Meant I'd been back on the market: free to be possessed.

Looked like he'd been eager to slip on the collar.

Still, if I was going to be Fernando's lab rat, then I'd demanded results: names and locations sent directly to Hartford's iPhone.

Aedan had gifted the snazzy little number to Hartford. How's that for a get well pressie? That way Hartford could work even whilst healing in Aedan's bed. Hartford's dark despair was now tinged with determination. It was bloody terrifying.

I wouldn't be the Blood Life Council for the world.

'There'll be a pattern; there always is,' I'd told Fernando. 'It's just a matter of looking right. Someone's hushing it up. A terrorist's M.O. is fear, right? Panic? Control? So where are the corpses? The fires? If these Renegades hate the slavers anywhere close to as much as I do? They're not going to be asking nicely for them to free their property over a cup of tea.'

Now I should be going home again, except Sun and her silent accusations sucked up the air until I choked.

Sun had been this pissed at me only once before.

We'd just moved into the apartment – with the holes in the wall, the taps that never worked and Mr Rat – and I'd discovered Grayse's crimson evening dress balled at the bottom of the bedroom wardrobe. Bloodstained and still smelling of gorse and sunlight: Grayse in every bursting miraculous breath. The memory had cocooned me; I'd been safe in it.

I'd straightened out the dress, curling around it, as if I could bring back the shape of Grayse out on the moors. It'd held me in its embrace: how I'd bleeding craved I could hold her one more time.

That night had come crashing back: when Grayse's dad – *Master* – had shot her. The moment – that agonising moment - when I'd known I was going to bring her back as a Blood Lifer.

Yet Ruby hadn't been one to share her secrets. I'd been led like a puppy on a string, rather than apprenticed into the dark arts of second life. In my hesitation, both Hartford and Donovan has grasped my hands, their fangs springing out to guide my own to the back of Grayse's neck and her spinal column: the very place *Sir* had desecrated with the tracker and branches of fire.

Then I'd injected the venom, as Grayse had died. Because our life? It's not only in the blood. It's in our venom. That's our evolution.

Our strength.

I'd felt Grayse's heart stop. Then there'd just been my own fast pulse. My venom seeping through tree-like nerves. We'd been one, as I'd authored her – and she'd evolved.

Into one of us.

When Grayse, however, had opened her peepers? I hadn't kidded myself. She hadn't been my Grayse any longer. She'd become someone else. New born to this brutal world. Born of my fangs.

And she was formidable.

'She's not me,' I'd opened *my* peepers to discover Sun standing over me. Her mush had been death white.

Tumbled in our wardrobe, wrapped in Grayse's dress? My nose pressed to the satin? Silently crying?

I'd been so buggered.

I'd tried to push myself up but tangled in the threads, I'd landed on my arse. 'I know that, sweetheart.'

'She's dead.'

'Again, I--'

'You're in love with a ghost.'

Sun had slammed out then – *bang*.

I'd sodding wished she'd clouted me instead.

Then there was Will. I couldn't even think about Will.

I couldn't work out what was worse: my guilt for not seeing him or the guilt I'd ever seen him at all.

I'd caught up with Trinity along the back of Borough Market, as she'd been strutting home. I'd wanted to know if she'd heard any *whispers* about Donovan's kidnap.

Trinity had looked me up and down like I'd crawled out of the Thames. 'That bare jokes, bruv. We your invisible army?' She'd snorted. 'Or this mean you be seeing mandem now we useful to you?'

'Bugger that. You and me? We're--'

Trinity shoved me in the chest. ''Cos you're sorry for us? Reckon we're the same as some *creature*?' I'd drawn back; Trinity knew how to grab a bloke by the throat. 'This Donovan? He be the same one as wanted to *snack* on my Will?'

'Heard about that, did you?'

Suddenly Trinity had been so close to my mush, her lips had been touching mine. 'It don't matter how much chocolate and BS you been feeding Will, I ain't helping you find no monster.'

'He's my bloody family, you stupid bint.' I'd twisted away before I'd been able to say – do – more.

I'd reckoned I was learning this friendship lark but I was still paddling in the shallow end.

Sighing, I slipped out my e-cig, clenching it between my trembling lips in the cold. A few more drags, then I'd have the balls to go home to Sun.

Crash.

Screaming agony.

Crash.

Blood dripping.

Crash.

Nose broken.

Dazed, I scrabbled behind me at the bastard, who was slamming me headfirst into the glass.

There was copper in my mouth. Lights fairy danced.

I shot back my elbow, hearing the satisfying *oomph* of a connection. Pressure was pushing me flat against the café's front.

The teenagers must be getting quite a show.

Elbows, neck, back... It was organised. A team.

First Lifers.

Not again. Not this time.

I kicked my foot out, before pushing back, thrashing wildly. I was desperate to at least see my hidden enemies: the bleeding cowards who'd attack a bloke from behind.

A holler, cursing, and then...

Crash, crash, crash.

I yowled.

Sun...a dark tunnel of grey...Sun...

She wasn't here. She was meant to be. Yet because of my secrets she was safe.

Sun was *safe.*

A sharp prick in my neck.

The wankers plunged the needle deeper. Somewhere in my scrambled brain, I remembered. The thick transparent liquid: our venom in pure form.

Silverman's experiments.

I was the lab rat.

I laughed – I couldn't help it - at the sodding irony, as paralysis cramped my limbs and our toxin held me prisoner in my own body. I couldn't even blink the blood out of my peepers.

I was a poseable doll.

True terror set in then. What did they want me for?

Strangers' hands seized me like they had every right to touch. Then fingers on my eyelids – intimate and wrong - closing them.

Forcing   me   into   the   dark.

NIGHT 6

You look...

Knackered? Like a dog's breakfast? Death warmed up? Starvation, sleep deprivation and five rounds of torture on the trot will do that to a bloke.

Mr Blickle, the Blood Life Council does not employ such methods. I was assured--

If *you* were assured...and you are again?

The woman who's trying to save your ungrateful – and rather worn – behind from an untimely demise.

If you wish to heal today and smoke that e-cig of yours, then secrets are on the agenda. If you also wish me to delve into your claims of unfair treatment..? That extraordinary mind of yours - I want it.

I'm only here – alive – because of my photographic memory?

I'd wondered at your *generosity*.

Talents are our genetic advantage. Why we've always been the apex predator.

What you're also not figuring, however, is that when you're persecuted, you use every trick and con to adapt.

That's what makes *me* the bloody king.

You won't be pulling the wool over my eyes, Thomas.

We'll see. But truth or trust? None of that means a thing when weighed in the balance with survival.

Dark.

Help, help, help...

I. Can't. Open. My. Eyes.

Chains.

Tight around my wrists and ankles, tying me down to the cold plastic of an examining table.

You feel that once? You never forget.

Can't move. Can't speak. Can't see.

Can hear though and *feel*...

Hands.

Touching every bleeding inch of me, probing and exploring, alien-like in latex gloves.

Bloody make them stop.

But they didn't stop; icy fingers owned me in the dark, as if I was a cadaver, ready to be sliced, before my lungs were pulled from my chest.

Inside panic coiled, but I couldn't even shudder or pant: the venom kept my heart pumping as calm as you like. I could hear it, mocking in my ears – *beat, beat, beat* – as those hands reduced me to nothing.

Yet Sun wasn't with me. Amongst the terror and despair – hallelujah to the golden heavens – Sun was safe. She should've been at the café. If I hadn't narked her off? She would've been.

Whatever they did to me? No matter what the bastards stripped from me this time?

They couldn't hurt me - not truly.

Because Sun was safe.

'Subject One is a proper job,' the hands' owner – a First Lifer – patted my stomach.

My name is Light, my name is Light, my name is...

But I couldn't even whisper it.

Dark. Violation. Dark.

Hours? Days? Weeks?

Trapped. Powerless. Lost.

Entombed inside your own motionless body, time doesn't mean a bleeding thing. All I knew? Hunger, blood pangs, nicotine craving, cold, cramps...

As a slave, I'd been strapped down: stripped of hair to be fetishized into a plaything. Suffered surgery with no anaesthetic: to be implanted with the wankering tracker or to have my fangs pulled out one by one by the Doctor.

I had no choice or control. Yet I'd freed myself, slaughtered the slavers and freed my family. But this time? I didn't even know who'd kidnapped me, why they'd taken me, or if it was a death sentence.

'Subject One's responding as expected, aren't 'ee? Let's increase the dose.'

Subject.

In one sodding word I was sticky labelled *nothing*. No identity or personhood.

I was the monkey in the lab, and when did he ever escape alive?

To lose my freedom a second time was... My mind fled into the slave dark.

Welcomed it.

There was no Grayse this time to save me by reminding me I was Light.

My name is...

Light.

A thin crack – angelic awe-inspiring glory – spilling through the bottom of my eyelids.

I could move.

Just a fraction but I'd take what I could get. I wiggled my toes.

Blinding – that'd never felt so good.

Next my fingers. They felt loose, as if I was a ragdoll, or had been on one hell of a bender.

Tongue next – serious one that, because not talking? You try it when you've got a big gob like me. My tongue was like a sleepy snake but still...possibilities.

I risked opening my peepers half-mast.

Bollocking hell.

Retinas scorched, with tears running down my cheeks, I let out a strangled yelp.

Voice box was up to snuff then.

Gasping, I waited for the blaze of glory to settle. Fuzzy shapes spectred out of the strip lighted haze. A glass barrier directly in front of me out into a narrow corridor, which was panelled in bronze military style, as if I'd been swallowed by a beetle and was pinned to its metallic guts.

Let's all scrutinize the bug on the slide.

I could see my own starkers, strapped down reflection bounced back: I wouldn't be winning any Miss Britain sashes.

An IV set-up was running into the back of my left hand; there was a steady ache where the thick needle pressed under the skin. A crimson bag hung limp from the stand; it was stamped with a logo: a branching black tree.

I sniffed: *human blood.*

My hollow belly groaned.

They were keeping me alive like a sodding coma patient.

Suddenly the slavers' baby bottles were looking more appealing.

I licked my dry lips. No water or food. Of course not, because I wasn't human, was I?

'Paralysis has reduced in subject.'

I rolled my nut to one side to see my chief tormentor in the long dark: a spindly bloke with neat grey hair and intense peepers, like a decrepit spider. His white lab coat, over cord trousers, was too short and his shirtsleeves were rolled back, revealing thick forearms.

The tosser was scribbling notes in a file on a '60s oak desk, which was out of place amongst the laptops, Blackberries and gleaming steel trays of scalpels, pliers, saws...and the sliced remains of Will's green bracelet.

I was going to hurl.

The scientist scampered to my side, running his latex gloved hand down the centre of my body with casual ownership. His fingers curled around my todger: weighing and measuring. 'As noted earlier, Subject One is...average.'

I shot out my fangs. 'No touching the goods, Frankenstein.'

'Subject One is teasy 'cos it's still tired. You have the gag?'

'Yes, professor, but surely we don't need--'

'Call me Ivor. Dusta think I care about titles like *professor*?'

I twisted to the other side.

A frumpy bird in an oversized lab coat was banging through a glass cupboard of scientific equipment.

Torture devices.

If you're the rat it's one and the same.

The bint was flushed and wouldn't meet my eye. She brushed a stray brunette strand, which had fallen out of her haphazard ponytail – cry for help if ever I saw it – as she handed Frankenstein a steel gag. It even had the black tree logo on it: thorough branding that.

'Thank you, Ms Shah,' Frankenstein held out the gag like it was a gift, 'now if the subject is a babby and don't open up, remove the IV. Do it some good to go without vittles. See if the subject won't knuckle-in then.'

I glanced between them. Sometimes you have to lose a battle to win a war. And sometimes?

You don't even know who you're fighting.

Reluctantly, I withdrew my fangs and opened my gob. Tremors took hold, as Frankenstein fixed the gag at the back of my nut, wrenching my jaw. And then as the experiments began.

Sometimes as I drifted in and out of paralysis in a pain induced fog, I just wished they'd bloody get it over with.

Whatever *it* was.

Because this was playing silly buggers, like a kid pulling off a fly's wings. I tried to remember if I knew the bastard: it felt personal. If I'd noshed his family or feasted on his lover back in the bad good old days with Ruby. Yet there'd been a rule: no witnesses. Ruby had drilled it into me with kisses and clouts.

I couldn't have been that careless?

Despite the relish Frankenstein was taking, however, there were also the soldiers, with their hands smartly behind their backs, observing me in all my naked, battered glory, as they stood behind the glass.

The soldiers had curt chinwags, but because my cell, which masqueraded as a lab, was soundproofed (after all, it'd be a crime for my screams to interrupt their morning coffee), I couldn't hear them.

Their expressions – like an army of clones – were always the same: a dumb smart blankness. As if experimental research on a Blood Lifer was just another day at the office. Maybe they were dissecting a bulbous headed alien in the cell next to mine: I was nothing special at all.

But somehow?

I reckoned this was all to do with Blood Life.

Our venom: how it paralysed, and how the military could use that to carve a crimson path in whatever war they pleased.

Everyone reckons it's about defence, but there'll always be terrorists. The enemy.

Others.

There'll always be an excuse to fight like the beasts we are. Yet it's needing an *excuse*, which raises us above the animals.

None of us should kid ourselves though, First or Blood. We pretend we want peace, when in fact our blood calls for war. We cherry pick the battles we can win and then to be the victor we create the best warriors, with the deadliest weapons.

Any First Lifer stole the advantage of our venom?

They'd be conquerors of the world.

All I knew? I couldn't allow it to happen. I didn't have a scooby though – trussed up, gagged and brutalised as I was – how I was going to stop it.

I blinked the sweat out of my peepers. That was...nine increases now?

I couldn't help having a butchers at the black box in the wanker's hands, as his thin fingers turned the knobs: when the wires were attached around my bollocks for a spot of electro torture before bedtime, I was long past playing it cool.

'Handsome: Subject One's heart rate be significantly increased. Let's see how loud the subject can screech. Level ten coming dreckly.'

The hum leapt. Furious wasps all flying to fry my privates, except they weren't so private anymore. My tender balls were out there: free to be shocked, thumped, and burnt.

I shook from the stink of my own sweat, the agony, which had swallowed me in searing waves and the shuddering fear of level ten because Frankenstein loved to build the anticipation: until it struck – lightning bolt. A shock worse twice over because you couldn't prepare.

Tosser knew what he was doing.

A low whine. Like a mutt.

Then I realised it was coming from me.

Cool fingers were on my brow, brushing back my hair.

I forced myself to glance away from that black box – and level ten. Shah was – trying – to smile at me. This wavering little thing, as frightened as I felt.

'We've proven the sensitivity of Subject One's...of that part of a Blood Lifer's anatomy surely by now?' Shah concentrated hard on the notes she was scribbling on her stainless steel clipboard, 'I don't think we--'

I shrieked into the gag, my fingers clawing at the arms of the medical table. My body bow rigid.

White hot searing agony: I recognised it from the tracker. But not *there*.

Not like this.

I was floating. A crescendo of sparking agony with no end. Maybe this was how it was always meant to be. Sun rose before me on the clouds of the ceiling in her flint-speckled top; she cast it aside for an Alex Highbury-Lord suit, as she transformed into a trader. Our family's leader: powerful and ambitious. And Will? He watched me through his sunshine curls in a halo of light, Trinity at his shoulder. No longer dragged into the dark with me: his false angel. Now he was left to live his mortal life, as I'd allowed Kathy to live hers.

The nancy boy tears fell then.

Dimmed, I could just make out panicked voices far below.

'He's not responding...'

'Subject's a bleeding tuss. If I give him another dose--'

'Don't you dare, Ivor.' Shah protectively cradled her arms around my chest.

Ivor shook his nut. Then – like a kid denied his treat – sulkily ripped the wires from around my bollocks.

And that? Sodding. Hurt.

At last, Shah let go of me, straightening her lab coat. 'Professor, I had no intention--'

'Hush, no harm done, and it's Ivor, remember?'

Movement. Down the beetle bronze corridor. On the other side of the glass.

Whilst my muscles were still cramping from the strain, my throat was still sore from screaming, and my balls still fizzed on fire.

The bustle of two soldiers, stony-faced giants in the narrow space, dragging a tiny First Lifer between them. Caught still between the real and dream worlds, I let myself watch, as if it was all an illusion. Just another false future, except this time a nightmare one.

Then, however, like a boot to the gut, all dreams were chased away.

Will.

Will's arms had been wrenched behind him in handcuffs, but he was still struggling, even though his ankles were in shackles too. His peepers were puffy, like he'd been bawling, but he wasn't crying now. He was furious: struggling and trying to fight.

Like I'd taught him.

The brave – stupid – little git.

Why the buggering hell did the military want some homeless kid?

Suddenly lead colossus gripped Will by the curls and cracked him across the jaw. The blood spurted.

That was e-bleeding-nough.

I fought my chains. They cut, breaking the skin and purpling rainbow bruises. I howled and cursed: garbled round my gag.

The cell was soundproofed, but when the lead soldier shoved Will, and he stumbled, Will glanced up – and our gazes met.

At first, Will's peepers widened with a mix of shock and hope. Just for a second. But then? I wished he'd never seen me: starkers, bound and bleeding. Because then he did bawl, as the soldiers hauled him off down the darkness of the corridor, until he was lost to me.

And I bawled too.

I'd understood the despair. I was Will's *angel*: I was meant to save him, but now he had no hope. If Will had been captured by these bastards?

Then I had no hope either.

'What..? Is the subject hungry? Do we need..?' Shah was patting my arm, as if calming a baby.

'Subject's a bleeding tuss, I told you. Now I'm jumping; this is not acceptable.' When Frankenstein snatched up his Blackberry, I didn't notice his blathering.

I couldn't breathe through the waves of sobs, which were shuddering through me: impotent rage. My hands were fisting repeatedly against the cold plastic; unable to fight, run, hunt, smash, boot, *bloody kill*, all I could do was lie there and wail, like the kid Shah seemed to be pretending I was.

Someone new was opening and closing the door. A shadow dark over me, then a laptop's screen shunted in front of my mug. Ghosted through my tears, it was blurred.

'Told you I'd have my vengeance, little man.' It was like being submerged in a bath of ice water. No more tears. Struggling. Despair. Because this betrayal was a bitter path I'd walked before. Now I knew the face of my destroyer? I was *me* again. I'd show Fernando just what Blood Lifer vengeance was all about. 'What? No clever comeback? Where's that witty sense of British irony now?' Alpha Geek traced a casual finger along my gag. Bloody hell, how I wanted to take just one bite... *Little man*: that was Will, and a blasphemy on this tosser's lips. Fernando laughed. 'Whoa, don't look like that; we had a deal. I get it, your end? Not so great, but the frackin' research? It's going to win us Nobels. You've no idea.'

Except I did, which was the sodding problem.

'No talking to Subject One.' Ivor shoved Fernando's hands, which were clutching the laptop, higher. Confused, I stared at the blank screen.

Then it sprang to life.

If I reckoned I'd been in ice water before? Now I was in an ocean of it.

Sun.

She was strapped – like me – starkers to a medical table, in a cell that was identical to this one. She was motionless and silent without the need for a gag. Desperately, I inspected her: no injuries. She must've been injected and paralysed. A living death. She was hooked up to a crimson IV circulating artificial life.

Everything crumbled. Resistance. Rage. Reality.

They had Will and they had Sun.

There was nothing they could do to me – *nothing* – that was worse.

I'd promised – fought – to keep them *safe*. My mind had fled through every torment to the cocooned hope of their better futures without me.

But now that was smashed, and me along with it; there was nowhere left to hide.

I shook, as I raised my gaze to Fernando.

He was watching me hungrily.

It's strange when you meet a bloke, you've only ever seen over Skype. He was shorter then I'd expected. His perfect black hair was messier. His white toothed grin was more crooked close up.

Yeah, he was no Mr Perfect.

I realised then something, which I'd been a daft berk to miss: just how dangerous Fernando was.

Because hell hath no fury like a geek scorned.

'Subject One needs to know that Subject Two,' when Fernando tapped the screen, I jumped, as if he was actually molesting Sun's helpless body, 'is also part of our research project. Come on, I'm a scientist. All experiments need controls. Professor here says you've been acting like a chowderhead, so let me paint a picture. If you be a good little man and play along with Mr Scientist here? Then I'll spend some quality time with the erstwhile Grayse Cain.' When Fernando wet his lips with his long tongue, I stiffened; decent bloke *my arse*. 'If you don't..?' He held my gaze, as he snapped shut the laptop – *bang* – cutting me off from Sun; I felt the loss keenly in every aching inch. 'And instead are a bad little man for Mr Scientist..? Then we'll have to see if Sun can be a better girl than you in these tests, and there's some wicked frickin' pissa ones coming up, which involve the heart and pointy things. How the frak do you reckon she'd handle those?'

Frantically I shook my nut.

I'd be a good *little man*, even if it meant testing a stake to the heart, before I let them play one game of research the Blood Lifer on Sun.

'Hey, I'm not convinced. How about--'

'You've made your point. We have work to get on with.'

'Sure thing, Ms Shah.' Fernando tucked the laptop under his arm, patted my nut as if I was his pet, and strutted out of the lab.

'Bellend,' Ivor muttered, as he shuffled his papers on the desk.

I lay unmoving, staring at the painful white of the ceiling, remembering the image of Sun on her own examining table. A twin of me: starkers, shackled and still. Fernando was with her right now, whilst I was powerless to stop him.

I might as well have had my fangs ripped out again.

I was no leader. No Blood Lifer. No man.

And now? I had to play perfect research subject to mad scientist or risk Sun taking my place.

Bugger it.

I was dragged back to the reality of the cell by the pain of the gag being loosened and then yanked out from between my teeth. I whimpered. Then I tested my jaw side to side; I'd never get used to that.

I glanced up questioningly.

'Subject will cooperate without the need for gagging,' Shah explained quietly, 'because of--'

'Threats to torture and kill the woman I love?' I rasped.

Shah reddened.

Frankenstein was clattering objects onto a steel tray. I wasn't going to look – I bloody wasn't. Then he rolled it over to my side. This was like sodding Christmas to him.

Slam.

Without warning, Frankenstein slapped a heavy silver crucifix across my chest. Right over the heart.

I gasped from the cold. Then I only just held back the snigger. 'I'm not a sodding vampire, mate.'

Clatter – there went the crucifix.

Slice.

I hissed, staring down in shock.

Frankenstein had carved right through my nipple.

Maybe shouldn't have made the vampire dig.

He flicked and... I howled.

Bleeding hell: that had better grow back.

Clatter – there went the scalpel.

Then Frankenstein was pouring clear water... It wasn't..?

The wanker, of course it was.

Holy Water over my abused nipple.

What was Frankenstein expecting? Bubbling blisters and steam?

'Bollocks vampire myths...' I got out through gritted teeth.

I saw a quirk of a smile from Shah, which was quickly hidden by her hand.

Clatter – there went the empty bottle of Holy Water.

Frankenstein examined me, in a way that made me want to scrub every inch. Then he carefully picked up a silver wand with a glass alien headed bulb in the middle and a sharp metal tip, like a giant needle; he was the picture of Doctor Frankenstein now.

'Xenon-mercury short-arc lamp?' Shah asked nervously.

'Sounds like a rubbish band name.' Then I twigged. 'Hang on a tick...'

Shine – bluish-white light burst a blinding path from the lightbulb onto my gut. Artificial sun ejaculated in a ray searing onto my skin.

I hollered, as the skin melted under the sunlight. Thrashing side to side – *white, white, white* – exploding snowflake flurries.

I'd burned in the sun before: I don't recommend it. But concentrated like this? Done slow? I hadn't even realised I was sobbing, until I tasted the saltiness on my lips.

Snap – Frankenstein shut off the lamp. 'Subject One do screech, don't it? I'll give it a bloody clip, if it don't stop squalling. Interesting response: Blood Lifers *do* react to sunlight,' he leant over me, scrutinizing the burn: it was like being enfolded by a dusty spider, 'like *vampires*.'

My stomach muscles were shuddering with spasms. The burn swirled in multi-coloured waves, the ripples dancing out across my chest, until I trembled with it. My cheeks were wet, but I couldn't wipe away the tear tracks.

This wasn't science.

I had no illusions. In the name of science the worst atrocities and inhumanities have been carried out: the strong upon the weak. Isn't that always the way? Good intentions or the greatest good. Grand speeches paving the way to abuse of power and genocide.

But this? It was...

Revenge.

I'd tasted it enough to know.

I just didn't have a scooby why.

'Prick,' I threw back: when you have nothing but words they become your weapons.

Frankenstein smiled. His peepers though? They were dark, with something even darker lurking in their depths, as he clutched the lamp. The angelic light was once more burning. 'Having taken a geek at the first burn site, we need a second test.'

'Are you certain? It appeared conclusive.' Shah was gripping my hand, her fingernails biting in hard, cutting bleeding crescents.

'On something more sensitive like...'

Frankenstein lowered the bulb towards my todger.

I panted, fixated on the path of the lamp. I hadn't meant *prick* literally.

Shah, however, caught Frankenstein's arm. 'Don't you need *that* intact for your tests later tonight?'

Frankenstein's beaming smile gave me the willies.

Clatter – there went the wankering torch.

Frankenstein rubbed his spindly hands together, as if anticipating his delayed treat. Then he nodded at Shah, before sweeping out of the cell in his short lab coat and stained cord trousers, which were rubbed bare at the knee.

I watched him potter off down the darkness of the metallic corridor, like he'd just left off working on his grandkid's science experiment in the shed, rather than brutally torturing another species for a secret wing of the military. Or Government. I hadn't worked that out yet. It was crystal clear First Lifers, however, had discovered our existence.

That had been Ruby's secret fear – mine too.

There was no partnership, joy or celebration. We were a bug, another animal to be exploited and experimented on. Stripped back and everything of worth stolen.

Maybe we were a weapon? Or maybe the First Lifers were attempting to drive us to extinction, like every other apex predator on this planet?

Either way: the test subject always ends up dead. Autopsied and stuffed on display.

It was only a matter of time.

But here's the thing: I wasn't ready to take my place mounted next to the gorilla behind the glass in the Museum of Death, as my Author Ruby had once prophesied.

I was Light. And I wasn't going down without a fight.

'You shouldn't antagonise him, you know,' Shah held a straw to my lips.

Surprised, I sucked.

Water.

I drank quickly, trusting Shah could read the gratitude in my peepers; she gave me this awkward half-smile, so I reckoned she could.

All too soon, Shah took away the straw; I guessed she didn't want anyone to witness her small kindness to a *subject*.

'Cheers,' I swiped my tongue along my lips.

She patted my arm: her habitual absentminded gesture. 'Just so you know? There's nothing – *average* – about you.'

For the first time, I smiled: what bloke doesn't need that ego boost? 'You're different to the others.'

'Excuse me?'

'You see me. You're bleeding talking to me for starters. Not like I'm a rat to be cut up. How about an e-cig or nicotine patch? Help a bloke out?'

'Contaminates.'

I tilted my nut. 'Why do you even work here?' Startled, Shah snatched up her steel clipboard, as if suddenly busy, before scanning through her scrawls. Yet she wasn't reading a word. 'Because the rest of them? They're sadistic bastards. Call this research? You could take my blood, a saliva swab or brain scan. These lot? They prefer Nazi regime methods. You don't seem the type.'

'And you,' Shah's brunette hair was wildly escaping from her ponytail; it swept across my mush, as she whispered low and fierce in my ear, 'need to keep quiet and stop pissing them off. Or this will only get worse.'

Shah took a deep breath, before rushing in a furious shuffle out into the beetle-guts corridor.

I'd almost manged to drift into an uncomfortable knackered kip, when (with predator's instinct) I became aware I was being scrutinized.

'Take a photo, Fernando, it'll last longer.'

A furious *hiss* – because what bloke likes to be caught out watching another bloke get his shut-eye? – followed by footsteps away, the *squeal* of the office chair wheeled back and the *click, click, click* of angry typing.

I smiled, as I opened my peepers.

Bloody hell, I needed to stretch.

I wiggled my arse on the plastic table. My smile exploded into a grin, when Fernando's clicking stumbled.

'Little man, concentrating.'

'Alpha Geek, not bloody caring.'

Fernando's checked shirt wasn't as pristine today; there were sweat patches wafting sickly stench clouds, his sleeves were turned back to the elbows and the bottom button looked like it'd been ripped off.

The venom had worn off Sun then...

Fernando stiffened – long-suffering martyr. 'What the frak? You're not getting this; I hold your life in my--'

'Yeah, yeah, heard it all before.'

Fernando stiffly reached up – *here it came* – but only twisted the aluminium blades of the ivy leaf light, which hung over the desk like a striking cobra. Repressed rage was never healthy for a bloke. 'Thing I can't figure is: you're a hacker. You should hate all these Government types, yet here you are in bed with them.'

'That's what happens when you say *hack* unencrypted. Not so paranoid much now, huh?'

Fernando was breathing hard, still fiddling with the LED leaf lamp, casting the lab through a rainbow of spectrums in infinite variety: endlessly adaptable. Yet these First Lifers couldn't see it in us – the good of it. Not when it was right in front of their noses in a sentient being.

When I rattled my chains, Fernando jumped, leaving us under a scarlet light. 'I reckon you're a prisoner, the same as me. Makes you Subject Three.'

'Great Scott! Being with Grayse Cain herself has taught you to be a frakin' drama queen too.

Only one of us is tied to a table, scheduled to have his...precious...stolen.'

'You what?'

Now it was Fernando's turn to grin. In the crimson light his large teeth were devilish. 'Hey, don't look so scared. It'll grow back...won't it?'

'Why are you doing this? I mean, I get *me*. I hated your guts way back, and you? Soon as you knew I was *something else*, you always looked like you were imagining me in your lab all trussed up. But Sun..? That's a bleeding crime because you two were like family.'

'*Grayse Cain, not Sun,*' Fernando launched himself at me, the swivel chair smashing backwards – *slam* - against the false blood red of the wall. *Smack* – his arms caged me in; his forearms were matted gorilla hairy. 'Grayse was mine. But she's dead. Sun? I don't know who the frak she is.'

'You're wrong.' Yet even as I whispered it, I knew he wasn't.

Fernando straightened, as he shrugged. 'This is my field of study: a whole new parasitic species. Evolved through their venom. An infection--'

'I take offence at that.'

In the hell red, Fernando gave his goofy smile, as he pointed at me like I was the prize in a game show. 'Little man, you're heaven sent.'

Later that night I learnt in graphic detail just how my *precious* would be stolen.

I lay in stunned silence, having listened to Frankenstein chinwagging to Shah about the procedure, as if hacking off my prick was as humdrum as sticking in a needle for a blood sample.

Shah was clutching my hand, like it was her privates (rather than mine), which were for the chop.

Frankenstein was taking his time with sliding on the latex gloves – each finger individually. Relishing the limelight and anticipation.

The terror.

Then he got up and personal: my body was no longer mine.

I was nothing. A subject. Flesh. To be cut and sliced. Harvested and studied. I wondered how long they intended to keep me here because on this IV of blood, it'd take a sodding long time to regenerate my todger.

If I even could.

It wasn't the kind of thing we Blood Lifers shared.

Oi, last time you were emasculated, grew back did it?

'Ivor, please...let's take something else. I mean, we talked about a finger?' Shah glanced at me apologetically. 'Or an internal organ? The liver perhaps?'

Frankenstein dropped my todger – *thwap.*

One way to humiliate a bloke? Don't even bother to drop his prick so it lies straight.

If I had to watch the whole procedure in the glass – touching, carving, removing – then at least let my last memory for months be of my goolies and todger looking *decent.*

'Squeamish? Betterway I do this procedure alone. You take a geek at Subject Two.'

Shah's hand tightened around mine.

A surge of hope – *please, please, please...*

'Ivor, I really think--'

'Don't be daft,' sharp and hard now, 'stop dilly-dallying and go.'

Shah nodded. Reluctantly, her fingers loosened around mine.

Crushed, I couldn't meet her eye. Couldn't let the tears I was holding back fall. Couldn't give Frankenstein the bloody satisfaction.

Suddenly the icy *slam* of the stainless steel clipboard on my chest, as Shah leant over me, flipping through her papers.

But underneath? Hidden by the clipboard?

Shah was loosening the chains around my left wrist.

I struggled not to react, as I kept my gaze forward and breathing steady.

Yet inside? I was predator roaring.

Now I had to wait.

Shah's fingers curled around mine just for a moment. I squeezed her hand and hoped – even in that fleeting contact – I'd translated my thanks. She'd betrayed everything to save another species.

I knew how that felt.

Prey. Predators.

I used to know which was which – First and Blood. But now? We're all capable of being both predator and prey. It's a choice. Sometimes we need to be one or the other. We just have to make the right decision at the right time.

Makes you think: *would you?*

Then Shah snatched up her clipboard, as she hurried out of the cell.

'Maids,' Frankenstein shook his nut in contempt. He pushed the steel tray with its regimented scalpels, saws and gauze next to me. I clocked Will's green bracelet buried beneath the metal. Then Frankenstein sprawled on a stool, so he was at a perfect height to separate me from my *precious*.

'May be dreaming here, but no anaesthetic?'

Frankenstein only picked up my prick like he bloody owned it. My eyelashes were matted wet, my breath was ragged, and even though I was bleeding willing myself to close my peepers, I couldn't. Look. Away.

'I remember you.' Frankenstein hadn't spoken directly to me before: about me but not *to* me. He was still staring at my cock in his hand but he'd said *you*, not *it*.

I eyed him warily. 'Yeah?'

'You swaggered around backalong, like James Dean. Don't look *all that* now.'

'Try being the monkey, instead of the scientist; I wager you wouldn't look up to much cop either.'

Frankenstein's hand tightened around my todger.

Buggering hell...

'Dusta remember me?'

I half-considered inventing a poncey voice for my todger, seeing as Frankenstein still hadn't lifted his gaze to my actual mush. Still, winding up the bloke who has his fingers squeezing your cock?

Even I'm not that much of a daft git.

Well, *maybe just a tad...*

'Supposed to, am I, mate?'

Frankenstein's mug ash-whitened.

I hissed, as he slapped my todger to the side. I could see the pink impressions of his fingers, like a branding. At least there was still something there to see.

'Professor Silverman: I bet you remember him? Genius, folks said.' I jerked. *Silverman*: a leonine scientist on a pirate radio ship of hidden horrors. Flames reflected flickering on the night sea. The cold stench of the burning...and my nightmares. You don't forget saving the world but you bloody wish you could. Frankenstein stared at me for the first time. Demanding, cold and triumphant. 'Doctor Ivor Glasse: Silverman's research assistant.

I did all his bleeding chores in the '60s, even though it was me who cottoned on to the separation: paralysis in half and pure death in the other. Silverman was agape. Then we had to test on humans. It's why they had me because this crossed the species. But Aralt? The uppish chucklehead wouldn't allow the next step: testing on Blood Lifers.' So there had been some lines Aralt wouldn't cross, not many but some. Frankenstein: *Ivor*? He'd already crossed every line. 'Silverman be given all the credit, but then he burned on that ship – not me.'

'I'd have happily toasted you, if you'd been on the ship.'

Ivor's shoulders relaxed. 'Kind of you to say.'

'Not to be the one to mention it, but you're no spring chicken. Just fannied around for half a century then? Couldn't be fagged to solve it? Or couldn't figure it out on your own?'

Me and my big gob.

Ivor snatched up a scalpel: it glistened in the light, the tip cruelly sharp. Then Ivor yanked my flaccid todger straight.

Good luck on getting that hard.

I sneakily tested the chain on my left wrist. It bit into my skin, but if I coiled it round and then yanked...

I glanced at Ivor from underneath my eyelashes.

He'd pulled back the foreskin and was holding the scalpel next to the red head like a threat.

'It's some cruel decision: do I cut it off all at once at the base? Quick. Or slowly slice by slice?'

I struggled to keep my breathing even, as I worked my arm back. The chain slipped. 'So this pure death..?'

I'd reckoned Silverman's research had burned and then sunk to the bottom of the sea in the '60s, but I'd missed Professor Glasse. Now along with the Government, Fernando and whoever else was mixed up in this unholy alliance, Ivor was developing something so bloody terrifying – so world transforming – that it shook every nancy boy inch of me.

'Silverman never tested. He was squeamish, unlike me. No one misses the homeless; they have no family, homes, or jobs. Of course we can feed you Blood Lifers off them too.'

Ivor glanced at the IV.

*My IV - a*nd *Will's blood.*

When I retched, Ivor chuckled.

Red. Red. Red.

I battled to remain still. Not to tear off the chains, sink in my fangs and make the bastard squeal.

Ivor pressed the scalpel into my prick's slit. Scarlet beaded. He gazed at it thoughtfully. 'I was invisible backalong. You don't remember me? You'll bleeding know me now.'

I slid my left hand silently free but then froze.

Two uniformed figures were pushing a gurney through the bronze tunnel.

There was something on the gurney. A black body bag. It was small. Just the right size for...

Then everything was crimson. Shrieking. Death.

When I came to? Sirens were whirring furious panicked scarlet. And the lab? Was painted a brilliant shade of Ivor.

And yeah, I'd chosen to pull off *his* todger at the base. So...*quick.*

I was buzzing. Muscles freed were bunched, tensed for a barney. Adrenaline surged.

I couldn't allow myself to think about that body on the gurney.

Will.

I howled.

My venom had killed Will; *I* had killed him. The boy who my Soul sang was meant to be born from my fangs, instead died at them.

Just as his blood healed and gave me life.

I was bloody toxic. Yet he'd had faith in me in a way no one ever had; Will had believed I could save him.

And I'd let him die.

Ivor had chosen Will because he'd reckoned him a worthless outsider, but all I could see was a tumble of curls.

No one would miss him? Then I was no one because I felt like I'd never be complete again.

I caught a glimpse of Will's snake green bracelet beneath the gory tray of torture devices: of course, it wasn't *my* blood...

It was Blood Lifer vengeance – justice – and all I wished was Fernando had been part of the show.

I brushed Ivor's remains aside, gently pulling out the bracelet. It'd been snipped off my wrist – the eternal loop broken – but I crushed it hard in my palm like it was a charm. Like it could magic Will alive again.

Like I truly was a bloody angel.

I wished - truly wished - I believed in the comforting opiate of heaven.

But this world? It was too real, and I had to rescue Sun.

I nabbed Ivor's security thingy, before stumbling to the cell door: starkers, sobbing and scarlet - I gave Carrie a run for her money. I was a sodding sight, as I staggered down the corridor.

Only to be bowled – *clang* – into the freezing metal by a dynamo covered head-to-toe in camouflage green, except for gold haloed amber peepers and bow lips.

Soft   lips   I   discovered,   when the...*bloke*...snogged me.

I tried to pull back but I couldn't. He was slight but with his arm wrapped around me, the – *Blood Lifer* – was steel.

A sodding Long-lived.

Magnificoe?

The passionate kiss was gentled with intimacy. He cocooned me in the scent of ripened oranges with a hint of cypress, like we were lovers under an Italian sun.

Yet here's the thing: once in those '60s tripped out days Donovan had snogged me, and it'd been like he and Ruby had learnt from the same lover.

When at last the Magnificoe drew back, I didn't know whether to clout him or haul him back in for a second snog. 'Plantagenet?'

The lips curled into a smile. 'Well-beloved.'

Then Plantagenet dashed me backwards *one – two – three* times.

As I fell towards the long dark only one word spiralled on cruel accusing repeat: *Sun, Sun, Sun*...

Then everything went black.

NIGHT 7

You fear the dark, Mr Blickle, yet do you not also fear the flames?

The thing about me, sweetheart? I'll never tire of staring into the glorious heart of the fire. The heat. The dancing, surging, freedom of those flames.

I don't fear death, only slavery.

In First Life you were a bright up-and-coming barrister: how was Captain saving you? From what was he freeing you?

I didn't need saving; I was happy.

I once knew a Blood Lifer, who believed in electing only the best, as if he was picking from a sweet shop. Advancement of the evolutionary superior. Aralt wanted to take over the world.

Most Plantagenets author differently; we burrow underneath to the enslaved: by families, societies or themselves.

Blood Life? Turns out it's freedom. It's not a loss.

Is that how you authored Sun?
Sun was different. Not electing her? That would've been the loss.

Pain. But that was nothing new. I groaned.

The sudden memory of having my nut smashed in by Plantagenet.

My peepers snapped open, and I sat bolt upright in...bed?

Bollocks.

I gripped the white silk sheets higher up my chest, like a starkers bird in some romcom after a one-night stand.

Not that I had any modesty left to preserve.

I carefully glanced around the cavernous bedroom. There was the cloying scent of cherry blossoms and no windows: that was novel.

Blood Lifer adaptations 101.

The dark grey walls were in that rich pigment, which bounces back until your temples ache. Biscuit carpets and pristine white ceilings.

Yet there was something off. Organic. As if the building was breathing, growing – *evolving.*

A spiderwebbed moon light cast me in twilight. The bedside tables had stainless steel bases but curled with fragile spirals of petals. Two oversized vases stood like sentinels either side of the – *thank Christ* – open door. One was black and painted with skeletal flowers. The other? A forest of green. They both had an unnerving beauty. The lilies inserted into their branches transformed the vases into blossoming trees.

I took a shufti at the threads on the bottom of the bed.

Blacks jeans and t-shirt? At least the wanker knew what I liked.

My blood screamed, punishing me for fighting the pull to Plantagenet.

Plantagenet would be one hell of a cult leader, except I reckoned it was more than that. He was a Magnificoe, a Long-lived like Hartford; I'd felt the power in Hartford too, but he hadn't been my blood.

And it always comes back to blood.

Plantagenet, however, hadn't even allowed me to speak. He'd silenced me instead.

I wasn't exchanging one gag for another.

I'd burned Aralt in the sun, when he'd been head of my family – rebel here, yeah?

If Plantagenet hadn't also saved Sun..?

He was going to wish I'd burned him like Aralt.

Resolved, I dragged on my jeans, before gently easing the t-shirt over my nut. Someone had washed the blood out of my hair; in fact, had cleaned every inch of me.

Considerate of them.

No socks or motorcycle boots. You forget how *reduced* you are in bare feet. Still, it was blinding for sneaking, and I was on a sneak mission.

I edged to the door, peeking out.

Long silent corridor. Same biscuit floors and grey walls. In hunt mode, I made no sound on the thick carpets. I slipped out into the corridor. It stretched like some wealthy bloke's idea of the walk to heaven.

Nothing.

Then Ronson's distorted Les Paul guitar riffs...drums...*and that voice.* "Ziggy Starburst" exploded in joyous eccentricity: a glam space fantasy.

I blinked. All right then, not what I was expecting.

I felt as far from home as Ziggy.

A splash of light – enchanted pale green – from an open door.

I glanced over my shoulder, before stalking shadow to shadow to the fairy light.

Peeper to the gap, I let my fangs descend, as I raised my fists.

Now I was bloody ready.

Forest baroque, like a world had sprung alive amidst twenty-first century tech. Steel, iron and titanium, but swarming with butterflies, moths and flowers. A breathing animal, which could swallow you. Screens of ivy in waves, and in the very middle? A humungous bed – big enough for...

Sun: she was dressed at least but back in Alex Highbury-Lord pencil skirt and ivory cashmere top. *Plantagenet*: at least I guessed it was him by the flicker of gold peepers; black curls cascaded to his waist. And some *tosser* I didn't know (twice my size), in poncey Savile Row purple suit, his haircut so precise it could've been scientific – the billionaire to match the pad – like a First Lifer god in the centre.

The First Lifer's jacket was thrown over a Louis XIV upholstered chair; his crisp white sleeves were rolled back, and his arms held out Christ-like (if Christ had been in ecstasy, rather than agony).

Sun and Plantagenet were on either side of the First Lifer, licking and nuzzling at shallow cuts along his arms: *blood sharing*. Their peepers were rolled to white, as they juddered.

Lost.

Me? I was the poor git peeping in at the door.

This? Meant the loss of my elected because I'd seen this before.

Blood sharing was sacrosanct. Yet Sun had broken it with one of our own. Worse? She was awake: but she hadn't been there when *I'd* awoken.

Had she even seen me since the rescue?

I craved to rent the world...that First Lifer...all three of them...in two. Donovan, however, was still kidnapped, and I'd made a promise.

So instead, I slowly pushed open the door. 'Alright?'

The three glanced up like they were doing no more than sipping tea together.

The First Lifer smiled. 'Our sleepy head awakes. You're too late to join the party.'

'Pity that,' I took a step forward, before realising my fangs were still out; I battled to force them back in. 'Sun, luv, you mind telling me, whether you're all in one piece after our adventure?'

At last Sun drew back from the human's – muscled – arm. Crimson dribbled down her chin; she licked it off luxuriously. I suddenly realised she'd never drunk directly from a human before.

Bloody hell, what were they thinking?

She was flying.

How was I ever going to... I flinched when I imagined the word *leash*. But Sun *unleashed*? She'd be a wild Blood Lifer as fierce as Ruby.

I'd never wanted that for Grayse...bugger it...Sun.

'Wanna try?' Sun gestured at the bloke's arm, as if it was ice cream. 'It makes you, like, see the stars.'

The businessman let out a bark of laughter.

'Blinding, sweetheart, but I've seen the stars: the real ones. And right now? I want a quiet word with Plantagenet.'

Plantagenet looked up from his licking, those lips curving into a smile. His peepers, however, were steel; he kissed the businessman teasingly, then – *sodding hell* – Sun too.

I bounced up and down on my toes, struggling to control the fighting instinct.

Plantagenet swung himself onto the edge of the bed.

Only then did it register that he was starkers: his slight form a piss annoyingly perfect warm Mediterranean olive. He raised an eyebrow.

Blushing, I turned around.

Still, that meant Plantagenet had been starkers in front of Sun.

I cut my tongue when my fang partially shot out. I whimpered, trying to hide it with a cough, as I sucked at the hole.

'I'm Jamie Blake by the way,' came a lazy drawl, 'but most people call me Blake.'

I already had some other names for him... For once I kept my gob shut.

A hand on my shoulder, and I was yanked round, so fast I stumbled. Oranges and cypress wove their spell. Then Plantagenet's neat hands were on my waist, steadying me.

A flash of silver: a ring on Plantagenet's left hand. A slave ring?

Plantagenet was a slave? So Blake was..?

I hadn't realised I was snarling, until Plantagenet took my chin hard between his fingers. 'My dear child, calm yourself. What is done, is done. We must reshape the future, not bewail the past.'

'You're a sodding slave?'

I didn't miss Plantagenet's glance back at Blake – or Blake's returning nod, before he answered, '*Was*, well-beloved. But I did not suffer at *Master's* hand, as you and so many others did.'

I took in Plantagenet's threads: the bloke was barely dressed. A silk white catsuit, slashed to the navel. Nothing but smooth golden skin and black curls. Two guesses who'd chosen it for him.

He had bare feet too, like me.

Yet those two lounging on the bed..? Sun was wearing embossed leather platforms. Blake: black Oxfords.

I could've bleeding wept.

'I wished to train Plantagenet myself,' Blake chipped in.

'Not helping your case, mate.'

'Indeed Jamie did take me in hand. But believe me, he discovered it not as easy as he'd bethought.'

Sun snorted. 'Frickin' join the club.'

Blake wrapped his tree trunk arm around Sun, as she burrowed down onto his laundered shoulder, like master and mistress chinwagging over the daftness of slaves.

I bristled, until Plantagenet shook my chin, and I was lost in his gold gaze again. 'Yet love? We're all her slaves, are we not? Master and slave alike? God's heart, I never bethought to follow Cupid's path to a First Lifer. Never that. For Jamie this was...it was new as well. Do not blame him: he's the reason for your freedom.'

'That right, is it?'

'He saw those most despicable pictures of you and the others. The ones you uploaded, whereby none may pretend ignorance of the infamy, and it changed him.'

I wrenched away from Plantagenet.

He'd seen. Blake too. Ironic: because that was what we'd planned, when we'd hollered the truth of the slavery empire onto the Tor Network.

Yet to finally meet the mythologised Plantagenet, only for him to have witnessed my greatest humiliation, degradation and abuse?

I twisted away, stumbling out of the *green, green, green*, sinking in the spidery strains of David Bowie and my own hot shame.

'Stay, my well-beloved. What ails you? You flame bright, not break at words.'

'You don't know me. Where have you been? 150 years is a long time to be missing.'

I sensed the sudden tension behind me. Note to brain: *Magnificoe here – he could snap me in half with one of those small hands.*

Instead, Plantagenet bounced around in front of me, his curls flying. To my shock, he was grinning. When he grabbed my hands, I fought not to flinch back. 'Then we must make up, must we not? You are the true rebel in this war with the evil doers; we have merely taken up your standard.'

You know when suddenly the penny drops? *And you sodding wish it hadn't*?

'You're the Renegades?'

'Guilty as charged,' Blake smirked.

'And...' I squeezed Plantagenet's hand, 'you're the leader?'

Please...no...don't let him say it...

Plantagenet dragged me close, his arms around my neck, caressing the strands at the base of my neck, as he swayed to the *beat, beat, beat* of the drums and blast of guitars, his snake-hips tight to mine, and - *sod it* - was it hard to remember *I don't dance.* 'In the country of the blind,' he whispered hot into my ear, 'the one-eyed man is king.' Then he chuckled, low and sensuous.

'Good on you,' *bugger, bugger, bugger,* 'but let's just slow things down and rewind.' I reluctantly pushed Plantagenet back, and he let me. I could never move him if he didn't. He looked shocked, however, and hurt. I wondered how often his spell was fought. 'The other night at that lab, there was a kid. At least...' I tried not to think about the black body bag. 'I would've told you, if you hadn't gone all caveman. We need to go back and--'

'Family?' Plantagenet was frowning.

'Bloody well he is.'

'Then I have offended, and as high heaven is my witness--'

'Na-ah, no way you're going back there on account of some First Lifer. Either of you. You're soft if you reckon I'll let that happen.' Sun shook her hand in the air imperiously. 'The boy's not family.'

I stared at Sun. Every moment I'd suffered in that lab thinking of her – loving her – taking it for her, so she didn't have to.

I wish love wasn't so bleeding blind.

'A First Lifer?' Plantagenet's frown deepened.

'What's Blake then? An ape in a suit? Hang on a tick, yeah – he is.'

Plantagenet's backhand slammed me so far across the room, I smashed through the ivy screen. I sprawled on the floor; the scent of cherry blossoms coppery now. I licked at the blood on my lips, as I hauled myself round.

Plantagenet was fidgeting on the spot, eyeing Blake worriedly.

Interesting.

'Well, help him up then.'

Plantagenet rushed to lift me to my feet: Christ he was strong. He gave an apologetic shrug.

Blake stroked Sun's hair slowly. 'Plantagenet isn't so keen on people insulting me. He's a good guard dog.'

'And me?' I turned my gaze on Blake. 'Not so keen on folks calling Blood Lifers mutts.'

A warm wetness on my lips... Plantagenet was licking the blood from my lips kittenish.

I guess I did always say *waste not, want not*.

'Your boy? My apologies, but he is not of need to our mission. It's a piteous look you bestow upon me, but a leader must make sacrifices. Make no bones about it – I shall.'

'Not your sacrifices though, are they?'

I wondered then, when I'd be of *no more need*, and it'd be my turn to be sacrificed.

'It's my responsibility,' solemnly Plantagenet studied the ring on his finger, 'to free all slaves. To work until this unfair world has equal rights for Blood and First alike.'

'Equal...what now?' I spluttered.

'Light...' I heard Sun's warning from the bed.

All right then, so my zealot of a touched ancestor was all for thrusting his hand into the fire too, but something had been niggling at me from the moment I woke up. 'What I can't figure? How you found Sun and me at that sick research lab?'

That quick glance by Plantagenet back to Blake; I wondered if he even knew he did it, or whether he was so conditioned, it was now automatic.

Blake stretched, before casually swiping the last oozing crimson off his arms to Sun, who sucked it with orgasmic fervour, and then turned his sleeves back down. He leapt up from the bed, sauntering over to Plantagenet: a giant and his captured fairy folk. 'Hartford,' Blake's expression was hard and blank, transformed to all business. 'This Blood Lifer shows up at the door. He knows about the Blood Club and about Plantagenet; he spins a tale about having discovered us via hacked names. Then an even more unlikely one about both you and some elected having disappeared. He thinks we'll help find you.'

'And you jump to help, just like that?'

Plantagenet was staring at the biscuit carpet, refusing to look up.

Blake swung his jacket off the armchair, sliding his arms into it, like cutting through water, in the way only the super-rich ever manage. 'We take precautions. To some? We're not freedom fighters: we're terrorists. Our identities are secret for a reason. It could be a trick. A trap. To lure us--'

'Where's Hartford?'

Silence.

I took a shufti at Sun, who was avoiding my eye, with her knees drawn up to her chest. 'You knew about this? You seen him then?'

Sun shrugged.

'Not really an answer there, princess. Just take me to him.'

Plantagenet nodded.

'I don't give a rat's arse if you're my grandfather...whatever...Long-lived...Magnificoe. If Hartford's not bloody alright? We're going to have a barney.'

The first clue? Plantagenet hadn't come into the room with me. The second? It was a bleeding BDSM dungeon: chains, paddles, and spanking benches. All present and correct. Unlike *Master's* training room, however, it had the pristine feel of folks who played at this bollocks: rather than the cold hard cruelty of a slave trafficker who knew how to break a man.

'I reckoned Blake fancied himself a Christian Grey,' I muttered, as I edged passed a rack of red ball gags under the ambient lighting: I bet he had handpicked soundtracks to go with his sessions too.

But then..?

In the dark shadows at the back, I discovered the only honest – true – item in that dungeon, which was devised to break a man - or Blood Lifer.

A medieval rack.

Hartford was chained, stretched by hands and feet across it, pulled so impossibly tight his ribs stood out sharply; his pale belly was hollowed to a cavern. His limbs were strained and dislocated. His skin gleamed with sweat.

Shocked, I couldn't make myself move any closer: *this was because of me.*

Hartford had come to this sodding place to get help but instead...he'd taken it for me, as he always did.

What could I ever say? Do?

Then I swallowed my bloody pride, kicked my arse and rushed to him: my family. I was here now and I'd never allow Hartford to sacrifice himself for me again.

Then I remembered Sun's shrug.

She'd known.

Up there blood sharing on those silk sheets, amongst the wool butterflies and steel trees, Sun had known Hartford was down here on the rack.

Hartford's peepers were closed; his nut was turned away. He was whispering something, over and over, '*Let my people go, let my people...*'

At once I was tearing off the padlocks around the freezing chains, choking on the dust, as they snaked to the concrete floor in angry coils. First one hand and then the other.

Hartford groaned, before his peepers snapped open.

'Little bunny,' to my shock, Hartford smiled, even though I saw the pain it caused him, 'you sure are swell; I knew you'd come for me.'

'Let's save the love-in and get you free.' I winced at Hartford's whimper, when I eased the chains off his ankles. I knew the level of agony he could take in silence: I'd witnessed it. So when he screamed as I lowered his arms?

Someone was going to pay.

I scooped Hartford off that wankering rack; his legs were knackered. No way was he strolling out. He was giving these small gasps of pain like he was trying to hide them.

I wasn't bleeding having that.

I cradled Hartford down to the floor. I knew starvation, and if they'd been feeding Hartford, I'd be a Dutchman.

I pressed Hartford's lips to my neck in invitation. He glanced up – just once – questioningly. Then his fangs sank in deep, and those stars Sun had seen? I saw in singing technicolour, backed by Les Pauls carrying me away on electric waves, as spiders danced. Blinding, pure communion. I vibrated with it, died and lived in the moment...

There was a hand pressing into mine. Hartford had stopped feeding and was resting our foreheads together.

'I'm going to bloody kill them, you know.'

Hartford pulled back, his expression serious. 'Don't get in a lather; they found you and Sun, didn't they? We can use them again: this time to free Donovan.'

I shifted, unable to meet his eye.

'What is it, mac?'

'We'll talk later. Let's get you--'

'Just don't take any wooden nickels. Promise me? They're not family, not like we are.'

I read the desperate question in Hartford's gaze. It broke my bleeding heart.

I clutched his fingers hard between mine. He flinched but for once, some things were more important. 'Family.'

The bath was like hollowed out soap, in glowing green porcelain. A swirling stainless steel mirror hung frameless above a double basin, which hovered ghost-like. The radiators were concrete scrolling flames.

Hartford sprawled luxurious amongst the green, soaking up the warmth into his torn muscles on the outside, as my blood healed him on the inside.

Blinding bit of evolution that.

I circled my fingers into the steaming water. Resting on my knees beside the bath, I'd washed the grime and blood out of Hartford's golden hair. I'd had to change the water twice already.

Sod it; Blake could afford the water bill.

Sun hovered in the doorway, biting at her nails; Hartford hadn't spoken to her since I'd carried him up. 'Plantagenet's put out a wicked cream wool suit for you.'

I didn't miss how Hartford's shoulder's tensed, when Sun said Plantagenet's name.

'Some poncey threads make up for it all?'

Sun booted the doorframe. 'You need to understand how frickin' difficult the decision was on account of they didn't know Hartford; he was a stranger and a Long-lived. Why should they trust him?'

'And don't you, Sun? Trust me?' Hartford didn't look round at her or raise his voice, but yet his words filled that small space until we were suffocating.

'Whoa, you don't put this one on me. I didn't choose any of this.'

I ducked my nut.

Sun was right. But wanker here?

How I sodding wish she had.

I snatched up a peach blossom scented bottle of some bubbly bollocks, dashing a dollop into Hartford's bath.

Atishoo...

When we both sneezed at the same time, we laughed. Then Hartford clutched at his ribs. Finally, he sobered. 'I'll level with you: I never expected...Plantagenet,' that flinch again at the name, 'to be...Donovan never let on he'd be...'

'Always idolise your Author. I should know.'

'Do you?' Sun's steely stare was dissecting me in a way, which made me feel like I was back on that examining table.

'Not as an Author, mac. As a lover.' Hartford had murmured the words, but I'd still caught them.

What was the bloke protocol here? Thump Hartford on the back in commiseration or swear blood pack revenge on Plantagenet?

I settled for growling, 'Wanker.'

The thing was, however, Plantagenet might've been a wanker. Scrub that, I knew he was in his own special way: hurting Hartford and blood sharing with *my* elected.

Yet the secret? The one I'd never tell?

Plantagenet was also Ruby's Author, who I'd heard stories, whispers and myths about for decades, and yeah, when did I believe in bollocks myths? But now the myth was flesh and bone in front of me? The pull was...excruciatingly beautiful...like rainbow numbers cascading in orgiastic waterfalls, and I *wanted* it.

Not him.

It.

The blood. Connection. Family.

If Donovan had experienced even a small part of that? He hadn't stood a chance.

Poor Hartford.

Still, I couldn't help remembering the aching loneliness, which I'd sensed in Donovan back in his wacky backy psychotic '60s days, as if there'd been a cog missing in his mechanical heart.

I'd figured it'd been love, when I'd seen him with Hartford at Abona, but now I reckoned it was loss. The loss of his Author – Plantagenet.

Donovan was going to have one hell of a choice if we got him back.

When...*when* we got him back.

I realised there'd been an uncomfortably long silence. I massaged Hartford's shoulders, pushing my thumbs deep into the torn muscles. He let out a sigh halfway between heaven and hell.

'What about Ruby?' Sun had wandered further into the bathroom and was leaning against the sink.

I stiffened. 'Don't bloody know, do I?'

But I did...because a kiss doesn't lie.

'Donovan's twin..?'

'Was too busy shagging Ruby; I saw the highlights.'

I shuffled uneasily on my knees, as Hartford eased his hands to cover his goolies.

Sun has that effect on you.

Then Hartford's hands clasped hard onto the edges of the mutant porcelain. 'Jeepers creepers, mac, Plantagenet and his sugar daddy didn't exactly welcome me with open arms, and I'm only the sheik of Plantagenet's ex-lover. But you, poor little bunny? Bumped off two of his elected. What do you reckon he'll do to you?'

I was so buggered.

When Hartford's slender fingers massaged *my* shoulders, I also felt the steel of his grip. He grinned around his bruises. 'Only reason I'm all balled up?' When he pressed his swollen cheek, it was me who cringed, not him. 'For crying out loud, don't you know me by now? I *chose* to take it. I was over a decade suffering every torture a twisted First Lifer's mind could conceive: to hurt and heal for more. And I took it. I survived. To start with it was for myself. It's no line that it became...more. For every Blood Lifer trapped there; of course then there was Donovan. Say, mac, after all that you reckon I'm no stronger than a pampered high-hat?' Hartford pulled himself up in the water, shaking the droplets in wild sprays across the luminous tiles from his blond hair. 'I'll do anything to get my lover back, and they're screwy if they reckon I'll let them harm my family.' Hartford brushed my cheek lightly. '*You're* my family, just so Mr Low Self-esteem is clear.'

I let out a shaky breath.

'Why the frig aren't we like that?' Sun blinked, as if surfacing from considering a deep problem. 'Plantagenet, his Author, Ruby, Donovan and Aralt: they all loved each other. Why isn't our family like that?'

I pushed myself up. 'We do love each other.'

'Naw,' Sun drawled, as if explaining to the dim kid in class, '*lovers*.'

Hartford and I exchanged a glance.

I took a cautious step towards Sun. 'I don't... I love you. Only you. I want--'

'*I want, I want, I want*... Who elected you boss anyway?'

Stunned, I gawped at the fuming bird.

'Give Light a break. All families are different, and folks change. A fella don't stay the same, does he? Donovan's my sheik now. He's with me and--'

'You hope,' Sun's peepers were frosty, yet so fragile, 'but what the frig do either of you really know?'

Then Sun swept out the bathroom, leaving us two blokes silenced.

We perched awkwardly on the edge of a vast sofa of moulded soft toys, which squeaked – *eek* – each time I shifted my arse.

It was like the maddest Hatter's tea-party ever.

Well, maybe not *ever*...

Blake's lounge looked as if a creative mind had exploded its raw emotion across a billionaire's unrestrained canvas. Chairs of timber offcuts or rubber: the poor exploited for the rich. The coffee table was untreated birch logs, held together by a steel band, like it was about to be hauled away by a lorry. The room was scented with – *sniff* – eau de blood: interesting choice.

Blake had certainly gone all out on his Blood Lifer adaptations.

A black rug puddled like tar; it reminded me of the rug in Grayse's Primrose Hill apartment. I tensed when I thought how easily Sun fitted in here, as she sprawled on the toy sofa. Hartford was balanced like me on the edge, holding himself still; it hurt me to see how hard he was working to hide his pain.

When we'd first prowled into the lounge at Blake's bidding, I'd noticed the wallpaper. There were still no windows, so the rich Victorian steeples, spires and cupolas had spun me back like I was truly there – *home*. For one disorientating moment, I'd been in another time and place, smelling the smog of London, the mists of London Bridge and tasting humanity. Then I'd shaken myself and snorted. I'd started to turn away when...

'Bugger me.'

The man under the tree? He had his todger out and was pissing against a grand old English oak. The bloke kipping in the leafy park? He was bloody bladdered.

I'd had a shufti at Blake, who'd been holding court on a chair made of hosepipe.

Plantagenet had been kneeling at his feet.

Yet this wallpaper subversion was genius.

Maybe there was more to Blake then the type of tosser who couldn't date a real bloke and instead bought a Magnificoe toy.

Unless Plantagenet had chosen the wallpaper...?

Suddenly Hartford had given a yell of delight and a clap of his hands. He hadn't been quite up for dancing but he'd rushed – and I'd hated the awkward way he'd held himself, gasping on each step – to a gleaming white grand Steinway, which huddled in the corner like a captive unicorn.

With a smile, Hartford had caressed the keys. He'd scrubbed up well in the glad rags Plantagenet had sneaked onto the bed as a peace offering: prisoner to guest. 'Do you play?'

'Don't touch; I don't want you breaking it.'

At Blake's sharp command, Hartford had withdrawn his pale fingers with a shudder, as if from blood.

I'd seen it, however, the flash of humiliation.

Now we sat on this sofa, self-consciously playing at afternoon tea, as if torture, secrets and murder didn't lie between us.

That's the English for you.

Sod this silly buggers.

'You're these Renegades then?'

Hartford slipped so far forward on the sofa in surprise, his arse practically tumbled off the edge. 'I'm sure one goof; I should've been the one asking the questions when I was on the rack, huh?'

'My dear child,' Plantagenet leant towards Hartford, his waterfall curls sweeping the deep carpet, 'you must understand how heartfelt my regret for the needfulness--'

'Hooey. And I ain't no child, fella.'

Plantagenet knelt back. 'I am aware. In trust, however, we must now work together.'

'You want us to,'...*eek*...sodding soft toys... 'Join you?'

Plantagenet's smile was infectious; I had to battle it. Hearing how hard Hartford was still struggling to breath around his fractured ribs helped. 'Imagine the glory; you are a miracle!' I jumped. Plantagenet didn't mean..? 'Sun has made intimation of your wondrous memory and play with numbers.'

Private, private, private... I was flayed bloody. Sun had stripped me bare for these...I didn't even know what they were yet. I couldn't look at her and that bleeding hurt.

'Sun's already working on our financial side,' Blake chuckled. 'She's making millions, whilst we sit here. Now that's what *I* call a miracle. I'm sure Hartford will be useful for something.'

I didn't miss Plantagenet's remorseful glance at Hartford, who was as still as a statue, which for Hartford was simply wrong.

'May I?' Plantagenet's fluid rise (just as Hartford had mastered as a slave), a nod from Blake, and Plantagenet was diving behind the sofa. He reappeared with a bag like you'd get from one of those poncey City department stores. Grinning, he swooped to sit on the coffee table, as if about to hand out pressies at a kid's birthday. He sinuously slid out a purple box, which was strung with so many ribbons, I could've hung myself with them. Then he pushed the box onto my lap. His hands were trembling: I hadn't expected that. 'I've been a saddle-goose.' That quick shufti at Hartford again. 'I wish us to be one. Sun made suggestions this would be of worth to you.'

I yanked off the lid.

Bottle of gin? E-cig? Fernando's nut served on a silver platter?

My leather jacket.

I wrenched it out of the tissue paper, wrestling my arms into the cool leather.

I was me again.

I lobbed that poncey box back at Plantagenet. I didn't want his – Blake's – bollocks touching me.

I remembered how Will had mended my jacket, passing it back to me in his grubby hands, in the needle-junked shadowed world underneath London Bridge. Even though he hadn't had a coat himself on the freeze of the streets.

I knew which gesture meant more to me.

Plantagenet was fiddling with the ribbons. 'Did I not get it right?'

'Cheers,' I said quietly, 'but what would be of most *worth* to me? Donovan.'

A flash of pain across Plantagenet's mush, which was hurriedly smothered. 'I as well, yet I spoke to you of sacrifices? They are mine too, alas. Jamie has a business empire, and we have a war to wage. Donovan will be saved: by this hand, I swear it. But for now--'

'Donovan ain't no sacrifice: he's the fella I love. Just so you're clear on that, mac.'

Plantagenet glared at Hartford.

They both radiated power; ancient, dark and dangerous.

'I am indeed clear. As long as you are clear that Donovan was the Blood Lifer *I* loved – and bedded – so very long before you.'

I gripped onto Hartford's knee to try (what would've been bleeding ineffectually), to stop his lunge forward, at the very moment Blake called out grimly, 'Blood time, Plantagenet. Where are your manners?'

I saw Plantagenet's shoulders tense at the rebuke.

I smirked. 'Earned a spanking, has he?'

'Why?' Blake clasped his big hands together: I noticed for the first time that he was also wearing a silver ring on his left hand. 'Want to watch?'

I flushed.

Why the buggering hell was Blake wearing a slave ring too?

Then all thoughts, however, were driven out of my blood craving brain.

Plantagenet was passing out packets of human blood from his expensive pressie bag: they looked like haggis. That explained the eau de blood.

When Plantagenet pressed a packet into my hand, I almost dropped it.

'Simulated skin,' Blake smiled at Plantagenet and it was the first – genuine – emotion I'd seen in him. 'I developed it for Plantagenet. There's only so much blood in my own veins, yet I wanted him to feed as he would in his natural habitat, as if he was in the wild.'

'This isn't a zoo.'

Blake's shrug was one of repressed rage.

Ever heard of too many alphas in a room?

'I have pigs' blood as well, just in case. I'm sure I can find a baby bottle for you..?'

I paled.

When I twisted to Sun, she had the good grace to look ashamed.

'Drink,' Plantagenet's soft fingers played down my neck, 'please drink, well-beloved.'

And in my fury? Shame? Hunger?

I sank my fangs into that blood bag and...

Christ in heaven, it was glorious.

I was transported in dark wonder to the beauteous violation of skin: that moment when your fangs slice through – deep, deeper – you hit the blood, and then the taste *explodes*. The drag, as you fight for each pull: the predator's conquest.

Then the savage climax: the purity of Blood Life.

When I dropped the empty packet on the coffee table and fell back amongst the toys – *eek, eek, eek* – still shaking, I saw both Sun and Hartford had experienced the same revelation. Except for Hartford? The blow seemed more powerful. After all, he was a Long-lived, who'd suffered a decade without feasting on live humans.

I experienced a sudden stab of worry. If Blake let Plantagenet feed from him and held these skin blood bags as doggy treats? He hadn't needed to break Plantagenet: rewards were as powerful as punishment.

Money? Status? Pride? Families, companies and societies are all based on punishment and reward. Be a good little boy and Father Christmas will leave pressies under the tree. Don't? A lump of coal or a switch to beat you with. Keep in line if you want your bonus. Speak out about the fraud? Instead there's the boot.

And you know what?

It's all bollocks.

Conditioned cradle to the grave, however, First Lifers follow it like sheep. I'd never figured Plantagenet for sheep.

Yet I knew what slavery did to a bloke, and there was more than one type. Didn't I sodding know that?

Plantagenet was watching us, with a wide grin. He hadn't drunk, and I blinked when I saw the array of sundries: Victoria sponge cake, cucumber sandwiches, and scones – arranged on the coffee table.

So Plantagenet was playing houseboy too?

'Cake?'

Nonplussed, I had a gander at the Magnificoe on his knees in silk catsuit, who was offering me a buttercream slice for afternoon tea; still, it was chocolate... 'I'd bite your arm off.' I snatched the white plate, gulping the cake in two gooey bites; he might be into a touch of torture but at least Plantagenet knew how to cater. 'I could be barmy, but is there sperm on this plate?'

Sun spat out her cream puff. I sniggered.

I flashed her the white plate: it was decorated with a giant-sized sperm, which was frantically swimming. Maybe it had places to be.

'You...'

'Chowderhead?'

I took a butchers at the cake stand: it was giving me the two-finger salute. I raised an eyebrow. 'Approve of your ceramics choice.'

Blake glowered. 'That's Plantagenet.'

The wallpaper? Yeah, Plantagenet.

'Bit of a rebel, are you?'

Plantagenet wiped his finger through the chocolate cake's thick cream, before sucking it slowly. 'Thou gained it some place.'

'Oi, I'm the original.'

Plantagenet laughed. 'Even *I* am not the original. Freedom is in our bloodline. In trust, it is in our blood. If that makes us rebels, then every Blood Lifer here is a rebel. We are family now.'

Hartford hunched in on himself. 'Even me?'

Plantagenet's voice was tenderer than I'd expected. 'Yet thou as well, if you so choose. We are all of us Renegades.'

'So where are they? The others?' Blake asked softly.

'Lost you there, mate.'

Blake leant forward on his throne. *He knew...bollocks, bollocks, bollocks...the bastard knew.* But if he did? Then how could he let Plantagenet discover it this way? 'Ruby? Aralt? Are they slaves? Were they abducted too?'

The silence in the room could've made my ears bleed, and that hopeful, desperate expression on Plantagenet's mush..?

When had I become the villain?

'Look, the thing you've got to understand is this was way back in the '60s. Aralt was set on murdering the world. He'd already done in his own elected. He was working with this scientist bloke – Silverman – to split our venom. We need to have a quiet word about that because those scientist wankers back at the lab--'

'It's all in hand.' I stared at Blake, who was twisting his matching silver ring, like we weren't talking about genocide and global apocalypse.

'If the pure death gets into the water supply..?'

'I appreciate you're new here,' Plantagenet flinched at Blake's stern tone, even though it was directed at me, 'but when I say something's *in hand*, there are no more questions.'

'And I appreciate you're a smug superior human playing at being master,' I launched up, dragging my jacket closer around me, 'but no one's managed to stop me asking questions yet, and it sodding well isn't going to be some baby Dom.'

Plantagenet's tackle knocked me over the skeleton-white cake stand, crashing my hip against the rough birch coffee table, as we tumbled to the carpet.

Blindfolded by black curls, I breathed harshly through the pain, as Plantagenet's hands pinned me like steel bands to the ground.

I heard Blake's smooth laugh. 'Plantagenet truly doesn't like people insulting me.'

It wasn't that, however, because when Plantagenet tossed his nut, and I was suddenly veiled and hidden from the rest of the world (alone with Plantagenet), behind his curls..? Those cat peepers of his were unnervingly close to mine, and I saw something in them. The question. Just as he read the answer in mine without needing to say a word.

Plantagenet's heartbreak felt like my own.

The narrowing of his amber peepers, however, was deadly.

'I had no choice,' I whispered, 'they were going to destroy everything. Everyone. I had to free myself.' A single tear rolled down Plantagenet's cheek; he didn't move, simply holding me still. 'And Ruby? I didn't want--'

Plantagenet let out a howl of grief, as if he was on the rack now, rather than Hartford.

Crack – he slapped me across the cheek. I gasped, as my lip split. My peeper swelled and bruised.

I knew what this was: I'd endured it before. It was the head of my dysfunctional family giving me a thrashing; it wasn't like I didn't deserve it. Yet this time it was a Magnificoe, and I didn't know if I'd survive.

Plantagenet backhanded me and – *snap* – there went my nose. I spluttered: I'll never get used to the warm gush of my own blood and the deep migraine ache spider-shooting out of my neb: because it's always a bloke's sodding nose.

Yet what I didn't understand? Plantagenet was holding back – even now. This was punishing the kid, not true revenge.

So I lay there, waiting to take my punishment.

A blur of cream on white – and Plantagenet was lifted off me in a wild flurry of limbs.

Confused, I agonisingly pushed myself onto my elbows, as I wiped a stream of blood from my nose.

Hartford had Plantagenet by the curls and was swinging him – *dash* – into the Victorian wallpaper: a lot of pent-up rage there.

Bloody blinding.

Finally, Plantagenet scrabbled away with an audible tearing of hair. Then it was like the dance of two powerful stags.

Long-liveds unleashed.

I wanted to stop it but...*Hartford was battling for me.*

The last time this had played out my Author had watched, as if it was a free show; Ruby hadn't protected me.

The two Long-liveds circled each other. Plantagenet wasn't holding back anymore: he bleeding couldn't. He grabbed Hartford around the neck, lobbing him across the timber chair – *smash* – and transforming it into *real* timber. Hartford dived back at Plantagenet – *jab, jab, jab* – and now Plantagenet knew what a broken nose felt like.

Plantagenet was getting the better of it – just - but only because Hartford was clutching at his ribs.

They rampaged through the cavernous lounge, rolling across the floor and smashing through furniture, whilst Blake leaned casually against the wall, flicking through his iPhone.

Blake only called time when Plantagenet tossed Hartford dangerously close to the grand Steinway. 'Plantagenet, stop.'

And just like that? He did.

It was eerie. I half-expected Plantagenet to drop into slave position. My gaze met Hartford's; I knew he was thinking it too.

'We all have choices,' Plantagenet wiped the blood from his nose, just as I had.

He was right, and I have to live with mine every day. I couldn't figure out, however, if Sun had made her choice. Because throughout everything..? She'd watched, just like Ruby in the '60s had watched Aralt duff me up, like a cold jewel between two gangs.

She hadn't even said a word.

When Plantagenet and Hartford warily limped back to us?

It was Plantagenet Sun cradled, fussing over his bruises and stroking his long hair.

Me and Hartford?

We didn't get a look-in.

Ghosted, I already felt Sun's loss; there was no longer anything to hold onto but ashes.

NIGHT 8

Mr Blickle, you do appreciate that if what you told me yesterday is true, then you've just saved yourself from burning.

Simply not being the Renegades' leader was not sufficient. Yet were you to hand over the true leader..?

Plantagenet.

You may warm your hands on his burning instead.

Like that, wouldn't you?

If the Council were to hear you testifying against Plantagenet at the trial, you'd live. I'd vouch for you--

That's right good of you. But here's the thing: I know I was betrayed. Yet I still won't testify.

What you do with this inquiry..? That's all on you.

Do you not consider it odd that Captain would grace you with two weeks and a trial?

I simply reckon Captain *odd.*

Your savant talent: there's no better witness. His – our – hunch has been justified.

I'm no science experiment, and since when have my darkest secrets become office gossip?

Since you were a slave. Slaves--

Have no secrets. Yeah, I got the memo, in fact the logoed rulebook, on that one, sweetheart.

If I'm such a prize, then why didn't Captain set the Jade Spider on me? He's done just about everything else.

I don't consider I've been so--

You don't keep your word.

An e-cig and your jacket. Delivered promptly.

You said you'd keep me safe.

You reckon I'd testify for that tosser Captain, after the fun and games he's put me through?

Graced me with two weeks?

I reckon Captain fancied a new plaything, before he threw his toy into the flames.

Captain swore he wouldn't--

Trust him, do you? Remember the first night? Cannibal Tarantula?

Certainly.

After that...just before dawn the two birds, who'd got touchy-feely on my strip search, shoved me down the bland beige corridors; I glimpsed through the vast windows out to London: a black jagged skyline above the slash of London Bridge. The cruel-bright stars were infinite above.

I could've lost myself right there.

The smirking bints in matching denim, however, grabbed my arms and hauled me to a door at the bottom. One more shove to the base of my back, and I was stumbling inside.

Captain told me sleeping arrangements had been made for you.

Did he now? Those sleeping arrangements are why I know I'm going to be all toastie in less than a week: trial or no trial.

Sometimes we need to open our peepers and see the true shadows of the world.

Blue: ceilings, walls and floors. It was like you were flying in the heavens, or had just snuffed it and were looking down from a cloud. It stank of antiseptic – that powerful chemical undertone, which claws at the back of the throat.

Captain wore dun cargoes, pale blue shirt, which was open at the neck, as if he was just back from the dullest swingers party ever; he was leaning in the centre with faux ease against...

I blinked.

Bugger me.

A closed coffin was raised up on rough oak plinths. It was shining black with silver handles and scrolling *BLC* initials in (what sodding else?), Gothic lettering. It was barely more than kid-sized. Its twin cosied up next to it.

It could've been a set in a play.

I wondered how long Captain had been waiting for me and whether he'd practised different poses.

He was the type.

I nodded at the coffins. 'My condolences. I'd ask if they're family, but you've already noshed your way through them.'

Captain gave a lazy smile. 'Not *my* family.'

I tensed. 'Come again?'

When Captain flipped open the lid, I jumped at the *bang*.

Empty – thank Christ.

Then Captain studied his fingernails, holding his hand away from him like a bird. *The tosser.* 'I'll see you at the trial, of course. Until then I'm awfully busy but I'm going to make time in my hectic schedule for you.'

'Dead kind.'

'I'm that sort of chap. One thing I'd like to know: were you not clear on my owning your fangs?'

'Crystal.'

Captain's baby-face reddened. He lost his hold on the shiny surface of the coffin. 'You *joined* the Renegades. I gave you a direct order to--'

'Not one for orders.'

Captain puffed up; he looked like a balloon with a perky Tintin tuft of hair. Then he let out a breath, as he deflated. 'Then how about this one? Strip.'

Bloody hell...

Reluctantly, I shucked off my jacket, pulling up my t-shirt and pooling it at my feet. I hesitated at the button flies on my jeans.

Captain raised his eyebrow. 'How precious: he's shy.' I yanked down my jeans so fast I nearly did myself an injury, before kicking them in a flying arc. They hit Captain in the goolies. Then went my socks to either side of the room. Boxers... Captain shuddered when they caught his forehead.

I grinned. *Tell me to tidy them up - bleeding try it.*

Instead, however, Captain's gaze flickered to the shallow coffin. 'I've promised to hold your hand and treat you like a guest this fortnight. Indeed, I shall. Do you like your bed?'

I stared at the coffin. If I'd reckoned *Master's* cages claustrophobic, they had nothing on the kiddie coffin.

I looked the bastard in the eye. 'A bit of a cliché..? This ain't Anne Rice.'

Captain bristled. 'Are you trying to be cute?'

I reckon the wanker had been expecting bawling wet your knickers terror. The scene wasn't playing out like he'd imagined – practised – in his pathetic dreams.

It was blinding to disappoint.

Even if inside, however, I *was* that blubbering boy, wailing with my hands over my peepers in case not seeing the nasties of the world meant they couldn't see *me*.

Because I knew what it'd feel like to be trapped in that box.

I'd been transported before in pine crates. Once to Grayse and once to *Master*.

Dark.

For a Blood Lifer to fear it? When we can see in the black?

Don't reckon I wasn't bloody ashamed.

Yet the sensory deprivation hood had buggered my senses and now they'd returned, they were amplified to pain.

When you're bound, helpless and constricted, the dark expands. It fills your mind until you fall into it, so deep there's nothing left.

Until you lose yourself.

I am Light, Light, Light...

This cruel Hollywood vampiric parody of a punishment replayed my every nightmare in the blackest night.

It was my hell.

And Captain knew it.

I attempted to shrug. 'Get on with it, pillock; I'm freezing my bollocks off here.'

Captain scowled at me, before stomping to the second coffin. 'Not for long.' He snatched off the lid with a snarl.

A burst of frantic breathing...

Donovan.

'Let me out... Let me out... Let...' Donovan scrambled upright, sobbing. His fingernails were bloody from where they'd scrabbled at the wood.

All I saw was a steel box, strapped and padlocked shut.

All I heard were the screams.

I dashed to Donovan, dragging him close, as I stroked his wildly trembling back to calm him. My hand was sticky with his slicked sweat. 'It's alright, I've got you.'

'You came for me?' Donovan gasped.

'Don't be a daft bugger: we're family.'

'When your bromance is quite finished,' Captain tapped his foot: the impatient torturer with PA and Blackberry. I glared round at him, never letting go of Donovan (who was starkers too). It's only insecure tossers who play power games. Unnerved, Captain stepped back. 'There are two coffins.'

'Congratulations, even Blood Life Councillors can count.'

Captain rapped the second coffin and then tried to hide the wince. 'Room for two.'

'Not bleeding likely.'

Captain's sneer was victorious. 'See your great leader? A coward after all.'

I gentled my fingers down Donovan's neck. His gaze was troubled. 'You have me now; you can get your jollies torturing me, but not Donovan.'

Donovan shook his nut, trying to pull back but he was too weak. 'Not cool, man. Don't come in here playing this crazy scene like the hero.'

I started...and I was back there again. Donovan in the steel chrysalis... *Let me out... Let me out...*

I was no hero. That was my secret, and Donovan didn't have a scooby: in fact I had more to redeem than I reckoned possible. Maybe this would count in the balance, however, if I believed the good could cancel out the bad – and I didn't.

Desperation though breeds self-delusion, and fantasies are prettier than reality will ever be.

'Adorable. You truly still believe you hold the power?'

I swung Donovan out of the coffin. He swayed, steadying himself on me, but didn't fall. 'I don't think, you wanker, I know. You want me to keep spilling my guts? Then you play this my way.'

Captain feigned boredom, affecting the pose with his nails again. 'Surely you wish to save your own life at your trial? I could ensure we have adequate...prison arrangements, instead of a bonfire. Don't believe you can threaten me.'

'Give it a rest,' I sauntered closer to Captain, which was difficult to do with a Donovan-limpet clutching round my middle like he figured the moment he stopped touching me I'd vanish – *puff* – into thin air. 'We both know this is your chance to prove yourself to the rest of the bastards in the Blood Life Council, and you don't get two of those. You want to risk that because of a game of box your enemy?'

Captain considered me – then Donovan. 'You have a deal.' He sidled towards us. 'I could do with two pets anyway. It's such a bore how easily that First Lifer boy tires.' I tightened my arm around Donovan. 'Into the coffin then. Chop-chop, I haven't got all day. Take your medicine like a man.'

'Light, I'm freaking out; I can't let you do this. You don't know--'

'I do.' I eased Donovan away gently; he was still shaking, but I knew it was for me now - for what I had to do.

There was no way I was letting Captain see me hesitate, however, so I hauled myself up into the coffin.

The coffin was so small I had to hunch to fit. I choked: it stank of antiseptic, like it'd been dowsed in the stuff. Just one more twist of the thumbscrews. Panic clawed at my shocking helplessness. I couldn't move. Every involuntary twitch of my already cramping muscles knocked me against the cold ebony. My nose would be touching the lid when it shut.

And that image? Of the lid descending and the dark swallowing me up..?

Paled me with terror.

Captain didn't need chains. He already owned me.

Donovan's mush – white against the blue of the heavenly ceiling – and then the lid was sliding across.

Nothing.

Nothing but silence, darkness and terror.

And I was lost.

I had no idea. Please believe it was no intention of this inquiry to subject you--

But you did, you are, and I already told you before, remember? You didn't believe me. What's different now?

The room you described; I've seen it. Captain is more of a delight to be around after he's spent time there. With you, I assume.

Question is: now you do know – what does it change?

Nothing.

I have my remit, and you have your witness to deliver. We have our arrangement. I will not be distracted by petty details.

Figured.

Because there's a world of difference between knowing something's wrong and doing something about it. And even if you do? Deciding what that *something* is?

That's the hardest part of all.

I tipped back my nut to stare up at the wild reaches of the night sky and the *real* stars. Bright, blinding, *mine*. The wind whipped sharp across my cheeks, stinging them red. I took a drag of my e-cig: turns out *no smoking inside* means the artificial type as well.

I prowled to the edge of Blake's flat roof, which was alive with yellow flowers that absorbed the sun's heat; the flowers were closed now against the moon. I rested my forehead on the laced chain-link: it was meshed into delicate ivy. There was a heart dead centre because doesn't everything come down to the heart?

Trust Plantagenet to have subverted even the security.

I booted at the fence; the padlock – a gurning monkey mush – shook.

I was beginning to feel we were less honoured guests and more prisoners.

I had a gander down at the courtyard of the beached whale of a mansion, except it was more than a home.

'Top floor? It's my hermit-like genius off-limits penthouse.' Blake had explained with a smug smile. 'It's the perfect cover, so you're safe. There are private lifts down to my garage, swimming pool and gym.'

'Hear that Light? A gym.' Sun had dug me in the ribs.

'This building, however, was designed for my company in seven sections, each a different department. Below here, the future's decided.' Blake had ruffled his hand through Plantagenet's curls.

'Ever heard of: all work and no play makes Blake a dull boy?'

'Or very rich.'

'Point made. So what's this company all about?'

Blake had stopped – grooming – Plantagenet, instead his fist had tightened, as it twisted; I'd flinched on Plantagenet's behalf. 'RE – Revolutionary Evolution. Our strategy? To be seven steps ahead of the trend; our solutions are unique because we base them on evolutionary advancement. How humans are evolving or may evolve. Then we invent: driverless cars, direct neural interfaces, metallic hydrogen... We work with Governments or the private sector. As our company always says: Let's evolve this!'

'Anyone would reckon you were after a Nobel.'

Blake had shrugged. 'A second one? Well, it would always be nice...'

First Lifer workers were still scurrying in and out of the cone-like departments, which were between the concrete ivy-clad plinths.

I wondered if Blake remembered humans slept at night; if Blake remembered *he* was human.

St. Paul's was a beacon, hazy in the black; it felt further away than the stars.

When I slammed my fist into the fence, it rattled. Again and again I pounded, until the wire heart was crimson with my blood.

'Stop acting so screwy and come rest your dogs.'

I twirled round. Lost in my impotent rage, I'd figured myself alone. I was getting sloppy and that meant dead.

Hartford was sprawled amongst the flowers: all cream linen suit and spun gold hair. Yet his expression was more *fight them on the beaches*, than strawberries and peaches.

I sucked the blood off my knuckles, as I swaggered back and threw myself down next to him. I took a deep vape. 'What's all this about then?'

Hartford nodded towards the CCTV cameras, which were perched like eagles on each corner of the security fence. 'They can't hear us beating our gums out here; it's the only place we can talk on the up and up.'

'I know this whole set-up's not pukka--'

'It's all wet. Blake? He's feeding us a line of bull. And Plantagenet?' Hartford's expression softened, before suddenly hardening. 'He's a regular guy, underneath the torturing and visionary leader hooey. But say, mac, there's only one thing we need to decide: how we're going to double-cross him.' I startled. It did me in to see the bitter flash of betrayal in Hartford's peepers. 'Not you too,' he was tearing at a loose thread on his trousers, unravelling it. 'If you've chosen them..?'

'Bollocks have I,' I grasped Hartford's destructive hand between mine, saving his new suit: he was cool and trembling, 'but there are other ways--'

'Dry up. What are they doing right now to Donovan? We already know what humans can do; these are Blood Lifers--'

'First or Blood Life: it's all the same.'

Hartford snatched back his hand from mine. 'Then let's blow this joint and--'

'Betray Plantagenet? That easy, is it?

'And how!'

I seized Hartford's arm, as he turned to rise. *Mistake.*

Hartford swung me up dangling into the air and then – *slam* – down again, crushing the yellow flowers.

'Bloody well won't be,' I choked out, 'I know I said turn your grief to rage but I was wrong. Turn it to *strength* because we need to plan a caper, proper-like. Don't be a pillock.'

I held my breath. If Hartford wanted to go rogue?

The Renegades would have a *genuine* renegade after them.

At last, Hartford grinned, as *he* took *my* hand. 'I can ab-so-lute-ski not be a *pillock*. For you.'

I took a shufti at our joined hands, trying not to miss the neon green snake of my bracelet. 'Hold on, I promise, just hold on.'

I'd left Hartford out on that wind whipped roof, flat on his back with his nut cushioned on his arms in his flowery bed. He'd escaped into the map of stars, adventuring beyond our concrete and steel prison.

I didn't blame him.

When I'd prowled down the biscuit corridors on the hunt for Sun, however, I soon realised I was the dim prat who was being hunted.

There was a *shuffle* style scampering behind me.

Slam.

A door on the right.

I sniffed: not First Lifer, nor Blood. But predator...every nerve screamed it.

A good barney would set me straight, yet the hairs on my neck were rising, as if I was in some poncey B-movie; I'd never been hunted like buffalo before.

Shuffle scamper. Slam.

Shuffle scamper. Slam.

The – *thing* - zigzagged across the corridor behind me.

Every time I twirled round, however, it'd hidden in another room, and there were only expanses of charcoal walls and doors stretching away, as if I was in *The Shining*.

I gulped.

We choose to be either predator or prey. That's the truth of it. I used to reckon it was God or our DNA, which birthrighted the glory or the shame.

But that was the bollocks.

We shift between the two, and right now? Fear had transformed me into prey.

So I ran.

Behind me I heard a loping *scamper*. A banshee *scream*.

I skidded round the corner to the ranks of pristine lifts. Brains beat...everything.

I smirked: *go evolution*.

Still, I couldn't stop myself pressing the underground garage button – *press, press, press* – frenziedly. As the steel doors clanged shut, I caught a glimpse of bristling black hair, yellow canines and a pink whiskery mush, which grimaced in infuriated rage at losing its prey.

I'd like to see any animal work out a lift.

When the doors pinged open, my heart was rapidly beating, and I was sweating. I hadn't got a hold of this being the prey lark.

'Still traumatized by enclosed spaces, Light?' Blake was leaning in inky black V-neck and trousers, against a BMW i8.

I attempted to swagger out of the lift but with legs like jelly..?

I didn't even convince myself.

Then I heard a *ping* behind me.

It couldn't be..?

Shuffle scamper...shuffle scamper...shuffle scamper...

That was sodding it: no more being the prey.

I spun round to face my tormentor.

A monkey.

A bleeding *monkey*.

He was now on all fours, with beady black peepers gazing up at me in cutest chimp at the tea party mode. No fangs or shrieking. Then he held out his disturbingly human pink hand.

'Clear off!' I pointed at the chimp. 'This...primate is a bully.'

'Nonsense. Shake Mr Darwin's hand.'

'Seriously? That's what you went with?' I sighed. 'Don't you dare bite me, you menace.'

I edged closer, taking Mr Darwin's hot rubbery hand in mine. When Mr Darwin squeezed so tightly my knuckles popped, I hollered.

'Mr Darwin, stop.'

At Blake's sharp command, Mr Darwin let go. It was disturbingly like Plantagenet's obedience; it made me wonder whether Blake had used the same training methods.

'You taught him to use the lift?'

'Just a party trick. He has a special one, as well as opposable thumbs. Plus opposable toes, which in some ways makes him better adapted than we are.'

'Only if I'm figuring on hanging around in trees. And I'm not.'

Nursing my swollen hand, I glared at the smug bastard, as Blake wandered between his sweet shop of luxury cars: Bentleys, Porsche 959 Coupe and an obligatory Rolls Royce Phantom. Of course the tosser also had a Ferrari: yellow because red ones are for the try-hards. Yellow are for flashy pillocks who truly do have it all.

Blake stroked his hand over the cars' bonnets; I reckoned he was only a whisper away from whisking his todger out and piddling over them to mark them. I wondered if he'd done that to Plantagenet... Then I shook my nut to dispel the image.

I frowned when I realised I was trotting after Blake in his shadow, just like Mr Darwin. I stood still, thrusting my hands in my pockets, but Mr Darwin continued to knuckle-walk his way after his...friend, owner, master..?

Mr Darwin was making these *pant-grunts*, holding his nut low.

Blake paused by a neon green McLaren F1, which was like a futuristic beast, standing with his hands on his hips, as if an Emperor awaiting tribute.

Mr Darwin squeaked, before crouching and presenting his rump.

Well, I guess it was a monkey tribute...and it was clear who was alpha in this troop.

At last, Blake grinned. 'Come on then, you.'

Mr Darwin turned and – God's honest truth – signed something furiously with his little fingers, before grunting softly and launching himself into Blake's powerful arms.

Blake cradled the monkey, as Mr Darwin clung around his neck.

'What's with all the..?' I gestured with my hands.

Blake sat on the McLaren's bonnet – *bloody sacrilege.*

'American sign language.'

'You're taking the mick.'

Mr Darwin gestured up and down in what looked suspiciously like a rude gesture.

'Did he just..?'

When Blake signed back, Mr Darwin clutched more tightly to him, as he howled with what sounded like laughter.

'Why do I get the feeling you two are making a monkey out of me?'

Blake's expression was stern and impossible to read. 'No speciesism, please.'

Under the garage's artificial lights, I shifted awkwardly. No one likes to be called out on being a...*what now?*

I nodded towards Mr Darwin. 'That bastard was hunting me.'

Blake stiffened. 'You're mistaken.'

'Not a chance.'

Blake stood. Slow and deliberate. Like everything he did it was measured and had an impact.

When he strolled towards me – his rich man's night black costume against my true rebel's leather skin – I had to remind myself at every step that *I* was the Blood Lifer.

Blake pressed so close, I could feel Mr Darwin's heat and smell his cabbage stench. Mr Darwin's lips were bunched back; his teeth a furious yellow.

Blake towered over me: he was tall, just like Sun. 'Let me make something clear. I do not make mistakes, and the people at RE - in my life - do not question.'

'More fool them.'

Blake leaned even closer. 'How do I know Mr Darwin wasn't hunting you? Because if he had been? He'd have killed you and he'd have eaten you. He knows better than to eat my guests though, don't you, Mr Darwin?'

Mr Darwin grunted: the picture of innocence.

The hairy wanker.

'Even wild animals can be tamed. Trained. Mr Darwin's mum died, when I was a kid, in what's now the Republic of Congo. I was out there with my dad, who was running a study into primates. Now there was a great man. Mr Darwin was...depressed. He wouldn't eat or play, so my dad gave him to me. We raised each other.'

'I can tell.'

Blake's smile didn't reach his pale peepers. 'Chimps? They have cultures just like humans – and Blood Lifers. They adapt to environments and to survive. They're bright with abstract thought and memories. Does that not fascinate you, when you have such talents yourself?'

'Simply like to know *I'll* survive mostly.'

Blake laughed. 'Follow me; I've something to show you.'

Just like Mr Darwin had, I trailed at Blake's shoulder, this time to the back of the garage.

By all that was holy, no...it was sacrilege.

A white striped travesty, as if some berk had stolen my best memory (Kathy blasting her way through '60s London in her little red number and saving me from the sun), buggered it, and then stuck a British flag on top.

All in the name of *reinvention*.

I glared at the new Mini; it glared back.

'Isn't she beautiful?'

'You're off your trolley.'

Blake looked thoughtful, as he did his heavy pace forward trick. I wasn't stepping backwards this time.

Sod it, listen to me feet.

'Evolution: even in cars. Retaining the original DNA but making it better. That's what RE strives for, and it's what *you* are.'

'You know,' this time I took a step forward – *good feet*, 'you haven't a clue what I am.'

Blake assessed me, which was bleeding disturbing with Mr Darwin's nut right next to his, giving me the once over too. 'Maybe not or maybe we'll all find that out together. Anyhow,' he rapped the Mini's nose, 'this is Plantagenet's. It was my gift to him.'

'Of course it was. Because it's hard to buy for, right? That occasion: I chose you as a sex slave and now I realise I'm a big fat guilty prat. So...Mini. Why not?'

'Do you have any idea what I'd do to Plantagenet if he spoke to me like that?'

'Unluckily for you? Yeah, I do.'

Blake pressed his left hand to his brow. Blinding – I was giving him a headache.

There was a flash of silver; Blake's ring (twin to Plantagenet's), caught the garage's light.

'Are you a slave too? Or married?'

'Both. You have a narrow view of love. When Plantagenet and your website educated me to the truth? I wouldn't have him wear the S.L.A.V.E ring, but he's still mine.'

'That right?'

'Of course,' Blake arched a brow, 'isn't Sun yours?'

That was different. Wasn't it?

I satisfied myself by shrugging.

'I'm also Plantagenet's, however, more completely than I imagined two creatures ever could be. In fact, before Plantagenet, I needed no one. These rings are bio: made from extracts of bone cells seeded and combined with silver. They're unique. This one?' Blake held up his finger, and I was spectre-chilled. 'Is Plantagenet. He wears me too at all times; I'm always with him.'

'This bone extract? How'd you get that then?'

I wished I didn't have to ask. I've written the...memoir...on obsessive love. I knew about needing someone, whilst being consumed by love's blaze. But this possessive control frightened me because its shackles were as small as a pretty ring, but were as powerful as any chain.

'Wisdom tooth.'

'And for Plantagenet?'

'Fangs, obviously. He has them removed anyway, when he has his venom drained. He sleeps through it regularly like a baby. Which reminds me, when shall we schedule your procedure?'

That was it: no more holding on to plan a caper. Now it would be me acting the *pillock* because no bastard was ever taking my fangs again.

And this First Lifer? He'd stolen Plantagenet's fangs? He was still stealing them?

My fangs shot out – *take that, you git, this is what a real Blood Lifer looks like* – and dived at Blake.

Shocked, it was Blake's turn to stumble backwards. When I clocked him across the jaw, he let out a nancy *yip* – and landed on his arse.

Scream...

Suddenly I had a mush full of enraged chimp. Mr Darwin clamped his long arms and legs around me, shrieking and barking. Then he opened his mouth wide and sank his teeth into my neck.

'Buggering hell...'

It wasn't like a bite from another Blood Lifer: a mind-blowing pain-pleasure. This was jagged, tearing agony.

I scrabbled at Mr Darwin's hairy back, before slamming myself backwards and crushing him against the bonnet.

Mr Darwin was heavy and powerful. How had Blake made him appear like a kid? His weight crashed me sideways over a motorbike, which was covered in a dustsheet. In my crazy thrashing, the sheet rose up, revealing a 350cc scarlet Triton.

Still staggering under Mr Darwin, I gawped at my bloody god.

'Don't thank me,' Blake offered, as if I'd been just about to, 'Hartford was droning on about it – between the screaming. Almost as much as about Donovan and your abductions; I couldn't get him to shut up.'

My peepers pricked with wet.

Mr Darwin bit harder; I spun round in a wild circle.

Blake was probing his tender jaw, as he watched the battle with cool amusement.

Sod. Him.

I stood still. Simply stood there, whilst that primate prat chomped on me. My blood was soaking my t-shirt sticky to my chest. I didn't drop my gaze.

Blake clapped lazily.

Smug prick.

'Mr Darwin, stop.'

Instantly the monkey let go, his lips smeared crimson, before shuffle scampering to Blake's feet. 'It's all about submitting. Anyone can be trained. Even you.'

'One day,' I pressed my hands tightly to the teeth marks, as the scarlet oozed between them, 'your security, guard dog Plantagenet and bodyguard monkey? They won't be around. And on that day? You'll be dead.'

A blood packet, followed by a quick wash and brush up in the green glowing bath and I was feeling more – myself – again and ready for a good kip.

At least Blake had decent sheets.

When...*shuffle, scamper, shuffle, scamper...*

I tucked the white towel (fluffiest I'd ever dried my arse with), closer around my body, as I edged into the bedroom. 'Mr Darwin?'

I wiped my wet hair back.

Now wasn't that taking the biscuit..?

A pink mush with whiskers was lying on the plush pillows, with white silk sheets pulled up to his large ears.

On my side of the bed.

'I don't think so. On your bike,' I stomped over, dragging off the sheets. I pointed to the floor, 'Out.'

Mr Darwin stared up at me – butter wouldn't melt.

'Your act's not going to work on me.'

All I saw were lips bunched in a terrifying scowl, before Mr Darwin was launching himself at me, and I was rolling to the side, losing the towel and all pretence at modesty.

'Bully!' I accused, as Mr Darwin wrenched off the steel base of a petal bedside light, before charging at me with it. I jumped onto the bed – not retreating mind – whilst Mr Darwin screamed, slapping his hands and stamping his feet.

Then I watched, shocked, as he dropped the bedside light, staggering instead to the black vase of skeletal flowers. There was a brief stand-off.

I slipped slowly off the bed. 'Good monkey, now don't...'

Mr Darwin picked up the vase, before holding it above his nut.

Of course he did.

I bared my fangs at him, but he wasn't scared. In fact, it only seemed to nark him off.

I only just made it to the bathroom, before – *crash* – there went the first vase.

Crash – there went the second.

When I peeked out an hour later?

Mr Darwin was asleep in my bed with his long arm slung over Sun.

Sighing, I picked my way around the shards of priceless ceramic, settling down to sleep on the floor, draping the towel over me, as if to hide my shame.

The next evening I groaned stiffly and stretched.

Bloody hell, had I pissed off Sun again?

Then I remembered why I was on the floor: Mr Darwin.

I shot up.

The bed was empty.

Relaxing, I padded into the bathroom. 'Alright?'

Mr Darwin grunted but didn't look up from grooming himself in the stainless steel mirror above the ghost double basin.

I ran my fingers though my pompadour; it needed some attention from the Brylcreem fairy. Even here, however, the chimp had me beat.

What did I say about too many alphas?

I turned on my heel back into the bedroom, dragging on my threads – still no shoes or socks – and went exploring.

Plantagenet and Blake only told us what they wanted us to know. Family? Love? Or their version of it?

It wasn't what I'd learnt, built or needed.

It was intense and dangerous. Yet here's the thing: I've always been attracted to the flames. That moment when the voice inside whispers to throw yourself on the bonfire, until you're consumed Guy-like?

For the first time, however, I'd found something different with Hartford and Donovan. I'd reckoned with Sun too.

Sun had always loved pretty playthings though, and the Renegades could offer a world, in which I didn't even believe.

Love – sometimes it truly isn't enough.

And that bleeding hurts.

Steely piano notes rattled out of the lounge like blues on a business schedule: straightjacketed into the refined neatness of classical perfection. "Rhapsody in Blue" evolved to the robotic.

I stalked into the shadows, pressing closer to the bladdered blokes wallpaper.

The albino Steinway shuddered under the onslaught. I slid over to the Victorian tiled mantelpiece: a black vase stood stark at its centre, which was scarred by cracks like branching veins.

Blake.

No security, Plantagenet or monkey bodyguard.

Blake was still playing, building to a clinically cold climax. He hadn't even glanced up.

I silently edged closer.

Blake raised his fingers off the keys. 'Most people request an encore.'

I stiffened, before sniffing. 'Hartford plays it better.'

Blake's cheeks flushed, as his hands clenched, before he pointed significantly behind my nut at the CCTV camera and pressed the outline of a Blackberry in the pocket of his purple suit. *So that was security then...* 'You don't like me. In fact, you hate me; Hartford does too. You think that's new to me? Being hated? I've been hated or ignored most of my life. Question is: do you think I care?'

'Wild stab in the dark here: you don't?' Blake gave a sharp, shark smile. I fiddled with the fractured vase, spinning it until the cracks were like holes in the universe. 'You might've broken this, mate.'

Blake's smile widened to a grin. 'I smashed it, right where you're standing now. As hard as I could because it was mine to break. I see it up there every day, remade by my hand: a reminder of that violence and that it's mine.'

I gave him a long look, as I balanced the vase on my palm. 'Whatever gets you off.'

Blake shrugged one large shoulder. 'Now you're getting it.'

'Well, cheers for the rescue from the lab, but I reckon we'll be off. Stuff to do and that.' I started to sidle backwards.

I could no longer hide my family in the shadows. There were no shadows left. No safety unless we acted. Here with Blake, however, we were prisoners in luxury, whilst the true nasties of the world – pure death and the Blood Life Council – were still out there.

The Renegades with their puppetmaster Blake were so radical they were missing the big bloody picture.

Freedom fighters?

Wankers more like.

'Leaving us?' Blake slowly stood. My heart beat faster, as he carefully closed the piano.

'I'd say it'd been fun but...'

'Back to that slum? Strip joint? Abductions and being used as lab rats?'

'It's not all so glamorous.'

'Plantagenet doesn't believe you're ready to head a family yet, and frankly? Neither do I.'

A hot flood of fury and humiliation prickled me pink.

I opened my hand; the vase tottered and – *smash*. 'Whoops.' *Let's see him glue it back together a second time.* A muscle on Blake's cheek twitched. 'Wonder what that symbolises now?'

'How about,' Blake strolled towards me, his hands casually in his pockets, but I could see they were curled into fists, 'are you sure your family would even leave with you?'

I stared down at the black shards, trying not to think about Sun nuzzling at Blake's scarlet arm and sucking at the gash, as she lost herself in the stars. The way she fit: two sets of shoes next to each other on the silk sheets. 'Anyway, with my company's abilities, I don't need to keep anyone against their will; we can track you from here. This is a prison without bars. So go where you like, but I thought you wanted our help with Donovan? Because if you do this? Go it alone and break up the Renegades, along with this family? Just know you'll also be breaking Plantagenet.'

'What are you on about?'

'I could've killed you any time I wanted.' I dodged back, as Blake paced towards me like a black panther. 'Hartford too. Do you have any idea, however, how desperate Plantagenet has been to find you? Since he saw you on that website? How frantic to save you? Not to mention the time, cost and resources I sank into the rescue at the lab. It was worth it though, to see Plantagenet's joy. A family, you see, is all he's ever wanted. If you knew him – bothered to – then you'd understand. Hate me but love Plantagenet.'

Confused, I nodded.

Controlling, self-destructive and obsessive as it was – Blake's love was real.

Still, I couldn't help feeling like another gift, frilly in ribbons and expensively boxed, guilt-delivered to Plantagenet to top even the Mini.

Blake threw himself down onto the rubber hosepipe chair, his leg across the arm: the picture of ease. I was better at reading him, however, and that muscle in his cheek was still twitching. 'If you're staying? There's a mission on tonight to liberate a slave. Plantagenet's leading it and he's asked you along. I don't need to tell you what it'd mean to him...or maybe I do?'

My blood was instantly racing...roaring...rushing. The air was alive with orange flames and the stink of melted flesh and ashes. I fidgeted, fresh to be out, free and on the hunt. Slavers were *my* prey. 'So this is what you do? Plan capers to rescue Blood Lifer slaves? All for Plantagenet?'

'He needs this. It's like a new family for him.'

'And you're looking out for him? Touching.'

'Of course,' Blake leant forward, 'this slave? Actually *is* family: the Plantagenet bloodline. His elected, the same as your Author: Ruby.' Blake wiped his large hands dismissively down his thighs. 'I told Plantagenet he should leave her where she is; she's...mentally unstable. Then there's the small matter that she's betrayed him once already. But family is family to Plantagenet, so I'm allowing him this indulgence. I do always prefer to look to the future; maybe our family should leave the past in the past.'

I saw Plantagenet's peepers, all fire and fervour in the dark, as we crouched either side of the panelled Jacobean door.

Plantagenet held up his gloved hand. 'One...two...three...'

Then it was like an explosion lit up the night – *bang*.

The door splintered; Plantagenet sprang through it, and I was at his shoulder. First Lifers with guns (because God help us if Plantagenet were allowed out alone), were hollering: *stay down, stay down*. An old bloke (minister of something or other), was squealing: this starkers flabby prat with a comb-over.

Mr Minister was gibbering, as Blake's team handcuffed him and hauled him out of the richly tapestried four-poster bed. The log fire spat and crackled, casting long shadows dancing across the walls; it smelled like nutmeg.

'Sweetums, call MI5. Call... Don't hurt her... She's not... She's no one...'

'Fie, sir! I most surely am. And look – my family come avisiting.' Mesmerised, I watched the Blood Lifer – my new family – stalk starkers on all fours to the end of the bed, her ivory Bristols swinging. A string of diamonds, like burning stars, was fierce around her neck.

'F-f-f-family, sweetums?' Mr Minister gawked between us. Uneasy, I was unsure who was truly the slave.

'Take the most wicked man outside,' Plantagenet stepped back to allow the First Lifers to drag the confused Mr Minister out and down the stairs.

The bird was still scrutinizing us, as if she was about to pounce; her blonde sweep of hair was like a Godiva. She was a beauty, like Ruby, but there was something off about her.

Was she one of those Blood Lifers who hadn't survived election? Or had she been touched before Plantagenet had even chosen her?

When her gaze swung to Plantagenet, I had the unexpected urge to step in front of him.

'How now? Where have you been? I'm just saying...' Then she gave a bright, false smile, which twisted my guts.

'It is merrily met, my dear child. Please, clothe yourself. We have business.' Plantagenet pointedly turned his back.

No licking, sniffing or snogging for her. No gentle intimacy or *well-beloved*. Just *business*.

Even if I knew how hard that must be for Plantagenet, he had to have a sodding good reason - and I wouldn't forget it.

As I turned away too, I clocked her expression: pained hurt but also a dangerous rage.

Plantagenet and I had ridden down to the caper in the back of a blacked out jeep. Plantagenet had been like a kid on Christmas morning. His slender fingers had wound round mine and for once, I hadn't been the only one bouncing up and down in my seat; I'd been buzzed for the barney, but for Plantagenet I'd reckoned it was the freedom.

'If this skirt is such a back-stabbing bitch...' When Plantagenet's fingers had crushed mine, I'd grimaced. 'Blake's words; not mine.' Plantagenet's grip had loosened, as he'd stroked my bruised hand contritely. 'Then why the white horse business? Let her get hung.'

'Mother's a slave,' Plantagenet's voice had been very low, 'I know what it is to be captured, enslaved and defanged.'

Plantagenet had been so subdued, I'd wished to tell him: *same here.*

Plantagenet didn't know what it was to be a true slave, however, not like Hartford and me.

Or did he?

'Mother is also family.'

Christ in heaven – now we sounded alike.

'Mother? Not going to tell me you came over all nancy and authored your mama?'

Plantagenet laughed this full belly laugh, as he slapped my knee. 'You jest! Mother named herself that because... Well, such is her tale, not mine. Although she is a witch...whore...traitor...'

'I get the idea.'

'She may be all but she's also my elected. I've been kept from my family. Held in the dark...it's no matter how or why. Only that in First Life I was a bastard. You were an orphan, were you not?'

I nodded, avoiding his eye.

Plantagenet gripped my chin, however, as he had when we'd first yakked in the penthouse, forcing me to meet his suddenly serious gaze. 'In faith to be different is a hard path. My father was a king, but my mother was the daughter of an Italian painter; she was the jewel of the Court. The fame of her beauty was both much spoken of and envied.

Edward the Third plucked that rose.' Plantagenet's fingers had trembled, before he'd steadied himself. In the rumbling shadows of that moving jeep, we could've been the only two blokes left on earth. 'I was raised on an Estate away from Court. Away from my mother, father, brothers and sisters. I was a shameful secret: *the bastard*. The servants who weren't thrashing or mocking me as weak and feeble issue, branded me with that name.

'Later, when my Author freed me to Blood Life, I watched as civil wars tore my family apart, and one by one they were executed for treasonable and wicked deeds. I learned then that my mother had begged for my seclusion because illegitimate or not? I had a claim on the Crown, and the brothers and sisters who I'd longed many piteous summers spent alone to play knights with, to ensure their own claim, would indeed have murdered me.' Plantagenet had licked along my lips, resting his forehead against mine, as if for comfort – touch – nothing more. He'd tasted of oranges and – *bugger it* – family. I could fight it, but it was stronger than it'd been with Ruby, even though she'd been like breathing to me for over a century. 'The world rejected me, and so I rejected the world. I forged a new family, even after my Author burned to save me. Because what is a good thing to a man if he has all the worldly wealth and power but not love?'

A *rustle* behind me.

I jumped when a delicate hand touched my shoulder. 'What's the sitch, bitches?'

I carefully eased away from Mother's hand.

Mother looked like a Californian Valley girl: tight gold trousers and pearly halterneck. Her diamonds were still sharp around her snowy neck. She'd slipped her highlighted hair up into a loose clip.

No chance she wasn't in charge of that poor old pillock's credit card.

Plantagenet turned without a word.

I shrugged, swaggering at his heels down the wide wooden staircase, under the sombre gaze of Mr Minister's framed ancestors. Mother clattered after us on her gold leather kitten heels.

At the base of the staircase, Mother's cool arms wound round my waist, her fingers wank-wandering, as she licked down my throat. Then she hissed, so close to my skin, I could feel her fangs, 'We are forced to woo because none dare woo us.'

Before I could react, she was shoved backwards against the wall panelling; Plantagenet's arm was across her throat. 'Light is not yours to... By this hand, you will not bite.'

Mother laughed: high and delighted.

I shuddered.

'But he's so bomb,' Mother pouted, 'and he's family; I can taste it.'

Plantagenet pushed away from her. Gently, he stroked down her cheek; she leant into his touch. 'Things are not as they were; you cannot simply take. We are all of us changed.'

'By my Soul,' Mother gave a robotic tilt of her nut, which was as disconcerting as her shifts in speech, as if she couldn't remember what time period she was in – slipping into past lives and roles, 'you have no fangs.'

Plantagenet reddened, his shoulders hunching.

Blake had been right: she was a *back-stabbing bitch*.

Mother smiled - vicious and victorious - as she stroked *his* pink cheek. Plantagenet didn't lean into her touch, however, in fact he shrank away, as if she was poison. 'Why do you look so melancholy? I am here now. Foolish man to think you did not need me; I am your creature, as you are mine. Now, let's go kill the kinky minister. I'm so psyched for this!'

Plantagenet finally grinned, before taking Mother's hand like he'd taken mine.

They twirled each other round, as they danced out into the courtyard garden, like I'd once danced with Ruby in the carnage and the flames – a kid let loose in the world. No conscience or battle for redemption. Nothing forcing me to grow up and face an adult world beyond my own will, wants and delights.

Together? A fanatical Magnificoe and his wicked witch?

The First Lifers didn't stand a chance.

Frowning, I prowled after them.

The courtyard was in front of a yew tree maze, which stretched labyrinthine into the dark behind the Jacobean mansion. Mr Minister – starkers, shivering and shackled – was on his knees, sacrificial in the centre of the courtyard. The stars above were blindfolded by cloud. The First Lifers in black with the guns were pressed against the red brick walls. Basil, mint and thyme from the raised beds washed me back to Abona and my servitude.

The scent strengthened my prowl.

When Mr Minister took a gander at us, the sobbing started. Then he pissed himself.

Plantagenet's mush was oddly blank again, as we stood ranked in front of the First Lifer. 'You are accused of the most wicked deeds against Blood Lifers--'

'I never hurt Mother. Never. Ask her. I've treated her like a princess.'

I took a shufti at Mother; Mr Minister hadn't used a slave name. I'd been reduced to *shadow*, yet he'd used her true name.

I half-expected Mother to jump to his defence, but she only gripped tighter onto Plantagenet's hand, as if for protection from some terrifying sultan.

'As high heaven is my witness, you shall pay: in this life and I am certain in the next. I give you one chance to make peace with your maker. The sentence is death.'

'Please, please, please...'

Mother waved, giving that false smile of hers, 'See ya.'

And I saw it. The deep – genuine – agony in Mr Minister's peepers: of a bloke who'd been played.

Just like we were being.

Suddenly I knew all this – the First Lifers with guns, the execution-style killing, Mother's gloating mush – was *wrong*.

Hartford, Donovan and me, we'd taken out the Blood Club crimson on the Isle of Man, but that'd been fangs and fists in the red-hot heat of battle. In the saving of our species from slavery all or nothing desperation.

But this was more like...

'Mother? Do you wish..?'

'Wait,' I held out my hand, knowing I couldn't stop them but having to say something.

It was too late.

Mother gripped Mr Minister's nut, screwed it round like the cap of a bottle, and then pulled – *plop*. When she tore it off, his lips were still wetly begging.

Mother hurled his nut next to his twitching body, which toppled slowly forward.

I heard one of the First Lifers hurl into the herb bed.

'The devil rot him,' Mother spat on Mr Minister's wrinkled back.

A burgundy pool puddled out of the headless neck. I was sickened at the urge to fall to my knees and lap every wasted – precious – drop.

Breaking abstention? Drinking human blood? Simulated skin?

Unleash a Blood Lifer and the predator will find a way to come out and play.

Plantagenet knelt down, dipping his finger into the blood. Then he spelt out, as if it was paint, onto the courtyard floor: **RENEGADES**.

Point made.

Plantagenet slipped his arm around my shoulder. His smile was mischievous. Mother snuggled on his other side – and he let her. 'Watch now.'

I had a butchers back at the red-brick mansion, which was above the sweep of steps.

Bang.

Plantagenet laughed, as I startled.

Whoosh.

Red flames dragon-like flew up into the silence of the night. There was the *shatter* of windows imploding. The *smash* of centuries-old walls falling in on themselves. The *roar* of panelled walls and that posh staircase turned to crackling, as ash billowed into the stormy sky.

I'd seen it before on Mann. I'd been the cause.

I've never been frightened of the flames. Yet this time..?

The slavers hadn't a scooby what they'd unleashed from the shadows – in all of us.

Now I knew what this was more like – what we were – and it wasn't freedom fighters.

It was terrorists.

NIGHT 9

What would you do if you knew the true identity of a terrorist leader? If you'd also been ordered to do him in? Yet your newly discovered family loved him hearts and cupid, and the woman *you* loved was caught in his web?

Blake.

You're insinuating that Blake is the real leader of the Renegades?

Are you expecting me to believe a *First Lifer* capable of taking on Captain?

A toddler could take on Captain.

Greatest mistake you can ever make is underestimating your enemy; humans aren't only prey.

They're vibrant, bright and deadly.

Blake? He could kill – or save – us all.

You'd say – anything – to exonerate your *well-beloved* Plantagenet.

He's a puppet; we all are to Blake. Good little boys to be trained.

You don't need starvation or torture to condition; you can lose your freedom without ever being chained.

Captain won't want to hear this. He has you – a Blood Lifer. The narrative is too strong. He can present his case to the Council neat and have a blaze on Easter Day as offering, cementing his standing.

Without Blake? There's no case.

'Just ask him. Then I'll have a shufti around and--'

'Why?' Sun contorted her legs underneath herself. She was practicing some Pilates bollocks in the gym; her hair cloaked her mug. 'It's fried the way you're so into Blake's business, when you didn't frickin' care before.'

I dropped onto the sweaty mat next to Sun. 'Don't get the hump; I'm asking now.'

No answer, just another unnatural twist of her legs.

The mat sucked – *squelch* – on my arse, as I shifted.

The gym stank of rubber, leather and that scent of new equipment never used. The machines gleamed out of every corner: shiny, electronic and expensive.

Pointless wankery.

*Bang...bang...bang...*muffled thuds from the room next door.

Someone was getting duffed up – *please don't let it be Plantagenet.*

I stroked back the ash blonde strands, which were over Sun's mush: not a single bead of sweat.

To my surprise, Sun was also smiling.

When I leaned in to snog her; she tasted of salt and...oranges.

I pulled back sharply, but Sun was still smiling. 'So you wanna know where I work now on account of I'm so wicked frickin' awesome, huh?'

'Something like that.'

'Ya huh! You're a big boy. Ask Blake yourself.'

Bang...bang...bang...

Troubled, I glanced at the steel door.

'It's not the same thing. Blokes like Blake? You ask them for something, it means they have you by the goolies.'

'You zoo'n' on me? Blake loves RE,' Sun rolled out of her pose, tumbling us both into a tangle of limbs. She pressed her orange tainted lips once more onto mine. 'He's like an automaton that won't shutoff on account of his business is his life.' Sun latched her arms around my neck, as she whispered in a singsong, 'Let's evolve this!' Then she burst into laughter.

Bang...bang...bang...

Now we were both staring at that steel door.

'Blake?' Sun was serious again, her arms clutching me close, 'He's a killer leader, but he's the man in charge. You need to step up if you want to lead too. So, do you?'

Cautiously, I pushed open that steel door.

Bang...bang...bang...

Louder now, it was like someone being clouted.

I stalked inside.

To be faced with a boxing ring: brand new in gleaming red, with pristine white ropes. And Blake: starkers apart from shiny emerald shorts and boxing gloves. His tanned torso glistened with more muscles than I knew existed. If I'd reckoned him tall before..?

Now I bloody did feel like fairy folk.

And the *bang...bang...bang..?*

Blake was beating a punchbag, which was hanging from a hook; punchbags were suspended around the ring like alien pods about to birth. The look of determination on Blake's mug..? No way he wasn't imagining someone.

I'll give you two guesses who.

I leant against the boxing ring's ropes, before giving a cough.

Those bloated shoulder muscles bunched. Then Blake clocked back his fist and whacked the punchbag so hard it flew off the hook and thumped against the far wall; a gnat mist of sand flew up like they'd burst early from the womb.

I raised an eyebrow. 'Better now?'

Blake turned to me. 'Security are--'

'Yeah, yeah. I'm not here to dismember you, or paralyse you, before I...' Blake had stilled. That muscle tic again. I smiled. '*Not* here for that. I just want a friendly word.'

'You box?'

I eyed those huge hands encased in crimson. 'I used to.'

'MMA champion, I believe?' Now it was Blake's turn to smile. 'I know more about my guests, than they even know about themselves.'

'No one likes a bighead. That mean you're into all this *my body is a temple* bollocks?'

'Why? Is your body a slum?'

Blake slipped off a – smaller – pair of boxing gloves from the wall, before passing them to me. Then he hopped up into the ring, as if its height was nothing.

I clambered up after him, the gloves slung by their laces over my shoulder. Then I pulled them on one after the other. Grudgingly, I held out my trapped hands to Blake; with a smirk, Blake wrenched off his gloves, before tightening my gloves' laces, as if I was a boy asking for help with his mittens.

No way was I admitting he'd pulled them *too* tight.

'All set, sugarplum?'

I pushed up onto my tiptoes, as I punched my fists together like a gorilla declaring war. 'You've no idea.'

Blake was big; a slugger, I'd wager. All he'd need to do was connect with those powerful paws.

'In some animal societies the status of a male is assigned by its size. Smaller – lesser - males play tricks to look bigger,' Blake circled, 'they arch their backs, puff themselves up...or stand on tiptoe.' Self-conscious, I rocked back on my heels. 'They flutter feathers, faking dominance with their coats. Where's that leather jacket of yours..?'

'Same place as your suit.'

'This is *my* pack; I don't need to fake anything.'

One moment I was standing there. Next? I was staring up at flashing lights.

And my jaw? Sod it if it wasn't broken.

Blake grabbed my bicep, hauling me up.

The world was bleeding into itself – a dizzy merry-go-round.

Blake's gaze was steady. 'Now we're even.'

'Not yet.' I raised my wobbly fists again.

'Don't challenge me; this is ended. Although, if you insist...'

Then Blake was sending a second staggering upper cut my way.

But this time? I wouldn't be distracted by his yakking.

I ducked.

A *snort* of frustration and another upper cut from Blake. I bobbed and weaved, slipping underneath or to the sides of the punches. Being the smaller bloke has its advantages.

Blake drove me back against the ropes. We were both sweating under the lights, but I knew his pattern now. I was a swarmer who'd been fighting for over a century before Blake was even a twinkle in his papa's eye.

I didn't need any tricks – I was the real deal.

There was just this moment when our gazes met: and Blake *knew*. A boxer's instinct, which screamed that our roles had switched – predator to prey.

I grinned, as I closed in on Blake, launching my attack: a flurry of hooks and upper cuts, which made his look like a warm-up.

Shocked, Blake fell back, covering up his mush with his gloved hands.

So I went for his gut instead – *bam* – *bam* – *bam*.

Blake shoved me back, until I was in the center of the boxing ring.

Conqueror of his world.

Whilst Blake was against the ropes: his peeper swollen, gut reddening and lip split.

Maybe I should've remembered he was a First Lifer? Then again I'd promised not to kill him, and he was still alive, wasn't he?

When he stalked towards me, however, wrenching off his boxing gloves with his teeth and holding out his hand, I tensed.

Then I had a gander down at his hand – he was holding it out to be shaken.

Wanker.

Blake sighed, when I waved my gloves at him, but began to unlace them. 'This animosity? You believe I abused my power and position to buy another person: Plantagenet. That's why you're behaving like such a brat.'

'Got it in one.'

Blake tossed down my gloves. 'You're right. I had no time or inclination to find a human partner, so I cherry-picked Plantagenet; he's perfect for me. But you know what? Get over it.'

'I reckon your motivational speaking could do with some work.'

Blake grabbed me by the back of the neck, shaking me as if he expected me to go limp.

No such luck, tosser.

'This isn't some sweet romance novel, in which everyone adores each other and is good; people aren't. That's not the real world. We still have to work together, however, because we have a job to do. A mission. I'm not a *nice* man. You can't fight genetics or evolution.'

'I'm living proof you can. You're what you *do*, not what you are. And your mission? It's not the same as mine. You can't just assimilate my family into yours.'

'*Assimilate*? Are you a secret nerd? Just think about this: isn't your real fear that your family are abandoning you? As you've always been abandoned?' I wrestled away from Blake's forceful grip, as I glared at him. I didn't give two sods that he was right. I'd lost too much – in First and Blood Life – to lose my newly created family as well to this bastard and to Plantagenet. 'Or,' Blake whispered conspiratorially, 'is the real fear: you should never have had a family? Now you've found your true home for the first time, and everyone fits here except *you*.'

I turned on my heel in silence, marching away before I could risk falling. The alien punchbags batted at me, as I passed.

'I told you I knew my guests better than they knew themselves,' Blake called after me, 'and by the way? Yes, you can have a tour of Revolution Evolutionary. I don't know why you didn't just ask. Anyone would think you were scared of me.'

A monkey.

Mr Darwin was projected across all four walls of RE Headquarters on his knuckles. As I watched, he stood erect, transforming into a purple suited Blake. The Ascent of Man: evolution's purest propaganda.

Kallis giggled. 'Mr Blake's idea: neat, huh?'

Blake dropped to all fours, and the cycle started again – *Christ help me*.

Kallis had collected me from the steel lifts, in her slip-on bright green shoes, which had honeycomb soles that *tap tapped* along the hard floors.

'Kallis,' she'd purred (although it'd come out more as a rattle of phlegm). She'd rapped a finger heavy with paint and wooden rings, which were like cavemen sweets, down my chest in jerky spasms, 'it means *beauty* in ancient Greek.'

'Good on your mum, luv, brave woman,' I'd caught her fingers, giving them a squeeze, before pushing them away from tracing patterns down my t-shirt.

Now Kallis was leading me into the central department of RE Headquarters, which was on the bottom floor of Blake's whale-like building. It was as if we were adventuring into an indoor town. There were no cubicles, offices or meeting rooms.

It turns out? I'm a fuddy-duddy.

Blake? More with the whacky unconventional.

There was a tearoom and patisserie with damask upholstered chairs, which were slap-bang next to mismatched stools, a humungous trestle desk that was big enough for each worker to be private but still part of the RE community, with clip-on lamps and plastic shelves; moon lights, which were like alien ships, hovered overhead.

Green, green, green...

Everything was in shades of green, including the neon hologram *RE*, which was projected up from the center.

And me? I was the risen Messiah.

I froze – cat caught doing the unmentionable – when the workers stopped and stared. Except for those who whispered and pointed.

Or the bloke who dropped to his knees.

He was my favourite.

'What's all this then?' I mouthed.

Kallis raised a radio device, and instantly her voice was booming through the open-plan office. 'Back to work people.' Just like that the clockwork drones in black slogan t-shirts were reset. 'How often do you see a myth? Your hero? The heart of what you've dedicated your life's work to?'

'Come again?'

'Take me,' Kallis wrapped her long fingers around my wrist, 'I dropped my Stanford degree, family...hell, I dropped *everything*. We all did to join RE. Blake headhunted us from forums, closed groups or our Internet histories because of what we believe, as much as what we can do. We wouldn't have it any other way. He's a genius, and this is our home.'

'*You're* the Renegades.' I yanked my hand free. 'The whole company?'

'Now wouldn't that be awesome? Just headquarters, of course, silly,' Kallis seized me forcefully by the arm, before leading me further into the futuristic town, her rings clicking. 'Now having one of the Blood Three visit--'

'Look, one of us is off their trolleys here,' as we passed, the Renegades would sneak glances, hidden behind piles of files, coffee mugs or their laptops. It was giving me the willies. 'I don't know what you're yakking about.'

'Hartford, Donovan – and you. You saved the Blood Lifers. You're the Originals: the Blood Three,' Kallis' peepers were burning feverishly. 'The website on Tor? That's how most of us discovered about Blood Lifers. Before that it was only whispers across the globe. Until Blake. There was always one name though: Our Light.' Suddenly Kallis' lips were touching mine. 'Our Light...'

Like an incantation, it was taken up around the room, 'Our Light, Our Light, Our Light...'

Cold with panic, I stumbled backwards.

Christ in heaven, what had I done?

We weren't heroes, myths or examples for First Lifers to copy in their rose-tinted berkdom. We'd simply been Blood Lifers seeking vengeance – justice for our enslavement. It'd been a warning for all other slavers.

Not a blueprint for baby terrorists.

But life has a way of biting you on the arse.

'Hey, wouldn't it be cool if Blood Sun dropped in too? Mistress and slave together. You know, it made me cry when--'

'She's not my mistress.'

That's when I recognised them: the slogans on the workers' t-shirts.

REBEL HERE, YEAH?

EVERYBODY KNOWS WORDS CAN NEVER HURT THEM...

I'M THE BLOODY SUPERHERO.

Buggering...bollocking...sodding hell.

'Where. Is. It?' I stalked towards Kallis.

She fiddled with her rings. 'What's the problem?'

'The t-shirts..?'

'Aren't they awesome?' Kallis struggled out of her baggy sweater – trapping her arms – before triumphantly thrusting her knockers at me, which were emblazoned with the words: YOU CAN'T FLAY A REBEL'S SOUL.

I hadn't reckoned you could flay a rebel's Soul.

I was wrong.

I twirled round, diving under the trestle table with a snarl. A bird shrieked; a bloke wailed.

They wanted a Blood Lifer? *Our Light?*

Then I'd let them have him.

A siren was spinning and wailing. Kallis was calling my name, but I wasn't with her any longer. I was back in Primrose Hill, sitting in a dining room with a pastoral mural of gentle hills and rivers; there were my Manx cats to find and count and the sun to touch. Buttery cream pages were laid out before me, with the scent of Italian calf leather.

Then I was writing...

I didn't notice the tears or Kallis and the other workers forming a barrier to hold back the security team, stopping them from shooting me. That was only after.

Instead? I was hunting, searching, ransacking the headquarters because I was certain Blake and his Renegades would've kept the book like a trophy, when they discovered it amongst my things.

The bloody bastard.

I caught a glimpse of the RE hologram, and just like that?

I knew.

I launched myself at the case, which was projecting the logo – *bang* – it sprang open.

There, like a holy relic, was *The Slave Journal of Light*.

My journal.

I rocked back on my heels, cradling the papers to my chest and smelling the leather.

For the first time in months everything was *real*.

The Grayse of these pages was dead, but I had Sun. This was all happening: Donovan was taken, pure death was a reality and Blake..?

We were his bleeding prisoners.

When I felt Kallis' soft touch on my shoulder, I looked up. Only then did I realise my cheeks were wet, security were being held back by a bunch of office workers and headquarters was trashed.

'I'm sorry,' I muttered.

Kallis beamed. 'That was epic! The journal is yours anyway. Blake should never have... We shouldn't have taken it. In case you haven't guessed? Every one of us would bleed out for you. You're Our Light.'

And if that didn't give me the collywobbles, nothing would.

'I hear you destroyed headquarters?'

'Turns out you had something of mine,' I held up the journal.

Blake made to take it, but I snatched it back close to my heart. No way was Blake contaminating it again.

Kallis had led me into the second cone of the building, after a furious bark through the radio from Blake's secretary.

Blake's office was a barmy mix of extreme surreal and minimalism. The walls were warped science fiction, like we were stuck in a cosmic comic battle. There was no furniture, except a giant mahogany desk, which had something etched into its surface (even upside down the pattern looked uncomfortably familiar), and a black leather chair: Blake's.

Keeping the other bloke standing? Classic trick to reduce him to sniveling schoolboy in front of the headmaster.

I wasn't taking a caning.

Blake sprawled back in his chair; it creaked. 'Some good reading in there. Really heart-wrenching.'

'Sod off.'

'*My name is Light...my name is Light...my name is...*'

'Again, sod off.'

Blake smiled around those perfect white teeth. 'It made my workers' – lives - to read that. Be generous. We're fighting to stop your extinction. This is a crusade for them.'

'That's what I'm frightened of.'

Blake assessed me. 'Did you know us humans aren't unique? Once there were four others, just as advanced? Yet they died out. It was luck alone that allowed our survival. We may even have made contact with these others; maybe we've made contact many times with Blood Lifers too?'

'And your point?'

'Listen, then maybe you'll learn something, like how only one percent of DNA divides humans and chimps.'

'Bleeding important one percent.'

Blake's laugh set my teeth on edge. 'It makes you wonder: by how much are First and Blood truly divided? You see, before they died out, we'd already interbred with those four species. We'd adopted their babies, raided and raped their women. There's no such thing as pure blood: we're all mongrels.'

'And this has to do with me..?'

'We've been running tests on Plantagenet; I want your blood and venom too. I intend to see if there's a genetic connection between some ancient ancestor, or if we interbred--'

'Now hang on a tick,' I thumped down on the desk; I hadn't noticed how fast my heart was thundering, until I couldn't catch my breath, 'I've seen where this type of science leads, and it's not anywhere good.'

'The world's moved on.'

'Don't fool yourself. Folks are just as hysterical, fearful and tribal as they ever were. Plus I'm nobody's lab rat.' My gaze hardened. 'Plantagenet? He's a Magnificoe. Maybe that doesn't mean much to you, but if you want to study us? Start there, not sticking us with needles and reducing us to spiraling strands of DNA.'

'Everything comes down to evolution,' Blake stroked the etched surface of his desk.

'You know what? We've evolved beyond the need to interbreed; we're a life born of fangs. It's in the venom. Death and life – it's all the same to us.'

I followed Blake's finger, as it traced the tangled web of a...*branching tree*.

Everything blurred.

Strapped to a cold medical examining table: starkers, starving and with a snaking crimson IV...the stand stamped with a *black tree logo*.

I grasped onto the edge of the desk, willing myself to keep my big gob shut.

Blake, however, had noticed my gaze.

'True evolution,' he crowed, 'isn't linear. It has unequal survival, extinction and an unpredictable end.' He rapped on the table. 'So a branching tree for my personal logo – private deals only. It's merely a little joke.'

But I wasn't bloody laughing.

Sun laughed. 'Blood Sun? Am I, like, in *The Matrix*?'

'Missing the point. That tosser's private logo was all over the research lab where I was sliced and diced. The one that's developing pure death.' I pulled Sun closer into the Wiccan circle with Hartford and me, until all our foreheads were touching. Our breaths dragon misted in the cold air.

I'd called them up to the flat roof, amongst the yellow flowers, casual as if I'd been arranging a picnic, rather than a war summit. The wind stole our words, masking them from the CCTV.

I hoped.

'I told you we should blow this joint,' Hartford whispered fiercely, 'this whole empire business is all wet.'

'Na-ah, there's a whole notha side to RE you just don't get on account of you've been Blood Lifers so long you've forgotten what it's like to be human.'

I couldn't fault Sun's brutal honesty, or the way it shanked me right through the sodding heart.

'And you?' Hartford held out his hand, and I took it tenderly. But Sun? She kept her mitts at her side. 'Beat your gums about bushwa because you ain't been a Blood Lifer long enough to know what it is to live as the Lost.'

I had a gander beyond the roof at the laced ivy heart, which webbed over the pale white moon face.

We were in gaol but since when did we have to act like prisoners?

'We're the Blood Three: we started this. We didn't mean to but we did. We have to stay and figure it out: stop Blake or help the Renegades...I don't bleeding well know, do I? But we do it together. Family.'

I reached for Sun's hand, but she pulled back.

Then Sun wrenched away, breaking the Wiccan circle.

Breaking us.

Breaking.

NIGHT 10

I need not remind you that only four nights remain.

Then don't. A counting clock of doom brings a bloke down.

A man cheating me makes me not care. Your secret – where was it yesterday?

And where's my ciggie today?

Waiting on a missing secret.

Fun as your game is, Liberty, I don't play games – not over love or death.

Then it appears you do break promises.

You broke yours first: how many days with Captain must I... After suffering with him, you reckon I'll still dance to your tune? I can barely stand. Now don't get all prissy, with your rustling papers and whatnot, as if I suddenly don't exist.

If you can't keep me safe, you don't have a witness.

I can do anything--

As long as it's ratified in triplicate first?

We can't all be rebels.

Try it on for size sometime; I reckon it'd suit you.

Let me be sure I have this straight: if I do something about Captain, then you'll bear witness?

It's all about choices. We have as many as there are stars in the sky: if we'd only look up from the ground to see them.

The stars were accusing peepers, furious and cruel; in the clear night sky, just turning to spring, they burned.

Yet I was out of RE, free and away from Blake. In the fresh (all right polluted) London air, but it was *my* London, which was the only thing that counted.

I knew I was being tracked; I'd immediately spotted the two First Lifers tailing me.

It was out on the blood bathed London Bridge, however, my own turf, as the cabs coughed by and the Thames silver-licked underneath, that I realised a bloke needed distance.

When you're caught in a trap, it's hard to see the bastard who's set it – or the way out.

Sun had pulled back.

When I ran my hand through my hair, there was my wrist – empty. No bracelet.

Breaking us.

I was a moron for reckoning I was free of any trap.

Blake's First Lifers were waiting for me on the other side of the bridge.

And Will was dead.

Where was Mutt?

I was guilt-cramped, when I thought of her shaggy black-and-white mug and her growling, barmy bravery, as she'd leapt to Will's defence against the world. Then I imagined Blake's expression, if I brought an adopted dog into his pristine home of silk sheets and designer squeaking sofas.

I'd like to see Mr Darwin try to bully his new brother...

Mutt was also something of Will's – I can admit that. Not him, but a memory. I needed that, at least.

Whistling to myself, I jumped down the side of the embankment in a crunching avalanche of sand. There was a holler on either side of me – Blake's wankers hadn't been expecting that.

I laughed, before I choked.

Barbed wire was looped around my throat, razor-sharp. I could feel it slicing through skin. One tug: I'd be headless.

'What's the drilly, cuz?' Trinity's lips were hot against my ear. When she twisted the wire, I gasped. 'You come like a tourist to my ends, acting all guardian angel. Next 'ting? My Will be missing. So where my Will, Mr Angel Man?'

I blinked back tears. 'I only came to fetch Mutt.'

'Why? 'Cos you wanna eat him too? I knew you were gonna switch on us. This be 'cos I made you drink my Will's blood, innit?'

And just like that I was crying.

For Will: the life born of my fangs that never was.

I knew Trinity was going to do it. Pull that wire. She'd meant to the moment she'd wrapped it around my throat.

It turns out the myth about vampire hunters isn't bollocks after all.

I was only still breathing because Trinity was desperate – terrified – I'd tell her Will was dead but she had to know for sure.

Although she was wrong I'd gone all Hollywood vampiric on him – she was also right. It was going to break her, the same as it had me.

The wire at my throat was proof of Trinity's love.

So I knew I was going to cop it on the murky banks of the Thames, under London Bridge, to the curdled tang of brine and piss, as the stars watched without giving one bleeding sod because why should they?

I can be all Emo when I feel like it, and when you're about to be done in..?

You feel like it.

The wire eased. Then it was whipped off, and I was kicked sprawling into the marshy mud.

I spluttered, holding my hand to the jagged slash. I hissed, as my blood trickled scarlet.

Trinity was scrutinizing me, her cheeks as wet as mine. 'No one cares. A tear ain't shed for one of ours.'

I pushed myself onto my knees. 'He was one of mine. No different.'

A *bark*. Black-and-white in sudden blur. Then Mutt – in all her wagging glory – tumbled me back into the stinking mud. Her warm tongue licked my tears.

'Mutts been missing my Will, same as all mandem. He stays with us; this is his yard.'

I stroked Mutt to hide the tremble in my hand. 'I'd only have got peckish and noshed him anyway.'

Trinity flung down the wire, before shoving her hands into the pockets of her khaki jacket: definite shiv reaching territory. Then she scuffed at the embankment; the gravel wept down the dark sides. 'Where be your crepes?'

I took a shufti down at the scarlet nicked soles of my bare feet. 'Lost a lot lately.'

'You ain't gonna tell me where my Will at? But you be telling me he dead?'

'I'm sorry.' She was a bright bird: that was enough.

Trinity nodded. 'Alright, blud,' her peepers were black with cold rage, 'now tell me who we shank.'

I wobbled to my feet, before edging towards her.

An enemy of my enemy was...

Still my psychotic, unstable, drug dealing enemy.

Yet we had a common goal and grief. Trinity could be my ears out into the world; First united with Blood.

Life consists of such crossroads: decisions that'll save you from the flames or roast your goolies.

Maybe it was an unholy alliance.

But for Will?

I'd have worn lipstick for the devil.

'If we work this right, you won't need to shank – fun as that is - because we'll make every bloody bastard care: about you, me and Will. We won't be the Lost. You won't be invisible. They'll see us at last.'

The lounge was in blackness, when I crept in just before dawn; I'd reckoned to kip on the sofa to save myself from She-Who-Must-Be-Obeyed.

When in the silence Blake touched the light by that ratty designer chair of his, and Plantagenet sprang to life kneeling at his feet with Sun at his shoulder, like Blake was a medieval king at an execution, I couldn't even convince myself I was surprised.

'Like that, is it?' I glanced between them wearily. 'You want me to tinkle the high notes on the Steinway, add some more dramatic tension?'

'Come and chat. Or do I simply call security..?'

'Those great elephants blundering after me around London?' I slouched over to the sofa, throwing myself down with an *eek* of dying toys; I was too knackered to keep running. I smirked, when Blake grimaced at the snail trail of scarlet on his biscuit carpet; he'd know better to give me boots next time. If they wanted a barney, then they wouldn't find me the rollover and take it sort anymore. Sun hid behind her veil of hair, as I pointed at her. 'Dead classy, grassing on me to teacher. What did Blake promise? A shiny head girl badge?'

Blake patted the back of Sun's hand.

My Sun Girl.

Not Blake's or his Renegades'.

Mine.

Blake smiled. 'Head of department, actually. She's our star.'

I burst to my feet. *No way, no bloody way.* Then I caught a glimpse of Sun's peepers: they were glistening. She looked as stricken as me. 'Still, most stars are just dying suns from our pasts, right?'

Sun exploded at me then, as I'd hoped she would, because I hadn't been able to see her standing there united with Blake against me. Not after what we'd fought for together. After all she'd lost and betrayed for me.

Not when she was my elected.

Sun bowled me onto my back, her arm pressed against my throat. It reminded me of how Plantagenet had pinned me under the curtain of his curls, as he'd wept for his lost family.

His legacy.

Sun's lips pressed hard to mine, as if to prove she was still burning molten, even though wet was dripping from her peepers like an anointing.

'Sun,' I mouthed, 'please...'

Sun was pulling away from me, however, leaving me alone on the floor.

It didn't hurt less the second time.

When I forced myself to look up, Sun was a shadow again at Blake's shoulder. Plantagenet was studying me tenderly – almost regretfully. 'Is this where you take me down to that dungeon of yours and get happy with the rack again, or am I demoted to lab rat permanently?'

'I told you not to ask questions,' Blake could've been a mafia boss, 'and accept what I told you. You're going to be a challenge to teach obedience.'

'I wouldn't hold my breath,' I pushed myself up: no way I'd let that wanker continue to recline there looking down on me. 'You're my... We're *blood*.' Plantagenet was shaking. 'I reckoned you were some sort of saviour, rescuing us from that research lab, but it turns out you were the bastards who put us in there.'

'Great gods, find no treason well-beloved! Nay, I knew not,' Plantagenet tried to rise, his slim hand outstretched to me, but winced when he was yanked back by Blake; I hadn't noticed that Plantagenet's curls were wound round Blake's strong right hand. For just a moment I reckoned Plantagenet would break free anyway, but instead he crouched back to *kneel*. 'I was ignorant of such...' Plantagenet glanced from underneath his eyelashes at Blake. 'Yet ignorance does not excuse my part. We wish no harm but only for you to listen to the winding path behind these wicked machinations.'

Another cruel twist on Plantagenet's hair; this time he groaned.

To my surprise, it was Sun who growled.

'It was before... I didn't know Plantagenet,' Blake was the most awkward I'd yet seen him, darting glances anywhere but me, 'or any Blood Lifer existed. This woman came to see me about a private and highly confidential subcontract. It's not unusual. It turns out they were a new department: the CIE.'

'Just what we need. Another sodding acronym.'

'They wanted a new military facility fitting out, everything from examining tables to our most advanced genetic tests, except when the specs came through – for my eyes only – it was to fit a human or something very like.'

'And you pulled right on out?'

'I tried to but I was committed. Plus they added a bonus,' Blake gentled his hold on Plantagenet's curls to a stroke. 'They opened my eyes to all of it: the Blood Life Council and a whole new species. They promised me the best slave.'

One stride and – *bam*. A hook straight to the tosser's neb.

Blake howled, as he cradled his smashed mush.

I told you that us blokes always go for the nose.

Whilst Blake stemmed the crimson with his poncey violet handkerchief, I stood back, waiting for the wrathful whirr of Plantagenet thrashing my arse.

Instead Plantagenet let me clock his master. And that? Was the most blinding thing of all.

Stunned, Blake opened his gob once. Closed it. Twice. A third time.

I gave a scornful laugh. 'Cat got your tongue? Some bint offered you enough lolly to tempt your greedy capitalist heart into overlooking the dodgy villain vibes. Then when you figured out the true darkness, you were bribed with a toy. Did I miss something out?'

Blake merely shook his nut.

'Now what are we going to do about it? Our venom? I'm guessing you didn't know about that fun part of the plan? *All in hand*? I should cocoa.'

When Plantagenet glanced at Sun, I felt like the new kid in school. 'Is not this sufficient? The Blood Lifers we save as Renegades and being together as a family? You are all hail and thunder, but glory comes from our mission. What has the world to do with us?'

Plantagenet meant it – bloody hell did he.

'Pure death won't merely be used as a weapon against other countries or political assassinations but the undesirables too. Our own country's misfits - to tidy up the imperfect, sway agendas or cut costs: immigrants, old folks, or those taking up hospital beds. The disabled and the homeless.' Will's dusky blond tumble of curls, as his manga peepers peeked up at me outside the comic shop, like he was waiting to be swept away with the rest of the rubbish: ciggie butts, chewing gum and abandoned coffee cups. Then the black body bag wheeled through the bronze guts of the lab – murdered by *my* venom. 'Who'd miss them?' When had I started yelling? Yet I couldn't stop. 'A spike in heart attacks in vulnerable groups like that? Who'd care?'

I finally noticed Plantagenet's gentle hand was on my shoulder; Sun's was on my other. Blake was left stranded – silent – on his throne.

'I would, well-beloved,' Plantagenet was all serious determination, 'because you do.'

Why are the Blood Life Council working with the CIE? Sodding First Lifer Westminster? Come on, give it your best because I don't have a scooby.

It's new Council policy – Captain's policy – to work with whoever best suits need: including First Lifers, governments or the CIE.

Cracking that is. Just who are these CIE wankers?

Committee on Interspecies Evolution. Julia Kane is human liaison.

Yet you have the cheek to call me *traitor*?

First you were sell-outs to slavers. Now military weapon developers. Did Captain and his cronies fly the nest from their Authors too soon to learn even the basic Blood Lifer rules?

They slaughtered them – so the records say.

I've been doing my homework, Mr Blickle, since we last chatted.

Well blow me down with a feather: the ruthless bastards are going to get us all done in.

This bird from the CIE isn't all sparkly dolls and fairy dust. She's studying us; how to hurt and *kill* us. But first? The CIE will use our venom. Wipe out a city. Slip it in the Thames and bye bye dear old London town.

It's more than a handy tool to assassinate Russian spies or terrorists in deserts. Pure death could enslave the world.

Or end it.

See beneath the paperwork, procedures and petty divides, you silly bint: *see me*.

That's not my job. All this other business is hardly your affair. We work with the British Government. The divide I see? We're legitimate; you're the terrorist. That's why you're the one who's going to be burned alive.

Am I still *silly*?

You're deluded.

We're slipping, one small choice and deed at a time, towards the edge of an abyss.

And it's bloody dark down there.

Now maybe that's none of my beeswax. But apathy? Not one of my weaknesses, sweetheart.

So I stole out of bed as soon as Sun was kipping, before riding the lift down to the ground floor. Something was going on in Blake's research labs, and although daft heroics had cost me in both First and Blood Life, I'd never lost the naïve hope that *this* time I'd pull off the caper.

Yet now I had a secret weapon. I wouldn't be alone; I had a fangirl.

I had Kallis.

'Awesome, you're...' Kallis struggled to explain why I was hanging about the back of the lift. I knew I was staying out of sight of the CCTV for as long as possible, whilst waiting for Kallis to sashay by, but I wasn't helping her out on this one. I smiled encouragingly. '...scoping the territory for other predators?'

'That'll be it, luv,' when I dragged Kallis into the lift with me, she gasped. Her heart was thudding – *beat – beat – beat* – like a tribal drum message straight to my brain. My fangs shot out, as I licked up her neck. Kallis sighed, pressing her thighs onto mine, before she giggled because my fangs weren't the only thing excited by the blood.

Sodding evolution.

I shoved Kallis back, as I shoved my fangs back in.

'Neat,' Kallis' fingers with the sweet rings were like soldiers; as fast as I batted back their raids on my fast wilting todger, they regrouped and charged. At last, I grabbed her wrists and squeezed. She squeaked, drawing back.

'I didn't come here for that. Instinct: hell of a thing. The blood--'

'*Blood is life.*'

'Appreciate it if you didn't quote me; it creeps me out.'

Flustered, Kallis nodded. 'So why's Our Light walking amongst us again?'

'Touch of the risen Christ, but first things first. I'm being a bad boy here; I haven't got permission. Blake's not gonna like that in a *he'll be doing more than spanking* me way.'

'Hold up,' Kallis rubbed the back of her hand down my cheek; it was surprisingly tender, 'Blake's hurt you? He would hurt you or any Blood Lifer?'

I bit my tongue.

Here was the crux: how much true darkness to unveil to a First Lifer.

It was the way Kallis had touched my cheek – that flash of awareness – which prompted me to admit, 'Blake's built himself a fortress here, training a team of fanatics, who he separates from family and friends. He's seated himself at the head. You do know you Renegades kill? Think about all that and then tell me you reckon us Blood Lifers stay here because we love being stuck with needles, defanged and wheeled out like prize exhibits? Blake's a bloody tyrant. Me? I'm the rebel who's going to burn this fortress to the ground. I'll free you all for real, but you have to decide right now whether you're going to turn me in, or join the true rebellion.'

There was a long moment.

Kallis stared at me. Then gave a quick nod, before holding out her long-fingered hand.

We shook.

A Komodo dragon.

Dead.

It was laid out on its side – a greyish green – five-foot-long (as tall as Kallis); its claws hung as motionless as its muscular tail. Its guts coiled worm-like, spiralling onto the plastic of the examining table.

A tiny bloke in olive operating overalls – a sodding kid – was jabbing a humungous needle into the Komodo's neck through its chainmail scales with gusto. He glowered at us when we tore into the research lab, slamming the door – *bang*.

I tottered to a meshed steel basket by the autopsy, before I chucked up.

'For God's sake, Kallis, why on earth would you bring in this creature, whilst I was engaged in..?'

'Don't blame me...'

I wiped my gob. The lab spun me back to Frankenstein's: the powerlessness, the burn, melting and the scalpel... *Do I cut it off all at once at the base? Quick. Or slowly slice by slice?*

I chucked up again. This time I missed the bin.

'Get him out of here,' the scientist hopped up and down like an enraged bug, 'he's contaminating--'

'You're the one contaminating, you little oik; Komodo died a natural death, did he?'

If the Komodo was still so green that meant he was only a kid too. The poor git's forked yellow tongue lolled out of its round snout; I remembered that indignity. I wished I could gently press the tongue back inside and give it some dignity at least, after this violation. Yet the guts gory on the padded plastic? How could I ever heal that wound?

I don't know why it was getting to me, but deep – biologically – there was a connection; it was my venom fizzing with fury at the outrage.

We weren't the prey to be sliced open with our insides on display.

'Neither did you,' the brat pointed the needle at me, 'that's nature.'

I slammed him against the wall, so fast he didn't even have time to *eep*.

More Komodo dragons. Another and another and... Photo after photo pinned to the walls. Living, mid-autopsy and dead. Green, grey and uniform stone. Close-ups of teeth, saliva and venom glands. In fierce barnies and slaughtering prey. I stared between them in silence, mesmerized.

'Your ancestor,' the brat was scrutinizing me like he was deciding where to jab the needle first.

'You say that about yourself whenever you see Mr Darwin?'

The tantrum scowl again. 'I wouldn't expect you to understand the finer points of the Island--'

'Monitor. Known to natives of the Komodo Island as ora, buaya darat, the land crocodile or biawak raksasa, the giant monitor.' Finally, the tosser lowered his gaze. 'See, I know more about these buggers than you do and I knew it before you were born. I've saved the world, you condescending prat. This is a dangerous thing you're playing with. Us Blood Lifers? We're not the school science project.'

'You're right: you're the Holy Grail, little man.' Fernando gave a casual wave, as he sauntered into the lab. He was wearing green scrubs, so had taken the time to be avenged on my ancestors too.

My world was spinning. *Even Blake couldn't have..?*

Yet Fernando had been working on the Komodo, as if he'd just finished up torturing me and abusing Sun.

When I dived for him, I found myself instead nose-to-nose with Kallis. 'Professor Zuniga Sanchez is on our team now.'

'Not my team. You reckon you had vengeance? You don't have a scooby but you sodding will.'

I met Fernando's glare: he was pressed against the door, sweat shining him doll-like. Yet he was too cool for a bloke facing death.

Why wasn't he playing the part of prey?

Then Fernando smiled, and it was my insides liquefying.

'You don't know what he did,' I muttered.

'We know,' Kallis shrugged, 'Plantagenet made him tell us.'

I could feel the heat like beacons in my cheeks, as Fernando's smile broadened to reveal those not quite perfect teeth. 'In a memo, was it?'

'More like a team bonding session.'

I recoiled. 'Bloody hell, why don't I just prance starkers through the office?' Then I regretted the outburst because of the way three pairs of peepers lit up for entirely different reasons. 'You all forgave the wanker? Trust him?'

Kallis' mush hardened. 'Never. I told you though, we arrive here by different paths; we don't have any other home. Now Fernando's the same.'

'*He* doesn't touch me: rule one. Rule two? You tell me right quick why I don't rip out his throat and none of this team bollocks.'

'Whoa, always the frackin' drama queen,' when Fernando pushed Kallis out of the way, there he was: the bloke who'd betrayed me into the hands of my torturers. Who'd started all of this out of jilted love – a love I no longer knew Sun even held for me.

Except everything had been set in motion long before Fernando had made his choice, one that'd ended in Will's death by my venom. One small choice, after one small choice. Fernando had been caught in a web, which had been spun by someone – or something – too large to see. Yet if you traced those silk threads back...

Suddenly it was so obvious.

Frankenstein's research lab was the Blood Life Council's, the same as it was CIE's: that's how Blood Lifers were sanctioned as lab rats. And lucky old me? With Hartford left on the outside to keep up the search for the Renegades, desperate to get Donovan back, it would've been like lighting a fire under the arses of your enemy - thumbing a nose at the Renegades to rescue me.

I was the trophy for either side: Our Light.

I'd made the ultimate mistake: underestimated the enemy. Captain was even more conniving than I'd reckoned.

'I'm still waiting on rule two.'

'I get it: straight down to business. I respect that.' Fernando leant closer, almost touching but not quite. I tensed. 'Because I'm the guy working on the antidote to the separated venoms.' I startled, bumping our noses. Fernando chuckled. 'Hey, come on, no touching now.'

'You've got a second chance here. Only one mind. We have some heroics ahead. So the question is: are you in on the rebellion or not?'

'It's not like I ever wanted to kill any...humans. But I can't just magic--'

'I'll pretend I didn't hear that first bit. Have you tried primroses for the paralysis? Maybe there are other natural antidotes to the pure death. Everything doesn't always come down to Blake's science of the future.'

When Kallis stroked my arm, I had a shufti: security. With a fuming Blake and Mr Darwin clinging round his neck, scowling.

Another round of playing monkey chew toy then...

I saluted Kallis and marched out of that Komodo graveyard, before I could be hauled away.

A bloke's got to have his dignity.

And a plan.

The truly blinding part? For the first time – I did.

I didn't even care when Mr Darwin pushed me out of bed again that night. Let him gloat.

My time was coming.

NIGHT 11

There are only three nights until the trial. I can't simply... You could save yourself if you testified to--

Plantagenet's not guilty, at least, not in the way you mean. Blake? He's a First Lifer. You reckon the Council's leaders would believe a *human* could make a chump out of them?

Our procedures are flawed. The whole system's--

Bollocks?

Quite. Blood Life is not what I'd imagined it to be. I've investigated your claims – Fernando, the CIE and research labs – it appears you weren't lying.

Well, doesn't that throw a spanner in the works? Or does it still change nothing? I burn; my witness is censored or buried, whilst you sit in silence.

Do you ever grow weary of thinking you know everything?

Why? Do you?

Sometimes. Then – just once – someone comes along. A terrorist, traitor and Renegade. The most irresponsible anarchist who has ever spread chaos and carnage through Blood Life. A multiple murderer of his own kin--

You're not painting me in my most flattering light, sweetheart.

Then I actually meet you and I come to understand that my Author – Captain – was wrong.

Everything I believed was wrong.

Yet none of that matters because indeed you will still burn, and there's no way I can save you.

There's always a way, we simply have to want it enough.

As a slave I was a product; Captain sees *all* Blood Lifers as products, however, merely useful weapons, pets or scalpels.

You?

You're the office stationary.

You have no idea, either what I am or what I could be.

Then show me.

I'll continue to give you my witness, if you promise to *sodding show me.*

'Abso-bloody-lutely perfect,' I slammed the soft pillow over my mush, futilely attempting to drown out Metallica's thrash "Master of Puppets"; the blazing guitars were taking a hammer to *my* dreams. 'Who the bloody hell *is* that, in the middle of the sodding day?'

Mr Darwin grunted his agreement, his palm patting my nut.

I stilled, before slowly lifting the pillow.

Mr Darwin peered at me from his side of the bed, primly holding up the silk covers to his whiskery chin.

I sighed. 'You're looking a bit rough today, Sun. Someone you ate?'

Mr Darwin gripped me around the waist with his feet, and before I could twist away...

Tickled.

'Stop it...stop...I bloody mean it.'

Now I got the meaning of *tickle torture.*

I doubled up, my muscles in spasms from the forced hilarity.

Mr Darwin shook with breathy laughter to match my giggles.

I only noticed there was someone else in the room, when Mr Darwin's grasping fingers paused in their play. Then I realized the music had paused too.

Mother was standing at the bedside, an iPhone wired to a UFO shaped speaker, which was clipped to her pocket, staring down at the two of us tangled together.

The covers had been kicked back in the commotion.

And I was starkers.

I struggled to roll Mr Darwin off me, as he embraced my neck (just like he had Blake's). The chimp was as much of a pillock when he decided to be my mate, as my nemesis.

Unless having proven he was the alpha, he was now playing nice again, dominating his troop.

I finally managed to shrug off Mr Darwin, as I hauled on my jeans.

'Fie, sir! Satisfy your longing. It is no shameful act of sin'

Both Mr Darwin and I gaped at Mother; I couldn't tell which of us she was encouraging.

I pulled on my t-shirt. 'I'm not laughing anymore.'

I pushed past her out into the long stretch of grey corridor.

Sun hadn't been to bed; she'd worked at night, trading and running finances. Yet she'd never been missing during the day, at least that I'd realized.

It prickled me in cold sweat.

Silence.

Blake would be down in his surreal cartoon of an office; I couldn't let myself imagine Sun with him. Not after their staged intervention the other dawn, when they'd waited in the lounge for me like parents trying to catch the teenager creeping back after curfew.

Sun had pulled away from Hartford and me out on the roof. Yet that dawn Sun had stood with me, choosing me.

Hadn't she?

Yet the image of Sun in Blake's office – blood sharing – over his branching tree desk, just like Ruby had with her brother over *his* desk, unmanned me.

My Sun Girl.

My girl.

Mine.

Click, click, click.

Mother's gold kitten heels clicked behind me, with the *rustle* of her crinkly gold trousers. She let out a breath, when she caught up, wrapping an arm around my neck, as Mr Darwin had done. 'Hey, slow down already, speedy much?'

'Things to do.'

When I tried to slide away from underneath her arm, Mother dragged me close. 'Are you mad?' She murmured. 'Are you out of your wits?'

'Not me, luv.'

Mother shoved me away, holding her iPhone and UFO speaker above her nut like a sacrifice. Metallica's distorted amps and aggressive revolutionary guitars burst out; I didn't need to have *Master* barked at me in any more lifetimes.

As if her puppet strings were being controlled, Mother danced: a pixie in a mosh pit.

Led on a string as well, I prowled after Mother, my bare feet sinking into the thick carpet.

'What an excellent shape you hath,' Mother yelled over the violent roar, 'I should have courted you, except that I see you.'

I stumbled. What had she just..?

Those dangerous peepers sparkled. 'I'm just saying.'

'No one sees me.'

'Damn, dude, that's heavy,' Mother mock pouted. 'You're bomb but you're sketchy. I'm Plantagenet's creature, and we? *Don't need you.*'

'Bleeding shame for you I'm here then.'

'Dontcha get it yet?' Mother stilled. 'You would create Sun one of your familiars, but she's not yours. Foolish man, this will never be your home.'

I realized then where we were.

Outside Blake's bedroom.

I was terrified to see what was inside.

I was desperate to turn and pretend I'd never woken up to find Sun missing.

Yet with a mind like mine? There is no forgetting. At times like this it's a curse.

Mother gave me a devilish leer, as she swiped her iPhone: the poignant rawness of "Nothing Else Matters" sang out. One bloke's agony at his separation from his love; his longing an open wound bleeding from vocals and acoustic guitar.

I stood frozen, caught in the ballad's web, as Mother pushed open the bedroom door.

When the electric guitar kicked in – the heart and Soul – I knew what I'd see. What Mother was leading me to will-o'-the-wisp.

But it was too late.

A giant's tangled steel forest. Butterflies and moths in confusion. An enchanted bed.

Sun.

Plantagenet.

They were shagging like it was the apocalypse, and if they didn't? They'd lose everything.

Like me.

I didn't move. Didn't speak. Didn't sodding breath.

It was Plantagenet who noticed me first mid-thrust.

He was polite enough to widen his cat peepers in surprise, before he rolled off Sun. He snogged her, however, with the same gentle intimacy he'd shown me.

For a moment, I didn't know who I was the most jealous of.

I was trembling with this wave of...fear...worse than when I'd been strapped down in the lab.

I remembered how M.C. had tricked me into believing Grayse had abandoned me to slavery: how it'd broken me. I'd lost my identity, even my name.

To be abandoned and lose someone I loved again..?

The cracks were still there. Yet this time? I wouldn't let anything shatter me.

Sun boldly met my stunned stare: no apology.

So I simply told Sun what I'd been desperate for her to understand since I'd authored her into this new world, 'I love you.'

Mother gave a disgusted snort.

Plantagenet pushed himself up onto his elbows. 'Under pain of death, Mother, you shall hold your wicked tongue; what ensues is your doing.'

Mother rolled her eyes, muting Metallica. In the sudden silence, the shamed couple looked twice as starkers.

I crossed my arms. 'Don't get narked at your creature here 'cos you fancied some hanky-panky with your mate's bird. See, Mother reckons we'll have a barnie, and you'll do me in or throw me out. Else I'll have a tantrum ('cos you're both lying tossers), and leg it out of here – like Hartford wants. But what she doesn't get?' I stepped closer to the green mouth of the bed and the magical world I could just reach out and touch or else be swallowed by. 'Is that *I bloody love you, Sun.*'

Sun edged towards me, her naked knockers brushing against my hand. I tingled – *Christ help me* – with a sudden rush of blood to todger (and don't let any bloke deny its dizzying hold).

But Sun didn't need that – the carnal.

We – Grayse and I – had never been about that. Considering she'd chosen me as a sex slave, it was ironic how (even though she'd come close to the edge once), she'd never used me.

Yet she'd loved me, and I'd loved her.

By the time she'd died in my arms, I'd been certain of that if nothing else.

But now?

Sun was someone new. There was a darkness coiled under her skin, which Blood Life had amplified – freed - and that was no one's fault but mine.

Sun clutched my hand. 'You're soft if you don't frickin' know I love you. Still, just 'cos you elected me, doesn't mean I'm yours.'

And there it was.

Bold, undeniable and the true bonfire of my dreams.

A world together to explore, joined by our love? Burned. The special bond between Author and their elected? Burned. My hope I'd ever be good enough – would deserve – to be loved again, as Kathy had once loved me?

Curled to ashes.

I was wrong. *Someone could shatter me.*

Then I felt Plantagenet's small hands behind me on my shoulders.

When had he risen? How long had I been standing there, lost in my grief?

Plantagenet was stripping me with practiced ease; like I was a puppet.

I let him.

'Well-beloved, it breaks me to see you so melancholy. In faith there are different loves. Family or home.' Plantagenet's soft curls were stroking down the curve of my spine; I shivered. 'Forever is too long a time to take one's pleasure with merely a single lass or single fellow.'

Sun pulled me up onto the bed.

Hands.

Stroking, pinching, caressing.

I quivered, overloaded; I struggled not to squirm, my skin alive with their kisses.

It would be so easy to choose this fall into their dual embrace. Black mane mingled with ash blonde veil. Familiar curves and the strange new hardness pressed to mine. Alabaster skin starkly beautiful against golden. A silk soft canvas of the known and the unknown calling to me – my blood.

This was home. Wherever Plantagenet was: I knew it. I'd always known it; I couldn't forget it.

I was his familiar.

Plantagenet's touch ignited me – I was bloody ablaze.

Two mouths: two kisses, both tasting of oranges.

And just like that? I was burnt to ashes.

I struggled out of their web of limbs, elbowing Plantagenet; he toppled off the bed with a startled *oomph*.

I bounced on the balls of my feet – ludicrous in the altogether – because Mother was right: I always had been the fists and fang type of bloke.

At least I had fangs, unlike...

All right then, wanker here.

I held out my hand to Plantagenet, who took it warily, allowing me to pull him to his feet.

Then he didn't let go. Instead, his fingers played across my palm. 'If I have offended...'

'This isn't about you. It's about the bird I love.' I had a shufti at Sun, who was perched on the edge of the bed, her knees pulled up to her chest; she looked more vulnerable than I'd seen her since her election. 'She's losing herself in this business: RE and the Renegades. We burned one slavery empire; why are we enslaving ourselves to another?' Sun was still avoiding my eye, but she was listening. That was the best you could ever hope for with Sun. 'Hartford was right: I was an arrogant pillock to reckon I could make a difference here. Change the world like some bloody hero. If I lead a rebellion but lose you doing it? It won't be sodding worth it. I need you, Sun. Now we have to--'

'Book it outta here?'

Thank Christ.

I grinned. 'Good on you, princess. Let's--'

'You zoo'n' on me?' My grin slipped; it hung precarious. 'We just found our new family; you already murdered my old one.'

My grin fell and broke. I bet I looked a sodding mess: I felt one.

Her family?

Slavers, rapists and torturers? Yet *now* Sun was getting all sentimental?

She'd taken a chance – Hartford, Donovan and me as well – we'd all taken a chance to bring them down. It seemed now, however, the decision was on me alone.

'Nizza job. Home. Money,' Sun counted each one off on her fingers, oblivious to my distress. 'It's fried how you reckon I'd wanna leave this.'

'Money?' I gritted out. Plantagenet had been tracing pretty patterns – branching trees – across my palm, but I snatched my hand away. 'That's claptrap, and you know it.'

'Na-ah, you don't get to tell me what to think. What Blood Life is or isn't on account of you're my Author. I won't be caged.'

Despair hit me in a black scream. My ears bled. I craved to huddle foetal, with my arms clasped over my nut, to block out all the nasties of the world.

Caged.

How had I made Sun feel that way?

After everything I'd been through – caged by *Master*, controlled by Ruby – I'd only ever wanted to set my own elected free.

Yet it turned out the bars to her birdcage might've been invisible but they were strong, and I was the bastard who'd ensnared her all along.

I simply nodded because what do you say to the woman you love to explain you never meant to take her freedom – only keep her safe?

Sun blinked, before giving this small smile. It shone: pure and joyful.

It was so different to how she'd looked at me lately that I knew I'd set her free, even though it was breaking my heart.

True love was a bitch.

Plantagenet – as courteous as any courtier – kissed the back of Sun's hand, before raising her to her feet. 'Let us play some more, my pretty lass.'

'Plantagenet, stop.'

Plantagenet froze.

Blake. An ink black gargoyle in the doorway.

He was glowering at the lovebirds, probably much like I had. I experienced a pang of sympathy for the bloke, until I realized the tosser was only narked he hadn't been invited to the party.

Mother was scuffing her heel against the skirting, her fingers tapping the iPhone in her pocket.

Blake must be plan B.

I was going to leg it, if they started the whole seduction routine on Blake, as they had on me. Freeing Sun was one thing. Watching her play out her fantasies with other blokes..?

Remember, I was no angel.

Sun immediately dragged the green sheet to drape over herself, however, like a toga. Plantagenet was motionless and giving these quick little gasps; I suddenly recognized it as fear.

'Did I give you permission to..?' Blake couldn't quite make himself say it.

Plantagenet shook his nut.

When Blake stretched out his arm, Plantagenet paced towards him with feline steps, his slender body quivering. Blake pressed their two bone rings together – fang meets tooth.

Slap.

Blake's backhand staggered Plantagenet away from Blake, breaking their touch. A purple bruise was already forming across Plantagenet's cheek.

Three Blood Lifers moved towards Blake – Sun, Mother and me. It was instinct – blood and love...I don't sodding know...but no First Lifer was beating a Plantagenet.

Plantagenet was right – we were family.

'In God's name, hold,' at Plantagenet's order, we hesitated, glancing between each other; I reckon I was beginning to get the hang of these unholy alliances.

Blake hadn't quailed. He hadn't even looked away from Plantagenet. I knew what that was like – the flame of obsessive love. 'You wanted to see Plantagenet spanked? He's earned a flogging now. Go prepare yourself.'

Plantagenet's mouth twisted, but he gave a quick nod.

'You're barmy if you reckon...'

Plantagenet caught my eye, silencing my outburst, as he slipped out of the bedroom. I noticed Mother tried to rub against him, but he pulled away from her.

Blake coldly assessed Sun. 'Your head girl badge doesn't look so shiny today. It's lucky you have Plantagenet as whipping boy.'

'No way you're thrashing him,' I prowled to Blake, forgetting in my fury that I was starkers, 'get your jollies over the internet: wank to porn, like everybody else. Don't take it out on a Magnificoe's arse.'

Blake tapped my bare chest with one manicured finger. 'The difference between you and

Plantagenet? He's learnt how to take his punishment.'

Then Blake spun on his heel and stalked out, pursued by one Blood Lifer wrapped in a silk sheet, a second clicking in kitten heels and a third starkers.

We found Plantagenet kneeling in the center of the dungeon – what a bloody surprise – with his hands clasped and his nut bowed.

Punishment positon.

He'd laid out a heavy buffalo hide flogger next to a St. Andrew's Cross – a wooden frame with leather cuffs, which was shiny and new, like it'd been inbuilt with this ready-made playroom. I flinched, remembering the flogger's *thud* and sting. Its cruel bite. Being manacled to that cross, helpless to the prison strap, cane or birch. Marked under the hand of my *Master*.

Now Plantagenet was willingly submitting, and I couldn't figure out why. He was a Long-Lived. Why was he allowing Blake to have this hold over him and us all?

When Plantagenet glanced underneath his eyelashes at us witnessing his humiliation, he blushed.

'Face the Cross.'

Plantagenet marched, like a knight onto the battlefield, before holding out his hands and feet to the cuffs. Blake slipped the leather carefully round, doing up the buckles. Then he pushed Plantagenet's Rapunzel curls to the front, exposing his back.

Only after he stepped back, did I notice Blake was shaking.

The black despair must've screamed through him, the same as me, and that made him dangerous.

Blake picked up the flogger, testing it – *whoosh* – through the air.

I cringed. Then Sun was pressed against me, her mush against my neck, like it used to be. Like I needed it to be.

Sun was shaking too.

I held her tightly: we were united in this.

Blake lifted the flogger high, before flicking it with practiced ease hard across Plantagenet's upper back. Angry red lines, as if Plantagenet had been clawed, scored his golden skin. He let out a pained gasp, after he'd breathed through the agony. He wasn't taking it silently though: Blake clearly liked to know the lesson was being learned.

Blake pulled his arm back again.

Sun and I stiffened.

"Ziggy Starburst" burst in tinny glam rock sacrilege from Blake's pocket.

As casual as if he was answering his phone between checking emails, Blake slipped it out. 'Blake here. What, now..? The CIE? Wait, I'll meet her... No, my private rooms are most certainly not acceptable. I don't care that she can track me. You must not allow...'

Blake twirled round, all coolness vanished. Punishment forgotten. Something scarier than him had spooked him.

'There's going to be an inspection. We have protocols to protect and hide our work in headquarters but my rooms...here...you..? *Hide.*'

Blake's panic was infectious.

'We're not chameleons,' I clutched Sun closer, 'we can't just camouflage into the wallpaper.'

Blake was banging about the dungeon, slamming open drawers, as if we could shrink down to fit. 'You don't understand; she's up there now.

Plantagenet's my slave: he can be here when she arrives. But if you're discovered..?'

Mother spun in circles. 'Stop tripping out, bitches.'

'Not helping.' I hissed.

'Mr Darwin's cage,' Blake threw off the thick plastic cover. The cage was large – more than man-sized. Steel, sturdy and shiny.

New.

'*Mr Darwin's* cage?' I lifted an eyebrow. 'Sure about that?'

Blake shifted his feet. 'It came with the room; I've never tried it out on Plantagenet. I wouldn't.' Blake undid the padlock, swinging open the door. He smiled, as he glanced between us Blood Lifers. 'I am delighted, however, to christen it with you.'

'Wanker,' I muttered, before dropping to all fours and crawling into the cage. It took almost more courage than I had to shuffle, my knees pressing painfully into the metal, into that cage. To trust Blake to trap me and repeat what *Master* had done, stripping away my manhood.

Then there wasn't time to think because Sun was pushing into the cage behind me, and I was being shunted against the front bars.

The bars rattled angrily.

'Hurry up. I need to get the cover back over before--'

'Hold on - what..?'

A final push crushing me against the bars – three Blood Lifers in a cage built for one man – the slamming *clang* of the door being closed and locked, and then the cover being drawn back and over. 'Wait...'

I couldn't stop the whining fear.

Black, black, black.

I was caged in darkness; terror infected, I moaned.

'Shh...' Sun's lips were warm on my ear. A kiss. Just one on the sensitive pulse point. Then her arms were sliding around my waist.

And I was safe. Home. The fear flew from her touch.

Sun loved me.

I knew it in that moment. That single kiss.

Everything else was snowflake patterns.

I could live with those differences. *If Sun loved me.*

'I'm not at all displeased to discover you are capable of disciplining your slave, Jamie,' some bint's uptight voice, so close to the cage that if she'd reached out, she'd have been touching us.

'The best gift anyone ever gave me, Ms Kane. I'll always be grateful for our business connection.'

'Why so formal? I hope our *connection* shall be fruitful for many years to come.'

'Hasn't it always been, Julia?'

'Quite. This Blood Lifer problem, however, is not a simple one; we need to develop a long term solution.'

'Agreed.'

Agreed? The tosser.

'Your slave was from a genetically powerful bloodline; they were most uncertain he could be tamed. That's why those Magnificoes, as they call themselves, rather than the weak children at the Blood Life Council, had possession of him. In a way, he was like tribute. Tell me then, how did you domesticate such a bitch? We understand you've used solutions such as defanging, and I can see here strict discipline. But what else?'

My fangs were out, as I struggled to remain motionless. Behind me, I felt two other Blood Lifers fighting the same battle.

'Conditioning. Punishment and reward. Blood Lifers are animals, when you come down to it; they respond to training, the same as a chimp.'

'Intriguing.'

'Of course, there's a magic ingredient: they have to be motivated behaviorally to change,' Blake was warming to his theme, 'with fear or pain. Aversion therapy to human blood, for example, would be most effective. I've found, however, that allowing him natural behaviour and environment is better – as far as possible in the artificial.'

'The CIE will bear it in mind, when weighed against cost. We're considering a range of...solutions to the Blood Life disease.'

'Wait,' blossoming alarm, which tickled spider legs down my spine, 'Blood Life is not a disease.'

'Infection then.'

'It's not a disease or an infection. It's--'

'Thank you, Jamie. Always an education.'

Silence.

Then light, followed by the *clang* of the cage's door banging open.

We backed out one by one. My knees were stiff against the cold bars. I stretched, as I pulled myself up.

Surprised, I clocked Blake undoing Plantagenet's cuffs, instead of continuing the flogging. When Blake hauled Plantagenet into a bear hug, Blake's powerful shoulders were suddenly rising and falling in waves, as he sobbed.

'I'm sorry,' Blake whispered, stroking Plantagenet's curls all the way down to his waist, before tracing the scarlet weals, 'I'm so sorry.'

Plantagenet pushed away. 'You cannot run with the hare and hunt with the hounds. Are you indeed with us?'

'It's too late; didn't you hear her? The CIE think you're an infection to be cured.'

'Where's Hartford?' I stood in the center of that dungeon, staring at the rack Hartford had been stretched on for me and felt like the worst mate, family member, leader...ever.

Because I'd only just noticed Hartford wasn't there.

What if the CIE bint had stumbled across him..?

I'd been too caught up in the blood spell that was Plantagenet and Sun: together it was home, family and love.

It was a fantasy.

A bloody dangerous one too.

I'd promised Hartford not to take any *wooden nickels*: yet my pockets were weighed down with them.

I'd told Hartford he was my family. Yet who had I forgotten (*we all* forgotten), in the danger and the fear?

Hartford had never forgotten me.

Then everyone started talking, yelling and accusing. All at once.

'Pipe down, for crying out loud!'

As one, we shut up, turning to see an astonished Hartford peering in at us.

I laughed then and once I started, I couldn't stop. Since when has a little hysteria hurt a bloke?

Slap – oh yeah, when he gets smacked in the mug by a Long-lived. 'Stop acting screwy and spill. What is all this?'

Hartford eyed the half-covered cage, flogger and us. Starkers – or at least Plantagenet and I were. Sun was just about holding onto her sheet.

'Life, helmethead, bloody life,' I was buzzing, as if I'd feasted on human blood, 'and we're going to start living it. We're rescuing Donovan and we're not going to be afraid. Why? Because *we're Renegades.*'

NIGHT 12

Have I been in any way remiss in my duties? Unclear as to the nature of this inquiry? Perhaps I should've kept things visual, making the adaptations you need for your particular style of learning?

Enough of that. Just spit it out.

Your statement taken from last night: *we're the Renegades.*

It seems clear enough to me.

Therein lies the problem. Today, tomorrow and then comes the trial.

The flames are already warming me; I've made my peace with it. Why won't you?

Because that's not how this works! I come in here and I untangle the witness, so the guilty can be punished. It's what I do.

Yet you hide truths and unmask lies. Confuse and manipulate, until I don't know...who I am.

Funny thing about who we are: no one can make us anything. Only we get to choose. Sometimes we get so buried deep under the controls of this world – family, society and love – we forget that and lose ourselves. Then we no longer know who we are or once were.

We can become whoever we want because we do have a choice, and coming from a bloke who was once a slave, you have no idea how precious that is.

That's all there is to it? I choose to act?

I tend to get booted in the goolies first, and then tortured. But...yeah.

Make the choice, lay the caper and act.

Thank you, Mr Blickle, that was a fascinating insight into terrorist mentality.

If I were you I'd make your remaining witness count. We only have one more session together after this.

Tell me a story of hidden truths and unmasked lies: of a man who chose to act.

'It's been ages since Hartford bolted. And you?' Aedan's green peepers sparked, 'You're a massive idiot if you reckon you can pull that on me.'

'Kidnapped. Researched on by mad scientists. Hartford to the rescue. Kept prisoner by terrorist Renegades. New caper to save Donovan: you in?'

Aedan sprawled in his crimson looped cock of a seat, his elven mush screwed up with the effort to process the barminess of our Blood Lifer world.

The Peter Pan was dark and silent before opening; it was eerie without its music, dancers and men in suits looking to lose themselves for one night at least.

Reinvent or hide: what's the difference?

Hartford and I sank into the brocade and damask, but it wasn't the same – because Donovan was missing.

Out of the corner of my eye, I kept catching glimpses of Donovan's dark mop of hair, as he danced sinuous in nothing but bowtie.

No wonder Hartford was so tense.

Aedan chewed at one braid in thought. 'I know I said we all had our histories? Remind me what a thick tool I am for not guessing yours. You're not exactly a choir boy, are you?' Then he glanced significantly at Hartford. 'Donovan wasn't going to give me a love bite that time on the dancefloor..?'

Hartford shook his nut, before to my shock – and Aedan's – dropping to his knees next to the First Lifer. 'I'll lay it on the line, mac: I'm goofy over my sheik. I'd do anything to save him; I'd suffer anything. We could've fed you a line, but you're my friend. I don't want to treat you like some sap. Please help us.'

Aedan threw himself to his knees next to Hartford, clinging around his neck.

I'd forgotten this intimacy.

Friendship.

Aedan had taken us in and given us a home. He'd accepted us, even when he'd discovered we were something other than human. I'd only known one other First Lifer like that, and now she was dead.

What else had Plantagenet's...spell...forced me to forget?

I coughed awkwardly. 'We're doing this then?' Two resolved mushes turned to me – angelic gold hair, mingled with impish red – so close they were one. I couldn't help the chuckle. 'Are you climbing off him anytime soon?'

'Why?' Aedan rested his cheek against Hartford's. 'Am I frightening the horses?'

I snorted. 'Yeah, right.' Both Aedan and Hartford goggled at me. *Buggering hell...* 'It was nothing,' I wagged a finger at them, 'and this is a council of war, not a--'

'Plantagenet,' Hartford's voice was flat and cold.

'Look, I'm not--'

'Says you. But from the moment you met Plantagenet, you were stuck on him. Sun was the same. Why do you think she let him...didn't help me? See, what I can't understand is why. A high hat, with his head up his ass.'

Aedan sniggered.

'You don't have to understand, because I don't. I know Plantagenet's not bad, he just--'

'Tell it to the marines. Because you see how you feel about a fella after you've been broken on the rack by him.'

Aedan wound even closer around Hartford, and the look he threw me, should've staked me – with a sodding spoon.

'Nothing's changed,' I said softly, 'you're still my family.'

'And Donovan?'

'Bloody hell,' I exploded up, knocking them tumbling back in a tangle of red and gold, as I paced the dancefloor in front of the cross-shaped stage. 'I'm not perfect. I'm falling from crisis to crisis, surviving the best I can. It's what I do. Only before? It was just me. And now there's you lot. These others, who I love by the way, are looking to me for decisions, and I'm getting it wrong or getting it right, but the rug's still pulled out from under me. I'm trying, alright? To do the best for everyone. If I could take it all on me – every hurt and blow – I would but I don't know how. I'm sorry. This is new to me. This is--'

'Being a leader.'

Hartford fluidly rose, pulling Aedan after him. Then he sauntered to me, pausing my agitated pacing with a slight yet powerful hand on my shoulder. '*Our* leader.'

I managed to smile. 'Sure you want to choose me?'

'In Blood Life leaders aren't chosen. They're authored. You're my leader, poor little bunny, so stop acting like it's giving you the screaming meemies, and let's rescue my sheik.'

Aedan patted my arse. 'Not my leader, just so as we're clear. I'm in though.'

Hartford's expression clouded. 'What I can't work out, mac, is how you plan to get Donovan outta there. The way I see it? There are only two ways: we double-cross the fella you're now goofy over, or I sacrifice myself.'

I wrenched back from Hartford, tremors bawling through me nancy. 'What the buggering hell are you on about?'

Hartford smiled sadly. 'Captain wants the leader of the Renegades. But that's bull. He just needs the big cheese to parade in chains before the Council to show how hard-boiled he is. He doesn't care who it really is. You hand me in: I'm a Long-lived and an ex-slave. You reckon he won't believe it? I confess to being leader of the Renegades, and then Donovan will be free.'

'Hey, mac, you certain you heard..? What did you hear?'

'You know...screams, like Blake was hurting--'

'Plantagenet?' Hartford spun round. I'd expected him to give me that same hard look, but instead there was only the anxious compassion Hartford had worn whenever *Sir* had laid into me at Abona.

I flamed with guilt. 'In that bloody playroom dungeon.'

'Nothing play about it, fella.' Hartford dove down the corridor so fast I couldn't keep up with him. 'Get a wiggle on! You want to save him or not?'

Smash – there went the dungeon door splintering.

I traced the sharp outline of the needle in my pocket; Kallis had half inched it for me, all overexcited in spy mode, from the research department.

'Say, there's nobody here,' I heard Harford's bewildered call.

Hartford was hesitating in the heart of the dungeon, his feet almost touching the cage, which I'd hidden in from the CIE bint: he was transfixed by the rack. He was making these frightened panting gasps, so like the ones Plantagenet had made when Blake had discovered Plantagenet in their bed with Sun, that I had to steady myself.

I could do this.

I had to bleeding well do this.

I tried to give a reassuring smile, as I sidled closer. 'Don't look at the rack. Sometimes things happen; we don't want them to, but they do. I'm sorry, I wish I'd been better, that's all.'

'What's all this baloney? And where's..?'

I stabbed the needle into Hartford's neck. I pushed down, letting in the venom: Plantagenet's venom, which had been separated by Fernando in his search for an antidote.

Hartford didn't react, as if my betrayal couldn't be real.

Then – for the first time – he unleashed his full Long-lived force on me, scrabbling the needle out of his neck and shoving me back. I flew the length of the room, slamming against the wall.

Crack – there went half my ribs.

I coughed, as I bent over.

When I looked up? Hartford had slumped to the concrete, shuddering with cramps, and then collapsed onto his back, as the paralysis took hold.

When mixed together our venom bite isn't toxic to another Blood Lifer. It's that ecstasy-thrumming line between heaven and hell. Yet when it's separated to paralysis alone..? It's none of the heaven and all of the hell.

I sighed, trudging to kneel by Hartford.

Hartford's glare of hate filled accusation sliced me in two.

He was trying to speak, but the paralysis was overtaking his control, trapping him in his own body.

I leaned closer to catch his whisper and then bloody wished I hadn't, 'Double-crosser.'

I avoided Hartford's glower (the only thing he could now control), as I dragged him to the cage.

When I unlocked the cage's door – *clang* – carefully pushing Hartford in like a doll, mindful to leave his nut facing out towards the room because I remembered the crushing boredom of having nothing but wall to stare at, I noticed the slick of sweat on his forehead.

I was a git.

Because Hartford remembered that boredom too. He'd been caged – just as I had – by *Master*. The only difference was that I'd been at *Master's* mercy for only a month, whereas Hartford had copped it for years.

I'd never be able to understand everything Hartford had suffered. Yet here I was betraying him, entrapping him in his own body and caging him.

I was the leader though. And sometimes? Leaders have to make the tough decisions.

Wankering responsibility.

I slid my fingers through the bars and then through Hartford's sweat dampened hair, neatening it back into his matinee idol style. 'It'll wear off soon. I couldn't let you sacrifice yourself, and we both know you're too stubborn to... I've got a plan, but it has to be me who... I promised to rescue Donovan and I will.' I cradled Hartford's lifeless hands between mine. 'It's not goodbye or any of that nancy bollocks. But Sun has Plantagenet now, see? And Donovan has you. So if one of us has to play at hero and go out bloody..? I'm voting for me: I'm the one who won't be missed.'

...A black body bag in military bronze corridor... A tumble of blond curls...

Rivers of tears were leaking from Hartford's peepers.

Tear ducts not paralysed then.

I wiped the wet away: Hartford wouldn't be comfortable like that. Yet as fast as I tried, the tears streamed.

I gave up, pushing myself to my feet. 'Soon as you're together with Donovan? Take your fanboy – and don't pretend you don't know who I'm talking about – and go. Be wild Blood Lifers again, free in the world. Donovan can run a music business, and you're a singer: it's perfect. Find your talent and live it. I wish I could've given you that. I wish...it doesn't bleeding matter now, does it?'

And it didn't.

Every step I backed away from that cage and the motionless, weeping Hartford, who'd been silenced good and proper, I lost part of myself: family and home.

I was swallowed into the darkness.

Here's the thing though: it was my choice.

Plantagenet would always be wrong: a leader mustn't make sacrifices.

He was the sacrifice.

Plantagenet was stretched out like a panther on the bed. Except he wasn't wild. Under the Oberon green cast by the ivy screen, the moss sheets and the steel roses..?

He was an exhibit in Blake's zoo.

It was time to set him free.

Plantagenet studied me lazily, his arms crossed behind his nut, as I stalked. Then pounced.

Lips soft as I remembered, opening on a gasp. That scent and taste of ripened oranges. No fight, only surrender. Black curls coiling round my fingers. One hand slipping down the slash of his silk catsuit, questing onto golden skin. Stroking over one peaked nipple.

Plantagenet mewed, squirming under me, as if I was working his todger.

I had a quick shufti at the CCTV camera, which was winking at us from the corner, before tweaking Plantagenet's nipple again. Plantagenet pouted, as his hips worked. I leaned in, allowing myself – just once – to feel closeness of blood.

Just once.

Then I twisted Plantagenet's nipple, and as he closed his peepers caught between agony and ecstasy, I edged out the shiv from the back of my jeans.

Trinity had sworn it would do the business: small enough for a bloke to hide but deadly enough to do in a Blood Lifer. She'd bought it for Will to carry, except he'd told her that he didn't need it. Not now he had a guardian angel.

I was no bloody angel.

As I raised the blade, I wished I could shut my own peepers, so I wouldn't have to always remember this. The feel of it and the blood on my hands.

But my name was Light: I was cursed to remember. Even when the world forgot.

So I raised that blade, as Plantagenet shivered and purred his delight underneath me, and I brought it down over his chest. Into his heart.

Just enough...

Plantagenet's gold-flecked peepers flew open. Then he screamed, as his back arched feline.

I rolled away from Plantagenet, staring dumbly at the shiv sticking from the wound, which was oozing thick burgundy down the white of his catsuit.

Blood. It was staining my hands. I shook.

Death. All great stories need a death. Weren't you hoping for this?

I raised my panicked gaze to Plantagenet's. He ripped out the shank, hurling it – *clang* – against the wall. He was breathing hard, as he pressed his palm over the wound to slow the bleeding.

'We talked about this,' I rushed to explain.

Christ, I felt like a wanker.

'Indeed?'

'Realistic, yeah? So when I show those Blood Lifer tossers the CCTV recording... They'd see through anything staged; we just have to edit it right. Now I can hand them me taking out the head of the Renegades; it gets me in.'

'Was it truly needful to bed me? May you not, well-beloved, have murdered me over cake?' Plantagenet whimpered, as he pulled himself up. I winced, knowing what it was like to have holes carved into you; when I'd been a slave, *Sir* had made sure of that.

'Hartford was about to sacrifice himself like the daft – heroic – berk he is,' I shrugged. 'I had to stuff him in the cage downstairs. He'll be furious when... I just wouldn't get into any more barnies with him because I wouldn't figure on you winning.'

'Still,' Plantagenet beckoned me closer. Reluctantly, I slid across the bed. You shank a Magnificoe? You're a dim pillock if you accept an invitation to see how big his teeth are. 'You tease and torment me, playing at my lover. You hold me down, as if you wish to do the deed of darkness. But instead, traitor? You hurt me, thus...' He held out his bloody hands to me.

'Put like that? It does sound bad.'

'In faith, it makes me wonder: do you love me? Or merely Hartford and Donovan?' Plantagenet traced a crimson trail down my cheek: a flaming brand. 'Would you betray us – the Renegades – if thou had to choose a side? Villainy of shame! I see the answer writ upon your face.'

'Weren't you the one who told me there were different loves? I don't have to choose. That's the point.'

'Wrong, I'm afraid.' Blake was leaning in the doorway, his mouth set in a tight line. He was examining Plantagenet's injured form, like he was only stopping himself from sweeping him up into his arms damsel-like by an iron will. 'Loyalty: it's the key skill essential to be employed at RE. No one gets in without it.'

'Lucky I'm not applying then.'

When Sun slunk into the bedroom, I smiled. She avoided my eye, however, slicing her fangs into her wrist, before offering the snaking scarlet to Plantagenet, who eagerly suckled.

I bristled, but Sun cut me off before I could protest. 'Ya huh! You didn't offer to help Plantagenet, even though you hurt him. I haven't forgotten a word you wrote in your journal. How Hartford and Donovan fed you from their wrists, when you were starving. We bleed for our frickin' family.'

Sun was right. Plantagenet was right.

Hartford and Donovan were mine to care for: my misfit family forged through slavery. After what we'd been through together?

They'd always come first.

So what could I possibly say?

I straightened my shoulders. 'Let's murder you. Deliver me to the Blood Life Council. And sodding save the day.'

Let me clarify: you intended to trick us? The entire Blood Life Council?

That's about the long and short of it.

Did you truly believe we'd be taken in by that CCTV footage? That we wouldn't also demand a body? Habeas corpus?

Bless you. You'd be gobsmacked what folks are tricked by: smoke and mirrors. We only needed enough evidence to get me in the door long enough to free Donovan.

But instead they double-crossed you, pretending *you* were the Renegades' leader..?

No need to rub it in. See what happens when you're not a team player?

Betrayal. It seems to haunt you, Light.

Or I haunt it. Either way, I'm the one in this Red Room, whilst you scribble down my witness. What I can't figure? Why didn't you let Donovan go?

Come now, did you truly believe we would?

So what happens if...when I die? To Donovan?

When...if you die..?

Captain will have two pets.

NIGHT 13

I'm sorry, Light, they were meant to walk you down a different way; you shouldn't have seen...

The bonfire? All that wood stacked up below in the courtyard, with the stake to tie me to, ready to burn the heretic?

Pull the other one; you wanted to put the fear of hell in me (or the Witchfinder Captain did), before the trial tomorrow. You've arranged an Easter to remember, with me blubbering out my guts today.

Did it work?

Here's your answer...except the two-finger salute works better when you *have* two fingers.

Good god, what happened?

Captain promised you wouldn't be hurt anymore; this is *my* opportunity to employ *my* methods. Torture is never effective at

**burrowing underneath the skin because
ultimately we'll all say anything – the lies
mixed in with the truth – to make the pain
stop.**

**Yet we all crave to tell our story. To be
heard and seen. There's power in words. I
weave them, without the crudity of pain.**

I don't even have to touch my--

Victims?

And they don't touch you, right? That's a cold
way to live.

Still, they die the same, don't they? Once you've
wormed under their skins, flaying them bare.
They're punished, the same as if you lit the match.

What happens after is not within--

Don't say your bleeding remit. We're
responsible for every moment we live. If you tear a
bloke apart - his secrets, weaknesses and guilt -
then you don't stand back, wash your hands
Pontius-like and call what comes after *justice*.

Right now? You're a cog in a machine, which is
grinding down the rest of the Blood Lifer world.
What's worse? When pure death is developed, it'll
be the First Lifers caught in its gears.

But I'm just a cog. How do I..?

We both know you're not *just* anything. It only
takes one cog to stop turning for the whole machine
to stop working: that's how revolutions start.

**I'm not one of your Renegades, Mr
Blickle.**

You're not Captain's puppet either...or his cog.

So tell me, how were your fingers burnt?

A reward.

Because here's the thing: when we chinwagged
about your sister? You never told me you had a
brother.

Black.

Banshee panic echoed through my mind so loudly I didn't know if I was hollering or only on the inside. My chest was sticky with blood from my torn fingernails; I'd scrabbled at the wood every day. A terror-stricken *let me out, let me out, let me out*...

A waking nightmare flashback to my slave days.

Swaggering bravado? It lasted just as long as it took for the lid to be nailed down.

I bet Captain had a right laugh. Or gloat: he was the sort to gloat listening to another bloke reduced like that because he'd never been broken. A beta like him?

I'd have given Captain a day tops in *Master's* hands.

Then I heard the sound, which was like angelic choirs: nails being ripped out.

The coffin lid slid across. I blinked against the heavenly blue, shivering at the sudden rush of frozen air.

'Diddums, he's cold. Maybe you can warm him up?'

Two mugs appraising me, as if I was the latest toy.

Captain's hand resting on the shoulder of...

Buggering hell – *Emo*.

I banged my nut against the bottom of the coffin; maybe I could knock myself out.

Captain chortled. 'Look how pleased he is to see you.'

When Emo leant over the coffin, his stripy scarf tickled my nose. 'He's mine?'

'You were such a good boy watching him and reporting back. I knew you could be motivated. You simply needed the right reward system.'

'Gold stars didn't work then?' I tried to clamber out of the coffin, but Captain slammed me back.

'Donovan could be substituted if..? No? Well, I have grownup's work now; you know how it is...'

'You're not leaving me alone with that psycho?'

Captain's hand clamped over my mouth and nose.

I flailed, as my peepers flew wide open, and my lungs speared sharply dissonant in agonizing bursts.

'That *psycho*?' Captain whispered; his mush was inches from mine. 'Is my elected, a karate champion and *your* owner for the next hour. You really do have authority issues, don't you?' At last, he lifted his hand.

I took a deep lungful of air and then another; I'd never reckoned breathing a privilege before.

'Just remember,' Captain straightened, before tapping Emo on the shoulder, 'no killing.' Emo's black rimmed peepers were so puppy-dog, you'd have reckoned his daddy had just forbidden him from texting his mates. 'But torture? Well,' Captain spread his hands expansively, 'it is your reward...'

When Captain met my gaze, his look was considering. Then he turned on his heel and he was gone.

Reluctantly, I had a gander at Emo, who was assessing me like he was deciding which limb to hack off first.

'Captain's your Author then? You work for him?'

Emo flicked his green fringe. 'Work for myself. Do what I like.'

'Didn't sound like it.'

Emo scowled. 'What does he know? He's old and stuff. After all, didn't tell anyone, did I? Didn't tell them about the kid.'

I hardly dared breathe – Captain might as well have still had his hand over my gob. 'Why's that then?'

'Told you: I work for myself. Keep my own secrets.' Emo ducked down.

I forced myself to remain motionless, when I heard rummaging, followed by the clinical *snap* of gloves being pulled on.

Nothing good has ever come of that *snap* sound.

And I should know.

When Emo loomed over me in thick black rubber gloves, clutching a metal tube with a look of intense concentration, I shrank back.

'When they burn you, how will we know what it feels like?' Emo traced one rubbery finger down my chest, all the way to my stomach and then up again, before crossing from nipple to nipple. I fought to keep my breath steady. 'Captain promises I can watch Easter night, when you go up like a candle. I told them: burn him slowly or wet the wood. Then we can make him tell us: how it feels as first his feet, then his legs, dick, guts, chest and arms burn.' I shuddered, when Emo slid his gloved fingers through my hair. 'Even as your head flamed – before your tongue melted – you could've screamed. Something.' Emo pulled back sulkily. 'They said no. The Council. Tradition and that.'

'Bloody shame,' I forced out through dry lips.

'But Captain said I could burn you now. That will still hurt, won't it?'

Emo scooped gooey paste out of a metal tube, before painting it down the path he'd traced on me – a cross down the center.

It was sodding cold.

Christ in heaven – white phosphorous.

If that ignited..? I was about to become sodding hot.

I watched, as Emo slipped his hand into his hoodie pocket. He smirked, pulling out long matches slow inch by slow inch, like a striptease.

I never reckoned I'd be frightened to look into the fire. Yet I'd never been seared by white phosphorous before.

This brat could learn about my pain, but he wouldn't learn about my fear. Instead, he'd get a lesson in how a bloke faced the flames.

'I don't smoke anymore but thanks for offering.'

Emo's smirk faltered. Immediately, he struck the match: a beautiful white flare. We were united by its fragile power. The heartbeat moment.

Then Emo held the match to the phosphorous...and I screamed.

White fire. A flaming cross. Searing agony, larger than me or the world. Bubbling, blistering and bathing me in blinding agony.

The fire burned out, sizzling down into a pattern of red scars. But the pain? It had burrowed so deeply under the skin that I didn't know how to free myself.

Emo had marked me.

Through my blurred peepers, all I could see was Emo's winged cartoon vampire, mocking me, as he asked, 'How does that feel?'

I shakily raised my hand in the two-finger salute, only to have the sadist in training clutch the fingers in his phosphorous smeared hand.

No way was I losing my swearing hand...

I tried to wrench back, but Emo had already flared the match to life and...

White fire.

And this time? Emo made me sing sounds I didn't even know I could make.

Emo scrutinized me, as I cradled my burnt hand. 'How does that feel? We have a whole hour to play. If you don't want to talk...'

'Maybe,' I forced out, as I shook from the shock of the sudden burns, and my whole body shut down, 'you should try out these fun games on yourself? Then you'd really know how it sodding felt.'

Emo tilted his nut, as if actually considering it. 'Did. Used to. Daddy said no more.'

'Daddy?' I hissed, as my skin split raw. 'We talking First or Blood Life?'

'We're talking dead. He wouldn't let me join the Black Parade, but Captain would.'

'And that's what this is?'

Deluded kid.

'Dunno. I can't feel. Anything. I think I'm dead. I'm everything I ever wanted to be. Powerful. Free. Only,' a crushing sadness swept across Emo's mush in one single lightning flash, 'you can't see the scars anymore. They always heal now, but I can see them on others when I make them pretty.'

My insides curled black.

That was why you didn't author kids.

In the '60s my best – and only – mate had been a kid. Alessandro. Trapped in a twilight world between First and Blood Life, he'd been controlled. Never allowed to grow up, no matter how many decades he lived. Never allowed to witness the glories of the world. Election amplifies emotions and hormonal teenagers aren't exactly known for handling those well. It botched the process.

No wonder this bastard was off his trolley.

I'd been blinkered to consider authoring Will. Deluded myself to reckon it'd be different.

I was making a piss poor attempt at redemption.

Yet love – in all its forms – will put out your peepers, until you're stumbling in the black.

Even though cringing agony was still washing over me in waves, I had a shufti at the kid, who'd never known anything of Blood Life but Captain, in his fanged vampire t-shirt and black-and-green fringe, which he hid behind.

I was shot through with hot shame that I didn't even know his name. 'So what do they call you?'

Emo shrugged. 'Who cares?'

'Power to a name.'

Emo considered this; his phosphorous gloved hand hovered dangerously close to my goolies. 'Blink. Does it help to know what to scream?'

'Helps if we're having a chinwag to know what to call a bloke.'

'*Rebel?*' That *sneer* again. 'I'm the true rebel 'cos you're all wrong: the Council, Government and Renegades. There's no such thing as rules. Family. Home. Only what you want. What you can take. I don't need anyone: there's just me. You shouldn't fear each other.' Emo bent closer, as fanatical as Plantagenet. 'You should fear *me*.'

Blink seized my blistered hand, bending the two scorched fingers – *snap*.

I howled.

'Now - how does that feel?'

You need blood to heal. I'll call Pet.

Is that the guilt talking?

The trial's tomorrow; you must look your most presentable.

That's like a soldier donning his best uniform for the firing squad, isn't it? Or fattening the calf for slaughter?

Wouldn't you be whole when you face the flames?

I haven't been whole for donkey's years, either on the outside or the in.

Reckon I'm one to go quietly with bastard death? When you tie me to that stake tomorrow I won't stop fighting, until the flames have ghosted me to ashes.

If I doubted that, do you think I'd have listened to you? Believed you? Conspired with you?

Conspired?

There's a flaw in all leaders.

All men.

They believe only *they* can change the world. So they overlook the women who work, live and love at their shoulders.

Ruby, Kathy, Grayse, Sun...even Mother. You don't reckon I can see their talents, power and danger?

You forgot one. My name is Liberty. And there's power in a name.

I'll ask again. Who the bloody hell are you?

Drink first. Slice a main artery on Pet, we can stich up after; you need the blood.

I bloody well won't. Scars don't heal on First Lifers: he's not Blink.

Who is he that you care?

A human. Haven't you been following? Sometimes they're prey, sometimes predator. But never my dinner.

Not unless they want to be.

Delusion. It's most self-serving.

Do you honestly believe the homeless living under London Bridge *wanted* **to be consumed? Money. You despise, belittle and bewail it but yet you steal? You use it to acquire your needs or influence.**

Never said I was consistent.

Even with Will. Coffee – wasn't it? Your very first gift. Do you think he'd have noticed you, if you'd possessed as little as he..?

Pet, if you raise your gaze one more time, I'll have you sent to Blink again for the night. He told me he'd *felt* **the most after his time with you, since he'd been authored. I was overjoyed.**

That's dead heartwarming. I've had my fill; Pet, you can go now.

How about you tell me Blink's secrets? The ones he was holding back from our Author.

I don't have the foggiest, sweetheart.

They were about the kid. Come on, if you move your pawn, I shall move mine.

How about you play with your brother instead? I was never one for chess.

We've been playing chess since the first night. We have your file: every strength and weakness. I've analyzed you: you're mine.

Another wanker wanting to own me? Now there's a turn-up for the books.

Listen, Mr Blickle--

How about you listen – *Jade Spider* – because let's cut the bollocks.

You were never here to help or save me. It's not been about truth or witness.

All this time you've been waiting, listening and spinning your web. Knowing I was condemning myself to death with my own words. And what's worse? Condemning my family too.

And what have you been doing, Light, if not spinning webs?

Me and you? We're the same. You play with words, just the same as I do.

The difference is, you bint, there's no fire with your name writ large on it at the center of my web.

So what is there? At the center?

That'd be telling.

Secrets – you're seeped in them.

And you're seeped in betrayal. I told you all great stories start with it.

Then death and hope. Do they come tomorrow?

You tell me. Except don't waste your breath because how would I trust you?

I'm the best at what I do. Trust? Isn't high on my agenda.

I've always had such green eyes; my mum said they were like *jade*. When I became a barrister… Everyone's frightened of spiders, but it's only the fly which needs fear.

The Blood Life Council understand that.

Bigger bleeding picture here than the Blood Life Council versus us Renegades. If the power of our venom's abused..?

Yet every tosser's shifting his feet like it's somebody else's responsibility. That's how wars tear worlds apart.

We could hide. I've tried it. But then our safety wouldn't be real.

Some bugger or other would use us as slaves, weapons or products. We're not safe in the shadows.

We have to step into the light.

What have you done?

What your Council should've, if it'd had the balls.

This Red Room? The guns? Captains bluster? It's all a screen for dramatic effect. The scenery in a play.

The real, raw power beneath? Quiet. Unassuming. Deadly.

Is me.

When – precisely – are you planning to scuttle onto the stage?

When I've spun a nest large enough to cage it – and no one can escape.

This inquiry is my chance; I warned you at the beginning.

Wait... Why am I getting..? This is outrageous...

Problem, sweetheart?

You don't play chess?

I stick to saving the world.

Why is Captain repeatedly messaging me about a disturbance on London Bridge? A...march?

What in god's name is this?

That's the bloody cavalry.

NIGHT 14

I should be dead. I reckoned I would be. Two weeks ago? I'd have bet money on it: I was a dead man talking.

Yet life's funny sometimes, or maybe nothing's ever as simple as you think.

And I'm to believe you now? Why would that be, Light?

Because I'm here of my own freewill. Because every inquiry needs a conclusion. Because you and me? We're the most unholy alliance of them all.

I'd have booted my own arse, if I'd even thought about joining forces with the Blood Life Council back in the day. But look at me now.

Here's the thing: you adapt to survive – and I'm not ready for extinction.

***Dramatic buggery*, don't you think?**

Pure death sorted then? All records destroyed? I didn't think so.

Dramatic doesn't even come close. With that CIE bint still in charge..? This is the beginning, not the end.

Tell me a story then this Easter night. Make me believe.

It all started with simulated skin blood packets – miniature affairs – that could be taped over the heart. You'd be gobsmacked at the river of blood, which comes out of one of them, when a shiv gets rammed through. Still, I'd had to burrow the blade deep enough to get the right reaction from Plantagenet – he wasn't *that* good an actor.

I'll never forget the flash of pain and hurt in those amber peepers.

As I said, Plantagenet is no Laurence Olivier, because in those moments when our lips had met..? The poor git had forgotten the caper, lost in the touch, taste and love.

Plantagenet was the one, however, who always insisted a leader had to sacrifice: he was right. Except the difference was, I reckoned a leader should give their own blood and flesh.

Bleed for their people.

And this time?

As Plantagenet had lain beneath me, still hard and panting, and so bloody broken?

I'd known it was Plantagenet who was bleeding out.

Of course, after the staged death, came the betrayal.

'My goodness, he truly was listening. I'd have owned your fangs before now, if I'd realised how useful you could be.' Captain arched his hands on the ebony desk, in his regimented front office, which was flanked by steel filing cabinets. Stress relief toys were lined like legal crack for executives across his desk: the sun yellow ball with smiley face was taking the piss. Everything smelled of new carpets and bureaucracy.

'I can even sing the alphabet,' the yellow face was freaking me out, 'backwards.'

'Precious. The thing I like best? I can make you sing anything I like.' Captain snatched up a bendy man from his row of toys, fiddling with its legs. 'Time is money you know; the Council doesn't run itself. So..?'

'Give over: you don't run it either. Far scarier bastards than you fucked or fanged their way to the top.'

There went bendy man's arms, as Captain twisted them all the way behind his back.

Captain gestured at the black masked freaks with their guns at my elbows. What did they reckon I was going to do? Make a run for it through the office's high glass windows into the sun?

A colossus nudged me with a shooter's snout: like I needed it spelling out. Or another bullet hole.

'He still thinks he can act the hard man: how sweet. I shall endeavor to find a solution for that. I'm ever so good at taking down fellows, who consider they can simply swagger through Blood Life like they did their First: as if they're legends. Is that what you believe, *Our Light*?'

Uncomfortable, I looked down. 'I don't believe in legends or myths.'

'Excellent,' Captain slammed his brown brogues – *bang, bang* – onto the shiny surface of the desk; the smiling yellow face rolled off, bouncing until it stopped against my foot, 'because I make it my duty to slay legends. I cut them down to size. Too long have the old dominated; now I reduce mythic Blood Lifers from ancient bloodlines to sniveling cry-babies. Just like your file shows you broke when you were a slave. Would you enjoy being broken the same way again?'

I fought to keep my breath steady. I slouched, as I stuck my hands into the pockets of my leather jacket. 'I'm not a masochist, mate. Don't add me into this new world of yours. You came smashing into our lives; we were simply getting on with it. Staying in the shadows. We were hidden from...everything. No one saw us. Then you kidnap my family and send me on a mission to find the leader of the Renegades or do them in. So – job done.' I started to slide out the disk from my pocket but then I heard fingers easing onto triggers. 'How much of a daft berk do you reckon I am?'

Captain gave a smug smile, before gesturing to his guard dogs.

Click – I breathed out.

Captain waved me towards him, but instead I chucked the disk at his nut.

Captain fumbled, dropping the disk onto his lap.

I chuckled – for about three seconds – before Captain signed for his minion to punch my lip bloody.

I licked my lip and then chuckled again.

Snap – there went Mr Bendy Man's neck. Captain hurled it against my chest, as if his toy's death was my fault. Captain smoothed his hair, before slipping the disk into his computer. Then he pulled a face. 'Sweets, if I wished to watch your homemade porn, then I'd...' Suddenly he peered at the screen with comical urgency. '*Plantagenet*? You're doing that with Plantagenet?'

'Hope so, else I was truly bladdered and went home with a stranger by mistake.'

Captain's leather chair squeaked, as he shoved himself up. 'Let me make myself clear: are you in bed with the Magnificoe of your bloodline?'

Something was off here: it was shadowed in my memory. Something Captain had once said about Plantagenet – or the bloodline.

'Why's that a surprise? He was a slave.'

'I was not aware.'

I frowned. I'd been right that there were scarier bastards than Captain – and they'd been the ones to hand over Plantagenet to Blake. The CIE bint had called Plantagenet *tribute* from the Magnificoes, but where had Plantagenet been before that?

Ruby had kept her family from me until the '60s, and by then Plantagenet had been gone. Just how long had he been missing?

Captain had his nose pressed close to the computer screen; he was entranced. I didn't blame him; Plantagenet had that effect. 'I've only heard descriptions,' Captain breathed, 'but none do Plantagenet justice. I must have him. He'd be the greatest legend of them all; so beautiful when he broke.'

I was cold all over. 'Shame that. You're too late.'

Captain's gaze flicked to me, confused. Then he saw the tiny me on screen raise the shank above the unwitting Plantagenet.

'No!' Captain shook the computer, like he could stop past me, flopping back into the leather seat in shock, as Plantagenet's scream echoed tinny, and the blood spurted.

Captain turned an appalled look on me, as if I'd just stomped on a butterfly. I guess I had. 'What did you do?'

'One leader of the Renegades: dead or alive. That was it, right?'

'He was..?' Captain shook his nut, as if clearing it of monstrous thoughts. You wouldn't guess the bloke had noshed his way through his entire family.

'First I got grabbed and tested on at these research labs. Then I'm rescued; it turns out by the Renegades. Plantagenet? He's their leader. Now I've kept my side of your blackmail, so you give me Donovan, and we'll be on our way.'

Captain considered me, steepling his fingers. 'Why? What does this prove? Except you're a murderer: I already knew you're a yob, and your files detail your penchant for familicide--'

'Not exactly a penchant...'

'But this latest? A Magnificoe? You'll be answering to the Order of Electors over Plantagenet's death. They're hardly in the twentieth century, let alone the twenty-first. They have no place in our future, but one thing I'll say for them: they will make you regret this. I only wish I could be the one to ensure that regret.'

I shrugged. 'If wishes were horses, then beggars would ride.'

Captain lunged over the table. Security held me still by my arms.

Fair fight, then?

I tensed, but Captain's Blackberry beeped. He paused mid blow to search through his messages.

Then Captain's mush lit up. He tucked the Blackberry back in the pocket of his cargo trousers, before forcing open my gob and tracing over my teeth...one...at...a...time.

No way was I letting Captain defile my fangs again.

'Three guesses who that was?'

'Prince Harry?' I garbled through his fingers, 'Adele? Robert Pattinson?'

Captain wrenched his hand out of my mouth and slapped me hard across the cheek. 'Wrong. It was a ghost.'

'Didn't reckon you believed in all that.'

'I'm a convert – since Plantagenet messaged me and sent evidence *you're* the Renegades' leader.'

'You're lying.'

'Maybe. It seems, however, that someone has betrayed you – *Renegade*. Oh joy! Now I get to break you again and I was so worried I'd have to restrain myself.' Captain placed his hand – almost tenderly – over the print, with which he'd marked me. 'I shall burn you. But first? Will come the dark.'

You gave yourself up to him? To us? Sacrificed yourself with a staged betrayal?

There was no Judas?

Got it in one.

Why? Such absurd--

Risk?

Stupidity.

You must've known Captain hated you more than most other Blood Lifers. I've heard the tale many times of your first encounter: how you cost him a fang. He believed you to be the worst of the posturing old bloodlines, suited only to be swept away.

And he's tried now: twice. I'm still here. All that? It's why I was perfect.

The CCTV of Plantagenet's death would only get Captain's attention, and me into his office. I needed something, which would excite him. Then he'd let down his guard, allowing me beyond into the heart of the Council.

Into the Red Room.

And that *something*?

Was me.

The Red Room's not most men's idea of entertainment. I understand that Donovan's here too, but being trapped with him..?

Captain wouldn't be able to help himself once he had me as a shiny new toy: he'd play with me, make an example out of me, and then break me to pieces.

In here - with you.

The Jade Spider.

Me?

You reckon I'm so daft I didn't always know?

But why am I..? You can't possibly have planned this whole rescue around me?

Power behind the throne: isn't that what you were singing before? A bloke like Captain could never run a joint like this, not without serious backup.

The only thing I had to figure was whether you'd step out from behind the throne...and help us.

'Why is Captain repeatedly messaging me about a disturbance on London Bridge? A...march? What in God's name is this? '

Liberty was gnawing on her long brunette fringe like it was some poor bastard's jugular; that was one of her many tells. The bint didn't reckon she had any, hiding behind a mask of cold efficiency, but I'd have cleaned her out at poker.

Liberty lobbed her Blackberry into her briefcase, along with copies of that night's inquiry, before clicking it shut; the *click* was harsh in the hard shell of the Red Room.

I fought to keep my expression blank and still my tapping foot. Because tells?

Yeah, I had them too.

I swallowed, as hope unfurled its moth wings, fluttering in my guts.

Don't let her cotton on yet...just a little longer...

Liberty's jade peepers were assessing. She didn't even need to speak to strip layers from my hide to wear as pretty looped necklaces.

Crimson. Scarlet. Red, red, red.

Every moment in that bleeding womb with Liberty, I'd been suffocated. Secrets Pied Piper danced from my tongue; I'd drowned in her.

I'd been fighting for my life with every word – every breath. From the very first night.

There's a reason we fear spiders.

Suddenly pounding footsteps outside. The door yanked open. Womb torn bloody.

My cue.

I leapt over the desk, gripping Liberty around the neck.

Liberty had some balls though because she did nothing more than lean back, as if knowing I'd wanted a final, private word, allowing me to whisper, *'That's the bloody cavalry.'*

Then there were hands clutching, hurting, ripping me away and slamming me against the wall, followed by a fist raised to smash across my mug. I glared Captain in the eye because this time when he duffed me up, it wouldn't be in the dark, at gunpoint or through his elected.

Captain wanted to hurt me?

Let him be Blood Lifer enough to use his own fangs and fists.

The blow, however, never landed; Liberty had caught it.

Captain stared at her neat hand encircling his fist; his mug swelling with childish outrage to match the colour of the walls. 'Liberty, will you allow me to...chastise the prisoner?'

Liberty squeezed.

Captain yowled, hunched over. When Liberty dropped his hand, he shook it, before hugging it under his armpit.

'This is my room,' Liberty smoothed down her black wool suit. 'My rules. No violence, remember?'

'No violence?' Captain held out his bruised hand beseechingly; I only wished she'd snapped off two of his fingers.

Liberty smiled slowly. 'Except by me. Especially when my inquiry session is interrupted on the final night before trial. It's terribly irregular.'

'Shall I show you *irregular*?'

Captain snatched me by the scruff of the neck, hauling me out into the busy Council offices. I could sense Liberty behind: a strong, quiet presence.

It made the hairs on the back of my neck rise.

Out here? It was bloody pandemonium.

Blood and First Lifers alike were rushing from office to office with the *slam* of doors, as if they were the ones set to be burned alive. Everywhere laptops, TV screens and iPhones blared out scrolling news.

I craned to see, but Captain dragged me on. I could earwig on snatches of conversation though... *They've closed it all... He's furious; they say he'll eviscerate... Anarchy...*

I couldn't stop the grin: until Captain smashed me into the window.

The vast window, along the corridor to the heavenly blue room: witness to my weeks of dark and fire-scarred torture. Blink's reward and Captain's toy. A legend to be broken.

Now crushed against that glass, I looked out at the black jagged skyline and the cruel bright stars infinite above.

I heard Liberty's sharp intake of breath behind me.

I wasn't broken: I was legendary.

My name was Our Light: leader of Light's Renegades.

And this was it – my rebellion.

Welcome to the Rebel Age.

You were waiting for the hope, weren't you? And like all the greatest stories, it always comes at the end.

There was no traffic on London Bridge *because the Renegades had come to take me home.* There were no black cabs or taxis honking, as motorcyclists weaved between. No drably suited businessmen staggering tense and cocaine-eyed from the strip clubs and brothels. No pickpockets, junkies or bladdered clubbers with cheesy chips and kebabs.

Nobody.

Except my new family.

Trinity swaggered at the head of her First Lifer crew, mutt proud at her heels. The homeless from beneath the bridge liberated for one night to walk magnificent on top of it. They clutched torches, large and small; the arcs of light swung angelic, burning across the hell red bleeding beneath the bridge.

Kids, veterans, single mums and smackheads. It didn't matter. They'd all donated blood to us Blood Lifers.

Me.

They were loyal to Trinity, and she'd voted in on the rebellion.

The first of my alliances. The second?

Aedan sauntered next to Trinity. He'd dressed for the occasion in a sharp russet suit, which matched his swinging braids. Trinity kept shooting him these glances, when he clung to her arm in excitement.

Yeah, not figuring on them plaiting each other's hair in a girlie night any time soon.

Alongside Aedan?

The Lost Boys from Peter Pan's – my Lost Boys now. Except from the moment we'd started working there, they'd been *ours* because Hartford had needed that. A new tribe to save and care for.

I caught a flash of Brendan's neon green hair in the throng; Kyle's determined mush was next to him. Even tiny Jamie.

Behind the dancers came the third alliance: Kallis and the Renegades.

They wore slogan t-shirts, with their declarations blown-up onto placards.

REBEL HERE, YEAH?

I'M THE BLOODY SUPERHERO.

YOU CAN'T FLAY A REBEL'S SOUL.

They waved the placards like grenades, as at their shoulders stalked the Blood Lifer slaves they'd rescued.

Alliance number four.

Mother led the Blood Lifers – if swaying from one to the other, licking and pawing was leading – dangerously in her element.

An army of tamed Blood Lifers? I shivered with anticipation.

I'd felt alone for so long – unloved. But here. Together?

Yeah, I wasn't alone.

Because at the heart of the march was my infuriating, damaged, confusing family.

I knew they didn't – couldn't – love like I did. Maybe we all love to different degrees. I crave every ounce of love squeezed dry because I give every drop myself. But try and hate them as I did?

I loved them.

Because there they were, riding to my rescue. They were the true heroes.

They were my home.

Sun and Plantagenet were grasping onto each other's hands like brother and sister on the first day of school: except I knew they were more than that. It was lovers marching to war, each afraid for the other. Maybe? They were thinking of me too. Maybe? They wished they were also holding *my* hand.

Fellah's got to hope.

I had to take a second gander at Plantagenet.

Gone was that wankering white silk catsuit – the symbol of his slavery. He'd been transformed to the original Blood Lifer, and the bloke had style. A billowing ivory shirt over tight black trousers, with RAF leather coat to the bottom of his patent knee-high boots.

That was one cracking coat.

It was Hartford, however, glorious in cream linen suit and Long-lived radiance, who led the army. Even I quailed at his expression, as he swept along the center of London Bridge.

Hartford's gaze raised to the Blood Life Council offices, never wavering. I wondered if he could see me. For a mad moment, I considered waving. Then I remembered the needle, venom...and the cage.

He couldn't still be narked.

I studied the fire blazing in Hartford's peepers.

He bleeding could be.

Yet even after I'd taken Hartford's place on the pyre, he was here. With the courage to stand up and lead First and Blood Lifer alike.

Hartford stopped at the edge of the bridge; his gaze was still locked onto mine. I shook at its intensity. Then he nodded to Plantagenet.

Plantagenet spun in a circle, as he waved at Mother. All of a sudden, a black ripple of iPods, speakers and phones rose in the air, like machine guns at a protest.

A moment of silence, then "People Are Strange" rang out in the black in all its gothic joy. But no longer alienation because as every sod on that bridge sang along – Hartford's bittersweet tones powerful underneath – we were joined.

Every one of us.

I noticed finally what my family had done: they had their fangs out.

I laughed.

This was the twenty-first century. There were no shadows or hiding, and this was my misfit rebellion: First and Blood Life united. No guns, just song.

And fangs. Mustn't forget the bloody fangs,

We'd never be invisible – or silenced – again.

When Captain twisted my arm, I hollered. He hurled me across the corridor – *clang* – against the opposite glass. Echo and the Bunnymen rose from below, filling the narrow space and hanging between us three like a question.

I glanced down through the glass to the courtyard below.

There was the bonfire, with the stake and ropes to tie me all pretty ready to roast for Easter.

I twisted back to Captain. 'Authority issues, mate. As in, I don't accept yours. Now let Donovan and me go.'

'The insolence,' Captain's shirt was skew-whiff. He pointed at me wildly. 'You're a terrorist, a disgrace and a--'

'Music lover who also likes moonlit walks along the beach?'

Liberty guffawed and then tried to smother it.

Captain swung an outraged glance between us. 'You've broken our most fundamental rule: you've exposed us to the humans. All of them. Every Blood Lifer worth their salt will want your head. This *demonstration* is already all over the Internet.'

'It'll be viral. Like us.'

Captain stalked closer.

Liberty was simply watching – like she always did: silent and calculating.

The singing below grew louder – like an unstoppable force – as Light's Renegades advanced.

'There's a balance,' Captain blinked rapidly, 'but what you've done? It's...this is the end of the world.'

'Now that's what I call dramatic buggery. The thing about the world? Traditions, rituals and rules? They're *bollocks*. The world is changing, so we need to change with it. That's what happens: it's called life.'

'It's called *Light*. You chose this.'

'I chose to allow all humans to deal with this new reality 'cos the idea of the CIE making the decisions alone gives me the willies. Now we all know the score – First and Blood alike. And the others – the wild Blood Lifers? At least they'll get fair warning about what's coming.'

Captain bit his own lip so hard crimson beaded. He licked it away with one furious swipe of his tongue. 'I don't believe you're on the same page as us, in fact you have the delusional notion you can rewrite the entire book.'

'Sometimes a system becomes so bleeding corrupt – abuses so much power – that some poor pillock has to stand up and make it stop. Today that someone is me.' I waved towards the window. 'Oh...and several hundred others.'

Captain took one step towards me, his body vibrating from his jaunty strawberry blond peak of hair to his quivering knees. 'Your nonconformity has ceased to be cute. If I can't break a legend, do you know what I do?'

'Send it home with a pat on the head?'

'I snuff it out.'

Then Captain shoved. Not hard – for a Blood Lifer. This building, however, hadn't been designed for Blood Lifers.

Crack – the glass shattered in one long sharp line, before spiderwebbing out.

Then I was falling.

Funny how time slows, as your stomach lurches. They say your life flashes before your eyes: they're wrong. I saw only two things as I fell.

Kathy in the heather at Ilkley Moor.

And Sun.

Her cold hands between mine, as caught in a bubble between past and present, we laughed in each other's arms on Peter Pan's dancefloor, whilst "People Are Strange" played and the organ rose to its crescendo.

I lived in that moment forever – one moment stretching on for eternity.

If I was going to die, then I'd die a happy bloke.

Because now there was no doubt or *degrees*.

I was loved.

So as I fell to earth, I smiled.

Suddenly something yanked my t-shirt. *Rip* – the cotton tore but it held. Then I was being hauled back in through the window.

I stumbled onto my mush. Breathing hard –
facing second death and then life were both equally
a shock – I stared up at Liberty.

Stronger than she looked that one.

Captain turned his astonished gaze on her.
'Has the entire Council gone quite mad? I'm your
Author. You don't override my decisions--'

'I think you'll find I do.'

Liberty swept her black briefcase into Captain's
stomach. He doubled over – *oomph* - before Liberty
drove him back to the missing glass panel, as if the
briefcase was a battering ram. Captain's heels hung
precariously over the ledge.

'Liberty...precious...'

'I was never precious. None of us were.'

One push. Then Liberty let go of the briefcase.

Captain flailed backwards, windmilling into the
night's cold air; I wondered if *his* life flashed before
his eyes? I imagine it was bloody but boring.

Then Captain was plummeting, as paper copies
of the inquiry – my witness and secrets – fell like
white tears around him.

Captain screamed, when he landed impaled on
the stake in the center of the bonfire, which had
been built to burn me. He looked like a spiked
voodoo doll.

Even I winced; look what irony does to a bloke.

I shot Liberty an anxious look, as I bottom
shuffled away from the window.

Was Liberty trying to hide a grin?

Bugger that.

I shoved myself up, crossing my arms in
customary slouch. 'Trial found me innocent then?'

'You're anything but innocent. The trial's been
postponed; the judge met with an unfortunate
accident.'

One of the denim bints gestured at Liberty from the end of the corridor; I didn't blame her for keeping Liberty at arm's-length. She lobbed an iPhone at Liberty, who caught it and answered without once looking away from me, like a teacher who reckons if they do, they'll miss the culprit spraying graffiti.

'I see,' Liberty arched an eyebrow, 'Well isn't that interesting? Thank you.'

'New reality show? Spurs lost? Bloody hell, the boy band you're crushing on aren't breaking up?'

'Downstairs. It seems your Renegades have delivered a gift.' I frowned. A fortnight I'd been playing this and for the first time I was off script. 'Something wrong?'

'I just got to watch Captain staked on *my* bonfire in a sea of *my* words. Everything's tickety-boo.'

Liberty studied me narrowly. Then she nodded. 'Follow me.'

The rest of the Council was in the same palaver as the previous offices; you'd reckon an apocalypse had broken out. Word of coups spread fast in dictatorships; these toadies were fawning over Liberty like she was the new messiah.

The pine crate rested at an angle across Captain's bland office: this was the *gift*?

I stumbled to a stop in the doorway, but Liberty didn't seem to notice. '*From Your Sun Girl,*' she read from the pink Post-it note, which was stuck to the front.

I knew that crate: it was identical to the one I'd been delivered in to Grayse from Abona, when I'd been nothing but a slave picked by a slaver's daughter.

It was everything I hated and feared.

It was the dark and nightmares.

It wasn't part of the plan.

They'd been holding hands. Plantagenet and Sun. Like Sun used to hold my hand.

Please...please...don't let Sun have betrayed me. Not now. Not like this. Any way but this...

To my shock, I realised Liberty's arms were round my shoulders and she was calling my name. 'Light, Light, Light...'

Two jade – concerned - peepers were scrutinizing me.

I pushed back from Liberty, before prowling to the enemy of my peace of mind. Then I sank my nails into the soft wood and ripped.

The wood smashed against the far wall.

Blake – starkers – was struggling against the red nylon ropes at his wrists, ankles and neck.

Red nylon – nice touch that.

Blake was shouting threats through the white catsuit, which had been used to gag him.

'Shouldn't mumble; I can't make out a bleeding word,' I patted him on the cheek, before turning to Liberty with a smirk. 'One leader of the Renegades.' I pointed at Plantagenet's bio ring, which had been forced (and sodding hell did that look painful), over the purple head of Blake's cock. 'Even decorated. You want your trial still? After what's happened today on London Bridge, I'm reckoning the Council will believe a human could be our equal or more than prey.'

'Maybe,' Liberty considered me and then Blake. 'This is the bully who subjugates our kind?'

I nodded.

A cold smile crept across Liberty's mush; I shivered. 'I shall enjoy this fresh inquiry. Very much.'

Blake began to truly holler then – but not threats.

'Shh,' Liberty leant over the crate. Her finger traced Blake's lips softly, whilst her other hand..? Let's just say Blake's not a daft berk: he got the message. 'You see,' Liberty stroked Blake's hair, 'it's all in the training. Punishment and reward.'

When Liberty straightened, I caught her eye.

'Guess that's us all paid-up? How about honouring Captain's promise? Give me Donovan and let us go.'

'You'll be wanting Will too..?' Liberty's cool look was amused.

I took a step back. My arse knocked off that bastard yellow face – he bounced leering up at me.

'I *am* the Jade spider. Do you think I played no part in this game of ours? Pet was without doubt the same boy you waxed lyrical about: he could barely be without you, as you could without him. The beatings Pet took for inattention... He was lost without you.'

Crack – the edge of the ebony desk snapped under my clawed hands.

'Not helping.'

'Captain took him from the research facility, after you and the Renegades rendered it worthless. For now at least. Captain delighted in playing with humans, except they broke too fast. There were a number of young human subjects at the labs.'

That black bag?

It hadn't been Will.

In my tortured, helpless state, seeing Will and being unable to save him, I'd buried him in my grief-stricken panic.

Love - it can do funny things to a bloke and love for the First Lifer destined to be born of your fangs..?

You'd suffer torture. Die for them. Resurrect yourself just to offer the sacrifice a second time.

You'd destroy worlds.

When I'd first seen Pet and known – Christ in heaven – *my Will is alive...* Yet he was bleeding out, sliced open for *me*, and I had to drink from him..? I'd nearly blown everything.

Because family make you weak.

Instead, I'd decided to leave Will to Captain's cruelty – in the heart of the Blood Life Council – for two weeks, treating him like a stranger.

It'd seared worse than the white phosphorous.

I'd hoped Will would cotton on to the game, however, because I'd trusted him, like he trusted me.

If Captain had ever realised who Will was to me? If Blink had told him? If Liberty had grassed?

Captain truly would've *owned* me.

He could've ended the rebellion at a word.

I would give up *everything* to keep Will safe. Yet neither Blink nor Liberty had used that, and I didn't know why.

Will was a bright kid. He'd played the game, and that flamed me with pride.

I tilted my nut. 'Will's coming with me.'

'I've become fond of Pet,' Liberty brushed at her fringe, as if imagining it was Will's fingers caressing her, 'he's like a foul-mouthed cherub. I'd considered keeping him for myself, and to bleed for picky eaters – like you – as well as political leverage in our future dealings, of course.'

'You know two weeks of my darkest secrets. All I'd suffer and the extremes I'd go to for my own. Do you want to unleash that on your own head?'

Liberty backed towards the filing cabinet, as she swung the door wider. 'That's why I've decided...'

An explosion of dusty blond curls burst across the room and into my arms; Will clung so tightly I could feel his heart – *beat, beat, beat* – next to mine. His quiet sigh.

This time I hugged Will just as tightly as he held onto me.

Then Will drew back. 'Angel of Light,' he stared at me like I was sodding...life. I blinked away tears, when I noticed the tramlines of white scars down his arms. That was because of me; I'd suckled there, lapping up his blood. I'd fed on him: *I'd made him prey*. Will softly touched my cheek. 'It ain't no thing. You're safe, remember? All that matters, innit?'

Little git was trying to make me blub. I caught his wrist. 'But how..?' A green bracelet – two entwined greens knotted together in an eternal snake – was wound round his wrist. 'The wankers cut it off.'

Will smiled shyly. 'Blink gave me the threads. Been making it 'cos I done know you lost yours.' He attempted to look stern, as he slipped it off his wrist onto mine. I couldn't stop staring at it: resurrected and green against my pale skin. I'd never take it off again. 'I ain't making another.'

'I'll be sure to look after it better, little man. But Blink..? Didn't he...hasn't he been..?'

'He's my mandem. He stopped his rents from, you know...'

'Captain?'

'Blink ain't be letting him hurt me, least not when he was there. The thing about Blink? He just never gets how things feel. So I tell him how the world don't feel so bad. We be tight now.'

'Good for you.' I wondered if I was allowed to veto Will's mates from now on.

I slipped my arm around Will's waist, and he let me, as I steered him towards the door. When he didn't even comment on the starkers bloke in the box, I felt a twinge of guilt.

I guess Will had seen a lot worse behind the scenes in the Blood Life Council.

When I'd first noticed Will, I'd reckoned him innocent but then I'd learnt his innocence had long been stolen from him. Now? Because I'd hunted him, drawing him into our Blood Lifer world, he'd never know anything but darkness.

After tonight's protest on London Bridge, however, *nor would the rest of the world.*

'You ain't no bad man,' Will nestled closer. 'You know, from the song? Blink lent me his iPod so I could... I listened to our song every night. It was like we were together. I knew you were coming for me.'

'Because it's what angels do?'

"Cos it's what true fam...*our* fam do. And that be shabby, man.'

All those days I'd been desperate to speak *one word* alone – away from Liberty and the cameras – to let Will in on the caper: so he knew he wasn't abandoned. And all that time? He'd had faith in me – more faith than I'd ever had in any one in Blood Life.

Christ I hoped I could live up to it; I was bleeding well going to try.

Donovan sauntered to join us at the wide foyer doors. He was resplendent in a purple velvet suit; Liberty must've planned that too. I suddenly wondered if the only reason Plantagenet had ever fancied Blake was because of his choice in threads. Blake had been nothing more than a wretched substitute for his lost love: Donovan.

Except Donovan wasn't lost now; he was coming home.

It was hostage release day.

Hartford – *my* angel leading the rebellion, who was ready to martyr himself for Donovan, was waiting out there...along with the bloke's greatest love.

'Alright?' I bumped Donovan's shoulder. He grinned, as he bumped mine back.

'Let's split; this scene has been a drag.'

'Couldn't have said it better myself.'

I grasped Will's hand on one side, Donovan's on the other, and we strolled out of those glass doors to the fanfare of Echo and the Bunnyman and the whirr of news helicopters above, which were like furious fireflies, towards a sea of faces, as if candlelit at an Easter Vigil.

Blood Lifers thronged amongst the First: predator and prey. I tightened my hold on Will. And for the first time? I realised what I'd done.

I'd cracked the world to save my family.

I didn't have a scooby what came next.

Yet after a fortnight trapped in artificial red and blue – worse coffin black – I stared up at the silent stars; their infinite freedom reached as far as any bloke could dream. Then I roared with a predator's victory: we'd done it.

We'd only sodding done it.

When Hartford saw me, a spark of rage blazed across his mush (so no hope the venom and cage had been forgiven and forgotten then), but fizzled out the second he clocked Donovan at my side.

A cream blur – then Donovan was swept up in Hartford's arms. Hartford's voice burst loud in joyful song, as he spun him round in the Charleston. Donovan laughed, clinging to Hartford.

They'd both been brought back to life; it was never the blood but love. Inside Abona? As slaves they'd needed each other. Out here? They needed each other just as much.

Icy fingers slipped around me from behind, teasing up my t-shirt and sliding over my shivering skin. They edged down towards my jeans, slithering under. I yipped.

'The frickin' fried thing? I forgot. It was, like, the new power, scents, drives and sensations were making me into someone different. It was wicked frightening to lose everything and feel changed: a whole notha species. I got confused on account of I love Plantagenet too. But I forgot,' Sun nibbled my ear, her teeth drawing blood, but on my gasp, licking over the marks, 'I'm still your Sun Girl, and that's my choice.'

I hadn't reckoned on hearing that again. Not said in that way. Not from Sun.

I could've danced – like Hartford and Donovan – right there in front of the Council's glistening glass monstrosity. I beamed. 'Still waiting to be scooped here.'

Sun dragged me round so fast and hard, I was pulled off my feet; I was flying. She was cradling my cheeks, like she was terrified I'd slip away – or fight her. But she'd already conquered me.

I was nobody's slave, yet I belonged to Sun, even if she'd never be mine.

Then Sun was snogging the life from me.

At once I was back in the bubble, which had embraced me as I'd fallen – caught in Sun's arms in Peter Pan's. My perfect moment for eternity. I didn't know where fantasy ended and reality started.

Until I felt a tug and realised I was still holding Will's hand.

'Work that nice!' Will winked.

I struggled to untangle my tongue from Sun's. Then tug my lips back. Her hands still held my cheeks tight. Embarrassed, I squirmed, as if I was

Will's dad caught out in some hanky panky. 'Oi, none of that, little man. Angel's don't like... Sod it.'

This time it was me snogging Sun. Stroking her soft hair like I'd craved to do when she'd sprawled with Blake or Plantagenet. Hoping that even if she didn't want to hear the word *love*, then she'd feel, taste and remember it in the kiss.

Sun smelled of...gardenias. Freedom – and our love.

At last, I drew back, and Sun let me. Bugger being *caged*. I was saying the two words, and she was going to hear them this time. 'I love you.'

Sun. I looked down. Then I felt her finger under my chin, however, lifting it, until our gazes met. 'I love you too, Light.'

And that was all the hope I'd ever need.

'Well-beloved, we are merrily met,' Plantagenet looked like a panther freed into the wild. And up close? I was beginning to have coat envy. In the dark Plantagenet's golden peepers were twin fires. 'Here are your Renegades to command and charge – and I too.'

'No, mate, you're free. No bloke's commanding you again.'

Plantagenet gave a quick nod, before he turned towards Donovan.

Even though I knew it was coming..? I still cringed.

As it'd been with Sun at the beginning, it was like the world (and Hartford with it), had fallen into darkness for Donovan. Nothing existed but Plantagenet – his long lost lover, there was no doubting it.

Donovan wrested away from Hartford, leaving him midstep in his dance. Hartford broke off his song in surprise.

When Donovan threw himself into Plantagenet's arms, I knew the routine: the silent snuffling, tender licking, fingers tracing the cheek and then...that gentle, intimate kiss. I could taste the oranges.

Donovan was draped around Plantagenet, as if Plantagenet was pure blood and Donovan was overloaded on him alone.

It was painful to watch because...Plantagenet...the blood...called to me as powerfully.

I was an addict too. No point denying it.

Seeing another in my place? It was like Plantagenet was shanking *me* through the heart.

Then I had a shufti at Hartford's mush: I wasn't the only one who was being heart-shanked. I understood the loss. Except for Hartford? It was a thousand times more bloody.

I tugged Will after me, as I edged over to Hartford; I was a sacrifice offered up as a distraction. 'You can boot me in the goolies; folks seem to get their jollies that way. Or clout me in the nose; that's also a popular choice.'

Hartford struggled to glance away from Donovan's snog to me. 'Tell it to the marines. I'm busy.'

'I drugged and caged you. Must've pissed you off.'

'What you doin', man? He's gonna switch on you.' Will tried to haul me away.

When Hartford prowled towards me, I had to bleeding agree.

'What you pulled? Double-crossing me?' When Hartford reached out, I flinched. 'Was nutty, screwy and...' Hartford smacked me lightly on the cheek. 'Just saved the fella I'm goofy over.'

I breathed out.

Plantagenet and Donovan were still at it. How did you make up for decades apart? It looked, however, like they intended to take a shot at it.

Even in front of an entire army, Hartford was alone.

I risked a manly pat on Hartford's shoulder. 'Families: love them one moment; want to rip out their throats the next. Yet you'd still battle to the last breath for them.'

'Say, mac, you're sounding dangerously like a Long-lived,' Hartford's features gentled, as he looked at Will. 'It's swell to see you too.'

Then Hartford grasped Will's small hand – a First Lifer safe between two Blood – and we swaggered together towards our family, lovers, army, allies and Renegades – the start of a new world on that night-time bridge over the tongue of the Thames.

We saw the world. And the world saw us.

Betrayal, death, hope.

It's how all truly great stories end too.

What comes next?

That's where the bollocks vampire myths finish, and the age of the Blood Lifer legends..?

It's only just beginning.

Need a conclusion to your inquiry?

I'll never be ashes but I'm on fire.

My name is Light. Predator. Slave. Freedom fighter.

And I'm the bloody hero.

✳✳✳✳

Blood Renegades over too soon? If you enjoyed *Rebel Vampires Volume 3*, you'll love the next book in the series, *Rebel Vampires Volume 4: Blood Legends*.

Prepare yourself for Age of the Blood Legends to begin...

Before the release of *Blood Legends*, comes the start of a whole new series from **Rosemary A Johns** in 2018: *Rebel Werewolves Volume 1: Moon Broken*.

Why not escape into a world where the fox hunts the wolf... She's the first female Wolf Charmer on CID; he's the first wolf on the Oxford Were Unit. Both are chasing their families' killers and hiding the dark secrets of their pasts. **Welcome to Were Town... Read on for an exclusive excerpt.**

REBEL WEREWOLVES VOLUME 1: MOON BROKEN

1

Omega's first day on the Were Unit at Oxford police station was much like a puppy's with its new family: petted for its novelty, before being smacked over the nose for growling at the Siamese cat.

Omega was sipping on his second mug of hot milk sweetened with rich honey, which had been heated by Detective Zach Little, the youngest member of the team - and definite pack material, Omega had decided with a determined nod – when the Wolf Charmer sidled into the office.

Omega stiffened. He could feel – the siren *call* of her – scratching under his skin. His *human* skin. Worming deep beneath to the wolf, who snarled his agony, clawing at his guts to escape, snap, *bite*...

'A rabbit...*thump*, *thump*...under the wheels, and it's my own fault for being #OverTheTop, like I'd hit a kid, but they convinced me to confess to Hawk. I was bricking it. You should've seen the Inspector's face when I reported the death of Bright Eyes.'

Zach sniggered. He was still nattering, as Omega perched on the Detective's regimented desk, which was alive with phones, computers and snaking cables, and casually swung his boots on the swivel chair. Still cracking jokes and trying to *impress*.

Sweet Alpha, Zach had called Omega in jest, *better make it something decent, before the others choose*... Omega hadn't needed Zach to fill in the blanks: Fiend, Baby-Eater, Animal, *Werewolf*...

Omega couldn't hear Zach now though. Not with that woman – all black hair and emerald eyes – stalking towards him across the open-plan office.

Omega was tense with the knowledge there was nowhere to hide.

The stink of the brand new carpets caught at the back of his throat: demonic red against the angelic white of the walls. There was a tangled web of *Good Work* letters, mixed with fuzzy photos of targets; someone had sketched cupid hearts between one couple. Omega smirked: *so had to be his boy Zachary*. As did the phone number for *The Jeremy Kyle Show* scrawled underneath the official list of Thames Valley contacts.

The Wolf Charmer had stopped next to Zach's desk. Right beside his shoulder. Although she was shorter than Zach, the way she held her head so

329

erectly on her neck..? Made her looked like she was taller. *And had a stick up her arse.*

Omega bristled, surging with unexpected protectiveness, before deflating: *by the Moon this was a Wolf Charmer – you wrapped them around your little finger with manipulation, mind games and your own charms, whilst you tested for weaknesses...but you could never protect against them.*

Omega hadn't reckoned his handler would be a woman; the ones who'd trained him had all been men. He didn't know why the *feel* of her already invading him, and her *smell* – a powerful wave of musk – choking him, was so much harder to take.

Maybe she'd still 'friend' him? He had a hilarious meme about a witch he could share...

Omega forced a smile. *Time to play the game.* 'Guess you're my new partner then?'

A snow white hand stroking his face; Omega hadn't expected that. Nor the words whispered for him alone, stinging and vicious as scorpions, 'Guess you're my new dog then?'

Omega jerked away, crashing back Zach's chair with a vicious – *slam* – as Omega overbalanced. When Omega heard Zach's gasp of pain, he whimpered. Wounding his boy? *Great job, Sweet Alpha...*

Silence. For the first time that morning in the office.

Omega flushed when he realised they'd become the freak show entertainment.

Nothing new there.

Omega scowled at his handler, baring just a little tooth: *even the enemy deserved a warning.*

The Wolf Charmer's expression, however, was so still, you'd have reckoned they'd been discussing stationary.

Come to think of it: a decent fountain pen? Omega wouldn't have minded chatting about that.

Nobody must ever learn of the nerd inside... His wolf could snap hard when he was cringing.

For a moment, the were and the Wolf Charmer scrutinized each other, and Omega shifted uneasily.

He knew what the Wolf Charmer saw: a tumble of pale moon blond curls and butterfly thick eyelashes heavy over golden eyes. He'd saved for suit trousers and an ivory shirt, in what he knew was a deluded attempt to fit in because he also wore the white woolen overcoat with moon symbol sewn onto the sleeve, as per regulation... *Yeah, like he'd memorized those.*

Omega also knew what the Wolf Charmer didn't see: a were crouching, hunched over and gaze averted from her strict one, sniveling in submission because if she was waiting on that?

She could just go wait on another partner.

Omega supposed the Wolf Charmer was beautiful, but she was also cold, cruel, powerful...and she hated him already.

Not much beautiful about that.

Suddenly scarlet tendrils grew out of the Wolf Charmer's hands; wisps of snaking shadow coiled, as if from her Soul: from her glowing eyes, chest and lips...a red, living *thing* intent on punishing him.

Omega could feel it pulsing; he could hear it hissing. Its sickly unnatural stench, like a rotting carcass or *death*, was reaching towards him. He started to pant and whine.

No Wolf Charmer had unleashed their charms on him. He'd behaved. Followed rules. He was one of the best in the Inclusion Program.

Call me Omega now, bitches.

The Charm slammed into him like a punch.

Omega cracked back against the desk. His mug of milk spilled, as if it was pale blood, in a pool across the papers, from his motionless hand. Pinned and spread-eagled, his wolf fought with rage, with its snout wrinkled in fury, it hurled itself against its cage.

Then Omega heard it: the music. Faint at first but still electrifying: a rowdy Mod revival of guitars and the joy of being young and free. Despite everything, as Kaiser Chief's "I Predict a Riot" rampaged, louder and louder, as if it too was inside him, Omega's lips curled into a smile. But then he jerked, gagging.

She was inside him. She knew: that's how the magic trick worked. Somehow it wormed out your deepest...desire...love...hurt...and used it to tame you.

He would never be tamed.

Omega gagged again.

'What's..?' Omega didn't need to see Zach to know his boy was running his hand through his carefully waxed hair and worrying at the horn buttons on his navy waistcoat (and who in the furless heavens wore those, like a Victorian doll?). No one else could see it: the snakes coiling though Omega and manacling his wrists to the desk. Violating. No one could hear the music. No one but him and the Charmer. He wondered if it was all a type of hypnosis, and why they'd never covered this at the Omega Training Centre: *probably reckoned obedience and cookery were more important life skills.* 'Hey, let up. Are you hurting him?'

'You saw the were go for me. They're not *puppies.*' Omega wrestled harder to escape, anger blinding him. 'See? Violent creatures.'

'But...' Zach again, this time closer; his fingers were soothing across Omega's tense shoulder, 'I've been with the bloke all morning and--'

'Lucky your little face wasn't savaged then, isn't it, pretty?' Not a flicker. The Wolf Charmer's expression was as closed off as before.

Omega shuddered, as a crimson shadow slid between his legs. The riot in his head was beating so hard, he wouldn't be surprised if his ears were bleeding. '*Witch*.'

The Wolf Charmer hovered over him; the black cloak of her hair transformed day to night. 'Yes, beast?' Omega felt her lips like dry leaves against his ear; her scent this close was pungent and overpowering. 'If you have trouble curbing your tongue, dog, I can do it for you.'

When the Wolf Charmer drew back, their gazes met. Omega noticed that her eyes were greener than he'd ever seen before. She was studying him, waiting for the moment when he discovered...

He couldn't move his tongue.

Omega choked; he couldn't breathe. A red shadow was weighing down his tongue. The thought that *she* was in his mouth..? He'd be buying a stronger mouthwash tonight: *did they make one with bleach in it*?

At least he could still glare.

He was so going to glare.

For the first time, the Wolf Charmer looked amused.

Could you ignite someone with a look? Omega reckoned it was worth a try – *then he'd have himself a burning*.

'Guys, is this how we greet new members of our team? I think not. Detective Fox, care to explain?' Inspector Andrew Hawkins' question – steel hidden beneath the soft velvet – was like being dragged by the scruff of the neck back to a reality: where this was Omega's first day on a new team and he was splayed over a desk with a woman crawling on top of him.

He was all for making good first impressions.

At last, the music possessing Omega's brain receded, leaving in its wake a lightning migraine, jagged through his face and behind the backs of his eyes. The light was too bright, every sound amplified to agony and the smells...

Hurling all over the office in front of his Inspector on the first day? Did they hand out commendations for that?

'Merely handling my were.' The Wolf Charmer – Detective Fox (and no, Omega definitely didn't reckon she was pack material), pushed off him with a casual flick of her hair.

'The correct term is Native Briton, Cora.'

Cora snorted. Just for a moment, Omega thought he saw the same laughter in her eyes, as was dancing in his own. But then it died. 'They're *Were Units*; I'm a *Were Handler*,' then Cora added as an afterthought, 'sir.'

Omega could hear the Inspector's shrug without needing to see it. 'We're heading the pilot project; they've invested a lot of faith in us and we're not cocking it up. So a woman as a handler..? You know me, I'm all for inclusion but--'

'Then why handicap me with a bitch from Were Town? I was promised a Met were.'

'Watch your language, Detective. Your...Native Briton...was trained in the London unit. Received highest marks, as it happens. He also grew up in Were Town, which gives him the edge in local knowledge. Use it.'

Omega was swinging between pride in being praised and humiliation at being discussed as if he wasn't there. Still, he'd be their good little police doggy, if it meant he was one step closer to Were Town. Local knowledge?

The single skins had no idea.

'I handcuff these Were Town beasts,' Omega could sense Cora's fury beneath her calm mask – the thrumming vibrations, 'I don't play at partner with them.'

The tendrils tightened around Omega, until even through the crimson gag, he yelped.

'No one on my team *plays* at partner,' Inspector Hawkins' voice was hard. 'My Office. Now.'

Omega's body was marionette-like tugged to his feet, before he was marched after the dark figure of Cora: *witch wasn't taking any chances she'd be mistaken for a were.*

Everyone had weaknesses and everyone could be played.

The witch's Goth chick look, leather corset and skirt with fishnet tights (nothing more than a mask), merely coiled her were hatred closer to her heart.

Weakness number one.

'Only you, Detective Fox, need delight me with your company.'

The red sea flooded out of Omega at the Inspector's sardonic bark, seeking comfort in its mistress, tendrils curling from Omega's mouth, chest, and every intimate...private...part of him. He staggered, finding himself caught in Zach's arms.

Omega allowed himself a moment's rest, as he rubbed the agony in his pounding forehead, needing the *touch*. He wished Zach knew to stroke him, nuzzle and lick.

Like he'd ever had that anyway... Maybe someone had invented an app..?

Omega ritualistically pushed his own curls back, combing his fingers through them to self-comfort. As always, it worked.

He'd faced more merciless monsters than the Wolf Charmer before – and now he was back? He was going to be facing them again.

Omega shook himself, as he grinned.

'Was that the CID initiation you warned me about? Because I imagined it'd be us getting bladdered, and then tying me naked to the front of the station.'

Zach bit at his lip, his expression troubled. 'Are all handlers like that then?'

'Nah, looks like the witch's just special.'

'Why do you call her..?'

'No reason she'd like.' Omega grimaced when he glanced down at the neat papers on Zach's desk, which were now sodden with milk. 'And they say it isn't all paperwork in the police. Need a hand?'

Zach nodded, but even before they'd started to sort through the damp files, Zach asked hesitantly, 'Why does Cora want to control you?'

'Who wouldn't? I'm adorable.'

But inside? Omega squirmed.

Good question: Goddess Moon, it was all.

Because beneath the coldness of those green eyes – the witch had *relished* every second.

She'd been consumed by the power.

✳✳✳✳

Want to find out what happens next in *Rebel Werewolves Volume 1: Moon Broken*?

Moon Broken is released 2018. **Then sit back and experience the thrilling mystery of Were Town...**

DID YOU LIKE THIS BOOK?

Let everyone know by posting a review on Amazon and Goodreads.

Remember, please feed this author reviews – they're better than chocolate (and Rosemary *loves* chocolate...)

Love Reading Gripping Fantasy?

If so, sign up to Rosemary A John's VIP Email List to be notified of new promotions and never miss out on hot new releases.

Indulge yourself, grab a coffee and then dive into a Fantasy Rebel book – they're fantasy for rebels.

Plus you'll also receive Rosemary's FREE and exclusive short story "All the Tin Soldiers".

It's our gift to you.

Visit Rosemary's website to subscribe: rosemaryajohns.com

ABOUT THE AUTHOR

ROSEMARY A JOHNS is the bestselling author of the *Rebel Vampires* series. She wrote her first fantasy novel at the age of ten, when she discovered the weird worlds inside her head were more exciting than double swimming. Since then she's studied history at Oxford University, run a theatre company (her critically acclaimed plays have been described as 'uncomfortable, unsettling and uneasily true to life'), and worked with disability charities. She's a music fanatic and a paranormal anti-hero addict who creates spellbinding worlds, thrilling action, gripping suspense and passionate romances, all uniquely told. When Rosemary's not falling in love with the rebels fighting their way onto the page, she heads the Oxford writing group Dreaming Spires. She can also be found listening to Nirvana. At full volume. Or not found at all. When she's dived into her secret worlds again. WINNER OF THE SILVER AWARD in the Wishing Shelf Book Awards.

Hooked on *Rebel Vampires*?

Let the world know. Go to Amazon and Goodreads to leave a review today. Remember, reviews are better than chocolate - and Rosemary *loves* chocolate...

Reward yourself with another enthralling book by Rosemary A Johns. Order *Rebel Vampires Volume 1: Blood Dragons* and *Volume 2: Blood Shackles* now.

Discover Rosemary's dark scribblings online:

rosemaryajohns.com
www.facebook.com/RosemaryAnnJohns
www.twitter.com/RosemaryAJohns
https://uk.pinterest.com/rosemaryjohns1
http://www.linkedin.com/in/rosemaryajohns

Follow Rosemary's writing here:

https://www.amazon.com/Rosemary-A-Johns/e/B01JOJVTNE
https://www.goodreads.com/author/show/15571684.Rosemary_A_Johns

Go ahead and drop Rosemary a line at: rosemary.johns1@btinternet.com

Member of a Book Club?

Share *Blood Renegades* with your group and delve into the free Reading Group Notes at rosemaryajohns.com

Books by Rosemary A Johns

Rebel Vampires Series
Blood Dragons (Volume 1)
Blood Shackles (Volume 2)
Blood Renegades (Volume 3)

www.ingramcontent.com/pod-product-compliance
Lightning Source LLC
Chambersburg PA
CBHW051329250626
47155CB00007B/2524